THE McCALL TRILOGY

THE FOUNDLING ∫ TO ECHO THE PAST ∫ AN OLD-FASHIONED ROMANCE

MARCIA LYNN McCLURE

Published by Distractions Ink
P.O. Box 15971
Rio Rancho, NM 87174

© Copyright 2012 by M. L. Meyers
A.K.A. Marcia Lynn McClure
Cover Photography by
© Robertplotz and © Olga Itina | Dreamstime.com
Cover Design by
Sheri L. Brady | MightyPhoenixDesignStudio.com

First Printed Edition: 2012

McClure, Marcia Lynn, 1965—
The McCall Trilogy: a collection of novellas/
by Marcia Lynn McClure.

ISBN: 978-0-9852740-3-0

Library of Congress Control Number: 2012933295

Printed in the United States of America

THE FOUNDLING
(Formerly released as *Desert Fire*)

To Dixie,
Ahhh, the memories!
Walks and wagons…mailboxes and homemade bread.
The White Ranger and Wind in His Throat…firecrackers and
egg hairstyles.
Thank you for being a central piece of my heart,
A nurturer to my soul,
And my treasured friend.

CHAPTER ONE

She felt something on her face. It was cool, soothing, moist. Her throat burned and constricted, and when she tried to swallow, she couldn't.

"Ma'am?" She heard the voice, but it seemed so far away. "Ma'am?" It came again, closer this time. "Can you hear me, ma'am?" A man's voice, deep and stern.

She attempted to speak but found it impossible. She tried to nod in response, but her head was pounding like a drum was pinned up inside it.

"Open your eyes if you can. Open 'em," the voice insisted.

She opened her eyes just a slit and quickly clenched them shut again as searing rays of sunlight burned through her. She sensed movement, and the demanding voice came once more.

"Now…try again."

It was a voice not to be ignored. She tried to lift her hand to shade her face, but her own body would not obey her mind's command. She opened her eyes slightly, and when the sun didn't blind her painfully again, she was able to open them completely. Everything was blurry for several seconds, but she could make out a dark figure bending over her.

"Can you see?" the voice asked firmly.

She blinked several times, clearing her vision slightly.

"Yes," she mouthed, though no sound escaped her blistered lips. A hand slipped beneath her head and lifted it.

"Here—keep still, and let this stay on your tongue for a minute," the voice said, and she felt the first cool, life-giving drops of water moisten her mouth. She couldn't move her tongue at first, but the second time the stranger offered the water from the canteen, she was able to swallow it.

After several mouthfuls of water, she felt more alert and realized her face, arms, and shoulders felt tight and hot.

"Now…what's your name, girl? And how'd ya end up out here?" the man asked.

She could see clearly then, and for the first time she looked up into the face that belonged to the voice.

"I don't know," she answered in a forced whisper.

The man let out a sigh, tipped his hat back on his head, and looked around with an expression of both bewilderment and annoyance.

"You don't know how you ended up lyin' out in the middle of nowhere, with nothin' or no one with you?" he asked, still looking around.

"No," she whispered, feeling suddenly terrified at the realization.

The stranger stood up and pulled his hat down into place again.

"Well…I guess I'll just haul ya on home, and we'll think on it from there." He walked over to a nearby tree and untied a horse. "Come on, Bill. Ma will love this," he muttered.

The man led the horse to where she was lying, and she sat up more terrified still.

"I can't possibly go with you, sir!" she whispered as loud as possible.

He smiled and chuckled. "Well, sweetheart, what do you plan on doin'? Feedin' the coyotes?" He hunkered down, looking directly into her face. "Or…there are all kinds of worse things you could feed…" Then his smile turned into a frown as he looked at the ground around her. "Do you feel anything crawlin' on you anywhere, girl?"

She thought it an odd question but answered, "No."

He pulled her up until she was sitting straight and began running his hand over her back and through her hair. She realized that her shirtwaist was torn because she could feel his hands on the exposed skin of her shoulders. She gasped as she looked down and saw that it was also torn in front and gaped open, exposing her entire collarbone.

As the frown on his face intensified, the man quickly ran his hand over her back once more and then moved to her waist. She instinctively moved to slap him, but he caught her hand and looked angrily into her face.

"I ain't out for a good time, sweetheart," he growled through clenched teeth. He pushed her back down, and she wanted to weep when he lifted up her skirts and began feeling her right leg. But her state of severe dehydration prevented any tears from even developing.

"Well, you certainly ain't from around here," the man stated as he unfastened her bustle, throwing it aside. "Women don't bother too much with these contraptions 'round these parts." Then he stopped. "Don't move," he commanded, and she obeyed as she felt something crawling on her flesh under the left leg of her pantaloons.

She watched with utter mortification as the stranger's hand slowly slid beneath the cloth of her pantaloons and toward her knee. His hand clamped around something, and he quickly withdrew it.

"Sorry little cuss!" he mumbled as he threw something to the ground and drew a large knife from his boot.

She then witnessed him smash a large, sandy-colored scorpion into the dirt with his well-worn boot. When she looked up again, it was in time to see him cut the palm of his hand with the knife and begin sucking on the wound. He did this several times, spitting his own blood from his mouth each time.

"That sorry little cuss stung me," he mumbled. "They don't usually kill you, unless you're allergic or somethin'. But they make you awful sick, and the sting gets terrible sore." He looked at her oddly for a moment. "You feel like you're gonna faint or somethin'?" he asked.

She swallowed hard and shook her head to dispel the awful dizziness in it. The man slipped the knife back into his boot and pulled her up to a sitting position again.

"Well, least you had sense enough to nearly drop dead 'round here," he muttered.

She watched as he pulled an odd-shaped plant from the ground and broke open a few of the strange-looking leaves. He squeezed out a slimy substance and began to apply it to her face. It smelled unpleasant but felt very cool and soothing.

When he finished, he wiped his hand on his dusty trousers and said, "Now, let's see if you can sit a horse."

He pulled her to her feet, but her knees buckled, and her mind began swimming. He caught her and sat her down again.

"I'm sorry," she whispered, wishing she could cry.

"Hang on there a minute," he said, with a hint more of kindness in his voice.

She watched, perfectly alarmed, as he actually proceeded to remove his shirt and wet it with water from the canteen. Even more disgraceful was the fact that he wore no form of undergarment beneath—none whatsoever! He was standing there bare from the waist up. And judging from the bronze color of his torso, he paraded around in such a state often.

When he looked at her again, she covered her eyes with her sore hands.

He chuckled. "I believe you're blushin' under that sunburn, girl. You're definitely from somewhere else."

He draped the wet shirt over her head and shoulders and pulled her to her feet yet again. She still needed a great deal of support to stand. She tried to push herself away when her hands touched his bare chest as they searched for support.

"Tarnation, girl," he grumbled, taking her hands in his. "This is no time for propriety." She thought the word sounded a little out of character with his odd, rather Southern-sounding accent.

He proceeded to run her hands from his shoulders slowly down and over his solid stomach. "See, don't feel any different than your baby brother. You must be an unmarried one as well." He steadied her again. "Now, let's get you home to Mama so she can see the damage." He then lifted her onto the horse, which sneezed and stomped his foreleg several times.

"Settle down, Bill. She's with me." He mounted behind her and pulled her tightly against his body. "Try not to fall off. It ain't far."

She was still too shocked by her recent lesson in anatomy to take much notice of the shameful way she sat astride the horse. But somehow she knew that until that moment, she had always ridden sidesaddle. A great wave of fatigue was overtaking her, and she couldn't help but let her head fall back against his shoulder.

"I'm sorry," she whispered. "I think I'm going to faint." She felt his arm tighten around her waist and the heat of his breath on her face as he spoke in her ear.

"It ain't far, girl. Now listen here. I'm Jackson McCall. This here feller you're on is Bill. He don't care much for nobody but me…so you sit real still and hang on tight."

She could smell leather, bacon, and perspiration, but it was somehow a pleasant and comforting combination. "Yes, sir," she whispered, trying to keep her eyes open.

"Yes, sir?" he repeated in an astonished whisper. "Where are you from, girl?"

She tried and tried to pull an answer from her fevered brain. But she truly couldn't.

"I don't know," she whispered, just before she gave into the need to be unconscious.

CHAPTER TWO

"I think she's comin' around, Mary. Close the curtains. Her eyes should be mighty sensitive yet." A soft, feminine voice was drifting into her dreams, and she fought the urge to wake up from them.

She was dreaming of the handsomest man she had ever seen—one of those rugged types that lived in the savage West that she had read about. His body was darkened from hours in the sun, brown hair lightened by the same hours in the sun, square jaw badly in need of a close shave. Perfectly shaped lips and nose, straight teeth whiter than white, and intense green eyes shaded by long dark lashes. He had rescued her from something, though she couldn't think what.

"Wake up, honey. Can you hear us? Oh, Mary, I do hope she's well." The dream swept away as awakening triumphed.

She opened her eyes and blinked several times. They felt dry and hot. When her vision cleared, she beheld two women hovering over her. One was an older woman, perhaps fifty, and the other was young, eighteen maybe. Both were smiling down at her kindly.

"Well, finally!" the elder woman exclaimed. "We were beginning to wonder if we should send for a doctor."

"Where am I?" the still-recovering girl asked the two women at her bedside.

The older woman answered, "You're at the McCall ranch. We're near Cortez, Colorado. I'm Maggie McCall, and this is Mary Henderson, one of our dear neighbors. What's your name, dear?"

7

Tears began to trickle from the corners of the girl's eyes, leaving moisture across her temples.

"I don't know. I really can't remember. It's so frightening," she sobbed.

Mary dabbed at the tears with a handkerchief. "Now, now. It's all right. It'll all come back to you in time. Meanwhile, you're with the best people in the world, and I could use someone near my own age around here. Jackson told us that you seemed to have lost your mind…um…memory…but we were hopin' that some rest would help."

"Let's get you all bathed and freshened up, and you'll feel much better, sweetie," Maggie said. "Let's see, what would you like us to call you? How about Annie? I always wanted a daughter named Annie. How's that? Just until you remember your own name," she added.

"Annie" smiled and nodded. "It's lovely," she encouraged, the kind woman smiling down at her.

"Mary, go tell Baker to bring the washtub in here so we can have some privacy, would you?" Maggie said, helping Annie to sit up.

Mary nodded and left. Maggie sat down on the foot of the bed, smoothed her apron a bit, and began chatting. Annie knew that she was trying to help her to feel comfortable, and it was working.

"Well, a little about us. I'm Maggie McCall, and I've got me three beautiful little boys. Their daddy, Colonel Robert Jackson McCall, was the love of my life and the handsomest man on this earth. He passed three years back, and it hasn't been easy on us. We miss him more than anythin'. We came here after the war and started ranchin' and loved it. My boys are hard-workin' gentlemen—even if I can't get their grammar the way I would like it. The oldest is Jackson, then Baker, and then Matt. They're just itchin' for you to wake up. When Jackson rode up two days ago with you on Bill…I nearly dropped my teeth!"

"Two days ago!" Annie interrupted.

"Yes, dear. You've been in here with a fever and restin' for over two days," Maggie explained, looking concerned. "We all took turns the first two nights sittin' with you for fear you'd quit on us. Your skin is lookin' so much better! It's almost completely peeled off now, and I'm sure that feels nicer to you."

There was a knock on the door, and when Maggie said, "Come in," a tall, very handsome young man that Annie judged to be in his early twenties entered, carrying a large metal tub. He looked familiar to her somehow when he smiled, removed his hat, and offered her his hand.

"Baker McCall, ma'am. Glad to see you feelin' better." His smile was radiant, and she smiled back as he shook her hand instead of kissing it, as she had expected for some reason. He nodded, kissed his mother's cheek, winked at Mary, and left the room.

"I'll bring in the water, Mrs. McCall," Mary said and left also.

"Baker. Your middle son, Mrs. McCall? He's so very tall!" Annie commented as Maggie helped her stand.

"Oh my, yes! All my boys are tall as redwoods, though Baker is the tallest. Six feet three inches he is…even! And call me Maggie, please." Then she went on.

"Jackson says you must be from back east…says you kept calling him 'sir' and were near to dyin' of embarrassment when he was checkin' you for critters. And a bustle even! I never could understand why a woman would want to make her backside look bigger! Mine's big enough on its own."

Annie giggled. Everything felt good here. The air was dry, and there was a cool breeze coming through the window.

After Mary had filled the tub with warmed water, the two ladies left, and Annie soaked for a long time before getting out and dressing in the calico dress that Maggie had laid out for her. She sensed that she had never worn anything quite so simple and comfortable, though she felt a little underdressed without a sturdier corset.

Maggie knocked on the door, and Annie asked her to come in.

"My! You do look like you feel better, dear. May I do your hair? My fingers are just itchin' to work with that mane of yours." Annie smiled and let Maggie braid her hair.

Maggie marveled at the lovely hair on their nameless guest. It was long, thick, and so black that it seemed to hold blue light. This girl's eyes were an unusually light shade of blue and flattered by thick black lashes. Her mouth was perfect and still held the lovely natural wine color of youth. In fact, the girl was physically perfect in every respect. Maggie had also noticed an unusual grace possessed by the girl. Even her simplest movements were lovely.

"What do you think, dear?" Maggie asked as she finished.

Annie looked in the mirror and studied the long French braid. It was so divinely simple! She loved it. Her attention was drawn to the reflection of her face. She frowned for a moment, not really recognizing herself.

"Who am I, Mrs. McCall?" She felt hot, stinging tears begin to fill her eyes. Maggie reached out, turning her and facing her sternly.

"Now, don't get discouraged, dear. It'll all come back to you. And even if it doesn't…you've got us now."

Annie smiled, and the tears escaped her eyes. "I can't just live here forever, Mrs. McCall! You don't even know who I am. What if I'm a murderess…a criminal? What if—" she cried.

"Now, you stop that. That couldn't be. You're too nice a girl. Don't be worryin' about it. I'm sure you're no murderer." Maggie smiled. "Now, come on out for dinner. The boys will be in any minute bellerin' for food."

Maggie took Annie's hand and led her out into the brightest-looking room the girl had ever been in. Even though she had no memories to draw upon, she knew she had never been in a cheerier room. The walls were brightly whitewashed, and there were three windows through which the evening sunshine poured. Jars and jars of freshly canned peaches lined one counter, and their sweet aroma still lingered heavily in the air. The curtains were red-checked, as was the tablecloth on the table in the center of the room. Annie smiled from the pure delight that it sent through her. This was a home, not just a house with a mother and her three sons. A real home.

Baker was the first one through the squeaky screen door.

"Mama! That ol' Root tore up the north fence again! I am sick and tired of chasin' down that ol', ornery bull. I gotta tug myself to death on that ring to get him to stop. I tell you his nose is made of steel…'cause tuggin' on that ring in it don't slow him down one lick," he said with a frown. He looked over at Annie. "Well, good evenin' to you, miss. You're as pretty as apple blossoms in springtime," he said, his frown turning to a radiant smile.

Annie returned the greeting with her own fascinating smile. "And you've been taught well the art of flattery, Mr. McCall, sir."

"Weren't taught, ma'am. Got it from my daddy. Purely natural."

"Don't let him fool you, miss. He works hard at it. I got all the natural good looks and talent." Another tall, handsome young man had entered the room through the door. He smiled slyly, took Annie's hand, bent, and kissed it lightly on the back. "Matthew Robert McCall, miss. And I'm right pleased to see that you're up and about and lookin' so very lovely."

Annie giggled softly with delight. Never had she seen two more attractive men in all her life! Not only handsome—both had brown hair and brown eyes and were tall and boiling over with personality. Something told her that it took an overwhelming amount of positive personality to make people feel the way she did just then. The door squeaked again, and another man entered the room.

"Now, that…that there is our big brother, Jackson. He weren't endowed with nothin' but a mean streak. He's a smart-mouthed tease, and he works too much and too hard to be good for any feller," Baker teased.

Jackson McCall's eyes captured Annie's. Something about his very presence was overwhelming, and Annie couldn't help but take a step backward when he approached and offered her his hand. His was the face she'd seen in her dream, and a vision of him standing before her bare from the waist up flashed through her mind, and she went crimson. He reached out and took her hand, shaking it twice, very ceremoniously.

"Glad to see you're up and about, miss. I wasn't too sure myself that we found you in time. And don't listen to my brothers. I'm the handsomest and the smartest! The spittin' image of my daddy."

Somewhere Annie found her composure. "I thank you, sir, for finding me and bringing me here. I surely would've perished if you hadn't."

The three brothers looked back and forth at one another with raised eyebrows, then back to Annie.

"Darlin'…I hope you'll loosen up a bit around us boys. You're too polite. Now, what do we call you?" Baker asked.

"She let me pick a name for her, boys," Mrs. McCall chirped, smiling proudly. The three men looked at their mother. "I've decided on Annie," she announced, beaming.

"Annie!" came the simultaneous exclamation from all three.

"For Pete's sake, Mama! We've had three cows and an old sow named Annie," Jackson grumbled.

"Well, now we have a beautiful girl in our home named Annie. And I'm sure she's starving." She helped Annie sit down in one of the chairs at the table, and Baker and Matt sat on either side of her, with Jackson, Mary, and herself across from them.

Matt leaned over and whispered, "Mama always wanted a daughter named Annie so bad that everything that come along stock-wise that was female, she named Annie. It's really a compliment, you see—to be named after three cows and a sow."

Annie smiled. She felt safe. For the moment. But something in the back of her mind was nagging at her sense of security. How she wished she could remember.

Never had Annie tasted such delicious food! She was convinced Mrs. McCall was truly a culinary expert. After dinner, everyone retired to the front of the house. A refreshing breeze filled the room, and it was comforting to sit and listen to the family's conversation about the day.

"You know, ol' Buck Woodly is sellin' that bull of his, Mama," Baker began. "He wants a piece for him, but I'm willin' to buy him myself if we can get rid of ol' Root."

"Ol' Root isn't any more difficult than any other bull, Baker. He just has it in for you," Maggie said.

"That's right, Baker," Matt added. "You never shoulda done his tail that way three years ago. He remembers. Don't think he doesn't."

"He don't act up with me or Matt," Jackson said, smiling slyly at his brother.

"Well, fine then. Fine. You boys run alongside him ayankin' on that ring in his nose from now on. I'm tired of the ol' cuss," Baker added.

"He has a ring in his nose?" Annie asked out loud without thinking.

Everyone in the room looked at her, mouths gaping open as if she bore a ring in her nose.

"You ever seen a bull up close before, Annie?" Mary asked.

"I don't think I have, actually," she said, feeling ridiculous for letting such a question slip from her thoughts and out through her mouth.

"Well, I'll take you out to meet ol' Root tomorrow. And you can tug on his ring a bit if you want. Maybe you can start runnin' him down for me," Baker chuckled, smiling drowsily.

"Mary's comin' over tomorrow to help finish up my peaches, Annie. It'll go so much faster havin' you here to help now," Maggie said, smiling excitedly.

"Oh my, yes! I better be gettin' home, Mrs. McCall. It's late. I'll be here first thing though," Mary said, standing.

"I'll take you, Mary," Jackson said, yawning as he stood and headed toward the door. Mary followed.

Annie was horrified. "Aren't you going, Mrs. McCall?" she asked frantically.

"Maggie please, dear," Mrs. McCall answered. "Whatever for?" she added lightly.

Everyone in the room was waiting for Annie's answer. She felt silly again, but every logical nerve in her body told her that a woman always had an escort with her when she was with a man.

Jackson answered for her. "Mama, I think she means why aren't you goin' to make sure I don't misbehave. Isn't that right, Annie?" Annie nodded, and he smiled slyly at her. "You're definitely not from around these parts, girl. I'm just makin' sure she gets safely home. Nothin' else."

Annie felt a little annoyed at his mocking tone of voice.

"Don't worry, Annie," Mary said, smiling. "You'll get used to everything right soon. I'll see you all tomorrow." And they left, unescorted.

❧

Jackson returned later with a crate full of canned pears. "Mary's mama says she'll swap you three dozen quarts of pears for three of peaches, Mama."

Maggie stood up and clapped her hands. "Oh! I was hopin' so. Aren't they lovely, Annie?" she asked.

"Jack," Baker began, "do you think we oughta tell someone that you found Annie?" He seemed so serious that a chill ran down Annie's spine as he asked the question.

Jackson shot a quick look at her and then, looking at his mama, said, "No."

No one questioned him, but once again Annie's own questioning thoughts came bursting out.

"Why not?" she ventured.

Everyone in the room looked at each other for a moment, and then Maggie answered.

"Well, honey—now don't you be worryin' about it—but Jackson thinks maybe we should wait and see if someone is lookin' for you first. Girls just don't end up out in the middle of nowhere lookin' like they were runnin' from somethin'."

Annie looked at Jackson, and the serious expression on his face made her shiver involuntarily.

"Why do you think I'm running from something?" she asked directly and so strongly that she was even a little surprised herself.

He answered her bluntly. "You were either dumped there on purpose…or you were runnin' from somethin'. I rode all over that area—didn't find no carpetbag, trunk, clothes lyin' around, and no handbag. Nothin' that would lead me to think there was some kind of accident that you just wandered off from. I checked with Sheriff

Braddock in town too. No one has come lookin' for a lost girl. You're either runnin', or someone didn't want you around anymore."

Baker let out a long sigh. "Boy. You sure is a sweet talker, Jackson. Ain't no one can soften the blow of disturbin' news like you can."

Annie ripped her gaze away from Jackson's unsympathetic one and looked to Baker.

He flashed a dazzling smile and said, "Don't worry about it, Annie. We'll all take good care of you, and you're a blessin' for Mama. You ain't got nothin' to worry about. Even good ol' smooth-talkin' Jackson won't let nothin' happen to you. He brung you home, didn't he?"

She looked to Maggie, and the woman seemed to read her mind. "Now stop that, darlin'! You hear me? You're not a criminal. We're sure of that. So don't even think that way. In fact, Jackson thinks you're probably from a right good family. And that's one reason we'll wait to see if anyone comes lookin' for you."

Annie looked back to Jackson. His eyes seared hers as they met again.

"Why do you think that I'm from a good family?" she asked.

"The way you were dressed. Fancy. And your skin is too…too… pampered for you to have been workin' outside for any amount of time. Especially your hands. Soft as silk. They haven't been workin' hard lately. Look at them fingernails! Ain't a workin' woman on this earth that has fingernails as long as that…all perfectly shaped."

Annie felt like bursting into tears. He seemed so disapproving! Shouldn't a girl be as soft and as feminine as possible?

"Mark another one up for Mr. Subtle, Mama," Baker groaned disgustedly.

"Well, I think it's time we all turned in," Maggie suggested, taking Annie's hand reassuringly.

"Yep. I'm sure ol' Root will be out and about at the crack of dawn," Baker agreed, standing up and stretching. "Where is your mind off to, little brother?" he asked Matt.

Annie noticed that Matt hadn't said a word nearly the whole evening.

"Just thinkin'," he mumbled.

"You think too awful much," Jackson grumbled before leaving the room.

Maggie took Annie back into the bedroom where she had awakened earlier.

"Now, there's some clean nightdresses in here for you and another dress. We wear 'em out quick here. Don't have time or need of a lot of fancy wear. You get a good night's sleep, and don't worry about a thing. Everythin' will come back to you when you're ready. I'll leave the lamp burnin' all night if you like. The hitchin' post is right straight out the back door a ways if you should need it."

Annie frowned. "The hitching post?" she repeated, completely baffled.

Maggie chuckled. "The outhouse, honey. I'll leave you be now. Good night. And in the mornin', we'll put up a heap a peaches. Maybe do some preserves as well."

She kissed Annie lightly on the forehead and turned to leave.

"I'm sorry, Mrs. McCall…for the inconvenience. I just don't know what else to do or where else I should go. Maybe we should let the sheriff know that you found me. Surely that would be best."

Maggie put a soft, warm hand on the girl's cheek. "Trust Jackson, Annie. He can be mighty severe at times, but we've all learned that he has a special gift for figurin' things like this out. It's a little unnervin', but if he thinks it's best that we keep you to ourselves for now… then it's best. Now, get some sleep. Think about apple blossoms and rainbows, darlin'."

CHAPTER THREE

The smell was so strong and familiar. Yet she seemed to be having trouble breathing. The air felt heavy and wet. She stood in a grove of enormous black-barked trees. They were very beautiful but sent fear and anxiety riveting through her. What was the familiar odor in the air? She couldn't identify it, but it seemed as familiar to her as breathing itself.

Suddenly then, she knew true terror. The need to flee. To run—anywhere! She had to escape! From what? She didn't know. Just that she had to get away!

"Help me!" she tried to scream. Over and over she tried, but no sound would escape her throat into the nightmare. "Please, help me!" she cried out. She began to gasp with panic. "Help me!"

"Wake up!" she heard him say. "Wake up, Annie. You're dreamin'. Listen here. You're dreamin'." It was Jackson's commanding voice, and she opened her eyes to find her chin held tightly in one of his strong hands.

"You're dreamin', girl. That's all." His face softened for a moment, and he smiled ever so slightly at her. "You're fine. Tell me what you were dreamin'."

Annie looked over at Maggie, who was smoothing the perspiration from her brow and smiling.

Maggie nodded and mouthed, "Tell him."

She looked back into the eyes of Jackson McCall. They were so disconcerting! She glanced the other way as she spoke.

"I had to run. I couldn't breathe. The air felt so heavy! I could smell something. I know what it is…but I can't remember…and there were enormous trees. Black…oaks…I don't know how I know that. I had to run…and no one would help me. There was no one there to help me." Annie let the tears trickle down her face. She didn't care if they thought her weak.

Maggie smoothed her hair back. "It's over now, darlin'. You go back to sleep. You need to rest."

"Oh, no! I can't! I don't want to go back to sleep," Annie pleaded, sitting up in bed as fright gripped her.

Jackson stood, and Annie's panic was abruptly interrupted as she noticed his lack of attire. He wore no shirt—only red flannels that had been cut away at the waist and made to tie with a string.

Maggie laughed as Jackson turned around to leave and Annie clamped her hands over her eyes as she caught a glimpse of the trapdoor in the rear of the flannels. "Jackson, darlin'," Maggie said through her giggles, "you may have to learn some modesty now that we've got another female in the house."

He turned and looked back at his behind. "Why? They're hitched up and fastened good enough. What's she all fire blushin' about?"

Maggie chuckled, and when he had closed the door behind him, she stood to leave as well. "Forgive my boys, Annie. Their daddy didn't care much for modesty either. It's like bangin' my head against a brick wall tryin' to keep them decent at all. Go to sleep, pretty baby. It'll all be right in the mornin'."

❧

Amazingly enough, Annie did fall asleep, and quickly. And slept soundly until morning. The first thing she heard as she drifted away from slumber and into the day was a meadowlark's song carried through the open window on the cool morning breeze. The smell of peaches was sweet and strong in the air too.

She could hear low-pitched voices coming from the other room, and she guessed that the McCall boys and their precious mama had been up and about for some time. She felt happy and safe again. For the first time since…since she couldn't remember.

18

Quickly she dressed and braided her hair, taking a deep breath she opened her door. Sunshine radiated through the kitchen windows, and she had been right, for the three men and their mother were finishing up breakfast. Annie began to salivate as the aroma of frying bacon and hot maple syrup filled her senses.

"Good mornin', Annie!" Maggie chirped with a broad smile.

Baker smiled broadly at her, and she returned the greeting. Annie had already decided that this man's moods were contagious. "Well. Let me just tell you, Miss Annie…that you better be dang glad I ain't the one who found you lyin' out there…'cause I would've just run off with you all to myself. Jackson ain't got the sense given a pig."

"I'm done, Mama. I'll be in the north pasture if you need me," Matt said, rising from the table and kissing his mother's cheek. "Baker can complain all he wants to about chasin' down ol' Root, but seems like I'm the one always gets stuck with repairin' that north fence when he busts it down. You have a good day, Annie…and don't let Mama run you ragged just yet." He tipped his hat with a smile and headed out the back door.

"Hello!" Mary called from the front door.

"Come on in, honey!" Maggie said, wiping her hands on her checkered apron. "I'm glad you're here. Now we can get started as soon as Annie's had her breakfast. Have you eaten, Mary?"

"Oh, yes, ma'am. You know my mama—don't matter if she starves you the rest of the day, we all eat breakfast whether or not we want to," Mary said as Annie noticed her eyes lingering on the back of Jackson's head.

"Me and Baker are gonna break in that new black today, Mama," Jackson mumbled as he wiped his mouth with a white napkin.

"Oh, no, Jackson. Surely not yet. He's so wild! I wish you would geld him instead of usin' him for stud. He frightens me," Maggie said. "I hate when you go abreakin' in horses as wild as that one. Bill scares me even now."

"Oh, Mama…you worry too much. You know big brother can break any horse alive. I'd put money on it any day of the week," Baker assured her, looking at his brother, who grinned back at him.

"Dang right," Jackson said, slapping Baker's broad shoulder.

"You see, Annie," Maggie began, "my boy Jackson here thinks there ain't a horse on this green earth that he can't ride. I'll admit, he's bred some mighty fine colts and fillies—made a heap of money doin' it. But you watch him a bit today and tell me, if it was your baby out there, how you'd feel. Besides, there's always your daddy to consider, Jackson."

The boys' smiles faded.

"Now, Mama, don't you worry about me. I won't take no unnecessary chances," Jackson assured her.

"It's unnecessary to break him at all, son."

Baker stood and kissed his mother affectionately on the forehead. "Don't you worry, Mama. That's why I go with him—to keep his head on his shoulders 'stead of smashed in the dirt. Ladies," he said, tipping his hat as he put it on. "Do come out for a visit later after Mama has you sick of peaches." And he left.

Jackson stood up and kissed his mother as well. "Don't you girls let her sit in here and fret all mornin'. He's not as bad as you think, Mama. Girls," he said with a smile and followed his brother out.

Annie didn't miss the look that passed between Mary and Jackson as he had turned to leave, and for some reason she felt resentful of it.

"I hope they're careful, Mrs. McCall," Mary said, frowning.

Maggie let out a heavy sigh. "Well, darlin's…when you have boys, you better strengthen your faith. Now let's do some peaches. You haven't said one word this mornin', Annie. Not that you could get one in around here during breakfast."

"It's far more entertaining to listen to ya'll talking," she said, smiling. "By the way, Mrs. McCall…I'm afraid I don't know whether or not I've ever done any canning."

Mary giggled. "Well, it's easy enough, Annie. Just takes time."

❧

They canned for nearly five hours without a break, and Annie found it exhilarating. They talked, and Maggie and Mary gossiped. Annie learned a lot just listening to them. The most disturbing to her was Mary's habit of bringing the conversation around to Jackson nearly constantly. She didn't know why it bothered her so. Jackson obviously looked upon Mary with some affection, at least, whereas he seemed to think Annie a great inconvenience.

"Those boys get so busy. I hate when they don't come in for lunch. Mary, take Annie out there to the corral to call those two in for lunch. I'll go holler for Matthew," Maggie sighed.

Mary gleefully slipped her arm through Annie's and led her out through the door and down to the corrals.

Annie had never seen such a sight, she was sure. There was Baker, sitting atop the fence hollering as he watched his brother. Jackson was astride a magnificent black stallion, which was jumping and arching his back furiously, trying to throw the determined-looking man off. Mary leaned up against the fence, but Annie felt nervous and stood back a few feet.

"Is he gettin' anywhere, Baker?" Mary asked.

"Oh yeah! Look at that! He's nearly got him now!"

"He does?" Annie inquired doubtfully. She couldn't help moving closer to the fence to get a better look.

"Oh yeah!" Baker chuckled, reaching back, grabbing her arm, and pulling her flush with the fence. The dust being kicked up made it hard to breathe.

"Yeee-haw!" Baker hollered. "You got him now, brother! He's wearin' down."

"He is?" Annie asked again. She wondered how in the world Jackson was staying on that horse.

And in the very next moment, he wasn't. She watched in horror as Jackson's seat left the horse's back and landed hard on the ground. Then she stifled a scream as she watched the horse stomp at him as he ran to the fence and jumped it. The horse snorted and shook his head furiously, rearing and stomping savagely.

"You sorry cuss," Jackson muttered, clearing the fence just in time.

"Jackson, your mama wants you boys in for some lunch. But you're covered in dirt!" Mary laughed. "She'll have your hide if you go trackin' in like that."

"Then I won't go trackin' in, Mary. Now give me a big hug and a kiss, girl," Jackson said, moving to capture Mary in his arms.

"No!" she screamed as she giggled and moved away. "You're filthy!"

Baker chuckled. "It's just good ol' dust, Mary."

"He's filthy!" she laughed.

Jackson grinned slyly at her. He was dusty, Annie admitted. But it was different than being dirty.

"Soil doesn't make a man filthy," she thought out loud. "A man can be as clean and smell as fresh as evening and still be the filthiest creature on this earth." Annie hugged herself tightly as she broke out in goose bumps. Something was making her feel sick to her stomach. Something dreadful.

"Well, thank you, Miss Annie," Jackson said, bowing. "Coming from you, that's a real compliment."

She was suddenly rather vexed. Why was he so mocking? "What do you mean by that?" she demanded, and his eyebrows rose in surprise. "What have I done that has caused you to label me as arrogant? Nothing I'm aware of. In fact, I would say you are the more uppity of the two of us. Overly judgmental of people that you know absolutely nothing about! Why did you even bother bringing me here if I'm such an annoyance to you?"

Jackson stood staring with a stunned expression on his face.

"Well," Baker said, grinning. "We know she has a fuse about as short as Mama's at least."

"I'm sorry, Mr. McCall," Annie said, smoothing her skirt self-consciously. "I'm just overly fatigued, I guess. I must seem terribly ungrateful to you." She put a hand to her head as she felt a sudden headache hit.

"Not at all, Annie. I'm sorry if I made you feel unwelcome," Jackson apologized, grinning almost kindly at her.

"Your mama is gonna think we got lost comin' to get you boys," Mary reminded. "You all right, Annie?" she asked when she noticed the frown on the girl's face.

"I'm fine," she whispered.

"Maybe it's this hot air not agreein' with you," Baker suggested, tipping her head up and searching her face.

"No. No. Actually, I find it much nicer than all that sticky dampness. A body can't even dry off after bathing there's so much moisture in the air there," she mumbled as she began to feel dizzy. Suddenly she was shaken back to her senses by Jackson's strong hands on her shoulders.

"What do you mean? Where is it damp? Where?" he growled into her face.

"Dang it, Jack. Give her some air," Baker said, removing his brother's grip and scooping Annie up in his arms. And then everything was dark.

Annie regained consciousness almost immediately. "Put me down! Please, Baker!" she demanded, feeling completely aggravated. "I'm fine. It's only a headache." She was not the weak-blooded, silly girl they were taking her for. She pushed firmly against Baker's broad chest until he put her down.

"You sure you're all right, Annie?" he asked, sincerely concerned.

She looked up into his handsome face and felt the urge to smooth the frown from his brow. Smiling, she said, "I'm fine. I'm sorry to be so much trouble." Mary and Jackson looked at each other and then at her.

"Where is it so damp and all, Annie?" Jackson asked casually.

Annie tossed her head and rolled her eyes. "Louisiana, of course! Where else would I be…" Her voice trailed off, and the others watched as the color drained from her face.

"Louisiana? Where in Louisiana?" Jackson asked, taking several steps forward until he stood directly in front of her with his eyes burning into hers.

"Just…Louisiana," she choked out.

"Jackson," Baker said, taking his brother firmly by the arm. "That's good, darlin'," he continued. "You're beginnin' to remember. See. Now, let's get in there for lunch before Mama has kittens."

Still holding his elder brother by the arm, Baker pushed Jackson ahead of himself and through the screen door.

"What's the matter with you all?" Maggie asked when she noticed the two brothers glaring at each other as they washed up in the basin.

"Nothin'," Baker answered bluntly.

"Mary? Annie? Now I know you girls will tell me what's goin' on. You weren't hurt tryin' to break that horse were you, Jackson?" she asked.

Mary looked at Annie and then cast her eyes to the floor.

Annie responded, "I think I must have come here from Louisiana, Mrs. McCall. In fact, I'm sure that's where I'm from. I think your eldest son is impatient and irritated with me because I can't remember anything else. That's all."

The cloudy memory, as small as it was, was gradually helping Annie's confidence and personality to reemerge. She felt that maybe she would eventually be able to remember everything—and that, no matter what, she could endure it. She had felt like a little lost puppy until now. But that would change—she hoped.

"That's wonderful, honey!" Maggie exclaimed, but Annie thought she sensed a look of regret in the woman's eyes. "Now, you take Jackson with a grain of salt, dear. He's an impatient boy. And, Jackson McCall, you find some manners and compassion in that hard heart of yours."

"Oh, he's not so hard-hearted, Mrs. McCall. It's an act, I think," Mary said, coyly smiling at Jackson.

Annie didn't miss the look in Mary's eyes as she watched Jackson sit down at the table next to her.

"Got that mean thing broke yet, Jackson?" Matthew asked as he came through the back door and began to clean up at the basin.

"Give me another hour or two, little brother. He ain't as tough as he lets on," Jackson answered, smiling.

"Most people ain't either," Baker said, winking at Annie and motioning subtly at his elder brother.

As Matthew sat down, Annie noticed how his eyes lingered on Mary for a moment then darted around nervously to see if anyone had noticed. Mary's gaze never left Jackson, though he seemed oblivious to the fact. Annie felt a little stitch form in the pit of her stomach. Obviously Matthew had feelings for Mary, and obviously Mary had eyes only for Jackson, who didn't seem to be aware of it.

"Why don't you tell us about Louisiana, Annie?" Jackson suggested after they had begun their meal.

"Good gravy, Jackson! Leave the girl alone," Maggie exclaimed.

"It's okay, Mrs. McCall," Annie said, sensing the tone of almost *I don't believe you* in Jackson's voice. "I don't remember much, Mr. McCall. It's a feeling almost more than a vision. Moist, heavy air. Rain. The smell of a million different green things and a million different bug noises in the breeze. Magnolias come to mind. And grand old black oaks." Suddenly a shiver went through her. The dream she had had the night before returned, and for a moment she was silent as she tried to remember more about it.

"What makes you sure that it's Louisiana you're rememberin'?" Baker asked.

"I'm uncertain," she answered, hugging herself to dispel the goose bumps that had sprung up all over her.

"I take it that our Annie here is from Louisiana," Matthew stated. "Not that anybody bothers tellin' me anything nohow."

"I think she's the very picture of what I've heard a Creole girl should look like," Mary added. "They've all got dark hair and milky skin and are as beautiful as princesses," she added in a dreamy voice.

"Well, then I'm surely not a Creole girl," Annie added in complete sincerity. When she looked up from her plate, everyone at the table was staring at her with odd expressions on their faces.

"At least she's humble about it," Jackson said, chuckling and returning his attention to his food.

Matthew stood to leave. "Thank you, Mama. I feel a whole lot better. Ready to run down ol' Root now. He got out while I was repairin' that fence. Wanna help me, Baker? You seem to have a regular talent in catchin' that bull."

Baker shook his head vigorously. "You kiddin'? What would ol' Jackson do without me out there to make sure he don't get hurt? Naw, you better take care of ol' Root yourself, Matt."

"I'll come with you, Matthew," Annie volunteered, standing up and folding her napkin neatly.

"I don't know, Annie..." Matthew began to protest.

"I'll be fine. I just can't imagine a ring in a cow's nose. I've got to see that for myself."

"Bull, Annie. Ol' Root is a bull," Maggie chuckled.

Matthew glanced at Mary, who was still staring dumbly at Jackson, who was still cleaning his plate.

"Okay, Annie. You a fast runner?" he asked, and they left laughing.

CHAPTER FOUR

"What's the matter, Matthew?" Annie asked, surprising the man.

"What do you mean?" He stopped walking and looked curiously down at her.

"You like Mary, don't you, Matthew?" she asked.

He looked away, rolling his eyes as if he thought it a silly question. "You're loco, Annie. Mary's been in love with Jackson since she was six years old. She asked him to marry her when she was thirteen. Why would I be interested in her?"

"Because she's pretty and sweet. You're nearly completely silent whenever she's around, you know."

He began walking again. "Where has that bull gone off to?"

Annie was beginning to feel that maybe her feet weren't used to walking through pastures and climbing fences. But as far as her encouraging Matthew where Mary was concerned, she was undaunted. "Maybe if you weren't so silent—more yourself when she was around—she'd notice you," she went on.

Matthew laughed and stopped, looking down at her. "You're a persistent little gal, you know that? You don't even know me, Annie. How are you so sure who I like and what I should do about it?" His smile was like sunshine.

"It's a gift I have, Matthew. Truly it is. You just need to catch her attention."

He took her hand in his own and patted it with the other. "I've seen other men try to take women's attention away from my big brother, Annie. It don't happen. They're always second choice once the female realizes that Jackson won't ever be interested. I don't want to be second choice, Annie. I'll wait for a girl who sees me first."

"She's just infatuated, Matthew. He's quite rough, mysterious. She'll get over him, I'm sure," Annie encouraged.

"You are a sweet thing, Annie. But I'm a lost cause. Hey, there he is! Come on!" And he took off toward an enormous bull standing some one hundred feet away.

Annie hiked up her dress and petticoats and took out after him. She stopped when they got close and the bull lowered his head and snorted. He looked mean, and Annie didn't like the ominous look of his horns.

"Matthew?" she whispered. She could clearly see the shiny copper ring that pierced the animal's nose.

"Oh, he's full of beans and other stuff, Annie. Don't worry."

But when the bull started on a headlong run straight for her, she turned and began to run.

"Jump the fence, Annie!" she heard Matthew holler, and she obeyed, rather ungracefully, when she reached it.

The bull charged headlong into the fence, and she let out a startled scream as she turned to see him ramming it over and over again with his massive head. Matthew reached him finally and jerked hard on the ring protruding from Root's nose. The bull turned his head, and Matthew began to lead him back to the pasture.

He looked back at Annie, who was still panting from her sprint, and called, "He'll get to know you, Annie. You run on back to the house and tell ol' Baker he ain't the only one 'round here that sticks in ol' Root's craw!"

Matthew's laughter was contagious, and Annie giggled to herself. What a sight she must have been!

When she entered the house, it was to hear Maggie's concerned voice scolding Jackson.

"I knew it! I knew it! That horse is mean, Jackson. Look at this! He could've really hurt you!"

"Mama, I've been nipped before. It ain't no big—" Jackson started.

"Nipped? Nipped? Jackson, it's beyond me, son, how this is considered a nip!"

Jackson was standing in the kitchen taking off his shirt, and Maggie was frantically wetting a towel at the basin.

"Mary, fetch some water, and get it boilin'. Oh, Annie, thank goodness! Get that boy to sit down!"

Annie looked at her, dumbfounded. What did she mean? Was she to command him to "sit"?

"Just look at that! Will you look at that?" Maggie exclaimed.

"Mama, go out and gather the eggs or somethin'. Please. Baker and Annie can take care of this," Jackson said calmly.

Annie stood still, not quite knowing what to do.

"Jackson, quit ordering me around. I'm your mama!" Maggie wailed frantically.

"I've helped with horse bites before, Mrs. McCall. I can do it. You go out for some air," Annie said, understanding the situation at once.

"I just don't handle it well when my babies get hurt, Annie. I don't handle it well at all," she said, wiping the perspiration from her brow.

Mary returned and handed the water to Annie.

"Mary, take Mama out for a walk, will you?" Baker said, winking at Annie and handing his mother to Mary.

"Come on, Mrs. McCall. Let's get you some air," Mary suggested, leading the woman out the door.

"Those boys!" Maggie sighed heavily as she left. "They keep my stomach in knots! I'll probably end up with twenty-five grandsons and not one granddaughter in the litter."

"It is a pretty bad one, Jack," Baker said, examining the bite mark on Jackson's shoulder.

"Well, it feels pretty bad. That ol' cuss. Nipped me when I had my back turned. I've gotta break him now, Baker. I can't let him get away with it."

"You wanna clean this out, Annie? I ain't too thorough at cleanin' wounds," Baker said, wrinkling up his nose.

Annie walked over to inspect the wound herself with great reluctance.

"Neked men make her nervous," Jackson whispered to Baker, and they both smiled broadly.

"Perhaps," Annie agreed. "But unclad adolescent boys do not concern me in the least."

Baker snickered. "She's gettin' wise to you, Jack," he mumbled to his brother.

The wound was more severe than Annie had first thought. "Do you receive these kinds of injuries on a regular basis?" she asked.

"Yep. Impressive, ain't it?" he asked, though he grimaced as she pressed on it.

"Where I come from we call it 'stupidity,'" she stated.

Baker and Jackson raised their eyebrows at each other.

"Well, well, well! Miss High and Mighty, I'm sure that where you come from the boys all smell like girls and ride sidesaddle too," Jackson chuckled. "You come sit here on my lap, and I'll show you what a real, hard-workin' man feels like." And he pulled her to sit down on his lap.

She was caught off guard and automatically clutched at his arms for support. He grinned slyly at her, and she felt like slapping him. He was either flirting or rude every minute of the day! No in between, it seemed.

She intentionally squeezed his wounded shoulder as she righted herself.

"Where I come from, Mr. McCall, men like you are welcomed only in brothels and drinking establishments," she informed him as she began to dress the wound.

"I think that it weren't no rag doll you brung home, big brother," Baker chuckled.

Jackson never quit smiling at her the entire time she was dressing the wound, and it made her very self-conscious, though she did an excellent job of hiding it.

Mary returned with Maggie, who immediately began smoothing her son's hair and clinging to him. "I wish you wouldn't break so many, son. You know it unnerves me," she pleaded quietly.

"I'm a big boy, Mama. And horses need to be broke if we're gonna sell 'em." Then he stood up, took Annie's hand, and pressed it against his bare chest. "And thank you, Miss Annie. You did an excellent job of dressin' this bite." He smiled as she began to blush and tried to pull her hand away from his hot skin.

"I take it that you never had brothers, Annie," Mary said, smiling as Annie was able to detach her hand at last.

"You're rotten to the core, Jackson. And put a shirt back on. For cryin' in the bucket, son! Have some manners," Maggie scolded, although she wore a broad smile like everyone else, except Annie.

"Come on, Baker. Let's break that ol' sucker," Jackson said, putting his blood-stained shirt back on and heading out the door.

"You're going to let him go out there again?" Annie questioned Maggie in disbelief.

"I don't want to, honey…but that horse has gotta learn who's boss," the older woman replied.

CHAPTER FIVE

After two weeks, Annie was feeling quite comfortable at the McCall ranch. She hadn't remembered anything else significant, just bits and pieces of Louisiana life. She had fallen into a routine of daily chores—milking a cow every morning, gathering eggs, churning butter, making soap, mending, and helping to bring in the herds in the evening—and she loved it. She loved the life the McCalls led and secretly hoped it would go on forever.

The boys were wonderful to her—except for Jackson, who seemed to like her one minute and be irritated with her the next. Matthew still pined for Mary from afar, and she was still unaware of it. Mary spent a lot of time at the ranch, and Annie found herself annoyed each time she would see the girl smiling cutely at Jackson and tugging at his shirtsleeve to get his attention.

One morning, Annie went out as usual to milk Flossy. She went to the corner of the barn for a stool and heard voices. Jackson and Mary were coming into the barn, and she was certain that Mary sounded upset. For some reason, Annie quickly hid in an empty stall instead of revealing that she was there.

"Jackson, don't you care for me at all?" Mary sniffled in a pain-stricken voice.

"Of course I do, Mary. But not like you're wantin' me to. We've had this conversation before." Jackson sounded angry.

"But, Jackson...I've grown up now. I'm old enough for you. I'd do anything for you!"

Annie found a knothole in one of the boards of the stall and peered through it.

Jackson spun around and took Mary by the shoulders. "Listen to me, Mary. I don't want to upset you, and I never, ever wanted to hurt you. But it's just not gonna be, darlin'. I always thought you'd outgrow your crush—"

"It's not a crush anymore, Jackson!" Mary interrupted furiously. "Just let me prove it to you, Jackson. I'm old enough to be everythin' you need…and want."

Annie's eyes widened as she watched Mary lock her fingers behind the man's neck. Her expression then changed from hurt and frustration to something quite different.

"Mary, I'm serious. I'm not for you. You're a sweet, beautiful young lady. You deserve much better than a smelly ol' cowboy like me," Jackson said quietly, trying to remove her arms from about his neck.

"You are for me, Jackson. You've always been for me. I grew up… just for you." The girl raised herself to kiss him, but he turned his head from her, and she only succeeded in kissing his handsome, unshaven face.

Jackson forcefully removed her arms from around him and held them to her sides. "Enough, Mary. It won't ever be. You need to go on with your life."

"You are my life, Jackson!" she pleaded.

"No, Mary. I'm not what you need, and I'm sorry, but you're not what I need. And…and you're not what I want."

Annie suddenly felt sorry for the girl. The look on Mary's face was that of utter and complete heartbreak.

"I'm sorry, Mary. If I ever led you to believe anythin' could happen between us…I'm sorry," Jackson soothed as the tears began to roll down Mary's cheeks.

"You've nothin' to be sorry for, Jackson. It was me. I know that. You never led me on in any way. I'll leave you alone. I'm the one who's sorry."

She turned to flee, but Jackson caught her arm and pulled her to him, holding her in a sweet embrace. "You've always been special to me, darlin'. I don't want you hatin' me or stayin' away because of me. Everyone loves you here. You're like one of the family. Don't stay angry with me. I'm just a nasty old bear…not much good for anythin' but breakin' horses and fightin' with my fists." Then he cupped her face in his hands and kissed her lightly on the mouth. "Now then… we've had our kiss. Someday, when you're married with ten babies runnin' around in the barnyard, you'll look over at your handsome devil of a husband and think, 'That ol' Jackson McCall…he weren't hardly worth all the fuss.'"

Mary smiled up at him through her tears. "You're wrong, Jackson. You're wrong."

He grinned at her as he gently pushed her away from him after a final hug. "Nope. I'm right. You'll see, darlin'. You'll see."

Mary smiled at him once more, turned, and left, wiping her tears on her apron. "I better get back and help your mama with those berries."

Annie wiped a tear from her own cheek and whispered to herself, "How sad." Then, terror struck as she saw Jackson turn his attention to her hiding place.

Looking as fierce as Root, he reached over the wall, grabbing the back of her dress and pulling her up to face him.

"I understand why you hid. You didn't have much time to do anythin' else. But if you care anythin' at all for our little Mary, you'll forget everythin' you heard. She's a sweet girl, and I won't have her embarrassed."

Annie grabbed his arm that held her dress and dug her fingernails in deep. "Let me go!" she growled at him. "I'd never do anything to hurt Mary! Even you should know that."

Jackson released Annie, and his expression was now that of discouragement. "I hate situations like that. I never handle them right," he mumbled, picking up a pitchfork and starting to clean the stall. It really bothered him. Annie knew that it did. It dripped from every part of him.

"You handled it wonderfully. Many men would've laughed at her—or worse, taken advantage of the situation."

"I suppose," he mumbled.

He was so incredibly handsome! Annie understood how a girl could be in love with him from the day she was born.

"You better get to milkin' that cow before she busts," he said, smiling at her.

She blushed when she realized that she had been staring at him.

"I have to say, Miss Annie, I misjudged you. You turned out to be a right good worker. Even if you ain't got calloused hands," Jackson chuckled when she had finished milking Flossy.

Annie smiled as she lifted the bucket full of milk and began to leave. "Thank you. I know how it pains you to admit you were wrong."

Annie left the barn and began to walk toward the house, but she stopped in her tracks when she saw them. A group of wild-looking Indians was approaching on horseback. When they saw her, they stopped, and the one who appeared to be their leader dismounted his horse and moved toward her.

"Jackson?" her voice squeaked out. She couldn't yell. She was too frightened. So she slowly set the bucket down and began walking backward toward the barn. They looked so menacing!

As she walked backward, the Indian still walked toward her. When she felt a pair of hands on her shoulders, she gasped and spun around. Relief flooded her as Jackson pulled her into his arms and against his strong, protective body.

"What do you want here, Black Wolf?" he asked angrily. There was no response. "We've nothing to trade today. I want you to go," Jackson growled.

"The woman. She is very good to look at," came the rough reply of the Indian.

A chill of horror traveled down Annie's spine, and she wrapped her arms tightly around Jackson's waist.

Jackson said nothing at first and then began stroking her hair as he said, "She's mine. Don't look at her."

The Indian chuckled. "I will trade many horses for her, Captain. I know that you want horses. I want the woman. We have seen her in the field many times. I will take her, and you can have horses. Or I will take her, and your life can bleed from you." Annie clenched her arms tightly around Jackson's waist, but he broke the embrace and pushed her aside. Without Jackson's support, Annie's knees weakened, and she found herself trembling and sitting on the ground at his feet.

"Don't threaten me, Black Wolf. You know I have no fear of you. And you also know that I can kill you easily. Now leave. Or *your* life will end. You're never to come here again. Never come near this land…or you will die."

Annie looked up at Black Wolf. His expression was one of barely controlled anger as he looked at her. His chest rose and fell with his angry breathing.

"She is your woman?" Black Wolf asked.

"Yes," Jackson replied. "Never dare to even look at her again, Black Wolf."

The Indian took a deep breath and forced a smile. "Of course, Captain. Black Wolf understands." And he offered a hand to Jackson.

Jackson shook his hand briefly but never smiled. He stood like a granite boulder watching them ride away. Then he turned to look at Annie. She still sat on the ground next to him, shaking with fright.

"I saw them out near the north pasture two days ago. I had no idea what he was lookin' for…until now," Jackson mumbled.

Annie felt an odd guilt rush through her. She had put this wonderful family in danger. She wanted to find a hole and crawl into it.

"He called you 'Captain,'" she whispered. Jackson just shrugged his shoulders and offered her a hand to help her up.

"Let me tell Mama, Annie. It makes her mighty nervous whenever they show up."

She put her hand in his and quickly removed it once she had stood. "They're very shocking…aren't they? I mean…the first time you ever see them." She tried to speak calmly, but her voice still quivered, revealing the state of her nerves.

"They're renegades. A mess of different tribes—Apache, Crow— all pretty mean. But they're alone out here, so they stay pretty much in hand." Then he took her by the shoulders and glared into her face. "Never show your fear! They take it as a sign of weakness. Talk confidently, trade with them. But never give them anything."

"You think they'll come back…don't you?"

He shrugged again. "You might wanna get that milk into Mama before the flies get to it." And he turned and walked back into the barn.

⁂

"Well! I was wonderin' where you had gone off to, honey," Maggie chirped as Annie entered the kitchen. "What's wrong?" she asked immediately as she continued to look at the girl. "You're as white as a sheet."

Annie tried to smile. Why shouldn't she be pale? In the last ten minutes, she had witnessed Jackson breaking Mary's heart and nearly been abducted by renegade Indians. "I'm fine, Mrs. McCall. Too much sun maybe."

Maggie wiped her hands on her apron and felt Annie's forehead. "Too much sun, my foot! Now you tell me what has you lookin' so peaked."

"Ol' Black Wolf just paid us a visit, Mama. I suspect little Miss Annie was a little…unnerved," Jackson said, striding through the back door with a broad smile.

"Black Wolf!" Maggie gasped, all color draining from her face as well. "What did he want, son?" she asked.

Jackson cleared his throat, grabbed a fresh peach from the basket on the table, and began peeling it with a pocketknife. "Annie," he answered, nodding toward the girl.

Maggie's mouth dropped open, and she looked from Jackson to Annie and back again. "Annie?" she whispered. "Tell me you're teasing me, Jack!"

"Nope. He wanted little Miss Porcelain Complexion here."

Annie felt tears of exasperation brimming in her eyes. He could be so insensitive!

"What did you tell him?" Maggie asked, pulling a chair from the table and sitting down.

Jackson's smile faded. "Don't worry, Mama. He won't be back."

Maggie clutched his hand firmly in hers and spoke gravely, "Jackson…how can you be sure?"

Jackson looked up at Annie, then back to his mother. "I didn't have to say anythin'. He got a closer look at her and changed his mind."

For a moment Maggie's expression was still that of worry, but it slowly changed to a smile.

Annie, however, found nothing soothing or humorous in his remark, and as the tears of frustration began to escape her eyes, she slammed the bucket of milk down on the table and fled out the back door.

As she angrily walked away, she began to realize that she felt more hurt than vexed. She didn't like the fact that she was a burden to Jackson McCall—an irritating inconvenience. The two times she had been in his embrace—when he held her as they rode home after his finding her and as he spoke to the Indian only a few minutes before—she had felt safe, protected, and as if she wanted to stay only there forever. But he obviously saw her as nothing more than an ignorant girl who was a burden to the family.

"Wait a minute, jumpin' bean," Jackson chuckled as he caught her elbow and spun her around to face him. "You know I was only kiddin'! Mama gets so upset when Black Wolf is roamin' around. I had to calm her down."

Annie yanked her arm from his grasp and began walking away. "Fine. Now let me go for a walk. It has been a very fatiguing day." She wiped the tears from her cheeks and continued marching off.

Again he grabbed her arm to stay her. "Looky here, Miss Annie," he said, glaring at her, "I don't go chasin' after emotionally high-strung women as a rule…so you hear me out."

"I am not emotionally high-strung, Mr. McCall! I've just been nearly abducted by wild renegades and drug off to who knows what…and you're making light of it." He took a deep breath as Annie continued her venting. "I am sorry that you had to be the one to bear the burden of finding me out in the wilderness. But until I remember some shred of my life before you were forced to rescue me, I'll have to stay here and be the proverbial thorn in your side. Forgive me! Will you? And quit bringing the fact of my complete dependency to my attention every living minute of the day!"

Jackson's eyebrows raised in slight surprise at her outburst.

"Okay," he said. Annie took a deep breath and smoothed her skirt. "Maybe you didn't run away, Annie. Maybe you talked somebody crazy, and they dumped you out there," he muttered with a grin.

She moved to slap his face, but he caught her hand and twisted her arm behind her, pulling her body flush with his. The ache in her chest of hurt at his words started again.

"Why do you hate me so much?" she whispered as more tears escaped her eyes.

She looked up into his face, which was solemn again. His eyes left hers and seemed to rest on her mouth for just an instant. She glanced away from him when she realized that she had been studying his mouth as well.

"I don't hate you. I just like to tease, that's all," he whispered. Then he abruptly let her go. "If you ever see Black Wolf again, Annie… you get on back to the house at once and tell one of us boys. Do you understand?" He was so commanding, she felt like saluting with a strong "Yes, sir!" But she only nodded.

"Now, go for your walk and think hateful things about me." He smiled, tipped his hat, and began walking away.

He paused for a moment and said, "You won't let anyone know what you heard in the barn before, will you?"

"Of course not! I like Mary, and I'd never want to embarrass her," she replied.

"Did I…did I handle that all right, do you think?" he asked, adjusting his hat.

Annie was astonished. He actually seemed unsure about something. "Yes, of course," she muttered and watched him leave.

CHAPTER SIX

That night at dinner, the inevitable subject of Black Wolf came up.

"What did he want, Jackson?" Baker asked.

"Annie," Jackson replied, glancing at Annie and then his mama.

"Annie?" Matthew repeated.

"Well, I think that's mighty understandable," Baker said, smiling at Annie and adding a wink.

"It's terrifying!" Maggie reminded.

"Well, what did you tell him, Jack?" Matthew asked.

Jackson spread some butter on a biscuit before answering nonchalantly. "I told him that he couldn't have her 'cause she was mine."

Baker and Matthew raised their eyebrows at each other. Matthew let out an amazed whistle.

"Now my question is this," Baker began, smiling. "Did you tell him that to avoid a situation like the Smithes had…or were you thinkin' 'finders keepers'?" Baker winked at Annie again.

But Annie noticed that Maggie had dropped her fork.

"The Smithes?" Maggie asked as an ill-looking paleness washed over her.

"Good job, Baker," Matthew mumbled, hitting his brother hard in the ribs with an elbow.

"Now, Mama, don't get all upset," Jackson began.

"The Smithe girl! They took her and…well…Jackson, are you sure Annie's safe now?"

"What happened to the Smithe girl?" Annie asked as she felt the hair on the back of her neck stand on end.

"Mama, Bill Smithe didn't know a thing about dealin' with them renegades. These renegades…they aren't like the friendlier tribes. You gotta play tough. I told Black Wolf that she was mine. He knows not to buck any of us boys. He thinks she's mine. Bill Smithe told them other renegades that his daughter, Lilly, didn't belong to nobody. Black Wolf won't cross me, Mama. You know it."

Maggie threw her napkin down. "I don't know it, son. This frightens me!" Then she turned to Annie. "Lilly Smithe was taken by renegades. They did unspeakable things to her, Annie! Then they took her back to her daddy and murdered her right in front of him."

Annie looked at Jackson, who returned to eating his meal.

"Um…Mama," Matthew ventured. "I don't know if you wanna get too all detailed about that story just now." Then he turned to Annie. "Black Wolf is scared of Jackson, Annie. He's scared of all of us boys. You ain't got nothin' to worry about."

"That's right, darlin'," Baker said, reaching across the table and taking her hand. "You got three knights in shinin' armor here to protect you. You're safer here than you've ever been in your life, I'll bet."

His smile was so contagious, but Annie startled when Jackson reached out and slapped Baker's hand, causing him to release hers.

"She's mine, remember, little brother?" he said, chuckling.

"It's not funny!" Maggie cried out. Everyone looked at her. She wore a terrified expression. "Are you sure, Jackson?" she asked in a whisper.

He smiled warmly at his mother. "I'm sure, Mama. And if he did come back, I can whip him. So don't worry."

"He's a beast, Jackson! He'd carve you up like that girl!" she sobbed.

Jackson got up from the table. He walked over and crouched down beside his mother. "No one's gonna carve me up, Mama. I'm too mean," he whispered lowly.

The woman took the man's face in her hands, kissed his forehead, and smiled. "You're my pretty baby, son. I just worry," she whispered.

"Nothin' to worry about, Mama," he assured her.

Annie felt panic rising in her bosom. She had to get away! She was putting this precious group of people in obvious danger. But what could she do?

"Excuse me," she said, smiling and pushing her chair back.

"You all right, darlin'?" Maggie asked.

"Fine. Fine," Annie said, smiling. "Just need a little air." And she walked out the back door and toward the barn.

Her mind began racing. How could she get away? Where could she go? These people who had taken her in and cared for her were in danger! She could go to the sheriff. Maybe someone was looking for her. She could have Mary go into town tomorrow and check. She didn't have any money for a train ticket to anywhere, no horse or supplies to ride away with.

"Stop it right now, Annie," Jackson spoke from behind her. She spun around, startled.

"What?" she asked.

"I know what you're thinkin'. Stop it. You're not goin' anywhere."

"But I've put you all in terrible danger! If I leave—"

"If you leave, it'll break my mama's heart. And we don't like to have our mama upset. I'll tie you up in your room if you don't stop thinkin' this way. Understand?"

She looked up at him with desperation in her eyes. "You could help me. Just give me the means to buy a ticket east. I can go somewhere and get a job. I'm a burden to you all here."

"Oh, quit playin' martyr, Annie. You're no burden. Mama needs to have you here. You're good company for her. And besides…it gives us boys somethin' to look at besides the hitchin' post." He flashed a brilliant smile at her.

But there was more that she couldn't tell him. She was following in Mary's footsteps. She felt nervous whenever he was near her. Her bosom ached whenever he almost touched her in some way. She dreamt of him, thought of him almost constantly during the idle and working hours of the day. She found herself watching his mouth when he talked and wondering what his kiss would feel like.

"Hey!" Baker's voice boomed as he approached. "What are you two doin' out here? Are you tryin' to start sparkin' with my girl, Jack?" He laughed and put a comforting arm around Annie's shoulders. "We all know what you're thinkin', sweet pea. And Jackson may mean well, but he's got as much charm as ol' Root. You ain't puttin' us out or in danger or inconveniencin' us in any way…other than I gotta listen to Jackson talkin' in his sleep every night now. But we couldn't very well let him sleep in his old room with you, now could we?"

"I don't know," Jackson said, grinning. "I never thought of that before. I'm sure Annie don't snore as loud as you."

Annie reached up and patted Baker warmly on one rough, unshaven cheek. "You always make me feel better, Baker. Thank you."

He smiled and pointed to his other cheek. "Well, then I at least deserve a little peck…don't you think?"

She giggled and smiled as she stood on tiptoe and planted an affectionate kiss on his cheek.

"Hey!" Matthew called from the door. "What's goin' on? After all, Annie, ain't I the one that shares secrets with you?" he said, pointing to his own cheek and bending down.

Annie giggled again and placed a quick kiss on his cheek as well.

"Well, I'm the one that fought off them renegades today, ain't I?" Jackson added, pointing to his cheek.

Annie's smile faded, and she felt butterflies take flight in her stomach.

"He don't bite, Annie. Really," Baker chuckled.

She stood before him, and just as her lips would've brushed his cheek, he turned his head, causing her to kiss him directly on the mouth instead.

"Slap him, Annie!" Matthew chuckled. "He's slick as ice."

Jackson smiled slyly down at her, and she blushed.

"Red is definitely your color, darlin'," he whispered, grinning triumphantly before heading for the barn.

"He's still a kid when it comes to some things, Annie. Now come on in. Mama's still upset," Baker laughed as he put a comforting arm around her shoulders.

After convincing Maggie that she shouldn't worry, Annie went to her room to prepare for bed. She was still shaken by Jackson's boyish gesture at stealing a kiss. He was a puzzle. Serious one minute, boyish and playful the next. And even though it had lasted only a split second, she could still feel his lips brushing hers and smell the familiar scent of leather and hay that was his.

CHAPTER SEVEN

Several days passed before Mary visited again. When she did, she looked solemn and was quiet. Maggie sent a questioning look at Annie more than once, and Annie played ignorant to knowing what was wrong with the girl.

At lunch when the boys came in, Annie watched Mary closely. She never once looked at Jackson. She hardly joined in the conversation.

"You feelin' okay, Mary?" Matthew asked.

"Fine. Just quiet today, I guess," she answered, forcing a smile.

"How's your mama, Mary?" Jackson asked, smiling at her warmly.

She glanced at him only briefly before answering, "She's right as rain. We're workin' on our dresses for the Harvest Dance already. Sewin' tires her eyes more now than it used to."

"Harvest Dance?" Annie asked.

Mary's eyes lit up. "Oh! It's just the best thing all year, except for the Christmas Dance, of course. Punkins with faces cut in 'em, apple cider, punkin pie, waltzin'! Mr. Daniels plays his fiddle, and he's wonderful. You'll love it, Annie! I can help you with your dress. Maybe you could do my hair all fancy up for me. I can never do it myself."

Annie smiled. With her simple question, she had managed to break the bleakness of the girl's mood.

"Are you gonna go this year, Mrs. McCall?" Mary asked.

Maggie looked skeptical.

"Oh come on, Mama. It'll be so fun if you go with us this year. I mean…someone will have to go with us to chaperon Annie here. It wouldn't look good at all to have us three boys goin' alone with her," Matthew said between food bites.

"Oh…I don't know," Maggie whined.

"Oh, come on, Mrs. McCall. I need someone to keep me company while Annie's dancin' all night long. I'm sure she'll be the prettiest girl there," Mary said, patting Annie's hand.

"Well, I don't think either one of you will be wallflowers, girls. I know several young boys that have their eyes on our own Miss Mary," Jackson remarked before standing up to leave.

Mary smiled at him finally, and he winked at her.

"You wanna go for a walk with me, Annie?" Mary asked unexpectedly.

"Of course. Goodness knows I need some exercise. Mrs. McCall, your cooking has turned me into a complete piglet!"

"Sow," Jackson corrected her. "Fully grown female pigs are sows."

"Thank you for enlightening me, Mr. McCall," Annie sneered. "I suppose that would be comparable to referring to a colt's hindquarters instead of a fully matured horse's behind."

"She's gettin' good, Jackson," Matthew mumbled.

Jackson tipped his head in agreement.

The girls linked arms, exited through the back door, and headed toward the pasture.

"I guess you've noticed that I'm not quite myself lately, Annie," Mary began and took a deep breath to help hold in tears. Annie knew it was time to listen.

"I spoke to Jackson the other day. You see…I've been so terribly in love with him for as long as I can remember, and I was tired of waitin' to see if he felt anything for me. I just need to talk to someone about this, Annie. I told him how I felt the other day…out in the barn. I was so sure that he felt somethin' for me. But…as it turns out…he doesn't." She wiped the tears from her cheeks. "I just love him so much, Annie. I feel like I'm just gonna shrivel up and die inside."

"I do understand, Mary," Annie said, smiling at her. "More than you can imagine."

"There'll never be anyone else for me, Annie. Never."

Annie put a comforting arm around her friend's shoulders. "I know you think there won't be, Mary. But there will. There might be somebody close, right this moment, that'll treasure you and love you more than you can fathom. And I think you'll find that he's more suited to you…and you'll love him more than you ever did Jackson."

Mary looked up at Annie and smiled. "Nice speech." They both chuckled and hugged.

Just then the back door slammed, and the girls turned to see Matthew walking toward the barn.

"Matthew is so sweet," Annie remarked. "He's got a special way of knowing how people feel. He's very understanding and compassionate."

Mary looked at Annie and smiled knowingly. "You wouldn't be trying to steer me toward my old lover's brother, would you, Annie?" she asked.

Annie shook her head innocently. "He's very handsome too. Don't you think?" Annie added.

They giggled. "Well, Miss Annie," Mary started, "I've got an awful handsome older brother myself who is very interested in meetin' you. Collin is a dream and—what's the matter, Annie? Annie!"

Annie put her hands to her head. The pain was excruciating! Everything was going dark, and the name *Collin* kept echoing through her mind.

"Help me!" she whispered just before she fainted.

CHAPTER EIGHT

She could hear voices. They sounded far away at first. Then closer.

"Is she all right?"

"Yeah. Annie, wake up."

"We were just talkin', and she grabbed her forehead and fainted. No warnin' that it was comin' on at all."

"Annie?" It was Jackson's voice. "Annie? Wake up now."

"Malaina," she whispered as she began to regain consciousness. "My name is Malaina." She opened her eyes to see Jackson searching her face.

"Malaina?" he repeated. She watched his mouth as he repeated her name. "Malaina. Can you hear me?" he asked.

"I can hear you."

"Do you know who I am?" he commanded.

"You're Jackson McCall. Do you think I'm ignorant?"

Malaina heard chuckling, and Jackson smiled. "You know darn well I think you're ignorant. She'll be all right, Mama. Looks like the memory is comin' back too. Malaina. At least we can go back to namin' the stock 'Annie' now."

Maggie leaned over and smiled at her as she smoothed her hair back. "Malaina. That's a beautiful name. It suits you much better. You had me worried, sweetheart! As if these three boys don't keep my insides stirred up enough as it is."

"I'm sorry," Malaina whispered.

"Anything else? Do you remember your last name?" Jackson asked.

Malaina's head ached brutally. "No. But there's someone evil…a man. I don't know why—but I know he's evil. Collin something. That's all I can remember."

"We were talkin' about my brother, Collin. It musta triggered a memory for her, Mrs. McCall," Mary said.

"We'll go and let you rest, honey," Maggie said with a smile.

"Oh, no! No. I'm fine. Really. I need to get busy if Mary's gonna teach me how to sew a new dress for this Harvest Dance," Malaina said frantically. She didn't want to be left alone.

"Okay, sweet pea. Why don't you and Mary have Matthew drive you into town? The general store should have some cloth that'll do for a dress."

Malaina paused as realization hit her. "On second thought, Mrs. McCall…maybe I better just wear one of the dresses you've already given me."

"Nonsense, child! You'll be needin' some clothes of your own. We might as well start with a dress for the dance," the woman exclaimed.

"But…I don't…" Malaina stammered as she looked up into Jackson's scowling face.

"For cryin' out loud, Mama," he growled. "She's flat broke. Ain't that what you're tryin' to say, girl?"

Maggie broke into laughter. "Is that what you're worried about, sweetie? Well, I'll be. You're part of the family now! Money we have is yours too."

But Malaina shook her head. "Oh, no, Mrs. McCall. I'm a big enough burden as it is. I can't possibly expect you to—"

Jackson heaved an exasperated sigh. "You know, Miss Malaina… you're sickenin'ly sweet." Then he reached into the pocket of his well-worn pants, pulled out a wad of paper money, turned Malaina's hand palm up, and put the money in it. "Now, go to town, buy cloth, and make yourself a new dress. We can't have you lookin' like a ragamuffin at that dance. We got our own reputations to protect."

After rolling his eyes to show his irritation with the situation, he put his hat on and left.

Malaina sat stunned for a moment and then looked up at Maggie and Mary. Mary's mouth was still gaping open in surprise, but Maggie was smiling maternally, as usual.

"I can't possibly!" Malaina exclaimed at last.

Maggie laughed. "Of course you can, dear. Where do you think I would've gotten the money anyway?"

"Oh, but, Mrs. McCall—a lady just doesn't accept money from a gentleman," Malaina began to explain.

"You're out west now, dear…and this is family. We all work together to keep this ranch goin', and we all get paid for it in one way or another. Now let me get Matthew." And she left Malaina staring at the wad of money in her hand.

"Jimineeee!" Mary squealed. "What I wouldn't give to trade places with you!"

Malaina counted out the money. "It's far too much, I'm sure. I guess I'll just use what I need and then return the rest. But, Mary, taking money from a man—it's so improper!"

Mary giggled. "She's right, you know, Malaina. You're gonna have to change your way of thinkin' now. You do chores around here same as anyone else, don't you? Just think of it as your wages. That's all."

Malaina frowned. "I guess so. Well, let's go then. I haven't been anywhere besides church yet, and you can't see the town from there."

❧

Half an hour later, they set out for town. Baker decided to go with them too. Malaina had managed to get Mary to sit up front in the buggy with Matthew, and she sat behind them with Baker.

When Matthew and Mary started their own conversation finally, Baker winked at Malaina and whispered, "I know what you're up to. Don't think I don't."

Malaina giggled. "Now all I have to do is to find a suitable young lady for you, Baker." His smile faded, and as he looked away, she felt she had said something very wrong.

"Not just yet, darlin'," he muttered. He was quiet for a few more moments and then looked at her with an apologetic smile. "I ain't quite ready again. And when I am…well, I got you right here, now don't I?"

But she didn't laugh at his flirt. "What do you mean…'again'?" she asked.

He looked away for a moment. "Well, I guess you might as well hear it from me. I got married, Malaina. Two years ago next month." Malaina's eyes widened. "Yep. Not every young filly finds me as homely as you do, you know." She smiled. He went on. "Elizabeth. Elizabeth Johnson. Purty name, ain't it? And she was a vision, darlin'! A vision! Deep brown eyes—so dark you could hardly tell where that little black spot in her eye was. And yeller hair. Yeller as gold and soft as silk. A purty spunky little thing too. She kept me in line all right." He paused, and Malaina began to feel depressed.

"We got married in October. She died in December, darlin'." Malaina gasped and put a hand to her mouth. She couldn't say anything. She couldn't even begin to think of what to say to such a revelation. Baker continued, "Doc Pritchard said her appendix busted. It was all so unexpected…and so fast. It was over before I even knew what was goin' on. Mama's got the weddin' picture up in the attic somewhere if you ever wanna see her."

"I'm sorry, Baker. I had no idea," Malaina whispered, feeling miserable through her tears.

Baker put a finger under her chin and lifted her face to look at him. "Here now! What are you sorry for, sugar?" He took a handkerchief from his shirt pocket and began dabbing her tears. "It's clean, don't worry," he said with a smile, and Malaina laughed.

"How devastating for you, Baker. I'm so sorry," she said as she took the handkerchief from him and finished wiping her tears.

"Yes," he said, looking thoughtful. "Sometimes I wonder. Was it harder to lose her after only a few months of knowin' and lovin' her? Or would it have been harder to love her for twenty-eight years and lose her…like Mama did Daddy?"

An opportunity that Malaina had been waiting for ever since

she had come to this family presented itself at that moment. "What happened to your daddy, Baker?"

Baker smiled at her. "Our daddy," he began. "Our daddy was the wisest and handsomest man ever born on this earth."

Malaina smiled as Matthew agreed with a hearty, "You bet your sweet bacon, he was."

Baker went on. "He met Mama durin' the war. He was a Johnny Reb, you know…and Mama was a beautiful young daughter of a Yankee officer. Mama's family had got caught behind enemy lines in Georgia tryin' to help some relatives escape the burnin'. Daddy found them while on patrol one fine Southern afternoon and helped them escape. It's an awful long story. Get Mama to tell you about it. Anyway, after the war, he kidnapped her, and they eloped, moved out west, and started havin' us boys. Jackson was the first—and if you wanna know my daddy, know Jackson. He's the spittin' image of Daddy in every way there is."

"That's fer dang sure!" Matthew added firmly, and Malaina noticed a smile appear on Mary's face as she looked at him.

"It was three years ago that he died," Baker stated.

"I was still away," Matthew muttered.

Baker nodded. "Daddy was breakin' a horse out in the corral. Mama was out there with me and Jackson watchin'. It was a mean one! Meanest I ever seen to this day. He threw Daddy, which weren't no easy thing in itself. Then, before Daddy could stand up, that ol' cuss reared up and planted his front hooves in the middle of Daddy's back. He lived long enough to tell Mama he loved her when she reached him. Then he passed. Jackson slit the thing's throat with that big ol' knife he used to carry." Matthew nodded.

Everyone was silent. After a while, Baker sighed heavily. "He was the best husband and daddy I ever seen," he said. He chuckled when he saw the skeptical look on Malaina's face. "Don't let him fool you, darlin'. Jackson is our daddy over and over. And Mama says that Daddy used to try and play tough ol' buzzard too."

"Mr. McCall was the handsomest old man I ever saw, Malaina," Mary added. "And kind to boot. He never passed the candy counter at

Johnson's store without buyin' me a licorice whip. He used to bounce me on his knee when no one was lookin'. I miss him. Everybody misses him."

"We thought Mama was gonna follow him there for a few days. It nearly killed her to lose him," Matthew said. "She keeps all his photographs in her room…to herself. I reckon someday she'll share 'em again."

Malaina sat silent. What loss this family had experienced in the past several years. It was unimaginable to her.

❧

The McCall boys helped the girls down from the buggy and into the general store.

"Hello, Baker, darlin'! How are you? It's been too long, boy," a beautiful blonde woman called from behind the store counter.

"Hello, Mrs. Johnson," Baker greeted as the woman rushed out and flung her arms about him.

Malaina recognized the woman from church and guessed that this Mrs. Johnson must be the mother of Baker's Elizabeth.

"And you must be Annie," she said, offering a hand in greeting.

"Actually," Malaina said, taking the woman's hand, "I prefer to go by Malaina."

"Oh. Forgive me, dear. I could've sworn that Maggie said—"

"The girls are wantin' to make some new dresses for the dance, Mrs. Johnson," Baker interrupted.

Mrs. Johnson smiled and spun around, motioning for the girls to follow. "Oh my, yes! We've got some lovely prints. This way."

After an hour in the general store, Malaina had chosen some lovely cloth for a dress and learned every bit of new gossip about everyone. Mary and Malaina stepped out of the store into the cool autumn day and began looking for Baker and Matthew.

"I'm sure they're off talkin' horse manure with someone," Mary said, grinning.

Malaina smiled. "Well, I guess we'll just sit here and wait." She motioned to a nearby bench.

They had been waiting for a few minutes when a voice penetrated her ears that made Malaina's flesh crawl.

"Well, well, well. If it ain't Miss Malaina."

Malaina and Mary had been looking at each other while they talked and hadn't noticed the grimy-looking man that now stood before them. Malaina looked up, and terror struck her. She recognized the man! She didn't know from where, but she knew that he meant her harm.

"What do you want?" she asked bravely.

The man raised his brows sarcastically. "It ain't what I want, missy...and you know it. I've been lookin' for you for weeks now, and I'm plum sick of it. You've been the cause of my havin' to be sleepin' on the hard ground for that long."

"I'm sorry, but I've no idea what you're talking about," Malaina mumbled, smoothing her skirt and smiling as Mary stood and walked casually away.

"Oh! My, my, my. Have we misplaced our memory somewheres?" the man said sarcastically. "Now, Miss Malaina, you'll come with me quiet-like, and we'll take you back to Mr. Collin where you belong."

At the mention of the name Collin, panic gripped her. "I'm not going anywhere with you," she said firmly and stood to leave.

The man took her wrist roughly in his hand. "Yes, you are! I'm gettin' paid for my time. I have my orders. You're goin' back—alive or dead. It don't matter to me none," he growled.

Malaina couldn't believe the man was serious in his intentions. But he was—she felt it. She was in danger. She looked around frantically.

"Don't try screamin'," he whispered, and she felt something sharp press against her waist. "I mean what I say."

She knew she would rather die than go anywhere with this vermin. She had to think of some way to escape him.

"Come along, Malaina," he growled and pushed her ahead of himself.

Mrs. Johnson came out of the store just then. She looked at the man oddly. "It was nice to meet you, Malaina. You come visit real soon."

"Yes. I will. Thank you," Malaina said, hoping the woman would realize that something was amiss and send for help somehow.

They began to cross the dusty road and walk toward a horse that was tied outside the saloon.

"Maybe I'll just keep you to myself," the man whispered into her ear. She wanted to vomit at the stench of his breath. "But even I know better than to cross a man like Mr. Collin." The man returned his knife to its place at his waist. "Now then," he began, "I can still kill you…easily. So just get on this horse, and we'll ride away. No one knows enough about you to concern theirselves. I checked on that."

But as the man moved to untie the reins of his horse, Malaina ran. She ignored his order to stop, and she didn't stop until she was stopped by someone.

"Please, let me by!" she screamed. But when she felt her arms clenched in two powerful hands, she looked up and nearly fainted with relief as Jackson's angry expression met her.

"Sorry, mister," the awful man said as he approached. "My sister is a little out of her mind. I need to get her home."

Jackson moved to stand in front of Malaina. "She is home, sir. I think you need to mount that dog-ugly horse and ride away."

The man was undaunted. "Look here, mister…I'm takin' that girl with me. And lest you wanna die where you stand, you'll keep your long, ugly nose to yourself."

Jackson spoke to Malaina, although he continued to glare at the man. "Now, you run along, darlin'. Baker and Matthew are over at the feedstore. You run along."

Malaina didn't move. She didn't want to leave him.

"Malaina," he growled, and she turned and began running toward the feedstore. She didn't dare look back, though she could hear them talking in low, angry voices.

A man was coming toward her, and he spoke as he neared. "Now, you keep walkin', miss. I'm Sheriff Braddock, and I'll help ol' Jackson out. Tell them other two boys what's goin' on, in case Mary didn't find 'em yet."

She felt hope and relief begin to wash over her. The sheriff was there to help Jackson. She slowed her pace to a brisk walk for a moment but began to run as she spotted the sign marking the feedstore. Baker and Matthew were standing outside and came toward her when they noticed her approaching.

"What's wrong, honey?" Baker asked, catching her in his arms.

"A man…he tried to abduct me! To take me back! Jackson…the sheriff…over in front of the saloon," she panted.

"Stay here, Malaina. Go inside, and stay here," Baker ordered, and they began running.

Malaina stood outside for several moments, watching them disappear around the corner.

Mary reached her then and flung her arms around her. "Oh! Thank goodness! I was so worried. I couldn't find the boys…so I told Sheriff Braddock. I just knew you were done for."

Malaina pulled away from Mary and started running toward the corner that the McCall men had just cleared. The man had a gun! She had just realized it. And Jackson, Baker, and Matthew weren't carrying any.

"Malaina! Wait!" Mary called after her.

But Malaina was panic-stricken! He was a vile man. She knew he'd do anything to get her back to Collin.

Just before she turned the corner, she heard a gunshot slice the air. Then, quickly, another. She stopped for a moment in horror and then rounded the corner.

The vile man was lying on the ground. But so was Jackson. "No!" she gasped as she slowed to a walk. Baker and Matthew were kneeling down beside their brother, and the sheriff was standing over the degenerate.

The sheriff motioned to another man, and he came over and felt the villain's neck. Malaina stopped several feet away from the scene. Then she began to shudder with horrific relief as she saw Baker helping Jackson to stand. She stood frozen, not even registering their conversation.

"Over here, Doc. Big, bad brother Jackson's been up to no good again," Baker called to the doctor, who had just informed the sheriff that the other man was dead.

"It ain't nothin'," Jackson muttered, opening his shirt to examine the wound to his left shoulder.

"Mama will have a livin' fit over this, Jackson," Matthew chuckled.

Malaina still stood frozen. She watched as Jackson took off his shirt and held it to the wound. The three walked toward her with enormous grins of triumph plastered across their faces.

Matthew called out to her, "You won't be bothered by him no more, Malaina. Jackson beat the…heck out of him, and then after he shot Jack, Sheriff Braddock shot him back. He's done."

"Dang right!" Jackson said, smiling as Baker slapped him on the back.

They stood directly in front of her now, smiling proudly and patting each other all over.

"You think this is funny?" she choked, looking at the shirt Jackson held to his shoulder that was now saturated with his own blood.

"Not at all, sugar," Jackson said. "It just means you're out of danger. From that varmint, anyhow."

"Dang right," Matthew said, smiling at Baker.

Anger began to add itself to the horror that Malaina was feeling. "How can you laugh about this?" she screeched. "He's been shot! You all stand there with your swollen-up egos, smiling and slapping each other on the back like a bunch of idiots. What is wrong with you?"

They looked back and forth at each other with puzzled expressions.

Then Mary spoke from behind, "Malaina, Jackson probably saved your life—again, I might add. What are you scolding him for?"

Malaina spun around, enraged. "He could've been killed, Mary! Killed! That means dead! I should've just gone with the man."

"Now wait a minute," Jackson growled, taking her arm and turning her to face him. "That's about the most ignorant thing I've ever heard you say. It's a scratch." He smiled down at her.

"It's a bullet, Mr. McCall," she said as tears began to stream down her face.

"So what? I'm sure Doc can dig it out."

Malaina shook her head and let out a hysterical laugh. "Forgive me! How silly of me! I was always under the impression that most folks die from being shot."

The boys all looked at each other. Then Jackson smiled at her, speaking softly to his brothers. "I know what's the matter with her, fellas. I've got my shirt off again. She always gets so upset when I got my shirt off."

They all three stifled snickering, and Malaina's teeth ground each other as rage took over. She moved to slap Jackson, but he caught her hand and twisted it behind her back.

"Excuse us, will you?" he said, smiling at everyone. Then he directed her forcefully into the alley nearby.

"I don't mean to be crude, little Miss Ruffled-Up Drawers...but that ain't the kind of man that keeps his distance when he's waltzin' with you. Do you get my meanin'?" he said, glaring down into her face.

"Thank you for the information. It's such a surprise," she spat, trying to move past him.

But he pushed her up against the wall, pinning her still with his bloody hand, which had dropped the shirt. "Malaina, don't be ignorant. You know what would've happened if he would've gotten away with you. Now, my brothers and me, we been hurt a lot. And bad. Don't be acting so ridiculous over this."

She felt ill. He had nearly been killed this time, trying to help her.

"It's too much, Mr. McCall. I've got to leave. I've put your family harm's way too often. Please...just lend me the money to leave here," she pleaded, pressing firmly against his chest with her hands as she stared into his face. "I promise that I'll find a way to pay you back."

He let out a heavy breath of aggravation. "Malaina, I don't want to hear that again. If you hate it here, I'll help you out. But I don't think you do. And it would destroy my mama." She looked away.

"Do you hate it here, Malaina?" he asked firmly. She didn't answer. He took her face firmly in hand and forced her to look at him. "Do you? Tell me. If you do…I'll send you away."

She looked up into his beautiful green eyes. She loved life with the McCalls, and she loved the land, the warm dry air, the smell of peaches cooking into preserves. And most of all, she loved him. She knew it like she knew breathing.

"I love…it here, Mr. McCall," she whispered.

He let go of her face and drew in a deep breath. "My name is, Jackson, darlin'. Now…let me pay the doc a visit." And he turned and walked away.

She smoothed her hair back, wiped her cheeks on her sleeve, and walked back into the street as she straightened her skirt. Mary stood there, looking at her with a stunned expression.

"I'm fine, Mary. Really," she said. Then she turned to Baker and Matthew, who both looked gravely at her. "I'm sorry, Baker… Matthew. It was just such a shocking experience. Thank you so much. You'll never know how much I thank you."

They looked at each other. "Mama is gonna tan our hides, Baker," Matthew said, studying Malaina from head to toe.

"Dang right," Baker added.

Mary began to hug Malaina but pulled away. "You boys are in big trouble with Mrs. McCall. You're gonna take Jackson home all shot up, and now this," she said, pointing at Malaina.

"What?" Malaina asked.

She looked down at her skirt. It was streaked with blood where she had touched it. She gasped and looked at her hands. They were covered with blood too. Then she realized that she had smoothed her hair and wiped her cheeks. There was also a large stain on the back of her dress where Jackson had pressed against her while directing her to the alley.

"We're really in the doghouse this time," Matthew said.

"Okay, folks. It's all over. Just had us a bad one in town today," Sheriff Braddock called to all the onlookers that Malaina hadn't even noticed. "You all right, miss?" he asked her. She nodded, feeling even more self-conscious now that she was covered in Jackson's blood. "Well, you're mighty lucky you've got good ones like the McCalls for friends," he said, smiling encouragingly at her. Then he left.

"After the doc patches Jackson up, we'll get home and face the music, Malaina. I guess me and Baker should finish up business at the feedstore. Give us a holler when he's done," Matthew said as he and Baker began walking away, leaving Malaina and Mary.

"I guess we could visit with Mrs. Johnson some more, Malaina. If you want," Mary said, smiling.

Malaina was feeling very weak and shaky. "No, Mary. Let's just sit out of the way for a while…please. What am I going to do, Mary?" Malaina asked, more to herself than to the girl.

"What do you mean?" Mary asked, taking Malaina's hand comfortingly between her own.

"I can't possibly stay here! All I am is trouble to the McCalls. He could've been killed, Mary!"

"He wasn't, Malaina. And you've got to realize that this is life out here. People have to be tough, hard, and able to survive."

If it meant people you loved died all around you, then she wasn't sure she wanted to stay. She pressed hard against her temples with her hands. "I've got to remember things, Mary. I've got to!"

They sat in silence for several minutes until Matthew approached them. "Sheriff don't know who that man is, Malaina. Ain't got nothin' with a name about him." He smiled at Mary.

Malaina seemed preoccupied. "His name is Beau Benson, and Collin hired him to pursue me after I ran away. I sold a diamond brooch that my mother had left to me, and the money took me as far as Cripple Creek. Beau tracked me there and had orders to bring me back to New Orleans. He forced me to go with him by holding a gun at my back, but when the stage stopped to change the stage horses, I hid and never got back on. I thought I'd be safe in that small town—I can't remember what one it was—but his brother, Dill, found me. I hit Dill over the head with a log when we were near Cortez. It only stunned him, and I started running. He must have fallen unconscious at some point—obviously—because Jackson found me first, didn't he?" She looked over at Mary and Matthew, who were staring at her with their mouths wide open.

Matthew regained his senses first. "Well, who is this Collin feller…and why does he want you? You ain't his wife…are you?" he asked.

"No!" Malaina answered vehemently. "I am not his wife! If nothing else, I know that." Then Malaina's eyes widened in horror. "Matthew! What if I killed Dill? What if I hit him so hard that I killed him?"

Matthew shrugged his shoulders. "If he's dead, he's dead…and that's one less varmint that'll be after you then, ain't it?"

Malaina was shocked to silence at his matter-of-fact answer.

"Here comes Jackson and Baker. Let's get home, girls," Matthew said, offering a hand to each of them.

Jackson looked up and down at Malaina, and she made a fruitless effort at smoothing her hair that was matted with dried blood.

He smiled. "Looks like you'll really be needin' that new dress now."

She looked at him, intending to respond smartly, until she saw the bandages at his shoulder and the sling supporting his arm. Guilt overwhelmed her, and tears brimmed in her eyes.

"I'm so sorry," she whispered humbly.

"Ain't no big deal. Ol' Doc just dug it right outta there, slapped on a dressin', and I'm ready for anythin'."

"You better be. Looks like a feller named Dill might be showin' up one day with the same intentions," Matthew stated.

Malaina looked at him, sickened.

"Who?" Baker asked.

"Seems this ol' boy that the undertaker just drug off has a brother who's workin' for this Collin feller too. Ain't that right, Malaina?"

Malaina nodded. "I've got to leave here!" she pleaded, looking from one brother to the other.

"You ain't goin' nowhere, darlin'," Baker said, putting an arm around her shoulder. "You're safer with us than anywhere on earth."

"But you all aren't," she said bitterly.

"She keeps askin' me to lend her money to go east. Hey, how come you always ask me, anyway, girl?" Jackson asked, suddenly curious. "Baker and Matthew—they got as much money as me."

She cast her eyes down, unable to answer at first.

"Well, it seems to me she knows me and Matthew want her here no matter what. But you, Jackson, you see, you're a grouchy ol' bear, and she figures you want rid of her. Ain't that right, darlin'?"

But she really couldn't answer. Maybe it was really because he was always the one coming to her rescue.

She scowled as a pounding headache started in her head, and lifting her skirts to climb into the buggy that they were all standing before now, she said, "Let's just get back. I feel horrid."

"Bill's over at the blacksmith, Baker. He threw a shoe this mornin'. You think you could ride him home for me? I'm a little sore."

Baker laughed. "I ain't ridin' that maniac of yours, Jack. We'll tie him to the buggy and lead him home."

Jackson and Matthew looked at each other and laughed.

"Not if you wanna actually get home, Baker. You know he won't have none of that," Matthew said. "Why'd you bring him to town for shoein', Jackson? You usually do all the shoein' at home."

Jackson climbed into the buggy and let out a heavy breath as he settled himself. Malaina knew that the wound hurt him, no matter what he said.

"I threw the shoe on the way to town. Jerry Smithe came over awhile after you all left. He said there was a dirty-lookin' ol' thing in town askin' about Malaina. I came to see what was goin' on. Now, who's ridin' Bill home? I ain't leavin' him here."

Malaina stood up and hopped down from the buggy. "Me," she stated, walking toward the livery.

"Over my dead body!" Jackson shouted when he realized she was serious.

"Apparently so," she said, looking at his wound.

"You don't wanna ride Bill, Malaina. He's meaner than a sat-on yeller jacket!" Matthew warned.

They all thought she was kidding. She kept walking.

"Malaina," Jackson called as he climbed down from the buggy, "don't be ignorant." He caught up to her, grabbing her arm and spinning her around. She broke his grasp violently.

"I am not one of your horses in need of breaking, Mr. McCall!" She glared up at him, and he returned it.

"I'm not so sure about that. And I can break anything," he growled.

Her mouth dropped open at such a vulgar remark, and she moved to slap him yet again. And, yet again, he caught her arm with his free hand.

"You are not ridin' Bill. You can't. He won't have no part of it."

She ripped her wrist from his grip. "You can break anything, and I can ride anything. You just don't want anyone else to be able to ride him 'cause it'll detract from your superiority."

His eyes narrowed at her. "Fine. Break your uppity little neck, girl." And he turned and walked angrily away.

As she started for the livery again, she heard Matthew say, "You can't let her ride him, Jack. He'll throw her!"

She couldn't hear Jackson's response. "No, he won't. He likes her."

Bill was already saddled and ready to go. Malaina's heart began pounding furiously, as if the pounding in her head wasn't enough. Everyone stood stone-still in the livery as she untied Bill and stood in front of him. What a sight she must be! Covered in Jackson McCall's blood and standing here threatening to ride his stallion that everyone, including her, knew was a wild hair.

"Ma'am, uh…that's ol' Bill…Mr. McCall's horse. I don't know if you wanna—" a man said, approaching.

"Yes. I am aware of that, sir. I intend to ride him home, being that Mr. McCall is injured on my account. And why does everyone here insist on calling every animal 'old' something-or-other?" she said irritatedly.

Bill snorted and stomped a hoof. She stroked his nose gently, standing close to his nostrils so that he could smell her.

"Now, Bill…you know me. You're going to let me ride you home, aren't you?"

The horse nodded strongly and stomped again.

Malaina talked to him gently and patted his neck for several more minutes. She felt very self-conscious with everyone gawking at her. Finally, she found the courage and tried mounting him. He moved away neighing the first two attempts, but on the third, he only snorted and shook his head.

She eased herself into the saddle, and when she had the reins in hand, she pressed gently with her heels, and he shot out of the livery.

"Bill!" she shouted. But he was already in a dead run through the middle of town. "Calm down. Calm down," she told herself. She pulled up hard on the reins with every muscle in her body just as she reached the buggy where the others sat waiting for her. The horse reared and came down hard, snorting and stomping the ground. A mother walking in front of the store pulled her small child against her, looking at the wild-looking woman before her.

"She's on ol' Bill!" she heard a man say from the saloon across the street.

And within moments, Malaina looked around to see the entire town emerging from one building or another to look at the spectacle. Bill reared again and stomped around madly.

Baker, Matthew, and Mary looked at her with mouths hanging open and eyes as wide as saucers.

Jackson simply raised his eyebrows and said, "No need to wait for us."

"I won't!" she said angrily, and with a "Ya!" as signal to Bill, she rode off at a mad gallop through town and toward the McCall ranch.

CHAPTER NINE

Riding Bill was exhilarating! Even Malaina's headache seemed cured. The sound of the saddle moving with the horse's rhythmic run consoled her somehow. Bill was indeed a magnificent mount.

"Imagine," she said out loud, "naming an animal like you Bill!" After a time, she slowed him. "You are something else, boy!"

She realized that for the first time today—and it had been a long one—she felt like smiling. The sun was setting, and it turned the sky all shades of purples, pinks, and oranges. The sunsets were so beautiful in the West! She rode the rest of the way calmly, talking to Bill and trying to think more intently on the memories she had acquired earlier.

"So," she said to the horse as she rode, "I'm from New Orleans, my name is Malaina—Malaina something—and some horrible man named Collin is looking for me. But I don't know why. I can't remember who he is, what he looks like, or why he wants me. I can't remember if I have parents, siblings, friends to help me, family. Oh, Bill! What will I do?"

As the sun set, she rode up to the barn at the McCall ranch. She unsaddled Bill, brushed him for a few minutes, and gave him oats and water. Then, taking a deep breath, she headed for the house.

When she opened the screen door and stepped into the kitchen, Maggie turned with a smile to greet her. "Oh, honey! I'm so glad you all are…" The smile left her face as she took in the sight of Malaina, dried blood in her hair and on her face, hands, and dress. Her hair was a mass of windblown mess, and she looked as if she needed a month of sleep.

Maggie turned and put her apron under the pump to wet it and then started wiping Malaina's face. "There's so much blood, Malaina. Where are you hurt?" she asked, trying to appear calm, although her quivering voice betrayed her.

Malaina took her hands and smiled at her. "I'm fine, Mrs. McCall. I'm fine. There was some trouble in town—a man tried to take me with him. Jackson stopped him and was shot in the shoulder, but he's fine, and they're all on their way home in the buggy just now." She rambled it out as fast as she could, hoping the woman wouldn't panic over the news of a wounded son.

Maggie stared blankly at her for some moments. Then she began wiping the dried blood from Malaina's face once more and asked, "How did you get home?"

Malaina could tell that she was extremely upset, so she talked calmly as if nothing whatsoever had happened. "I rode Bill. Jackson was a bit sore." She smiled hopefully at the woman.

Maggie's eyes bugged out like a mouse with its head caught in a trap. "Bill? You rode Bill home?" Then she chuckled. "Now quit your teasin', doll. Who brung you home?"

Malaina smiled. "I rode Bill. He's in the barn. I brushed him down. I think he likes me."

Maggie smiled. "Well, I'll be. What did Jackson have to say to that?"

Malaina began unbuttoning her blouse. "I suspect he wouldn't have let me if he thought there was any danger," she said with a delayed realization.

❧

After she had bathed and put her clothes to soak, Malaina let Maggie brush her hair awhile as she told her the events of the afternoon. Maggie listened attentively until she was finished.

"My stars and garters, child! Who in the world are you?" she commented.

"I wish I knew, Mrs. McCall." Then she turned her pleading eyes to the woman. "Please, I've got to leave here. Don't you see? I'm putting you all in great danger!"

Mrs. McCall cupped the beauty's face in her hands and smiled lovingly. "You're ours now, precious. We won't let you run away."

"But Jackson was shot today, Mrs. McCall! And I believe this Collin won't stop until he finds me. You've got to help me leave," she begged.

But her hopes were dashed when she heard Jackson's voice from beyond the screen door. "Oh, now turn off them puppy-dog eyes, Malaina. You ain't goin' nowhere," he said.

The others followed him in, and Mrs. McCall went to inspect the wound. Malaina noticed immediately how tired Jackson appeared.

"I'll drive Miss Mary home, Mama, and then milk the ones need milkin'. They oughta be bustin' at the seams by now," Matthew said as Mary followed him outside.

"I'll go start milkin' now," Baker said, kissing his mother, winking at Malaina, and leaving.

"I'm goin' to bed, Mama," Jackson said, standing. He began to sway, and instinctively Malaina took his good arm and placed it around her shoulder. She was surprised when he didn't resist but leaned on her for support.

"You know, Mama," he began, his words slurring together, "I feel a might dizzy."

"He's lost a lot of blood, judgin' by what came home all over you, Malaina. Let's put him to bed," his mother sighed.

The two women helped him down the hall to Baker's room, where he had been sleeping since Malaina's arrival. Malaina helped him to sit down on the bed and, since his arm was about her, sat with him.

"Ol' Doc is right good at fixin' 'em up, but he never cleans very well. Stay with him, Malaina. We need soap and water," Maggie said, hurrying out of the room.

When Malaina attempted to stand, she found that Jackson had his arm clamped tightly about her. She looked up into his face. He was frowning down at her. The heavy beads of perspiration appearing on his forehead worried her.

"Mr. McCall?" she asked tentatively.

He grimaced. "Jackson," he corrected emphatically.

Malaina put a hand to his head and then cheek. He was feverish. "Lay down, Jackson. Do you hear me?" she said, pushing him back.

He still held her firmly, and when he did finally relent and lay down, he took her with him.

"Let go, Jackson," she said calmly, pushing against him. He was so strong, even in his present condition.

"You rode ol' Bill, did you? He likes you. I can't begin to wonder why. But he does. I wouldn't have let you ride him otherwise," he mumbled.

"Yes. Yes. Now let me go."

"Ain't you gonna thank me, Miss Malaina? I mean, for savin' you again? I think a proper thank you is in order." He was grinning slyly.

She looked directly into his eyes. "Thank you, Jackson. Again."

He closed his eyes, and he smiled. "Now, kiss me," he said, his speech even more slurred.

"What?" she gasped, and as his arm released her, he began to chuckle, and she realized that he was fine. A little sore and feverish, but fine all the same.

Within seconds, he was breathing slowly, and she knew he was asleep. Maggie returned with a basin of warm water and rags.

"My poor baby," she murmured as she began to bathe his face. Maggie looked over at Malaina, who was deep in thought as she stared at the wounded man. "That's enough, Malaina!" she demanded. "You're staying right here. If he hadn't of gotten shot, it would've been somethin' else. This isn't your fault. I know that it was meant for us to find you. You're ours now." She smiled and cupped the girl's cheek in her hand. "Now, help me clean him up. That doctor! Well, at least he patched him up anyway, huh."

Maggie handed a washcloth to Malaina after she had wrung it out. "See if you can get some of that dried blood off his chest. I'll go tell Baker to start bringin' in some clean water. We're gonna need a lot more than a bowlful!" Maggie left the room, and Malaina began dabbing at the blood.

She jumped when Jackson said, "I'm your knight in shinin' armor, ain't I, sugar?" She thought he was still asleep. His eyes were still closed, but he wore a slight grin. "How many times have I saved your bacon now?" he asked.

Malaina was very self-conscious about cleaning his bare torso now that she knew he was conscious. "At least three, by my count," she answered, sounding remarkably calm. "All you're lacking is a white horse, I'd say," she finished.

He opened his eyes just a bit to look at her. "Dang mess, ain't it?" he said with a note of irritation in his voice. "I'm so dang tired. Can't seem to keep my eyes open much."

"You need to rest. I don't know why you're even trying to stay awake."

Malaina wished he'd go to sleep. It made her very uncomfortable to have him alert while she was bathing him.

He chuckled lowly. "I'm still waitin' for my kiss."

She rinsed the cloth in the basin, causing the water to go red.

"Stop teasing, and go to sleep, Jackson," she ordered.

"I musta found another way of gettin' yer dander up," he mumbled. "Well, all right. I'll just corner you out in the barn one day and collect the debt." And with a final chuckle, he fell asleep again.

Maggie returned and could tell Malaina was flustered. "What's wrong, peach?" she asked.

"Your son is a flirt when he's out of his head," Malaina told her.

CHAPTER TEN

The family had discussed Malaina's newfound memories that next evening. But everyone was a long way from solving the puzzle, and life returned to normal. Malaina had become close to Mary and was overjoyed as she watched a new type of friendship sprouting between her friend and Matthew.

Mary would often visit so that she and Malaina could work on their dresses for the Harvest Dance and would somehow end up talking with Matthew as he did the chores. Malaina never said a word about it to either one of them but decided to wait until they chose to come to her. And so things went along.

One early evening about dusk, Maggie asked Malaina to run and get a hammer out of the barn. Malaina wrapped up in a shawl and headed out to do the errand.

The weather was cool, and Malaina was unaccustomed to it. She found it hard to warm herself at times. She guessed it was because she'd always lived in a warm climate. She entered the barn and began rummaging through the toolbox for a hammer.

"Whatcha need?" Jackson asked from behind her.

Malaina spun around startled. "Don't do that! You scared the life out of me," she answered.

"Sorry. What are you lookin' for?" he asked, coming to stand beside her and looking down into the box.

"A hammer. There's a nail out of one of the kitchen chairs, and your mama wants to fix it."

Jackson put down the brush he'd been using on Bill and began digging in the box. Malaina noticed that he was, once again, without a shirt.

"It's freezing out here, Jackson! How can you run around half-dressed like that?"

He chuckled. "I ain't a bit cold. I hope you start gettin' a little more used to this weather. It gets ten times worse than this, darlin'."

Malaina shivered involuntarily. "Really?" she asked. The thought was not at all comforting. "Well, you should put some clothes on anyway," she stated as he stood handing her a hammer.

"Why?" he asked with his sly grin spreading across his lips.

"It's indecent, that's why. Have you not one shred of modesty in your being, Jackson?" she answered.

"Not a shred," he whispered.

"I think you do it to show off," she mumbled to herself.

"You do?" he asked, raising his eyebrows as his smile broadened. He took a step toward her, and she stepped backward, bumping up against the barn wall.

"Yes," she answered, trying to appear unrattled. He put one hand against the wall behind her and leaned close to her face.

"Why do you think that I'm showin' off when I work without a shirt on, Malaina?" he asked almost in a whisper.

She opened her mouth to answer, but none came.

"What, exactly, do you think I'm tryin' to show off?"

"Your…your…" she stammered.

He raised his eyebrows. "My what?"

She gritted her teeth and took a deep breath. "Yourself!" she answered.

He chuckled and put the other hand on the wall. "You mean, my body. Is that what you mean?"

She felt herself begin to blush and was horrified that she should.

"It sure ruffles your feathers whenever we get on this here subject, girl," Jackson said, still smiling slyly at her and moving closer.

"We have a name for men like you where I come from," she told him, blushing a deeper crimson.

"Really?" he asked, raising his eyebrows. "And what would that word be, Malaina? Rounder? Cad? Or maybe it's more like the perfect lover."

Her eyes widened at his conceit. "You are impossible!" she exclaimed.

He chuckled and moved so close to her that she felt the warmth of his breath on her forehead. "Why don't you try me out and see for yourself?" he mumbled, taking her by the shoulders and locking eyes with her.

"You're a beast!" she scolded, though it came out in more of a whisper than mean and harsh as she had meant it to sound.

"I'm callin' in your debt now, Miss Malaina. Here and now," he whispered just before he kissed her.

Malaina struggled for a split second, but as the feel of his sensual mouth on hers engulfed her, she was swept away. It lasted only a few seconds, but it was long enough to prove to her that he had been right about himself. It took every bit of restraint in her being for her not to wrap her arms around his magnificent form and passionately return his kiss. When he broke the kiss, she glanced up at him and then away quickly.

"You're a shameless flirt," she whispered as she moved past him.

"Not really," he said, picking up a pitchfork and giving the cow some hay. "You're just so funny when you're embarrassed that I can't help it." She heard him chuckling as she walked quickly toward the house.

❧

"It must really be nippy out there. You're as red as a beet!" Maggie said as Malaina entered the kitchen.

Actually, she felt a little too warm. "Yes. I guess I'm not used to this cool weather."

Maggie smiled as Malaina handed her the hammer.

"I've just now remembered where I put that lace that I thought might look nice on the collar of your dress, love," Maggie said, sitting down on the floor and preparing to fix the chair. "Now, up in the attic there's a whole load of mess, so watch your step. There's four or five trunks up against one wall, and I think I laid that lace in the top one. Go have a look, will you? It's white with a pretty design woven in. Run along now."

Malaina smiled as she pulled down the ladder to the attic and began climbing.

The attic was stuffy, and she was glad she'd brought a lamp with her because it was pitch dark inside now that the sun had set. She began looking around.

"Mess?" she spoke out loud. "Treasure!"

There were old harnesses, an old dress form in one corner, and other wonderful things piled around. She quickly spotted the trunks up against the wall and went over eagerly. They weren't, however, piled up the way Maggie had described, but rather all of them were sitting on the floor. She shrugged her shoulders and opened one.

It wasn't the correct trunk, obviously, but her curiosity was piqued as she spied a uniform of some sort lying in it. She lifted it slightly. It was familiar—not Confederate or Northern from the war, but still very familiar. A photograph fell out of the folds, and as she held it up, she recognized the uniform worn by the man in the photograph.

"West Point?" she muttered as she stared down at the handsome face of Baker dressed in the uniform and standing in front of the sign that greeted all visitors to the institution. How dashing he looked! She couldn't resist looking deeper into the trunk. Below the uniform was another photograph—a very large one—and she knew at once that this was his wedding photo.

Baker looked so handsome dressed formally. Next to him stood Elizabeth. She had been a unique beauty, just as he had described her. They looked so blissful, and Malaina felt as if something had pierced her heart. She quickly replaced everything and shut the trunk. She dusted the top off to reveal a brass nameplate and read, "Baker Robert McCall."

She moved to the next trunk and dusted the nameplate. "Matthew Robert McCall." And the next. "Jackson Robert McCall. All named after their daddy, Robert," she said to herself. Jackson's trunk was locked. She wondered what secrets it held.

The next trunk looked much older and much more worn. She dusted it off. Instead of a fancy nameplate, the name was carved into the wood. "Robert Jackson McCall," she read, and she knew that she dared not open it.

Malaina moved to another trunk and lifted the lid. Sure enough, the lace was there. She quickly grabbed it, shut the trunk, and hurried down the ladder. She felt as if she'd been eavesdropping somehow.

"Did you find it?" Maggie called from the kitchen.

"Oh, yes! It's lovely, Mrs. McCall. I can't possibly use this! It's just too lovely." Malaina exclaimed.

She entered the kitchen to find the three men and their mother sitting at the table waiting for her. How long had she been up there?

"I'm sorry. I had no idea we were this close to dinner," she said, taking her seat. Her confidence had returned, and she smiled sarcastically at Jackson and said, "I'm glad you decided to actually dress before dinner."

Maggie rolled her eyes. "Jackson McCall! It is entirely too cold to be working without a shirt now. And I want you to start wearing your long johns."

Jackson smiled at his mother. "Better watch your backs, boys. Little Miss Proper Pants is a tattler."

"Jackson!" his mother scolded, trying to hold back a snicker.

Baker started the dinner conversation. "I saw horse tracks out by the north pasture today. Ten riders, I'd say. Unshod."

Matthew and Jackson looked at their brother, and all smiles faded.

"It's gettin' colder. They're hungry," Matthew said.

"I'm sure they're hungry all right. But I'm wonderin' what for," Baker said, directly to Jackson.

"Quit talkin' over my head, boys. Is it Black Wolf?" Maggie asked, and Malaina felt as if her blood had turned to ice.

"Can't think of any other ten unshod ponies 'round here, Mama," Baker said. "Don't worry, though. As long as it's the cattle they're eyin' up, I ain't worried."

They all looked at Malaina suddenly. "What? What are you lookin' at me for?" she asked, beginning to shiver.

"Did Mary come visit today?" Matthew asked, changing the subject.

"No," Malaina said flatly.

"You girls only got a couple of days to finish them new duds. I thought you'd be sewin' your little fingers blue by now," he said.

"We're nearly finished," Malaina commented, still preoccupied by the previous conversation.

"Well, I can't wait for that dance!" Baker said, smiling. "It's been a long time since we done anything sociable around here."

"Dang right," Jackson said. "I saw that little Justine Smithe in town last week. She sure turned out purty."

Malaina looked at him quickly and then away.

"Here we go," Maggie said. "Sizin' up the goods already," she giggled.

"Well, you want grandbabies before you're a hundred, don't you, Mama?" Baker asked.

"Oh, yes!" she answered.

Malaina was feeling nauseated. She hadn't considered that Jackson might be flirting with other women there.

"Ol' Jackson better beware this year, Mama. I heard that the Widow Thompson still has her eyes on him," Matthew said, laughing.

"Older women is like fine wine, little brother. Better and better with age," Jackson said.

"How would you know, Jack? You ain't never had fine wine," Baker teased.

Everyone laughed, and Malaina even managed a smile.

Baker continued, "Well, I got my eye on that little Susan Adams. She's got that purty auburn hair, and her eyes are matchin'."

"Oh, she *is* lovely!" Maggie added.

"Well, I know little brother Matt here will have his hands full enough with our own Mary...so who is gonna chaperon Malaina?" Baker asked.

"I don't need a chaperon," she stated.

They all looked at each other with raised eyebrows.

"You most certainly do!" Maggie exclaimed.

"The men 'round here ain't much on manners and the proper ways…as you well know, darlin'," Jackson said with a wink.

"Well, as you know, Jackson…I am most certainly aware of that. And I still don't need a chaperon."

"She thinks I'm a neked barbarian, boys. She caught me with my pants down today—well, actually with my shirt off—and then she went on in here and told Mama," Jackson said.

"That does seem to upset her every time, don't it?" Matthew snickered.

"It's a good thing it weren't with your pants down, I guess," Baker said, and they busted into laughter.

Maggie scolded. "All right, boys! That's enough. You quit your teasin'! Just 'cause Malaina has some modesty don't mean you can give her grief about it every day of the week. I'll keep Malaina company if and when she ever has time on her hands. I'm sure those young men in town will snatch her clean away from us."

Jackson snickered. "Naw. She won't like any of them boys. They'll all be wearin' shirts." Maggie sighed in exasperation as the three boys broke into peals of laughter.

Even Malaina had to laugh at their teasing. They all cared for her in some way, she knew. Even Jackson. Otherwise he wouldn't tease her all the time the way he did.

⁂

Two days before the dance, Mary and Malaina were in the north pasture. "Well, you got waltzin' down perfect. I guess you all waltz down South at least. But you still haven't got any reels or anything. So, let's get started," Mary said.

Malaina had awakened in the night several days before realizing that dancing out West might be very different than dancing in the South. So she had asked Mary about it and found that the assumption was indeed correct. As a result, Mary and Malaina had been sneaking off to the north pasture and practicing.

"I don't know what the point is anyway, Mary. I don't know

anyone here. I'll just be the perfect example of a wallflower, I'm sure," Malaina commented.

"Don't be silly, Malaina! I swear all the men in town take to droolin' like dogs whenever you're around. Let's try the two-step. We do it more than waltzin' anyway."

Malaina found it very easy to learn. It was similar to the waltz, and the gentleman held you the same way. As they practiced, they talked.

"You mean the women don't wear gloves then?" Malaina asked in surprise.

"Of course not, Malaina," Mary sighed. "You actually have to put your bare hand in his bare hand," she mocked.

"Well," Malaina began again, "does the gentleman at least put a handkerchief between his hand and your waist?"

Mary laughed, and Malaina spun around when she heard Jackson laughing as well. There he stood, in the cool October weather, wearing boots, pants, a hat, well-worn gloves—and no shirt.

"You beat all, girl. I swear," he said.

"What are you laughing at, Jackson? It's the proper way," she told him.

Jackson took Mary in traditional waltzing form. "Not out here it ain't, Malaina. Looky here! Mary's dancin' with a half-neked man, and he ain't got a hanky at her waist." Mary and Jackson began laughing so hard that they doubled over.

"You are impossible!" Malaina giggled. It probably did seem rather outlandish to them.

"Now come here. I'll teach you dancin'," Jackson said, motioning to her to join him. Malaina shook her head slightly and stepped back. It would be too much—too close to him. He'd sense how she felt about him, she was sure.

"Oh, go on, Malaina. I get mixed up trying to lead," Mary said as Jackson removed his gloves and threw them aside, motioning to her again.

"Chicken?" he teased. And with that, she placed her hand in his.

He tipped his hat back, put his other hand at her waist, and pulled her against him.

"This close?" she asked, shocked.

"Yes, ma'am," he said, smiling. "But only with me."

Mary giggled. As Jackson began to lead Malaina in an instructive two-step, Mary counted.

This was indecent! Malaina could feel the muscles in his thighs against her own, and her chest was flush with his.

"This isn't proper, Jackson!" she exclaimed, trying to pull away.

"You gotta feel where I'm leading you, Malaina," he chuckled.

"Oh, believe me, I feel where you're leading me, Mr. McCall. Does the word corruption ring a bell?" she said nervously. Mary giggled.

"Oh, relax, Malaina. Mary's standin' right there. I ain't gonna do nothin' improper," he said. And in a few moments, when she had mastered the step, he did indeed hold her out away from him a bit.

"Of course, the other men at the dance will have their shirts on… so it may not be as fun as it was with me," he teased.

She shoved him away. "You're horrid," she said, turning and stomping away. "Let me know when you're finished being corrupted, Mary, and we'll talk," she called back over her shoulder.

"I'm comin' too, Malaina," Mary said, waving to Jackson and catching up to her.

"He is impossible," Malaina sighed.

Mary smiled. "He makes people laugh and feel special and happy," Mary said.

Malaina smiled. "Yes, he does," she had to agree.

❧

That night when they all sat down at dinner, the boys were trying to control their snickering.

"All right," Maggie said at last. "What is it?"

"Jackson and Malaina were dancin' out in the north pasture half-naked today, Mama," Matthew said, and they all broke into laughter.

Maggie looked at Malaina, who had gone white. "Boys tease, darlin'. Just let it roll like water off a duck, and you'll be fine. Now, you boys act your age. Poor girl is gonna be half-mad before you're done with her. And, Jackson…you start wearin' your shirt! It's nearly winter out there."

"Yes, Mama," he answered when he could at last take a breath.

CHAPTER ELEVEN

Malaina felt as if she'd swallowed a cavern full of bats as they drove to the dance through the cool October evening. It was so delightful though—like a dream! Every time they passed a neighboring farm, the family would fall in line behind the others, and everyone joined in singing songs together all the way to town. It was a safe, friendly feeling, and Malaina reveled in it. Matthew had taken a separate cart because he was escorting Mary and her parents. But Malaina rode in the back of the buggy with Baker while Jackson and Maggie were in front.

The barn on the Smithe ranch was decorated with shining jack-o'-lanterns, scarecrows, and other harvest-type things. Several men were playing fiddles and other instruments while standing on a bunch of wooden crates that had been pushed together. One man was even blowing on a jug. Malaina thought it very odd.

People were already dancing, and Baker led Malaina to the floor. She was overcome with nerves for a moment until she realized that everyone was simply having a good time. Most of the men looked like monkeys jumping around or were as awkward as Root would be dancing. Baker, however, was a very proficient dance partner and made her feel more relaxed. Soon she was laughing and feeling as if she never wanted to leave.

The punch and refreshments were delicious, and Malaina found many familiar faces to chat with. Her spirits were only dampened by the moments when she would see Jackson smiling charmingly down into the face of an adoring, lovely girl. Once he caught her staring at him and winked at her. She turned away quickly, mortified. She caught bits and pieces of conversation among the women and girls, and the subject always seemed to be the McCall boys, especially Jackson.

One older woman was flirting shamelessly with Jackson, and Malaina surmised that this must be the Widow Thompson. He was as polite and charming with her as he was with the others. He hadn't once asked Malaina to dance after an hour, and she felt as if she'd been slapped in the face. She was sure that she was the only one he hadn't danced with.

Malaina had just finished a cup of punch and was setting it down when Jackson came to stand beside her. He pulled his pocket watch from its home in his pocket and eyed it closely. "Hmmm. I believe—yes—this is my dance with you, Malaina. Would you mind?" He had the familiar mischievous look about him.

"Very well," she said, cautiously placing her hand in his.

Just then the fiddler shouted. "All right, folks. Quiet down, quiet down now. It's that time of the year again. We're all celebrating a good and prosperous crop this year. Some folks do this as a tradition to bringin' in the New Year. But we do it at the Harvest Dance!" Whoops and cheers went up from the crowd. "That's right! It's turn-down-the-lamps time—the Kissin' Waltz for lovers!" And the crowd continued to whoop and holler as the lights dimmed.

Malaina looked up at Jackson in complete astonishment. She tried to pull her hand from his.

"You said, 'Very well,' remember? Now be a lady and dance with your ol' improper pal!" he said, pulling her toward the dance floor.

Malaina looked around. There were Matthew with Mary, Baker with a lovely auburn-haired girl. Even Maggie was dancing with a jolly-looking older man.

"See, sugar…it's all in fun and completely harmless," Jackson said, smiling. He no longer wore his mischievous grin. Simply a friendly smile.

Malaina relaxed and smiled up at him. "You like to…to…" she began.

"Ruffle your pin feathers?" he finished.

"Yes," she said.

"That I do. You're different, you see. Most girls, they just get all giggly and know I'm flirtin'…but you get so upset! It's very entertainin'."

"Who is this Justine person you're interested in?" she asked. "I don't believe I've been able to put my finger on her this evening."

"Who?" He looked sincere.

"This Justine girl that you think is so lovely."

He smiled as realization hit him. "Oh! Justine. She is a cute little gal." He pulled her to him suddenly. "See that little brown-haired girl right behind us? That's Justine."

Malaina felt unwell as she looked at the girl. She was a living doll. "Oh," she said.

"Have you found the man of your dreams tonight, darlin'?" he asked, smiling.

She had. He was holding her in his arms at that very moment. "No," she answered.

"Well, then, I guess I'll just have to do." Her heart threatened to leap from her bosom. How she wished he wouldn't tease about such things.

"I can't thank your family enough," she said, trying to distract him from their current conversation. "Thank you too, Jackson. For bringing me here. It's like heaven."

"Oh…you're more than welcome. It's a good time havin' you around to tease. And you do wonders for Mama."

Just then Baker and his partner danced up next to them.

Baker leaned over and whispered, "Better put a little space between you two, Jackson. You'll make our little Malaina nervous." He winked at her.

Jackson whispered a response. "I figure if I wanna really impress her and make her feel right at home…I better be strippin' my shirt off here pretty quick." Jackson and Baker suppressed snickers.

"Well, Jackson…are you gonna?" Baker asked.

"Dang right! You gonna?" Jackson replied.

"Dang right!" Baker said, smiling.

Malaina was curious. "What are you two going to do?" she asked.

Jackson seemed to listen intently to the music for a moment. Then he whispered, "Well, you see, darlin'…this here's called the Kissin' Waltz."

"Yes," she said, still not understanding.

"Well, you see," he continued, "it's called that for a reason." She waited for him to tell her the reason. He grinned slyly, and she began to feel nervous again. "Well, here in a minute, they're gonna blow out all the lamps. And between the time they blow 'em all out and the time it takes to get 'em all re-lit…well…everyone who wants to gets to do some kissin'."

It took only a moment for the meaning of what he was saying to sink completely in. Malaina's eyes widened, and she gasped as she understood.

At that moment, the fiddler yelled, "All right, boys—blow 'em out, and light 'em up!" And everything went dark.

The last thing she saw was Jackson's sly smile, and the first thing Malaina felt him do was wrap an arm tightly around her waist, pulling her against his powerful body. Her heart pounded furiously as he slid a hand caressively up her arm and then cupped her chin. When Jackson's lips touched hers tentatively at first, her entire body erupted with goose bumps. He kissed her harder, pulling her tightly to him with both arms about her.

Malaina surrendered. She let her hands slide over his strong chest and up over his shoulders. She pulled herself even more tightly against him. She sensed that the room was beginning to lighten, and realizing the passion of their kiss when she felt his tongue touch her upper lip, she broke the embrace.

She was grateful that Jackson held her for just a brief moment before releasing her, for her knees surely would've given way under her weight. She didn't look at him at first but looked around the room to see who might have witnessed their kiss. A wave of relief flooded her being as she realized that every other woman on the dance floor was as bright a blush as she was.

"I gotta trap you in the dark more often, darlin'," Jackson said, leading her from the dance floor.

"You're worse than any sailor I've heard of," she said, trying to steady her breathing. After he had pinched her cheek affectionately, he sauntered off, leaving her still blushing.

"You keep him in line, love," Maggie chuckled. "He can be mighty flirtatious at these get-togethers."

Malaina blushed an even deeper shade of crimson. "Yes. Flirtatious. I need some air." And she gave Maggie's arm a loving squeeze before heading outside.

Malaina was still a little stunned by the incident and didn't hear a man come in and announce, "I just seen Black Wolf and his varmints ridin' up this way!"

She took her coat from the hook on the wall and went out behind the barn. She was greatly surprised when she saw large snowflakes falling to the thin layer of snow already on the ground.

She apologized as she tripped over the feet of a couple cuddled up on a hay bale sparking. The thought went through her mind that she wished it were she and Jackson cuddled up on that hay bale.

Walking a good fifty feet from the barn, Malaina wrapped her arms tightly about herself and drew in a deep breath of crisp autumn air that was signaling the onset of winter. How she had grown to love it here—the dry air, the pink sunsets, the sound of the locust in the elms and willows, and now the silent beauty of frost and snow falling to earth. Whatever she couldn't remember about her life so long ago in Louisiana, she knew that this was infinitely better.

She whirled around when she heard the girl that sat in her sweetheart's embrace behind her scream. Her hand flew to her mouth in horror as she came face-to-face with the flaring nostrils of Black Wolf's brutal horse.

"Come with Black Wolf!" he commanded, and she shook her head and tried to run past him toward the barn.

Black Wolf reached down, catching her arm. In the next moment, she was lying on her stomach, watching the horse's hooves gallop away beneath her.

She heard shouting. It seemed to be the renegades, but Malaina was sure she heard other voices from the barn.

"Help me!" she tried to scream. But the mad race of the horse made it nearly impossible for her to get a breath.

For several minutes, she was too gripped with fear and panic to react. But then her instincts to survive, which had saved her once before, championed her, and she began to struggle.

"Do not move. I will kill you," Black Wolf commanded.

She stopped momentarily, but when Black Wolf looked over his shoulder, shouted at the others, and kicked the flanks of his horse to push him faster, she knew that they were being pursued. He wouldn't have time to kill her if she could just fall off.

They came to a creek, and Black Wolf's horse faltered. As Black Wolf fought to steady the animal, Malaina pushed herself from the horse and into the water.

It was painfully cold, like wading in liquid ice! It only took a matter of seconds for her arms and legs to begin numbing. The snow was falling heavily now, and it was hard to see through it.

She heard Black Wolf's blood-curdling yell and turned to see his horse fighting the water as it struggled toward her. When he reached out to grab her again, Malaina flung herself down into the freezing water, and his torturous grasp overshot her. She stood up shivering and watched as he turned his horse back around for another attempt. Malaina knew that she couldn't endure going under that water again! But she had to and slipped through his fingers, which tore at her dress, ripping out the back of the bodice.

She was freezing, disoriented. But she heard gunshots and wiped the icy water from her eyes. Several men from the barn had reached the renegades and were shooting at them. Two renegades fell into the water, and their blood stained it red. The others began using arrows and knives to defend themselves. Malaina screamed as she saw an arrow hit a man in the shoulder. Then she dropped on her knees, sinking into the frigid water as she recognized the wounded rider. Jackson!

He pulled up on his reins, and Malaina watched helplessly as Black Wolf started toward him, shouting and readying a weapon that looked like a small hatchet. She stood again, shouting Jackson's name as she watched Black Wolf getting closer. As Black Wolf reached him, Jackson pulled the arrow from his own body and speared the renegade through the heart. Black Wolf fell into the water, and Jackson, having lost his balance, followed him.

The remaining renegades retreated, and the other men followed. Jackson shoved Black Wolf's corpse aside as he waded through the icy water toward Malaina.

"Come on," he called, motioning to her to walk to him.

"I can't," she forced out in a whisper. "I don't think my legs will move." She felt panic rising in her chest. Her jaws were clenched tightly together because of the cold. "Help me!" she called, trying to extend an arm toward him. Then her knees buckled, and her brain began to feel numb. She began to crawl toward him through the icy water.

When Jackson reached her, he fell to his knees, panting. "Stay awake, Malaina! You're gonna have to save me first if I'm gonna save you later," he said through chattering teeth. He looked around and, finding no help, dragged her to ground. The snow was already several inches deep and coming down heavier than ever.

"Listen to me," he said, taking her face roughly in his hand as he fumbled with his pants pocket. "I got hit by an arrow. Now, ol' Black Wolf poisons the tips once in a while. If he has this time—it didn't go deep at all, but if it gets any further into my blood, if it's even there—anyway, it's probably a good thing that I'm frozen to the bone. It'll stop my blood from rushin' around as fast." He withdrew a pocketknife from his pocket at last and flipped it open. "Make an X mark over the wound and then suck out the blood there," he said.

Malaina didn't even feel cold anymore. "What?" she whispered in disbelief.

Jackson shook her by the shoulders, and his voice sounded angry.

"Do it! You heard me. Else we'll both die, girl!"

With trembling hands, she took the knife. Her fingers were blue, and she could hardly hold it steady. He tore his shirt away, revealing the wound.

"Hurry up, Malaina!" he yelled. The injury was just under his collarbone, and the flesh already looked slightly torn there.

"I don't need the knife," she said, realizing the fact.

"Fine. Just hurry," he commanded. She looked up at him. "Malaina! Don't get shy on me now. Do you wanna die out here?"

Taking a deep breath, Malaina put her mouth over the wound and sucked hard. Jackson's skin was as cold as the water, and she nearly gagged as warm, salty blood flooded her mouth for the first time.

"Spit it out!" he yelled. She did and repeated the process several times. "Does it taste strange?" he asked suddenly. She wrinkled her brow and looked up at him at such a ridiculous question. "Is there a bitter taste or is it just salty?" he asked.

"Salty," she said, spitting. He held her away from him, reached down, lifted up her soaking dress, and used its hem to wipe her mouth and then his wound.

"Come on," he panted. "I know where we are, and we better find shelter. This ain't no flurry."

Malaina couldn't move her legs at first. She was frozen stiff, but once they started walking through the snow, she began to feel warm and drowsy.

"Don't knock out on me, girl," Jackson said as he began pulling her.

It wasn't very long before they both collapsed into an opening in a large rock formation. It was so dark she couldn't see anything but its outline and the snow. The wind had begun to blow more fiercely by the time they entered the cave.

"Someone is lookin' out for us. I can't believe it," Jackson mumbled.

Malaina could hear him banging around, and suddenly a flicker of light pierced the blackness. He came walking back toward her holding an oil lamp.

"Me and Baker used to play in here when we was boys. It was our hideout. When we got older, we figured it would be a good place to weather out a bad storm, and we always kept supplies in it, for sentimental reasons, I guess. But farther back there's blankets and such."

"It's okay," Malaina said sleepily. "I'm warmin' up already."

Jackson frowned and put an icy hand to her face. "Come on. We better hurry," he said, pulling her to her feet and starting back into the shelter of the cave.

The cave turned and ran into a dead end twenty feet back where the wind could no longer reach them. Malaina watched drowsily as Jackson began to build a fire in the middle of the room.

"See…there's a hole up top. Wind don't come in, but the smoke goes out." The fire burned orange quickly, and he sighed, relieved. "Malaina? Wake up," he demanded as she began to lie down and close her eyes.

"I'm fine now, Jackson. I'm warming up nicely," she said, feeling like she couldn't fight sleep any longer.

"No you ain't, girl. You're freezin' to death! Now get up," he yelled, pulling her to her feet. "Don't go to sleep yet. I don't know if I've got the strength to get those clothes off of you by myself!" he said as he removed the remains of his own torn shirt.

Malaina's eyes widened at these words, and she even took several steps back.

"Get 'em off," he ordered as he began to strip off his pants.

"You're teasing, of course," she whispered.

"Not a bit, and I don't have time for your proper fussin' now," he said as he stepped out of his pants and boots and lumbered toward her.

"I'll dry out soon, Jackson. It won't take long," she said, smiling nervously as he reached her.

"Yes, it will, Malaina," he said, shoving her aside and opening an old trunk that was up against one cave wall. She sighed with relief as she watched him rummaging through the trunk throwing out blankets, wearing only his red underwear, which he'd sadly mutilated by cutting off the top.

She smiled with relief. "For a minute there, I thought you were going to…" But her smile faded when Jackson straightened and turned around, studying a completed pair of long johns.

"Take 'em off…or I will," he stated, his eyes piercing through her.

Every part of her was frozen. Her fingers were so blue and numb now that she wasn't sure she could, if she had the intention of doing so.

"Now," he growled, and she automatically began to step out of her drenched petticoats. He tossed the long johns on the ground at her feet and turned around. "Now, don't you be peepin', girl. I gotta get out of these as well," he said, rummaging through the trunk again. She whirled around with her back to him, mortified.

"You're wanting me to put these on?" she asked. "They'll just get wet. I'm soaked clear through to my underthings."

She heard the tearing of cloth, and he said irritatedly, "I wasn't meaning for you to wear your 'underthings' underneath 'em. Everything that is wet comes off, Malaina. Now hurry it up! I ain't gonna look 'til you're ready."

She wanted to cry. What indecency! She quickly stripped everything off of her frozen and now fevered body and put on the awkward men's underwear.

"Finished?" Jackson sighed impatiently.

"Yes," she answered timidly as she pushed up the incredibly long sleeves and legs and checked the trap door to make sure the buttons were secured.

"Move," he ordered as he began laying an old bearskin and blankets on the floor next to the fire. He had torn away the top to the dry long johns that he had put on himself. He worked frantically and kept looking up at her with concern engraved across his face. "Lay down here," he said, pointing to the primitive resting place.

"Gladly," she said as she began to feel dizzy and very hot.

But as Malaina lay down on the rugs, she began to shake uncontrollably. Her teeth knocked together, and her muscles were so tensed that they pained her. "What are you doing?" she asked as Jackson lay down next to her and pulled a blanket over them.

"You're gonna freeze to death if we don't get your body warmed up. Don't give me any trouble about this, Malaina. It's necessary if you want to live." As he tried to pull her against him, she put her hands on his chest to prevent it. "Malaina. Don't fight me," he growled. She looked up into his eyes and began to shake even harder. She pulled her arms tightly to her chest and let him pull her against his warm body.

Immediately, Jackson's teeth began to chatter, and Malaina heard him swear under his breath. "You're like ice," he whispered. He held her against him and panted into her wet hair. "Dang!" she heard him mumble as he put a leg over hers. "You're frozen!"

She felt something warm and moist on her cheek. "You're bleeding!" she exclaimed.

Jackson said nothing and simply reached behind them and produced his pocketknife. He held the blade in the flames of the fire for several seconds. Then he released Malaina, sat up, and drove the hot knife into the wound. The look of pain on his face was too much for her. Malaina was unconscious.

CHAPTER TWELVE

Malaina's eyes felt dry as she forced them open. She could still hear the wind whipping about outside the cave. How long had she been asleep? She gradually became aware that her hand and one arm were lying on Jackson's chest, which rose and fell in slow rhythm as he slept. He was lying on his back, and her upper body was flush with his. She felt one of his hands resting on her back, and she could see the other holding hers where it lay on his massive chest. She was no longer shaking, but she felt oddly warm and still dizzy.

Slowly, she raised her head, and when Jackson's hand slid from her back, he didn't even stir. She slipped her hand from beneath his and sat up. The fire was burning out so she got up, went to the woodpile, and selected wood to stoke the fire with. She could tell it was very cold in the cave, but she felt almost hot, so she assumed that she was with fever still.

After she had built up the fire and refreshed her dry mouth with some melted snow that stood in a bucket near them, Malaina sat down next to her sleeping champion. Jackson's breathing was still slow and rhythmic. He stirred slightly, and afterward his hands rested on his stomach.

As Malaina studied his rough, calloused hands, her attention was drawn to the new wound. It looked horrifying! Dried blood caked the area, and the black from the heated knife caused her to shiver. There had been no doctor to stitch it neatly closed, and she knew it would leave a rough scar. She noticed too the other scar just above this one—the one he had received at yet another attempt at saving her.

She brought her hands up to cover her face as the tears of guilt and thankfulness erupted. Malaina cried quietly for several moments, looking at the damage she'd caused to his magnificent form.

"All you lack is the white horse. Every little girl dreams of a knight coming to her rescue, you know," she whispered as she sobbed quietly. "I'm so sorry."

He looked so sweet. Like a little boy, she thought. His hair was tousled, and he slept so soundly. She wiped her tears and stood up again, taking a deep breath. "I must look a mess!" she whispered, trying to change her train of thought. She picked up the top of the long johns that Jackson had mutilated and dipped a sleeve into the bucket of water. She bathed her face and then turned her attention to her shoulder. The blood from Jackson's wound had stained her own shoulder while she had lain with him. She slipped the red flannel off of her shoulder and removed her arm, holding the garment at her chest. She wiped away the blood that had soaked through the cloth and onto her own skin. The thought of again being covered in the blood of the man she was in love with caused the tears to reappear.

"I'm so sorry," she whispered.

"For what?" The sound of his voice so unexpectedly startled her and she spun around so quickly that she nearly lost the grip on her underwear. He stood before her, clutching his own garment at the waist. These underwear had no drawstring rigged up by his mother to secure them.

There he stood—only half-dressed, looking just like the magnificent lover that he'd teased her about.

"I'm sorry for nearly getting you killed yet again," she said, looking down at her exposed shoulder and rubbing it harder with the wet cloth.

"I figure you'll be the death of me yet, girl," he said. But no smile crossed his face.

All the guilt she felt for his injuries exploded. She threw the wet cloth at him and burst into tears. "You are so cruel!" she screamed in a tear-choked whisper. She tried to move past him, but he caught her arm.

"Lie back down," he ordered. "You're still very flushed and hot."

"I'm fine," she growled, but the painful chills were returning.

"I said, lie down, Malaina," he commanded through gritted teeth.

"I just want to walk around for a…" But the dizziness hit her, and she stumbled. Reflexively she reached out for him to steady herself. He caught her with one arm and pulled her against him. She let go her grip on her garment and fell against him, weakened. Subsequently the other side of her garment slipped down, and both of her shoulders were exposed.

"I think I had better lie down," she mumbled. She felt him lay her gently down on the bearskin again, and she drifted off to sleep almost immediately.

❧

When Malaina woke next, she was again lying on Jackson's torso as he slept. She raised herself and sat looking at him. The hand that had been clutching his underwear had relaxed, and she hoped silently that he wouldn't move—otherwise she would be embarrassed to utter death.

She studied his wound for a moment, and it looked like he had escaped infection. "Oh, it is so hot in here!" she whispered to herself, slipping her other arm out of the long johns and tying the sleeves across her chest in order that the garment should not slip off. With shoulders and arms exposed, she lay back down and tried to rest. She wiped the perspiration from her forehead and frowned. Sitting up again, she muttered quietly, "It is *so* hot!"

"Well, don't slip anymore of them longies off. It's too hard on a man," Jackson mumbled.

Malaina looked questioningly at him. His eyes were closed, she was sure. She bent close to his face and whispered, "Are you awake?"

He smiled. "Of course I'm awake."

"Well, it's very hot in here," she stated irritatedly.

"You're tellin' me," he mumbled.

"What?" she asked, but he only grinned with his eyes still closed.

Malaina rolled her head back and forth, trying to soothe her aching neck. "I hope somebody finds us soon," she said to him.

Jackson's grin broadened.

"On second thought," Malaina corrected herself, "if anybody found us, they'd think…" Malaina's eyes widened, and Jackson chuckled. "Jackson! Oh, no! What will folks think?" He opened his eyes to look at her, and the look on her face caused him to break into laughter. "It's not funny. This is completely sinful!" she cried.

He erupted into more laughter. "Darlin'…this is survival. We ain't done nothin'. Folks 'round here know that. I guarantee you nobody, but nobody's out lookin' for us in this storm." He lay down again and continued to laugh.

She couldn't help but smile at her own comments. "You're right. People out here are different. They don't just assume the worst."

Jackson sighed as his laughter subsided. "How are you feeling?" he asked.

"Better," she said, reaching back and rubbing her neck. "Just stiff from lying on the ground. How's your shoulder?"

"It don't hurt much. Baker got arrowed once right in the hiney," he chuckled. "Poor boy couldn't sit down for a month. Mama had a crazy fit, of course. We just won't tell her about this. I bet she's worried sick about you," he said, frowning.

"She won't worry. She knows I'm with you," Malaina said confidently.

He chuckled again. "That won't give her no comfort necessarily." He winked at her, and she blushed. Then a frown crossed his brow again. "She might not even know you're with me. Don't know as anyone saw me get you back there." Jackson began searching the cave. "I need somethin' to hold up these britches."

Malaina stood and went to her drying clothes. "I have a pin in my petticoat that might work." She fumbled around and found it. "Stand up," she said, and he did. He hiked up the long johns and held his hand out for the pin. "No, no, no. You hold them like that and…I'll…just…there. See! Now you don't have to worry about…"

Her voice gave out as she felt his eyes boring into the top of her head. She slowly looked up at him.

Jackson's jaw was visibly clenched, and his chest rose and fell heavily. "I think you better go back to sleep," he mumbled. Malaina noticed how his eyes left her face for a moment and traveled the length of her body and back again.

She giggled nervously. "I must look a sight! Red men's underwear, trapdoor and all. Look at my hair! All unpinned and wild." She dared to look up at him again.

"You ain't helpin' me out any, Malaina."

She cleared her throat and looked away. "And look at you! Half-dressed…as usual…wounded…pants half falling off." She looked up to find his eyes still burning into hers.

"Go back to sleep, Malaina. Please," he mumbled, not moving. Malaina studied Jackson's flawlessly chiseled torso, square clenched jaw, soft tense lips, and boyishly tousled hair.

"I don't want to," she whispered as she took a step toward him.

He closed his eyes tightly and, frowning, shook his head. "Please, sugar. Go over there, and go back to sleep for a while."

It must have been the fever, for Malaina knew that had she been in her right mind, she would never have taken another step. But she did. She stood so close to him that she could feel the heat from his body.

She gazed up into his brutally handsome face and said, "Bet you a nickel that I can kiss you without touching you, Jackson McCall."

He raised his eyebrows and grinned. "Really?" Malaina smiled and nodded. "All right then. I ain't known as a bettin' man…but I'll call your bluff."

She reached up, taking his whiskery face in her hands, and pulled it toward her own. "Do you have a nickel?" she whispered, smiling.

"I'm good for it," he said.

Then she touched his lips very softly with hers, and the thrill of it caused her to tremble. Malaina stepped back to look at him. He looked just the slightest bit dizzy. She reached into the pocket of her long johns and pulled out the nickel that she'd discovered earlier.

"I guess I should stay away from gambling," she whispered, flipping the nickel into the air.

Jackson caught the coin and dropped it in his own pocket. Then he slowly took her into his arms and kissed her forehead.

"Don't go playin' with fire, Miss Malaina. It's mighty unpredictable," he whispered, and she thought he would push her away.

But moments later, Jackson had made his decision, and Malaina felt his coveted kiss on her forehead. Jackson bent and kissed one of her shoulders. Malaina couldn't halt the excitement that flooded her being. When his lips next found her neck, she tightened her grip on his arms, solid as granite. Jackson caressed her neck several times with his kisses, and then, as his mouth savored hers, Malaina let her arms slide around his waist, pulling herself tighter to him. His kisses were deep and filled with desire and passion, and she returned them with equally as much emotion. She caressed his back, reveling in the feel of the muscles hardening as he worked to hold her tighter. She ran her fingers through his hair, felt his unshaven face, gasped once when he nearly crushed her ribs with his strong hands.

Time was lost to them, until he finally tore his lips from hers and held her to him. His breathing steadied a little. Then he suddenly put her away from him and walked to where their clothes lay by the fire.

"We gotta get home, Malaina," he mumbled. She watched as he angrily pulled on his pants.

Malaina stood stunned and then embarrassed. "I'm sorry," she said as she reached for her clothing. "What you must think of me." She felt hot tears forming in her eyes.

Jackson grabbed her arm and spun her to face him. "What I think is that you are the only thing in my entire life that I have trouble resistin'! I don't go drinkin'…no gamblin'…no womanizin'…then I find you out in the middle of nowhere, and all my self-control goes right out the window. And if I don't get you home, Malaina, I'm gonna end up havin' to make an honest woman of you when I do." Her mouth dropped open in astonishment. "Now…get your clothes on. I'm pretty sure that the storm is over."

CHAPTER THIRTEEN

Jackson and Malaina entered the ranch house kitchen together, finding Mary and Maggie seated at the table, sobbing. Both women looked up with astounded expressions as the tattered couple approached.

"Hi, Mama," Jackson said matter-of-factly as he reached for an apple that sat with several others in a basket on the table.

Malaina didn't utter a word but flung herself into the parlor and in front of the warm fire. It had been a mere mile and half another home. But walking through two feet of snow with no extra clothing for warmth had put her back to the brink of freezing.

Maggie slowly stood, still staring at her son as he followed Malaina to the fire. "Hi, Mama?" she screeched. "Hi, Mama?"

Mary knelt beside Malaina and brushed the tangled hair from her face, studying her features with unspoken awe.

Maggie continued in an emotional voice, "We have been worried near to death, Jackson McCall! The entire town is out searching for you. And for Black Wolf!"

"Oh? Well, they can stop lookin' for him. I killed that dirty son of…I put him out of his misery. And me and Malaina weathered the storm just fine and are home safe and sound," Jackson said, as if he'd been out milking the cow all night and day.

Malaina saw the fury rising in Maggie's face.

"Oh. Fine. You killed him," Maggie cried, shaking her head. "We thought you were dead!" Her voice returned to the frightened state as before. "And you waltz in here with a 'Hi, Mama' and grab an apple like you've been out sparkin' after the dance."

Jackson stood and gathered his mother into his arms as she began sobbing. "I'm sorry, Mama. But we really are fine, and now we don't have to worry about Black Wolf anymore. We're nearly frozen to the bone, though…and too awful tired to have any emotions left in us. You get Malaina warmed up now, and I'll go find the search party and tell 'em we're home."

Malaina watched as the grief-stricken mother clung to her baby.

"I'll go tell Matthew, Jackson. He's home. He can ride out after them," Mary said, throwing on her coat and heading out the door.

Maggie held her son's face in her hands and smiled up at him through her tears. "You boys scare the life out of me!" Then she looked over at Malaina. Her mouth dropped open as she drew in a horrified breath and moved to her side. The tears began to flow again as she hugged her over and over and wiped her face with her well-worn apron.

"Oh, my baby girl!" she soothed.

"I'm sorry for all the trouble, Mrs. McCall," Malaina forced out in a whisper before bursting into tears of her own and throwing herself into the woman's welcome embrace. Malaina sobbed hard as the older woman consoled her with hushes and kisses on her head, rocking her where they sat on the floor. "I've brought so much trouble on all of you," she cried. "I'm so deeply ashamed of it."

Maggie pushed her back and cupped Malaina's chin firmly in hand, forcing the young woman to look at her. "That is enough, young lady!" she said. "I won't be havin' that kind of talk, 'cause it just isn't so. Do you hear me? We wouldn't have life without you now…no, we wouldn't. You're our own! Our very own. Do you understand me?"

Malaina nodded only to please the lovely woman. Maggie pulled Malaina to her again. "Now, let's get a tub filled for the two of you and get somethin' warm down."

Jackson chuckled from his resting place on the sofa. "I think it would be wise to run us each a separate tub, Mama." He grinned and winked at the two women.

Maggie let out a sigh of exasperation. "Well, at least I know now that he's truly unharmed."

Maggie left the room to prepare baths, and Malaina stood in front of the fire for several more moments until her teeth quit chattering. At long last, she turned to see Jackson asleep on the sofa.

"Jackson?" she whispered. "Jackson? Are you asleep?" No answer and steady breathing indicated that he was. She crept slowly over until she stood looking down at him. He didn't move.

Malaina knelt and put a hand softly on his knee. "Jackson?" she said again. "Thank you," she whispered as tears brimmed in her eyes once more. "Thank you…for my life…again."

As she stood and turned away, Jackson's hand caught her own, startling her. She turned to look at him and watched as he slowly stood up. It was apparent that every muscle and bone in his body pained him. He smiled down at her, and she smiled back as she surveyed the tousled hair and dirt-smeared face. He looked so boyish.

"I'll tell you what, little Miss Red Flannel Underwear…" She couldn't stop the blush. He held up one hand and bent one finger at a time down as he spoke. "Let's see—finding you in the desert, pullin' a scorpion outta your drawers, gettin' shot by some varmint who wanted to drag you off from town, killin' an Indian who wanted you—took an arrow, by the way—and keepin' you from freezin' to death durin' a blizzard." Her spirits began to fall again, but he went on. "I count at least five times that I've saved your dainty little hide. Tell you what…" He looked around sneakily and lowered his voice to a whisper. "You give me one more kiss like you did last night in that cave…and we'll call it even." He grinned down at her surprised face for a moment. Then his smile faded, and his brow puckered in a frown. "I won't ever ask again. And life has to return to just the everyday like before, you hear me?" It was a command, and she felt her heart sink into the pit of her stomach. "It was all too romantic last night, stuck in the cold with a dusty ol' rancher. I know you weren't in your right mind, and I wasn't neither." Malaina's eyebrows lifted at his use of the word *romantic*. "But I am a man, after all… and you look mighty cute in red flannels. So, I want a proper, 'Thank you, Mr. McCall.'" He grinned at her again, but she felt like running.

In other words, it would have made no difference if the ugliest woman in the world had been in that cave with him. It offended and hurt her. She thought they had shared a loving passion for only each other for a few blissful hours. Now she knew differently.

Malaina struggled to push herself away from him, but he held her tightly. "Take it like I mean it, Malaina…not how it sounded," he said, frowning, and she stopped struggling as she felt his lips on her forehead.

A warmth of desire passed through her as his mouth moved to her neck. She let her arms return his embrace and delighted at the feel of him against her. "I saved you for my ownself, you know," he whispered just before he took her mouth roughly with his. The passion was even stronger than before. His kisses were almost uncomfortable at times with their forcefulness and desire.

Jackson tried seven times to end their kisses. It took him eight before his self-control was finally in check. He held her head tightly against his chest once more before breaking the embrace, and when he did, he smiled as he ran his thumb over her lips.

"If there were ever gonna be a next time for this—which there won't—I had better cut off my whiskers first. I done a job on that petal-soft skin of yours." The skin around her mouth did feel damaged. His whisker growth was very heavy. "I'm gonna see if Bill made it home." And he turned and staggered out the front door.

Malaina stood deeply depressed for several moments. She hadn't seen Maggie peeking around the corner at them, with a smile as broad as the Mississippi across her face.

"Come on back, Malaina. Let's get you warmed up," Maggie called innocently.

CHAPTER FOURTEEN

Winter came and went without incident. Malaina found that Jackson was true to his word. He had seemingly forgotten her for anything but perhaps a sister now. Matthew and Mary had become a charming little couple, and Malaina, being Mary's confidant, knew that an engagement would soon be announced and was joyous about it. Baker was still comfortable in his solitude. Malaina wondered if he would simply forever mourn his long-lost sweetheart. Maggie was cheerful and smiling all the time, and Malaina would often catch her looking lovingly and a bit slyly at her.

"What?" Malaina would ask on such occasions.

"Oh nothin', dear. Nothin' at all," Maggie would chuckle.

Jackson was Jackson. Teasing most of the time, brooding some of the time, and grumpy once in a while. He never seemed to look twice at Malaina, whose dreams continued to be filled with him.

It had been six months since Black Wolf had tried to steal Malaina. She had remembered very little else of her life before she had been found by Jackson and had settled down into family life.

She still broke out in goose bumps whenever Jackson's hand would accidentally brush her in passing, but she knew that he had no interest in her other than as a friend—probably regarded her as less a chum than he did ol' Bill. Sometimes at night the tears of hurt and aching to be in his arms again would flow steadily for an hour or so, but she made it through each time.

One morning in early May, Malaina was in the kitchen with

a basket of strawberries to be made into jam. She was shamelessly spying on Matthew and Mary, who were out by the north fence wrapped in a loving embrace. A grin spread across her face as she peered out the kitchen window and snipped strawberry stems.

"Didn't know you was a 'peepin' tom,' sweetheart." She jumped guiltily as Jackson chuckled behind her.

"Hush!" she shushed him, giggling. "They're so cute," she said, smiling and returning to her spying.

He came and stood beside her, peering out the window. "They oughta be…after all your matchmakin' efforts," he chuckled, and her smile faded when he gave her a quick kiss on the cheek as he stole a strawberry.

She turned around to set a bowl of stemmed berries on the table and noticed that blood was saturating a place on the thigh of his pants.

"Is that yours?" she asked irritatedly.

"What?" he asked in return.

"The blood on your pants. Is that yours?" She stood with her hands on her hips in a very scolding and rather maternal manner.

"Well, of course it's mine. You ain't been in any trouble lately," he said, starting out the door.

Malaina stepped in front of him to stop his escape. "Well, drop 'em, and let's get it cleaned up before your mama gets back from the berry patch. She'll tan your hide if you've hurt yourself breaking another horse."

In the previous months, Malaina had developed a cast-iron stomach when it came to injuries, blood, and wounds. The McCall boys were covered in cuts and bruises more often than not.

"Forget about it, Malaina. It's a scratch," he said, trying to move past her.

"Jackson! It'll get infected. You probably cut it on something rusty as well." She innocently reached forward and unfastened his pants.

"Wait a minute! You ain't my mama!" he said, pushing her away.

"Now, Jackson," she ordered. "Do you want me to handle this one, or would you rather bear your mama's wrath about it?"

After considering the question for a split second, Jackson stepped out of his pants, backed up, and planted himself on the table.

"Eeewww!" Malaina whined with a grimace as she inspected the wound through the tear in his flannels. "How did you do this one?" she asked as she saturated a cloth in the water that was boiling jam jars on the stove.

"I'm breakin' that new stallion we got. He's purty mean, that one. He threw me, and I caught it on a broken fence post—which wouldn't even have been there if Matthew weren't so dang busy sparkin' Mary all the time."

Malaina giggled. "Oh, you're just jealous 'cause he's smooching with a girl and you're out smooching with another horse."

"I ain't jealous, Malaina. Besides, he can't even do a proper job of it. I need to teach that boy a thing or two yet."

Malaina rinsed the blood out of the cloth into the sink and wet it again. "Ha! Quit patting yourself on the back. He's a wonderful, sensitive man. And besides, I've seen them a lot more stuck together than that. It's just daytime and out in the open, that's all. I think it's wonderful." She inspected the wound again. "Hmmm. A splinter, I think." She used her fingernails to pull it out.

"Whatever happened to that gentle touch you used to have?" he asked.

"Don't be a baby. I swear! You get shot by arrows and bullets, and it's no big deal. Then you go on and on, whining about a little sticker."

"Well, now this is cute!" Baker chuckled, coming through the back door. "You better hurry up, Malaina. Mama's done pickin'."

Malaina quickly bandaged the wound—but not quickly enough. Maggie stepped through the back door in time to see Jackson pulling up his pants.

"Ah ha! Caught you with your pants down, I see," she laughed as the three guilty faces turned on her. "How bad is it, son?"

"It's just a scratch," Jackson said. "Mama, teach this girl some manners," he said, pointing to Malaina. "She's been spyin' on Matthew and Mary again."

Maggie chuckled, and Malaina stuck her tongue out at him in a childish gesture. "Well, maybe she just needs some sparkin' of her own! What do you think?" Maggie teased and didn't miss the look that quickly passed between Jackson and Malaina.

"Well, I oughta be the one to take care of that," Baker said, gathering Malaina into his arms. "What do you say, darlin'? Give us a kiss," he teased, puckering up his lips and trying to kiss her as she giggled and moved her head away.

"Now stop that, Baker. We've got berries to do up," Maggie said. She had noticed that Jackson's smile retreated immediately the minute Baker had touched Malaina. She saw his chest rising and falling with heavy breaths even now.

"No more cuts today, Jackson. My stomach can only tolerate one a day," Malaina said as she returned to the berries.

But Jackson simply turned and left the house, slamming the door behind him. Malaina didn't see Baker wink at his mother, who winked in return.

❦

Maggie and Malaina put up strawberry preserves and jam for the rest of the morning. Mary helped, and they all talked about wedding-type things.

"Oh, Mary! I can't wait. It's been so long since I've been to a wedding," Malaina sighed.

"He hasn't officially asked me yet, Malaina. Maybe he won't," Mary said, frowning.

"Of course he will," Maggie assured.

It was suppertime when Jackson opened the kitchen door, stepped in, and stood looking at them like the grim reaper.

"What is it, boy?" Maggie asked, drying her hands on her apron.

"There's a man in town. Collin Mereaux. From Louisiana," he said.

Malaina dropped the jar of jam she had been holding and put her hands over her mouth. She began walking backward, shaking her head, and muttering, "No! Please! No!" She cried out, and her hands pressed against her temples as an excruciating headache began to pound in her brain. The others watched as she crumpled to the floor, sobbing.

"Who is he, Malaina?" Jackson asked in an angry, commanding voice. "I asked you a question!" he yelled.

"Jackson!" Maggie scolded. "Just wait!" She went to where Malaina now lay on the floor crying. "Honey, what is it?" she asked in a soothing voice. "You've got to tell us what you remember."

But the memories were flooding back so painfully and so fast that it was several minutes before she could speak. When she did, she sat up and spoke directly to Jackson. "He owns me," she squeaked out.

"What are you talking about?" Jackson growled angrily.

The memories of her previous life in Louisiana and how she came to be out in the middle of the wilderness were restored to Malaina's conscious. Horrifyingly restored!

"He owns me. I mean…my stepfather sold me to him when my mother died last June. He gave my stepfather an old plantation that he owned, and my stepfather turned me over to him in exchange. I don't even know if he intended to marry me…but I was to be his to do with as he would."

Baker and Matthew had since entered the room, and everyone stood stunned.

"You mean you're a—" Matthew started, but he broke off as he saw defiance cross her face.

Malaina stood up and slowly walked over to him. "If it were anyone but you, Matthew, I'd slap your face for asking that," she said, holding her head up and trying to stop the tears of hurt. She looked around the room at everyone staring at her. "Is that what you all think of me?" she cried and began to shake.

"No, sweet thing. Of course not!" Maggie said, raising a hand to brush her cheek. Malaina stepped back and out of her reach.

"You do! All of you! You think I'm a—it's not true! I ran away! I would rather have died than…you don't understand. They still fight the war down there. They still think anyone can be sold for the right price!" She felt as if she would vomit. "He even has a so-called legal paper to prove it. He owns me, and I ran away."

Everyone in the room was silent for a few moments, and Malaina looked from one to the other.

"Nobody owns anybody, Malaina," Baker said at last.

She giggled nervously. "Maybe not here. But there they do."

"Nowhere, Malaina. Not in the United States," Matthew added.

Malaina felt as if she might faint. It was hard to breathe. Baker stepped forward to offer her support.

"Don't touch me!" She looked at Matthew. "How could you believe I could be capable of such a lifestyle?" Mary and Maggie were in tears, and Jackson stood staring at her.

"I didn't mean what you thought, Malaina. I wasn't suggestin' that you worked in a…in a…brothel or nothin' like that. I thought maybe you had slave ancestry, and that's why he was huntin' you down."

Jackson stood stiff and angry. "She's from the South. Either way, it's an insult, little brother," he growled.

"That's not true!" she cried. "I don't feel that way. I've no slave ancestry—but if I did, I wouldn't be ashamed of it." Baker reached for her again.

"Don't!" she cried. Mary burst into sobbing.

Maggie talked quietly. "Malaina, we love you! You're ours. We're you're family! Please, let us help you."

Malaina shook her head furiously. "No. He'll kill you. All of you. He's an evil, evil man." She began looking around frantically. "I'll have to leave! Right now." Then her eyes locked on Jackson. "Please, Jackson. Lend me some money. Help me get away where he won't find me. I beg you."

He looked down into her frightened, pleading face. Then he quickly grabbed her and held her tightly as she struggled.

"Mama, keep her here. I don't care if you have to tie her up! Do you hear me?" Maggie nodded obediently. "Baker, run on out to the barn and saddle up a horse. I want you to ride back to town with me. Matthew, go over to Preacher Pete's house. Tell him that if anyone asks…well, he's to say he married me and Malaina last month in private. Get goin'! Keep her here, Mama." And Jackson thrust Malaina into his mother's arms as he started out the door.

"No, Jackson! Don't go! He'll kill you. Please!" Malaina begged through her river of tears.

"Nobody kills me, Malaina. Especially where you're concerned. Calm her down, Mama. She's half outta her mind." And he left.

"Mrs. McCall! You have to stop him! You don't know Collin. Please," the girl begged, slipping to the floor in a near faint. She was unconscious for only a few moments and was a little more rational when she came to.

"There now, sweet pea. You're fine, and everythin' will work out," Maggie cooed.

"Mrs. McCall, please—you don't know this man," Malaina pleaded. "Jackson is overconfident, to say the least. He'll be killed!"

Maggie spoke sharply. "Get control of yourself, Malaina. First of all, in this family, everybody's problems concern everybody. Second, Jackson talks a big game because he's capable of it. Don't you know that by now?"

Malaina nodded. She did know it. She had no doubt that face-to-face, Collin was no threat to Jackson. But Collin Mereaux was an evil, vile, corrupt, yet spineless man who always traveled with his personal thugs. She worried, for Jackson could well find himself facing ten men to his one.

Maggie went on. "We'll wait here. The boys will take care of this."

So they waited. The three women sat together in ominous silence as the minutes passed. The clock on the mantel numbered those long, tedious minutes and eventually struck the hour. Malaina closed her beautiful eyes in unspoken prayer as the clock marked yet another hour.

And then, as if the clock's striking were to summon a dreadful premonition, their hearts leapt at the sound of approaching riders.

Malaina sprinted out the door. "Jackson! What's going on?" There was no answer, and her lovely hands gripped the porch railing tightly for support as she saw before her the heinous Collin Mereaux mounted on a violent black stallion, kicking at the dirt and snorting angrily as his master reined him to a halt. "Collin," she gasped, feeling as if someone had drained the lifeblood from her.

How could she have possibly forgotten this man? He was tall, not unusually handsome like Jackson, but considered very handsome just the same—black hair, black eyes, white teeth, and wicked smile. And now he was before her with at least four other men behind him.

"Yes, darling. So, you've regained your precious memory. We had been informed that it was lost for some time," he said mockingly.

As his repulsively familiar voice echoed in her brain, she ordered, "Go away, Collin," and hoped the fear in her intonation wasn't too apparent.

"Oh, but I've come to rescue you, my beauty." He dismounted, and Malaina resisted the urge to step back.

"I'm afraid you'll have to leave, sir. You're not welcome here," Maggie said, stepping through the door to stand next to Malaina.

Collin laughed. "Well, I'm certain that is an understatement, ma'am."

As Malaina looked then to Maggie, complete and absolute understanding sparked within her bosom. Maggie loved her! She loved her as she would her own daughter. A moment before she had appeared at her side, Malaina had contemplated conceding defeat to Collin, thereby preserving each precious life in the McCall family. But now she knew that she could never endure such an existence. Death would be more tolerable an anticipation. She further knew that if she were to be taken by him, the pain inflicted upon this uniquely brave and beautiful woman would be too cruelly administered. Baker and Matthew were both willing to protect her with their lives as they would, no doubt, their own sister, had they been blessed with one. And Jackson…yes, Jackson. Jackson had proven time and again that he would forfeit his own life to preserve hers. She thought of him now, her champion, her dream lover. She could not leave him. Better to perish and pass to the next life than to leave him, knowing she would have to endure the touch of another man.

"We're not alone here, Collin," Malaina stated bravely.

"Hmmm. Yes. So I hear," he mumbled, moving closer to them.

Malaina still stood her ground. The severe shock that the horrible memories rushing back had left was gone, and she was herself, in control again. Barely. He approached until he stood directly before her. Then he reached out and touched her cheek. She pulled away, sickened.

"I've been searching for so long, darling. Think how it must be for me, anticipating having such a beauty as you for my own, and then—poof—you're gone." He reached to touch her again. Malaina stepped back out of his reach. "How very rude and quite unbecoming, darling. After all, I've come to take you home," Collin chuckled.

"You know that I won't go with you, Collin. And I've friends now to protect me," Malaina stated flatly, though she felt everything within her quivering with fear. Still she would stand stalwart. Nothing could tear her from her course.

"I would suggest that you leave our property at once, mister. And for your own well-bein', I wouldn't be tryin' to bother my son's wife again," Maggie added boldly.

Collin sneered and said, "Don't tell me you've gone and married one of these…these…farmers, Malaina."

Malaina raised her chin proudly as Collin chuckled. Snapping his fingers, he motioned to the men that accompanied him and ordered, "Bring her forward, Jon."

Malaina watched as one of the riders dismounted, dragged another rider from his own mount, and forced him forward. She gasped in astounded horror as Collin proceeded to brutally rip the hat from the smaller rider's head, revealing the hauntingly familiar face.

"Charlotte!" she cried out.

"Yes. Our dearest Charlotte," Collin confirmed.

Charlotte burst into tears and was undoubtedly scared beyond rational behavior. Malaina stared disbelieving at the young woman who bore her similar likeness—blue eyes, black hair, and beauty. "If you've harmed her, Collin—" Malaina began.

"What, darling? What will you do?" he mocked. "Now, there,

there, Charlotte," he muttered to the girl, putting a hand caressively to her face.

"Don't touch her!" Malaina screamed, gripping the railing even more solidly.

As Collin sighed triumphantly, Maggie looked to Malaina for explanation. "Who is she?" she asked.

"My half-sister, Charlotte," Malaina mumbled.

"Yes," Collin chuckled. "Dear, dear Charlotte. The spoiled baby sister. Though you do love her, don't you, Malaina? Charlotte was always good to you. Even though your stepfather sold you to me so that his own daughter could have a dowry. Sad, but true. Now, come along with me, Malaina."

"Malaina, don't listen to him! Please!" Charlotte pleaded.

"What do you want of me, Collin?" Malaina asked defeatedly. Charlotte was her sister, and she loved her deeply. There was no other choice.

He smiled. "Why...you, of course, my dear. You come with me now—no more running away—and I'll leave dear Charlotte here in your place. Otherwise, I'll kill her here and now before your very eyes."

"Nobody's goin' anywhere, mister."

Malaina turned to see Mary coming out of the house, a rifle raised and pointed at Collin's head. Slowly she went to stand before him as she spoke once more. "You get outta here. Leave the girl too."

Reaching out quickly, Collin grabbed the gun barrel, tearing the weapon from her grasp. "Come now, miss. Don't be silly." Mary gasped and stepped back from him.

"You're a pretty one as well, miss," Collin said, tossing the gun aside. Then, in one swift motion, he had turned Mary to face the others, staying her with one hand while the other pulled a revolver from beneath his coat and held it to the girl's head.

"Mary!" Maggie cried out.

"Collin...please," Malaina began. "Let her go. Please."

"Now this is comforting, Malaina. Pleading with me...as it were." Collin nuzzled Mary's neck, however, commenting, "She's sweet as magnolia in summer. What do you say, honeysuckle? Perhaps you and I could enjoy a satisfying moment or two before I move on to my dear Malaina there. What do you say?"

"Get your filthy, smelly hands off her!"

Hope was renewed within Malaina as she saw Matthew approaching from one side of the house. He'd obviously returned and seen the trouble they were in. He now leveled his own rifle at the villain's head.

Chuckling, Collin turned to face him, still holding Mary in front of him with the pistol pressed firmly to her temple. "Ah. A farm boy. Don't trifle with me, boy…or this little miss won't be of any use to any of you. Except perhaps as fertilizer for your pitiful little crops come next spring. Put the gun away, boy. Or I'll start the job for you with her brains. You could plant a lovely little flower bed just here… where her blood first spills."

Malaina watched as Matthew's chest rose and fell with fiery anger. She watched as an anguished expression crossed his face when he realized that the risk of Collin successfully shooting Mary should he attempt to fell the monster himself was more than he could chance.

Angrily, Matthew tossed his gun aside. "Let her go then," he ordered.

"Your wish is my command," Collin said. However, in that next moment, he pushed Mary to the ground, pointed his gun at the young champion, and fired. Matthew's hand flew to his head, and he staggered forward slightly before falling to the ground.

Mary screamed and Maggie screeched, "Matthew!" as the handsome young man lay silent and motionless a few feet away.

Malaina began shaking her head and muttering to herself, "No. No." As she started toward the fallen hero, Collin kicked Mary squarely in the stomach and grabbed Malaina by the arm, staying her.

Yanking at her mercilessly, he pulled her against his powerful body. Looking down at the breathless, heartbroken, and battered Mary, he said, "No woman threatens me with a weapon, girl. Be glad you have your life." Then he turned to Malaina, still holding her securely. "I own you, Malaina. He's dead now. Forget your dirty little farm boy." Reaching into his inner coat pocket, Collin retrieved a folded document. "My papers, Malaina. A bill of sale signed by your dearly departed stepfather."

Malaina reached up and slapped him hard across the face. He instantly slapped her back, leaving horridly red welts fresh upon her tender cheek.

"Leave her alone, Collin!" Charlotte shouted. "I told you—I'll take her place!"

"I don't want you, Charlotte. I want your sister, and I own her. Legally."

Then the sickening, wet kiss of Collin Mereaux met Malaina's mouth. Her defeated heart cried out for Jackson—for his powerful arms to be protectively about her, for his mouth to be warm and tenderly passionate upon her own. At last her struggling won out, and he released the nauseating seal his lips had on hers.

"Get the other girl back on her horse, men. We're going home," Collin commanded, laughing triumphantly.

Charlotte screamed, "No!" as the men accompanying Collin dismounted. Two of them took hold of Charlotte, dragging her toward a mount, as another man assisted Collin in pulling Malaina toward the waiting group of horses.

"You promised, Collin!" Malaina cried, struggling with all the strength left in her. "You promised to leave Charlotte!"

"Did I?" Collin mocked. "Oh, fiddle. We'll bring her along—just in case you decide not to…cooperate fully with me."

"Malaina!" Maggie cried as Mary at last was able to rush to Matthew.

"Leave it be, old mother," Collin warned Maggie. "I would as soon shoot her than take such a large financial loss. Do you know how much I paid for this piece of fluff?"

Malaina watched helplessly as the sister she loved so was lifted onto the horse, her hands then bound to the saddle horn. Collin shoved Malaina onto his own horse, bound her hands as well, and mounted behind her.

"I do thank you, old woman, for keeping her in good repair for me," Collin said. Then Malaina felt all hope—the very will to live—draining from her as his repulsive lips toyed at her neck. She painfully looked at Matthew's still body and Mary hovering over him sobbing.

It felt suddenly as if some all-powerful force hit Collin solidly, sending him falling from the horse. Her eyes fell to where he lay on the ground, and resplendent joy was rekindled as she saw the man being beaten mercilessly by Jackson. Jackson's horse stood snorting and rearing next to the one she sat on. She hadn't heard him approach, yet he was there, ever her protector!

"You dirty…" Jackson mumbled as his fists dealt blow after blow to the surprised man. He stopped abruptly, however, when three guns were cocked simultaneously, pointing at his head. Collin's men encircled Jackson, and Jackson ceased beating Collin and stood.

"Jackson," Malaina squeaked out in a whisper. He looked to her only for a moment before returning his attention to the villain.

Collin stood, brushing himself off dramatically. "This is a silk shirt, sir," he informed Jackson.

"Yeah? Well, it figures you'd wear somethin' that came outta a worm's behind," Jackson growled.

Collin cleared his throat and smoothed his hair. "Am I to understand that I've disposed of the wrong…husband?" he asked sarcastically.

"That's my brother lyin' over there," Jackson confirmed. His face blatantly displayed anger, disgust, and hatred toward the man who stood before him. "Even though you killed my brother, I mighta shown some mercy and killed you quick. But you laid your filthy hands on Malaina. And for that I intend to make your death as slow and painful as possible. I ain't never skinned a man before…though I hear that some Indian tribes find that the most painful way to kill a man. Yer purty much neck-deep in bull manure, mister." Malaina had never seen Jackson in such a state of vindictive hatred and rage. She was sure he meant to kill Collin as gruesomely as he had just described.

"Jackson, no, please," Malaina pleaded, "I'll go with him! I don't want you to have to—"

"You'll never go with him, Malaina! Not as long as I have breath in me."

"Which won't be long," Collin sneered. He looked to Malaina. "Don't tell me you actually married this…illiterate trash? Oh, Malaina, Malaina, Malaina. You know that you're mine. Your marriage changes nothing." He pulled the document from his vest pocket once more, flaunting it in Jackson's face. "My papers, um… sir. I own this girl. I've just come to collect the property that is mine, by law," he said.

Jackson smiled, snatched the papers from his hand, and said, "I know some of you folks have a hard time accepting this, but the war is over. The North won, and Lincoln freed the slaves. No court is gonna hold to anythin' so asinine as papers that say you own a woman."

"She's my property," Collin said as his smile faded.

"Nope. It just ain't so. You see, every court in this good country would most certainly hold to the paper *I* have concernin' this woman," Jackson said.

Collin looked about him, motioning to the men who held Jackson at gunpoint. "Well, no court's going to enter into it, farmer. Either you're blind or else you're too ignorant to realize that you are at a severe disadvantage. The South will, indeed, triumph this time. Let's just shoot him and get on with our journey, boys."

"I'm really very surprised and disappointed, sir," Jackson addressed Collin. "I always thought you Southern boys were so brave and chivalrous. I never thought you'd be hidin' behind hired guns. I heard you boys always fought your own duels. But then I guess you'd be havin' to get that wormy ol' shirt all mussed up again. Is that it?"

Malaina looked at Jackson in dismay. She knew he'd struck at the pride in the enemy—a dangerous attack, for Collin was nothing if not prideful.

The rage of the insult shone clearly on Collin's face. "Do not toy with me, farmer. I'll easily dispose of you."

Jackson grinned. "Now, by law, Malaina here is my wife; you can't take her. But, since you're such a lily-soft boy, I'll let you pick the way I kill you. Gun, fists, or—"

"Sabers," Collin stated without hesitation. Motioning to his men to lower their guns, he took several steps toward Jackson.

"Sabers?" Jackson repeated.

"What's wrong? You said I could choose, you swine."

Jackson nodded. Malaina turned to Maggie, who had exhaled an audible sigh of triumph. Collin seemed to ignore her, while Malaina wondered if the strain had been too much on Maggie's mind, for she appeared to be somehow relieved slightly.

Straightening his vest, Collin said, "Very well. I assume you'll be needing a saber. I've several with me." He turned. But Jackson's next utterance stopped him.

"Nope. Got my very own right upstairs. I'll have my mama fetch it." Then, turning to his mother, he instructed, "Mama, would you run along up to my trunk and get my saber?" He tossed a key to her as the fear began to intensify in Malaina again.

"So," Collin began, "you've a little trinket from the war or some such thing."

"Nope. It's my own. To do a little pattin' my ownself on the back, I was best man with a saber for every one of my four years at West Point."

Malaina looked at Jackson in astonishment. Black Wolf slipped into her thoughts as she now understood why the beast had referred to Jackson as Captain.

Jackson grinned at Collin. "You see, sir, I'm not what you thought you'd run into out here...am I?"

But Collin was all too confident. "What a nice bit of exercise this will be. Should last all of three minutes."

"You think that long?" Jackson asked mockingly.

"It depends on how fast the blood will drain from that sun-roasted body of yours, boy."

"A lot slower than it will from your lily-white hide. Remember, I ain't the one who has to buy me a woman," Jackson chuckled.

Maggie returned then and handed a beautiful saber to Jackson. She glared at Collin, reassured in her knowledge of her son's skill, and said, "Well, Mr. Collin whoever you are…you're a mighty brave man if'n you think you can go saber to saber with Captain Jackson McCall and come out standin'."

"Is that so?" Collin mocked.

Malaina screamed as Collin took a swipe at Jackson with his saber, cutting him deeply on one arm.

"Just a little taste of the mutilation you're about to endure, farmer," Collin chuckled.

Jackson retaliated then, cutting Collin nicely across one cheek in response. "All right, you purty little pansy…come on. I'm gonna carve you up with the McCall brand before I finish you, you coward."

Malaina was unable to tear her eyes from the nightmare that was the duel. She found herself holding her breath every time Collin lunged toward Jackson and releasing it in relief as he parried and returned blows of his own. Oddly fascinated, she watched as Jackson's saber met again with Collin's cheek, the two wounds now forming what appeared to be an inverted V. Jackson lunged forward several times in sequence, forcing Collin backward, away from Maggie, Mary, and Matthew. Collin was startled as Jackson masterfully inflicted the wounded cheek with two more small lacerations, completing a perfect letter M there. The villain was stunned and raised his free hand to the wound. His face registered fear and shock as he pulled the hand away and saw his own blood forming an M in the palm of his hand. Malaina watched the beads of perspiration dripping from Collin's brow, and triumph rose within her when Jackson completed the McCall brand by adding a bar above the letter with one final stroke.

Her joyous elation was short-lived, however, as Collin, realizing that he was outmatched by the farmer, barked a final order to his men. "Shoot the Captain!"

"No!" Malaina screamed. Shots rang out in that moment, and she was utterly confused as she saw two of Collin's men fall to the ground.

"Move away from my brother, boys." Baker appeared from the opposite side of the house. In his hands, he held a rifle aimed squarely at Collin's head.

"Shoot him!" Collin shouted to his last standing man. Instantly, Jackson lunged forward, fatally wounding the remaining man with the saber he still held.

The horses that Malaina and Charlotte sat tied to began to rear, spooked by the gunfire. Malaina saw Baker grab Charlotte's horse by the bit, controlling the startled mare. Jackson turned from Collin and tried to grab the reins of Malaina's panicked mount. They eluded his grasp, however, and Malaina gasped in horror as Collin grasped his saber firmly with both hands and raised it above his head, clearly intent on ramming it through Jackson's back. Another shot rang out then, and Collin fell to the ground.

"Matthew!" Malaina heard Maggie cry just as her horse bolted away.

As the horse ran from the ranch at a fierce gallop, she could feel the saddle slipping. She found it utterly impossible to gain control of the horse or regain her own balance with her hands tied as they were. But, as always, Jackson was soon at her side on his own mount. He whistled and shouted, and the horse reared, stomping his hooves, and turned back toward the ranch, slowing its pace in the process. Malaina could see the house again—beacon of safety and love. Maggie and Mary were helping Matthew to his feet. Baker was holding Charlotte protectively in his arms. Malaina was feeling the warmth of security beginning to ebb through her when the horse lost its footing. She heard the snap of leather and felt the sensation of falling. Then her soul memorized the looks of horror on the faces of the family as she plummeted toward the ground.

"Malaina!" Jackson's anguished voice called. Her last thoughts before the terrible weight and darkness were, *He's alive. My Jackson is alive.*

※

"She's breathing." The voices sounded distant and distorted.

"Pull him up! We've got to get him off!" It was Jackson's voice, and there was something frantic about it.

Malaina tried to open her eyes. She tried to force her throat to speak, but nothing would come. She was aware then of a great weight being lifted from her legs.

"He's up! He's up!" Baker shouted.

"Malaina? Malaina? Please…open them beautiful eyes and look at me, darlin'," Jackson's voice echoed in her mind. "Baker, get her hands free from the horn. Come on, honey. Look at me. You know you want to. Ain't too many ol' boys 'round here that can beat me in good looks. You know that," he said. "Baker," he shouted, "get these dang ropes cut, will you? Mama, her wrists are bleedin' somethin' awful." His intonation was harsh and unstable.

"I'm workin' as fast as I can, Jack," Baker assured him.

The stinging pain in her wrists as the ropes came free caused Malaina to gasp, filling her lungs with life-giving air. Still she could not speak.

"Dang!" she heard Jackson mutter under his breath, and she felt herself being pulled into his urgent embrace. "Don't you dare leave me, darlin'!" His calloused, gentle hands tenderly stroked her hair. Though she longed to gaze into his soft green eyes, to speak, reassuring him that she would be fine, her body refused to respond.

"Malaina. It's Maggie." Maggie's voice was so soothing. "I'm wrappin' those little hands of yours in my apron, sweet pea." Malaina sensed the pressure of Maggie's hands on her throbbing wrists. "Charlotte is safe with Baker, Malaina. Everything is fine now. Matthew was only grazed in the head." Maggie's concern and fatigued emotions were evident in the cracking of her voice as she continued, "Mary's fine too, and you're gonna be fine. Do you hear?"

"Please, Malaina," Jackson's voice pleaded. Malaina could feel the warmth of his breath on her cheek. She smelled the familiar aroma of leather and bacon that was his. "I can't lose you now, darlin'. Do you think I saved your hide time after time to let you go now? I even had the white horse this time, Malaina."

"White horse?" she heard herself whisper.

She was aware of Jackson sighing heavily and hugging her tightly against him. As her eyes at last opened, they beheld the magnificent face of her champion.

"You said yourself, way back when, that all I needed was a white horse," he said, smiling and kissing her cheek softly as he stroked her hair affectionately.

As she gazed into his handsome face and her mind became clearer, she realized fully the danger they had all just endured. She was angry with herself for subjecting them all to such peril. Especially Jackson. She looked at the blood dried on his sleeve, the blood from the wound inflicted because of her.

Pushing him away, she cried, "How dare you? Sabers, of all things! Why did you have to make it into such a game? It was awful! He could've killed you!" She buried her face in her hands, sobbing violently with emotional relief.

Taking her gently by the shoulders, Jackson again drew her to him. "Sshh, darlin'. It's all over," he whispered into her hair.

Malaina let her arms slip around him, hugging him tightly against her own body. "He could've killed you, Jackson," she reminded.

"He didn't, Malaina," he reminded in return. Then he chuckled, "He couldn'ta won anyway. I didn't spend no four years at West Point to get whipped by some man who wears ruffles on his chest."

"It's not funny. How can you laugh? I thought I'd have to see you be killed!" she cried, hugging him tighter.

His smile showed compassion, not mockery. "I know, darlin'. But it's over now. No more worries. No more strangers showin' up to try and steal you away." He kissed her cheek tenderly and began playing with a lock of her soft hair. His eyes hypnotized her as he spoke. "Now, I figure…I've saved you again, right?" He kissed her other cheek. "That's six times now, ain't it?" He kissed her forehead. "I figure…you marry me, and we'll call it even."

"But you said—" she began. Her words were silenced and her eyes widened in disbelief as he pressed a lovingly passionate kiss to her mouth.

"I was afraid, Malaina," he confessed, and his smile was gone.

"Afraid that you'd suddenly remember someday…someone in the past that you loved before. Someone you'd regret losing. Someone that you'd come to realize you loved more than your smelly ol' cowboy."

Tears rolled from Malaina's eyes and down her temples, and she tried to smile.

"But I own you now. And I've got the papers to prove it." He kissed her quickly again, waved Collin's "legal" bill of sale in her face, stuffed it in his shirt, and smiled as she pulled his head to hers to return his kisses.

Maggie and Mary were wiping their tears of joy with their strawberry- and blood-stained aprons. "A double wedding!" Maggie sighed.

"Malaina!" Charlotte exclaimed in horror as she watched her sister receiving and returning passionate kisses with Jackson. "Malaina! How can you? It's so improper! Such intimate behavior. In public! Not to mention kneeling in the soil…with a man!" Malaina laughed as she looked up at her sister's blushing face.

Jackson chuckled and winked at Baker. "I saw you lookin' at that girl, Baker. Take off your shirt and start breakin' her in!"

Baker grinned and turned to Charlotte. She was quite beautiful herself. He'd felt something toward her instantly. She clutched her shirt collar.

"Baker!" Maggie warned. But he ignored her.

"Ma'am," he said, taking Charlotte in his arms and forcing his proficient kiss on her mouth. She struggled at first but then relented and returned his kiss for a moment before he released her.

Maggie smiled when she saw the look that passed between Charlotte and her middle son. *Yes*, she thought. They'd all be married soon.

Happiness for Charlotte caused Malaina's heart to swell to near bursting. For she too had seen the undeniable expression of love at first sight that passed between Baker and her beloved sister.

Jackson pulled Malaina to her feet after he'd stood himself. Everyone was going into the house. Mary was chattering to Matthew about tending to his wound, Baker was looking dreamily down at the blushing Miss Charlotte, and Maggie was babbling about her new daughter.

"I've loved you from the very first moment, Malaina. I tried and tried to talk myself out of it," Jackson said, pulling her to him.

"Why?" she asked, nuzzling her forehead into his neck.

"I'm a sweaty ol' cowboy who's always beat up and couldn't talk good grammar if my life depended on it. And look at you… all beautiful and soft like a peach in summer. What do you want me for?"

She looked up at him, and he played with a strand of her hair in his mouth.

"You smell like heaven," she said, smiling. "You're every girl's dream—handsome, strong, intelligent, a survivor, a protector—and I'm sure you're every bit the lover that you make yourself out to be."

"That I am, my darlin'. That I am." And he kissed her again to prove it.

TO ECHO THE PAST

To Tina,
For hiking the hills and conquering the valleys…
Together, my friend!
Always!

CHAPTER ONE

Brynn Clarkston gazed despondently through the parlor window and out into the dusty, abandoned street. Even though it was a warm, bright summer day, her spirits were cool and blue. She abhorred the small town where her family had recently moved. She was a stranger to everyone, and they were strangers to her. There were so few young people her age, and she missed the grand set of friends she had enjoyed in the east. There were no grand shops, no scented bakeries, no park with a band playing in the gazebo. No automobiles, no opera, no medicine stores with soda counters. She sighed heavily, reflecting on her memories of the colorful, musical city that her family had left behind them. Yet she had no choice but to accept this brown, lifeless town that she lived in now. She must call it home.

Her father, Richard Clarkston, was an educator. And a good one at that. He had relinquished his position as a professor at the university and accepted a teaching post at the local school in the isolated western town. He explained to his wife and children he harbored a craving for adventure, and he felt the West would provide it. Therefore, what choice was left to Brynn, his eldest daughter? None.

And so, Brynn hadn't complained when the family arrived to find the township and its people a little primitive compared with others she had always known. These people all bore a sort of drawling manner about their speech, and very few of the women were properly corseted.

Heathens, her Aunt Rebecca had called them.

Brynn knew the people in town and the farmers and ranchers that lived on its outskirts were honest, hard-working folks for the most part. But as she watched Mr. Beevis Bellmont walk past and flash his rotting-toothed smile at her, she wondered this day if any of the honest, hard-working folk were in the least attractive.

Sighing heavily once more, Brynn deserted her post at the window and went to the mirror standing in one corner of the room. Yet another heavy sigh escaped her lungs as she studied her own reflection. She was a tall girl with a slender yet pleasing figure, humbly boasting the perfect curvature placement for an ideal feminine form. Her hair was dark, long, and brilliantly soft, accentuated by red and highlights, while her eyes were of a blue that was equaled only by the pure hue of the heavens.

However, Brynn, being blessed with an overabundance of modesty and a pleasing lack of vanity, saw none of these greatly sought-after attributes as she gazed at her reflection on that warm summer day.

"Darling…" Brynn's mother chimed as she entered the room, immediately noticing the dissatisfied expression on her daughter's face.

Ophelia Clarkston was a woman above all others. She was the matured version of her daughter in every physical aspect, at the same time possessing the knowledge akin to a woman of experienced years and wisdom.

"You're looking uncommonly lovely today," she said.

Brynn sighed, knowing her mother was trying to dispel her negative thoughts. "Thank you, Mother," she said. "But you'd say that if I were Medusa herself."

Brynn looked at her mother, wondering how such a beautiful woman as she could be ever so blissfully happy with her lot. After all, hadn't her mother been one of the most beloved divas of her time? So many admirers were heartbroken when she retired from the opera in order to wed the man she loved, Brynn's father.

As Brynn studied her mother's flawless complexion and brilliant blue eyes, she wondered how it would feel to possess such beauty.

"True," her mother admitted. "But you're not. Venus, more likely."

"Mother, I detest this dreary, dry town," Brynn sighed, going once more to the window.

"You only need to adjust, darling. Make some friends! You never go out." Ophelia smiled understandingly. "This very minute…why don't you go out for a stroll? Wander down to Mrs. Johnson's store, and pick out some cloth for that new dress I promised you."

Brynn smiled, relenting. "Very well. Perhaps the fresh air will do me good."

Fifteen minutes later, Brynn crossed the threshold of the general store.

"Good morning, Mrs. Johnson," she greeted the jolly elderly woman deposited in a worn chair behind the counter.

"Good mornin', Brynn. Yer lookin' particularly purty this morning," Mrs. Johnson complimented.

Brynn wondered at the elderly woman. She had heard talk of Mrs. Johnson's being well into her seventies. Yet she was quite alert, friendly, and able-bodied.

"Thank you, but I'm afraid I'm feeling far from pretty today." Brynn smiled when the woman shook her head in disagreement. "Mother has sent me in to choose cloth for a new dress. Do you mind if I have a look?"

"Not at all, peach. Go right ahead. Let me know when you find somethin', and I'll put it back for you until your mama comes in."

"Thank you," Brynn said, smiling kindly. She liked the old woman. Her eyes constantly sparkled as if she harbored some secret knowledge that amused her.

Halfheartedly Brynn began browsing through the bolts of cloth that stood nearby. At last she decided on a pretty cream-colored calico with tiny blue flowers.

Picking up the heavy bolt of cloth, she returned to the counter.

Holding the bolt of cloth near to her face, she asked, "Well? What do you think, Mrs. Johnson? Is this the one for me?"

As she raised her eyes to look for the woman, she was stunned to utter heart palpitations when she saw standing just inside the store the most inconceivably handsome man! So startled was she that her grip on the bolt of cloth faltered, and the heavy thing dropped to the floor, violently landing mostly on Brynn's right foot.

"Ow!" she exclaimed. She was horrified as the vision of pure masculinity then stepped forward and retrieved the toppled bolt, setting it on the counter.

"That there musta hurt, miss," he said as he squatted before her and brazenly took her injured foot in one hand. "Do ya think it's broke?" he asked.

Brynn could only shake her head in silent response as the blue of his eyes captured the blue of hers.

"Glad to hear that," he said, straightening, towering over Brynn, and extending his right hand in greeting.

Brynn took his hand, and he shook it firmly. "I don't believe I've met you before…Miss…Miss…"

"Brynn Clarkston," she managed to sputter at last.

"Miss Clarkston," the young man repeated, flashing a dazzlingly white set of teeth as he smiled. "I'm Michael. Michael McCall. My family's been ranchin' 'round here since right after the war 'tween the states. I don't get into town often…but maybe I oughta make a point of it."

Brynn blushed as he winked at her. "We just moved here from back east," she explained.

"Well now…that's right refreshin'," he chuckled. "My mama will be dern near to splittin' a gut with excitement when she finds out there's new folk in town. Both a my aunties will too, I reckon."

"You…you have a lot of family around here?" Brynn asked, desperate to keep the conversation going with such a profoundly attractive young man. He seemed quite nice and friendly too.

"Shoot, yeah!" he confirmed exuberantly. "This place is crawlin' with McCalls."

Brynn smiled joyously. It seemed there were actual civilized human beings nearby. Attractive ones. "How encouraging," she said.

"Hey, Mrs. Johnson," he addressed the elderly woman. "Why didn't you tell me there was a new—and right purty—young lady in town?"

The old woman chuckled. "I figured you'd find out for yerself soon enough, boy," she answered. "You sniff 'em out quicker than anybody."

Michael looked back to Brynn and smiled, still talking to Mrs. Johnson. "I come in for some liniment and witch hazel," he said.

Brynn found it difficult to look at him directly. His eyes were too probing, as if they could see her innermost thoughts.

"Been breakin' them horses again, have ya?" Mrs. Johnson asked.

Brynn cast her eyes to the floor, and Michael McCall bent his head as well until she was forced to meet his gaze again once more. He smiled at her and nodded, still talking to Mrs. Johnson.

"Heck, yes! Them boys need to be broke if'n we're gonna get 'em sold. It makes Mama so awful nervous to have Daddy doin' it, you know."

At last the handsome cowhand looked to the elderly woman. "S'pose ya better throw in a new shirt too, Mrs. Johnson. I done ripped this one near to shreds, and Mama will have a fit when she sees it."

Brynn hadn't noticed before, for she had been so entranced by the pure attractiveness of the man. But now she looked to see his shirt untucked from his Levi's and hanging open, exposing the browned, muscular torso beneath. There were several tears in the garment, and one shoulder was blood-stained, obviously from a wound that lay beneath.

Gasping at the unexpected sight of a man's bare chest, Brynn reflexively closed her eyes to shade them from it. She opened them again, however, when she heard the amused chuckling of Mrs. Johnson and the young man.

"Ain't used to blood, huh?" Michael McCall asked her. "Don't worry, Miss Brynn. It's just a little ol' scratch." Reaching up, he pushed the shirt from his shoulder, revealing a painful-looking laceration. "Though I don't normally admit to it…I got bucked off this mornin' and hit the fence. It don't hurt much now."

Brynn looked away shyly. The blood was far from making her uncomfortable. It was the sight of a half-nude man that did so.

"Let me get those things together for you now, Michael," Mrs. Johnson said, standing and going into a room that adjoined the store.

Brynn took a deep breath as she looked up to find the man again smiling at her.

"So what brings your family out here?" he asked.

Brynn swallowed with difficulty and answered, "My…my father has accepted a teaching position here."

"He's a teacher?" he asked.

"He was a professor at the university, but he wanted to move west. So here we are," she explained. She was aware that her hands were nervously wringing her skirt, but she was unable to will them to cease.

"How many Clarkstons are there?" he asked, smiling and taking a toothpick from a small dish on the counter. He opened his mouth slightly, setting the pick on his tongue. Then he closed his mouth again, the toothpick protruding from one side of his mesmerizing grin.

Brynn cleared her throat and cast her eyes down briefly before answering. His smile was all too intriguing! "Five," she answered. "My father, my mother, myself, my sister, Sierra, and my brother, Scottie."

"You're the oldest child?" he asked.

She looked up to him then. "Yes, sir."

He chuckled. "Darlin', I can't be more'n two years older than you now, can I? You call me Michael."

Brynn smiled. "Very well."

He chuckled again. "My mama will like you. It's been some time since she had a conversation with someone so proper. She's darn near nagged herself blue tryin' to get us childr'n to talk right."

Brynn smiled and was again mesmerized by the toothpick as she watched it slide to the middle of his lips and begin flickering up and down rapidly.

Michael chuckled and took the pick from his mouth. "Nasty habit, I know. But Mrs. Johnson keeps these out here just for us. It's a sight nicer than tobacca, don't ya think? 'Sides…tobacca turns yer teeth all yeller and black. Ain't a girl on this earth that wouldn't rather a man had white teeth than yeller. Especially come time for sparkin'. Don't you agree?" he asked.

Brynn cleared her throat again nervously and muttered, "Yes. I suppose that's true."

"Here you go, boy," Mrs. Johnson called as she returned. "Witch hazel for all them bruises yer bound to have collected on your seat. Liniment and a nice white shirt. Don't go tearin' this one up tomorrow, you hear me?" she said, smiling.

"No, ma'am, I won't," Michael said, taking the items from her. "In fact, why don't we save Mama the trouble of havin' a fit today, Mrs. Johnson?" And before Brynn could attempt to shade her eyes or turn away, Michael McCall stripped off the tattered shirt and threw it into a basket meant for garbage that stood nearby.

Heathens! Aunt Rebecca's voice echoed in Brynn's mind as she stared at the shirtless man before her.

The thought quickly passed through her mind that maybe heathens weren't so bad. Provided they all looked like Michael McCall and not Beevis Bellmont.

"I better get back," Brynn choked out anxiously. This man was truly unsettling. Retreat was the only alternative. "My mother will be in to pick this up as soon as she can, Mrs. Johnson," she assured the woman.

"Now, don't rush off on account of me, Miss Brynn. You and Mrs. Johnson go on about yer girl talk. Thank you, Mrs. Johnson," he said. "Our little secret?" he added with a wink.

"Yes, boy," Mrs. Johnson chuckled. "Now get."

"And what a pleasure to meet *you*, Miss Brynn," he said, smiling. "I'm sure we'll bump into each other now and then." Then he turned and left the store.

Mrs. Johnson dropped her voice to a whisper when he'd gone. "He's a fine young man, isn't he? Handsome too. He's his daddy over and over except for them blue eyes. He gets them from his mama. Young Michael McCall's a might more pleasin' to look at than a mud fence, ain't he?"

Brynn was unable to deny that he was truly a dream, so she nodded, blushing.

"I knew his grandma, Maggie McCall, real well. Real well. She died a few years back, but his mama and daddy, Jackson and Malaina McCall, live on the main farm. He has two uncles with families that live on their own properties. There's Baker and Charlotte McCall—they've got six kids. Matthew and Mary McCall, and they have five. Michael's got a brother and two sisters. I bet young Annie is about yer age. She's sixteen, I think. You can't dodge the McCall clan 'round here no matter how hard you try."

Brynn nodded and whispered, "He's very polite. Charming, actually."

Mrs. Johnson smiled. "He took right to you, didn't he?"

Brynn shook her head and sighed discouragedly. "I'm not the kind of girl he'd look twice at, Mrs. Johnson," she whispered.

"Well, sugar," the woman chuckled in a whisper. "He looked more'n twice just while you were standin' here a showin' me this cloth."

Brynn smiled. "Well…I better get back! Now, you'll save this cloth until Mother can come in, won't you, Mrs. Johnson?"

"Of course, Brynn. Of course."

The day seemed to have brightened considerably since Brynn first left the house. As she walked home from Mrs. Johnson's store along the dusty street, she didn't even mind the dry smell of soil as it filled her lungs. Something was beginning to whisper to her that perhaps living in the small western community wouldn't be so terrible. Hadn't he said that the place was simply "crawlin' with McCalls"? That in itself gave her hope. Of course, she didn't really care about any other McCalls. One, the one she had met, was more than enough.

"Mother!" Brynn called as she entered the house through the kitchen door. "Mother! I've something to tell you."

"In here, darling. Come quickly. We have our first visitors," Ophelia called from the parlor.

Brynn walked quickly to greet her mother but stopped abruptly when she saw her mother sat in the company of three women. One woman was undoubtedly a very unique beauty. The dark-haired, blue-eyed woman rivaled her own mother's loveliness. There was also a lovely blonde woman, and next to her sat another dark-haired woman who resembled somewhat the first one.

"This is my eldest daughter, Brynn," Ophelia said, motioning for Brynn to greet the women.

"Hello. How do you do?" Brynn greeted, forcing a smile.

The three women nodded and returned sincere hellos.

"Brynn, these lovely ladies have come to welcome us to town. This is Charlotte McCall."

The second dark-haired woman extended a tiny, gloved hand to Brynn. Brynn took her hand for a moment, smiling.

"And this is her sister-in-law Mary McCall," Ophelia said as she indicated the blonde woman.

"Hello," Brynn said, taking the second woman's hand.

"And this is Malaina McCall. She's Mary's sister-in-law and Charlotte's sister and sister-in-law! Oh, it's all so confusing, ladies! However do you keep track of everyone?" Ophelia chimed.

"Hello, Brynn," Malaina McCall greeted, taking Brynn's hand.

Brynn could only smile, for the realization was washing over her that this was the mother of the handsome vision she had only just met. As she looked into the woman's beautiful blue eyes, she recognized their similarity to her son's.

"You're lovely, my dear," Malaina commented. Then, looking from Brynn to her mother and back, her smile widened, and she added, "The image of your mother."

"Actually, she looks a great deal like her father," Ophelia added.

"I'm so very pleased to meet you, Mrs. McCall," Brynn breathed, awestruck by the woman before her and what she represented. "I've only just come from Mrs. Johnson's store, where I met your son, I believe."

"Which one, dear?" Malaina asked.

"Michael," Brynn answered.

Malaina giggled, and Brynn found it delightfully intriguing that such a graceful woman would have such girlish laughter.

"Oh, yes! My Michael. He's been into the general store, has he?" she asked. "Was he appropriately dressed or not, my dear?"

Brynn thought it an odd question. "Well, he…he…"

Charlotte spoke then. "He bought a new shirt, I've no doubt."

"Why, yes," Brynn exclaimed, astonished.

"And some liniment to boot, I reckon," Mary added.

"Yes. Yes, he did," Brynn confirmed.

Malaina turned once more to Ophelia. "Let me explain, Ophelia. My charming son takes after his father. They break horses as part of their labors, and I've no doubt that Michael has soiled, if not utterly destroyed, yet another shirt in the process. He thinks I'm innocent to the fact that he spends part of his earnings almost weekly on new shirts, attempting to hide the fact that he's been roughed up by some wild stallion that he's determined to break."

"Michael's very handsome, isn't he?" Mary inquired of Brynn unexpectedly.

"Well…well…" Brynn stammered.

"Of course he's handsome," Malaina answered for her. "He takes after his daddy." Malaina smiled beautifully then. "I've a daughter just about your age, I think. Annie. She's sixteen."

"I'm seventeen, yes," Brynn confirmed.

"Oh, wonderful! The two of you will get along beautifully. She looks like me. Fortunately, she lacks some of my most unbecoming flaws. And Mary and Charlotte both have sons and daughters that are near your age."

"How many children do you have, Malaina?" Ophelia asked.

"Four. Only four. But they're wonderful. Michael is the eldest; he's twenty-two. Then Robert, he's twenty. The girls are next. Margaret is nineteen and Annie sixteen," she answered.

"How delightful!" Ophelia sighed.

"Baker and I have six children," Charlotte said. "We've three sets of twins in the litter. Two boys, twins that are twenty-two. Two girls, twins that are nineteen. And a boy and a girl, twins that are fifteen."

"My goodness, Charlotte!" Ophelia exclaimed in amazement. "Do you lean toward triplets, Mary?"

"No. Ours are singles. Our eldest is twenty-two as well. He has the same birthday as Charlotte's boys. Then we have a daughter twenty-one, a daughter twenty, a daughter nineteen, and a son fourteen," Mary explained.

Ophelia released a sigh of astonishment. "I'm surprised that the town hasn't been named McCall with all of you living here."

"Do you have other siblings, Brynn?" Mary asked.

"A younger sister, Sierra, and a younger brother, Scottie," she answered. "Both terribly bothersome."

As the three ladies giggled, Ophelia smiled too, scolding, "Now, Brynn. Be kind."

"How charming," Malaina said. "But we shouldn't keep you any longer, Ophelia. That dashing schoolteacher husband of yours will be livid if he finds a group of giggling old crones in his parlor when he returns."

"Dashing? Father?" Brynn questioned, for she saw him as her tender, caring protector. Her beloved parent.

"Yes, of course dashing, my dear," Charlotte agreed. "You've got his eyes too. Yes, I do see the resemblance you referred to, Ophelia."

"We met your father this mornin', Brynn. He insisted that we not waste another moment in coming to meet your dear mother. And I'm glad we didn't," Mary explained. "Oh, Ophelia, we're so glad to have you and your family here! It will be so wonderful to have a friend in town."

"Yes," Malaina agreed. "Now, Matthew and Mary are having a barn raising the end of this month. We'll let you know exactly when."

Mary and Charlotte nodded their heads enthusiastically.

Malaina continued, "You simply have to come and meet everyone!" Then, turning to Brynn, "Annie will be thrilled to meet you! And if I know my Michael, he'll be looking forward to your family attending as well."

"I don't think I've ever seen a more beautiful woman, Mother," Brynn said that evening as the family sat down to dinner.

"Malaina McCall? Yes, she's a rare beauty. I tell you, Richard, I would've thought her not a day over twenty-five had she not told me her age," Ophelia responded.

"Quite a story there too, I understand," Richard Clarkston said as he took a bite of mashed potatoes.

"What? You mean the way she met her husband?" Ophelia asked.

"Yes. Extraordinary story," he answered, taking another bite.

"What story?" Sierra, Brynn's ten-year-old sister, asked.

"Well," her father began, swallowing his third bite of potatoes. "It seems that Jackson McCall—that's her husband—simply found her in the wilderness one day. She was weakened from exposure and had no memory." The family waited impatiently as he helped himself to a large bite of bread and butter. "To condense the tale, Mrs. McCall, Malaina, was a native New Orleanian, and some horrid villain was stalking her. It all met in the middle one day, it seems. Jackson and his two brothers—all three honored graduates of West Point, I might add—dueled to the so-called death. Triumphant, Jackson McCall married his beloved Malaina. Seems there was something or other about a renegade band of Indians as well."

"Indians? Really, Daddy? Indians!" seven-year-old Scottie squealed excitedly.

"Indians?" Ophelia asked, obviously unsettled at the thought.

"Yes, Ophelia, Scottie. Indians. It seems some violent leader-type took Malaina hostage at some point. Her gallant hero helped the beast to expire and saved the fair maiden. I think she even had to extract a poisonous arrow from his shoulder."

Brynn smiled, completely enchanted by her father's telling of the tale. He had such a way with the retelling of stories. "You're making it up, Daddy," Brynn giggled. "Renegade Indians? Poisoned arrows?

What did she do, Daddy? Cut him open and drain out the poison?" Brynn smiled. Richard Clarkston could really invent a tale.

"No. No. I believe she extracted the arrow and then proceeded to suck the poison from the wound. Yes, yes. That's it. No, wait…yes, Mr. McCall pulled the arrow from his own shoulder and used it to impale the renegade. Yes, that's how it went."

"Oh, Daddy. How nauseating! And at dinner!" Sierra whined.

"It's the truth. Young Grant McCall, their nephew, related the story to me only yesterday. Truly."

"He's embellishing, Daddy. Surely!" Brynn said.

"No. I think not. In fact, they tell me that the villain from New Orleans that was stalking Mrs. McCall is buried in the cemetery just outside of town. You've seen it, Brynn. The one we passed on our excursion last Saturday."

"Well, what was his name then? This man who tried to abduct her. We can all go just after dinner and look him up, can't we?" Ophelia suggested. "It's a beautiful evening, and it will be light enough yet."

Richard Clarkston chewed a piece of meat thoroughly before responding. "Yes. That would be nice, dear. As for the man's name… Collin something. Collin Mereaux. That's it. We'll all go then, just after dinner."

Brynn began to wonder then if her father's story did indeed have a basis. But to imagine the beautiful Malaina McCall sucking poison from someone's shoulder? Impossible.

"Well, I'll be," Ophelia exclaimed as she stood before the tombstone. "Look here, Brynn. 'Collin Mereaux.' That's all it says."

Brynn gazed at the slab of granite that lay on the ground. Indeed, the name was there. But only a name and a date. No epitaph.

"Why should it say more, dear? He was a villain, as the story goes," Richard reminded them all.

"Do you think it's true, Daddy?" Sierra asked. "Do you think someone really tried to kidnap Mrs. McCall? Do you think Mr. McCall really fought bravely for her, winning her in the end? Oh, how romantic," she sighed.

"I bet it was bloody," Scottie interjected. "Nice and bloody."

"Scottie! How gruesome!" Ophelia scolded.

"He's a man above men, they say," Richard stated.

"Who, dear?" Ophelia inquired.

"Why, Jackson McCall, dear. They say he can break any horse alive."

"I think you spend entirely too much time listening to gossip, Richard darling."

"They say he's a handsome brute too," Richard added, winking affectionately at his wife.

"Not as handsome as my brute," Ophelia whispered to him.

Brynn smiled contentedly as she watched her father place a loving kiss on her mother's forehead and hug her securely in his arms. They were deeply in love, even after so many years. It was evident every day of their lives.

Brynn looked again to the tombstone. It seemed there was some truth to the story that had been related to her father. She thought to herself how horrid it all must have been. How "bloody," as Scottie had put it. She was suddenly very curious to actually set her own eyes on this Jackson McCall, the legendary man who rescued and wed the beautiful Malaina. The handsome man that was the father of Michael McCall.

As if in answer to her thoughts, there came a low greeting from behind her.

"Hello, there. You must be the Clarkston family."

Brynn turned with the other members of her family to see Malaina and Jackson McCall standing before them. She drew in her breath, astonished at the uncanny resemblance this man bore to his son. His temples were graying, and his eyes were green, but this was Michael McCall's very image.

"Oh, good evening," her father greeted, extending a hand toward the other man. "Yes. I'm Richard Clarkston. We've met your lovely wife, and am I correct in assuming that you are Mr. Jackson McCall?"

"That's me," the handsome man confirmed. "We rode out tonight to freshen the flowers on my mama's grave. She's right over here. I see you're givin' ol' Collin the twice-over."

Brynn blushed, humiliated at being caught hovering over the villain's grave.

"Yes," her father confirmed again. "Young Grant was relating the fascinating story to me yesterday. I retold it tonight at dinner, only to find four sets of very skeptical eyes sharing my meal."

"It's all true," Malaina said, going to stand next to Brynn and gazing down at the tombstone. "Horribly true."

"Even the Indians and the arrow part?" Sierra asked, her blue eyes widening to the size of china plates.

"Yes, sweet thing. Even the arrow part," Malaina answered, smiling sweetly at the child.

"Dang right! Especially the arrow part, sugar," Jackson McCall added. Then he quickly unbuttoned his shirt and pulled it aside to reveal a large, blackish scar on one shoulder.

"Jackson McCall!" Malaina scolded. "Button that shirt! You're as bad as the boys!"

"Naw! They wanted to see it, didn't you, kids?" he asked directly to Scottie.

"Yeah!" Scottie whispered, moving closer. "It's so ugly!"

"Scottie!" Ophelia reprimanded.

"It is, ain't it, boy?" Jackson agreed. "But don't you think my Malaina was worth it?"

Brynn giggled as Scottie glanced briefly at Malaina and shrugged his shoulders. Jackson chuckled and tousled the boy's fair hair. "It's good to have new folks in town. And you," he said, turning his attention to Brynn.

Immediately her hands went to her skirt and began viciously wringing the garment. "Yes, sir?" she responded.

"Michael told me he met a member of your family today. Judgin' from his description, I'd say it was you."

"Yes, sir," she confirmed.

Jackson McCall grinned knowingly and chuckled, "Had his shirt off, didn't he?"

15

Brynn blushed slightly but was relieved of responding when Malaina took hold of her husband's arm tightly and said, "That's enough, Jackson." Smiling, she looked to Ophelia. "It was so nice to bump into you out here. We simply must get together for a chat. I mean that, Ophelia."

"We will, Malaina. We will," Ophelia assured her. "We'll be off and leave you to your visit," she said.

Jackson and Richard shook hands again. Then Jackson turned his attention to Brynn once more. "Now, next time you meet up with Michael, don't feel like ya gotta go on blushin' so. Though I did have the same effect on his mama—and still do, for that matter—whenever I take off my—"

His words were silenced by his wife's lovely hand as it clamped tightly over his mouth.

"Forgive him, Brynn dear. 'The apple doesn't fall far from the tree,' they say," Malaina whispered, winking.

"Charming couple," Brynn's father commented on the walk home. "Charming."

"Yes," her mother agreed. "There's something very unique about them. They're deeply in love."

"It's a blessing, dearest. A blessing that unfortunately many aren't endowed with." Then, taking his wife's hand in his own, Richard added, "Thankfully, we are."

"I think he's the handsomest man I've ever seen in my entire life," Sierra sighed.

"You're only ten, Sierra," Scottie reminded his sister.

"So? Did you see the way he caressed her cheek with the back of his hand? He's a truly romantic man."

Scottie made a rude noise, indicating that his sister's remark had upset his stomach.

"Scottie! That's enough," Ophelia scolded. "You're terribly quiet, Brynn. Whatever is your mind conjuring now?"

"Oh, nothing. I was just thinking what a nice family they seem to be," Brynn responded. She didn't add, however, that she had also been thinking about the ruggedly handsome face that had first appeared before her in the general store earlier that afternoon.

CHAPTER TWO

Brynn began to long to behold Michael McCall's face again. As one week turned into two, Brynn still hadn't seen him since the day in Mrs. Johnson's store. Furthermore, the weather had turned gray, gloomy, and endlessly wet.

It seemed the rain would go on for hours at a time. Then, as if to tease and titillate the townsfolk, it would stop. The clouds would disperse, the sun would shine brightly, and everyone, it seemed, would dash out into the brightness of the day. However, moments later clouds would quickly gather, drowning out the sun's rays, and the monotonous sound of falling water droplets would recommence.

It was on a day such that the weather succeeded in tricking Brynn into venturing out. She'd decided if her moods were dampened by the weather, then indeed those of Mrs. Johnson must be as well. Brynn pitied the elderly woman, who had no one. Apparently, her only child, a daughter, had died tragically years and years before. Her husband had passed on, leaving her lonely and without any family.

The Clarkston children, all three of them, tried to fill some of her lonely void by visiting with her as often as possible. Brynn found the woman possessed a wealth of historical knowledge about the town and its inhabitants past and present. She enjoyed their visits and, of course, secretly hoped each time she entered the store it would be to find Michael McCall calling on the old woman for liniment.

Half the distance between her home and the store on this day, the rain began to fall with tremendous force. It took only moments before Brynn was drenched, her teeth chattering from the cold of being wet.

As she dashed into the store, Mrs. Johnson fairly leaped from her chair behind the counter and went to the girl.

"Brynn! Dear child. What, for pity's sake, would drag you out into this weather? You're soaked to the skin," the woman exclaimed.

"I wanted to visit with you, and it looked like I would have plenty of time to get here when I started out," Brynn explained.

"You'll catch your death, sugar," Mrs. Johnson mumbled as she began drying Brynn's face with her apron. "Run back to the other room now. I've got a fire goin', and I'll bring you some warm cocoa in a jiffy. Just let me finish helping ol' Beevis pick out a shovel," she instructed.

Brynn nodded and smiled. She liked the store's back room. It was always warm if the weather was chilly and cool if the weather was hot. It was the coziest place on earth to Brynn. Pictures hung here and there on the walls, ferns from the ceiling. The furniture was worn and comfortable, and it was simply a pleasant place.

Upon entering the room this day, however, Brynn was startled to see someone else there. Sitting in a large chair before the fire, his bare feet propped lazily on a hassock, sat Michael McCall.

"Miss Brynn!" he exclaimed upon seeing her. "Fancy meetin' you here! And on a day like this. Got caught in the rain too, I see."

Brynn was flustered, for she realized what her appearance must be. Most likely akin to that of a cat only just escaping from a near-drowning in a bathtub.

"Yes. Caught in the rain," she mumbled.

"Well, here now," he said, removing himself from the chair and standing. "Sit yerself down and warm up. You'll catch yer death."

Brynn's eyes were fixed to the man's face, for when he stood, she was immediately aware of the fact that he was again shirtless. She shook her head quickly, forcing her gaze to his anatomy above his neck.

"No, no, no," she stammered. "I'm fine. Really."

"Nonsense, darlin'. Yer soaked to the bone. Now take my seat.

I'm warmin' up now," he insisted, stepping forward, taking her hand, and guiding her to the chair.

Brynn sat down stiffly and began staring nervously into the fire. Her intention was to keep her eyes off the bare and, yes, magnificent physique that stood in the room. But as if to intentionally thwart her determination, Michael sat down abruptly on the hassock, which, of course, was placed directly in front of the chair.

"I heard you met my mama and daddy," he said.

She looked up into his grinning face, which wore an expression of utter mischief.

"My mama's a real beauty, ain't she?" he asked.

Brynn nodded again and smiled at the thought of the lovely woman.

"Did you like my daddy? He said he showed yer little brother his arrow scar. It's one of his nastiest. Though I'm gettin' my own here and there," he said. When Brynn could only smile in response, he continued. "Mama says yer only seventeen. Is that right?"

Brynn felt ashamed somehow of her young age, but she nodded truthfully.

"Dang. I coulda swore you was at least nineteen," he added. When Brynn could only smile again, he asked, "You cold, darlin'? You ain't gettin' a fever already, are ya?"

When Michael McCall put his hand to her forehead as a gesture of concern, Brynn thought she might melt into a puddle of warm water right there before the fire. His mere touch provoked feelings and sensations in her that Brynn had never before experienced. She wondered at that moment if she did indeed have a fever, for she was instantly warmed. At the same time, her entire being was nervous and agitated.

"Hhhmm. You feel fine," he said. "Still, I reckon we best get you cozy." And before Brynn could move out of his way, he stood up and leaned forward, reaching for an afghan that lay folded over the back of the chair. As he leaned over her, his body was only inches from her face, and she could discern the aroma of leather and bacon. She turned her face to one side for fear that the bareness of his chest might actually touch her face. The thought went through her mind that her mother would absolutely perish were she to see her daughter in such an improper circumstance.

He retrieved the cover and dropped it sloppily over her lap.

"There. Now you can talk to me," Michael said, grinning. He reached over to a small bowl that sat on a nearby table and took a toothpick from it, which he promptly placed in his mouth. He replaced himself on the hassock and rested his arms on his knees, looking at her expectantly. "Tell me somethin' about yerself," he commanded.

"For instance?" she was able to verbalize at last.

"For instance…are you likin' it out here? As compared to where ya come from, I mean?"

Brynn paused and then answered, "Yes. It's very nice."

"Yer lyin'," he chuckled, his grin spreading further across his face. "Yer lyin' like a dog, darlin'."

Brynn cast guilty eyes to the floor for a moment. Then, meeting his amused eyes, she corrected herself. "I'm adjusting," she sputtered, momentarily distracted by the toothpick flickering up and down rapidly again.

"Now why don't you like it? We got all a body needs out here. Food, water, air…McCall boys," he added, smiling.

Brynn felt an entertained smile sweep over her face.

Michael chuckled, "Now…that's what I like to see. That purty little mouth of yers curled up at the corners." Reaching out, he tweaked her cheek quickly, and Brynn was deflated at receiving a gesture meant more for a child.

"I hear yer mama was some big fancy singer back east 'fore she married yer daddy," he said, leaning back toward the fire. As the muscles in his upper body tensed to support the weight of his position, Brynn gulped uncomfortably again.

"She…she was a diva with the New York opera," she explained awkwardly. "She retired when she married my father, yes."

Michael raised his eyebrows and flaunted an expression of being impressed. "Remind me never to sit next to her in church. I'd send her screamin' down the aisle."

Brynn smiled and muttered, "I doubt that." Again she found herself mesmerized by the trick his mouth played with the toothpick.

"Impressive, ain't it?" he asked, chuckling.

Brynn smiled. "I admit, I can't do it."

"I'll teach ya sometime," he whispered, winking flirtatiously.

Brynn was instantly agitated. This man was far too attractive. She felt unsure of herself, unable to stay calm. So she rose from her chair, allowing the covering to fall from her lap and to the floor as she turned and walked to one of the pictures that hung on the opposite wall.

"Is this her daughter?" she asked upon discovering the photograph was of a lovely young woman. She immediately regretted her inquiry when she sensed that Michael had risen and was standing directly behind her.

"Yeah," he whispered. "That's Elizabeth. See this one here?" he asked, pointing to a photograph hanging next to the one Brynn had been studying. Elizabeth stood with a very handsome young man in the photo.

"Her wedding photograph?" Brynn remarked, noting the veil and bouquet the girl donned.

"Yep. That's my Uncle Baker, you know. She was his first wife, before Charlotte. Elizabeth died very young."

"How sad," Brynn whispered. Then realizing that Michael's uncle now had a wife, she felt silly. "I mean…at the time."

Turning, she saw that Michael wore an amused grin as he looked down at her. "I know what ya meant, Miss Brynn," he chuckled. Then he looked past her to the photograph once more. "I think Mrs. Johnson likes to look at me as the grandbaby she never had."

Michael's gaze fell once more to Brynn, and for a moment their eyes seemed to capture each other's in an instant of mutual wonderment. Brynn watched as his eyes narrowed slightly. The toothpick in his mouth ceased its fluttering momentarily.

"Why do I make you so nervous?" he asked in a whisper.

"I'm…I'm not nervous," Brynn lied.

She watched anxiously as his hand removed the toothpick from his mouth, and he moistened his lips with his tongue. "You're lyin' again," he chuckled. Then she was paralyzed beyond rational thought as he bent to her ear. His mouth hovered just next to it, and she could feel the warmth of his breath on her neck. She thought her heart might burst from her bosom as he whispered, "I 'spose you'd slap me smack 'cross the face if I tried to steal a kiss from you, wouldn't you, Miss Brynn?"

"Yes," she whispered in a shaky, uncertain voice.

As he leaned closer, she instinctively put her hands out to stall him, thus placing her palms flush with the bareness of his chest. Quickly she drew them away, replacing them when he continued to move closer, drawing them away, and replacing them again. The feel of his warm, smooth skin was alarming. When he at last stood straight once more, she felt as if the warmth of it had burned through her hands, traveled the length of her arms, and settled in her cheeks.

"You got a mighty cute blush, you know it?" he chuckled. "And I'm a pantywaist for teasin' ya like that and not followin' through." He put one hand under her chin and tipped her head upward so that she looked at him. Taking the toothpick that he still held in his other hand, he put it in his mouth, moistening it. Removing it from his own mouth, he pricked her lip tenderly, causing her to gasp slightly, and then placed the small sliver of wood on her tongue. Brynn's mouth reflexively closed on the pick, and Michael smiled, tweaking her cheek once more.

"I'll teach ya that trick another day, darlin'," he said. "I gotta get on home 'fore my mama thinks I'm drowned. Which I will be if Mrs. Johnson comes in here and finds me flirtin' with you like this."

Brynn began to turn away from him. She needed to escape. But he caught her arm, and when she looked up to him, his mirthful grin was gone, and he wore an expression of extreme sincerity.

"I *am* sorry, Miss Brynn Clarkston. You've just formed a weakness in me, that's all," he whispered, shaking his head as he released her arm and went to where his boots stood next to the fire.

"Oh, Michael!" Mrs. Johnson exclaimed as she entered the room. "You ain't ridin' off already, are ya, boy?"

Michael looked up to the old woman and then over to Brynn before he continued pulling on his socks. "I gotta get home 'fore I get myself in trouble, Mrs. Johnson."

"Well, boy, ya ain't hardly dried out yet."

"Yeah, well, it's too awful warm in here for me today, thank you," Michael chuckled. He quickly pulled on his boots, and as he was putting on his shirt, he said, "Thank you, Mrs. Johnson. It's always so nice to visit with ya." Then Brynn began wringing her skirt as he walked to her once more. "I believe that's mine, darlin'," he said, plucking the toothpick from her lips and placing it in his own mouth once more. "Now you ladies have a nice visit this afternoon, ya hear?"

He put on his hat, tipped it, and with one last dazzling smile left.

Mrs. Johnson giggled and lowered her voice to a whisper as she asked, "Did I leave the two a you alone in here long enough, honey?"

Brynn cleared her throat and pulled at the collar of her blouse. "Too long, Mrs. Johnson."

Mrs. Johnson chuckled knowingly. "He gets under yer skin, don't he, Brynn?" When Brynn only blushed, Mrs. Johnson continued, "He's like a flea that needs scratchin', that one. And he's taken a fancy to you. I can tell."

"He's a grown man, Mrs. Johnson. I'm only seventeen. I'm sure he views me as no more than a schoolgirl still in bloomers," Brynn stated.

Mrs. Johnson smiled to herself. "Well, you come on over here and have a cup of cocoa with me, sugar. We'll have us a nice little visit."

Mrs. Johnson talked almost endlessly, but Brynn registered little of her babble, for her mind was simply spinning, reviewing over and over the moments she had shared with Michael McCall in the back room. She could think of nothing but the feel of his breath on her neck, the scent of his body, the taste of the toothpick he'd placed in her mouth.

Some hours later, Mrs. Johnson yawned and said, "I'm tuckered in, Brynn. And you need to be gettin' on home. You tell your mama hello for me, won't you, honey?"

"Yes, yes, of course, Mrs. Johnson," Brynn stammered, rising to leave.

They heard someone calling from the outer room then. Mrs. Johnson toddled into the store, followed closely by Brynn.

"Oh, good gravy," Brynn heard Mrs. Johnson mutter gloomily as they entered together. "Help us all, it's Annabelle Barrington."

Brynn looked to see a noticeable young woman standing at the counter.

"Oh, there you are, dear Mrs. Johnson! Why, you haven't aged a day since I left last fall," the young woman nearly sang.

"What brings you home, Annabelle?" Mrs. Johnson asked plainly. It was obvious to Brynn that Mrs. Johnson was not excited about this particular customer.

Annabelle laughed all too femininely. "Why, Mrs. Johnson! I've completed finishing school! Have you forgotten? I only had one year left."

"Went awful fast, didn't it?" Mrs. Johnson mumbled.

Annabelle began looking about the store curiously. "I heard Michael McCall was in here today. Is he still about somewhere?"

Immediately Brynn felt her own teeth clench tightly and every muscle in her body tense.

"No. No. He's gone on home. He got caught in a downpour and dried out in the back room with Brynn here," Mrs. Johnson answered. "Oh. I guess you haven't met Brynn yet, have you, Annabelle?"

Brynn didn't miss the mischievous twinkle in the elderly woman's eyes as she reached back, taking hold of Brynn's arm and pulling her forward.

"This is Brynn Clarkston. Her family's purty new in town. And Brynn, this is Annabelle. Annabelle Barrington."

"No doubt you've heard of me, Brynn. So nice to meet you," Annabelle said, feigning sincerity.

"Hello," Brynn managed through still-clenched teeth.

"Well, if he's not about…" Annabelle said, looking around once more as if expecting to find Michael despite what Mrs. Johnson had said. "I guess I'll just float on home now. It was so nice to see you again, Mrs. Johnson. And to meet you, um…um…"

"Brynn," Brynn stated.

"Oh, yes. Brynn. Odd name, isn't it?" And she turned and floated from the room ever so gracefully.

"That one there," Mrs. Johnson began. "That one there is a true and utter pill! Can't stand the girl myself. I was all too relieved when she went away last fall. And she just moons over Michael McCall somethin' awful! It's embarrassin', if you ask me. He don't pay her no mind though."

"I better get home," Brynn whispered, feeling suddenly depressed.

❦

The rain clouds seemed grayer and the air seemed damper as Brynn walked toward home. Not that she had expected Michael McCall to really harbor any interest in her. After all, he was a grown man of twenty-two. She was only seventeen. And Annabelle Barrington did look the part of the ideal woman. Still, she knew it would be difficult, nearly heartbreaking, to have to watch Michael with anyone else. But hadn't he threatened to steal a kiss? Of course, boys—men—were like that. Always teasing. Always breaking young female hearts.

Straightening her posture, she drew in a deep breath and said out loud, "I don't care! He's a rogue, that one. There's not a serious bone in that man's body." The thought went through her mind once more of what a perfectly formed body it was.

As she entered the house through the back kitchen door, it was to hear her brother and sister squabbling as usual.

"Mother, Scottie pulled my hair!" Sierra whined.

"Hair? That ain't hair, Mother! It looks like an old rag mop dyed in tar," Scottie sneered.

"*Isn't* hair, Scottie. Isn't hair. And you know that your sister has lovely raven hair. Quit irritating her," Ophelia scolded firmly yet calmly. "Hello, Brynn dear. Dinner is nearly finished. Could you mash the potatoes?"

"Of course," Brynn answered, opening a drawer and removing the potato masher.

"Did you have a nice visit with Mrs. Johnson?"

"Yes. I got soaked going over though."

"I hope you dried off sufficiently before starting home. I don't want you catching cold. That reminds me," Ophelia began. "Mary McCall dropped in on me this afternoon and invited our family to something called a 'barn raising' out at their farm the end of this month. Doesn't that sound interesting?"

The potato masher clattered to the floor as her mother's announcement startled Brynn.

"Careful, dear. Be sure and rinse it off," Ophelia reminded her.

"What's a barn raising?" Brynn asked, feigning indifference.

"I'm not certain. I guess we'll just have to wait and see. All I know is that I volunteered to bake two cakes. I can't believe I volunteered for cakes! You know the trouble I've been having with this oven. Brynn dear, whip them nicely when you've finished mashing."

"Your cakes are marvelous, Mother. You've nothing to worry about," Brynn giggled.

"Anyway," Ophelia continued. "I suppose we better get busy and finish that new dress of yours so you can wear it. Oh, I hear there's a young lady in town just about your age that's returned from an absence of some time. Annabelle Barrington."

Brynn sighed and began attacking the potatoes with the masher. "I've met her, Mother. She and I will not get on together, I assure you of that."

"Well, now how can you know that upon only just meeting her?"

"I know, Mother. I know. Please don't force the issue," Brynn pleaded, whipping the potatoes mercilessly.

"Very well, then," Ophelia conceded, recognizing a sensitive subject. "Your father came home at lunchtime, and it seems there's been another stage held up not more than fifty miles from here."

"That's three since we've been here," Brynn commented, feeling a bit insecure. "And they're getting closer, aren't they?"

"It would seem that way," Ophelia answered.

"Daddy says they shot the stagecoach driver clean full of holes!" Scottie expounded.

"Don't exaggerate, Scottie," Ophelia corrected. "He said the perpetrators shot him, that's all."

"I bet he was clean full of holes!" the boy exclaimed again.

"Scottie! You're so gruesome," Sierra cried out, grimacing.

"Children, let's not start that again. I tell you, I'm nearly sick to death of your squabbling today," Ophelia sighed. "Brynn dear…I'm sure those potatoes are sufficiently whipped by now. Run along to the schoolhouse and fetch your father. He's probably got his nose buried in papers and hasn't looked at his watch."

Brynn set the bowl of potatoes aside and left the house. She was relieved to find the weather was being benevolent and letting the sun shine once again.

She did indeed find her father working feverishly at his desk in the schoolhouse.

"Daddy," she spoke, startling him.

"Brynn. How nice of you to visit me. I…" Then realizing the reason for his daughter's visit, he quickly plucked his watch from his vest pocket and examined its face. "Oh, my. Your mother has sent you to bring me to dinner, hasn't she?"

Brynn smiled and nodded. Her father was so dear. Always reading some novel or another, some professor's essay, even the dictionary. She admired his diligence.

"Tell her I'll be along shortly. Just want to finish up these examinations," he said, returning his attention to his work.

"Yes, Daddy," she giggled as she turned and left the small schoolhouse. She wondered as she walked toward home what fascination her father could find in leaving a reputable university and coming to a small-town schoolhouse.

"Well, there you are, Miss Brynn," a voice called to her as she was crossing the main road through town.

Upon recognizing the voice, Brynn immediately remembered that she hadn't even run a comb through her hair since she had returned half-damp from Mrs. Johnson's. Bravely turning to face him, she answered, "Hello, Mr. McCall."

She caught her breath as she caught sight of him. Why was it that she always forgot how perfectly handsome he was until the moment he popped up again?

"Dried up purty nice out, didn't it?" he asked, coming to stand directly before her.

"Yes…yes, it did," she stammered as she began wringing the fabric of her skirt nervously.

The ever-present toothpick in his mouth flickered quickly. Brynn wondered for a moment if it were the same one he'd taken from her earlier in the general store's back room.

"I got somebody over here I want ya to meet. Can you spare a minute?" he asked, taking her hand and pulling her along without waiting for an answer.

A young woman stood not too far from where they had met in the road, and Brynn knew at once this must be Michael's sister, for the girl was the very image of his mother.

"This here's my sister Annie," he said as he stopped next to the girl.

"Hi," Annie said, smiling. "Michael says he thinks me and you will get along just fine."

Brynn was enchanted by the lovely girl. "I'm Brynn," she announced.

"He told me," Annie giggled.

There was an uncomfortable silence, and Michael finally broke it, saying, "Well, looky who we have here. If it ain't Miss Annabelle. I thought you was back east somewheres finishin' yer schoolin'."

Immediately Brynn looked away from Annie to see Annabelle Barrington approaching as gracefully as silk in the breeze.

"Michael!" the young woman sang. "There you are! I had no idea you were still in town today. And you've brought little Annie with you too. How sweet."

"Yeah, I'm helpin' Mr. Bellmont break that new colt he brung in," Michael answered, smiling.

"And, yes, we met in Mrs. Johnson's this afternoon…um…Fynn, isn't it? Odd name," Annabelle said.

"Brynn. It's Brynn," Brynn corrected her.

"My, yes. That's it. Interesting hair dressing, child. You may want to run a comb through it more often," Annabelle said, lowering her voice.

"That there's my fault," Michael interjected. "I mussed it up when I…when I…bumped into her earlier at Mrs. Johnson's."

Brynn gasped and her mouth dropped open in horror at his insinuative remark.

"Oh, I see. Forgive me, dear, will you?" Annabelle apologized. Quickly she took hold of Michael's arm and began leading him away. "You'll lend him to me for a moment, won't you, girls? It's been so long that I've been away. Michael and I must catch up."

"Um…I'll meet you back at the stables in a few minutes, Annie," Michael said. "Don't go runnin' off. Ma will have my hide if you get into any scrapes today."

Then, as Annabelle tugged at him impatiently, he took Brynn's hand in his own and shook it firmly. His touch was sensational, and Brynn was paralyzed for a moment by it. "Good evenin', Miss Brynn. Sorry about that…little incident in the general store. Next time I'll be more thorough," he said. And as he walked away, Brynn looked to find his toothpick lying in the palm of the hand he'd just shaken. The small sliver of wood was still moist at one end from being held in his mouth, and the knowledge sent a thrilling shiver through Brynn's being.

"Good riddance," Annie mumbled. "She makes my stomach churn." Brynn looked quickly to the girl, who continued to vocalize her opinions. "She's the devil in a girl's face, I tell you," Annie whispered, nodding with affirmation at Brynn. "She's been after Michael since she was walkin'. It just makes me sick." Annie looked expectantly at Brynn. When no response was offered to her remarks, she prodded, "Come on, Brynn. You know she makes you wanna shove her in the waterin' trough."

Brynn smiled. She liked Annie's honest forthrightness. "Yes. She does. She's the most obvious fake I've seen in my life."

Annie nodded. "Dang right! Don't worry though. My brother Michael is the smartest man on this green earth. He knows her ways."

Brynn smiled at Annie, and she smiled back. Annie giggled and said, "I can tell we're gonna get along right well, Brynn Clarkston."

"I believe so," Brynn agreed. "I was just on my way home for dinner. Do you want to walk with me a ways?"

"Oh, yes! Michael will be forever and a day at the stables, and I've been bored to tears since Mama went home earlier. If I had known he was going to hang around so long, I probably would've gone home with her. But then I wouldn't have gotten to meet you yet, would I?" Annie babbled quickly as the two girls began walking together.

"No. I'm glad you've been bored to tears until now anyway," Brynn said. "You look so much like your mother that I can't believe it."

Annie shook her head. "Don't I only wish! I got the color of her hair maybe, but that's it. Now, Michael, he looks just like my daddy. Don't you think he's just as handsome as anything on earth?"

"Michael or your daddy?"

"Well, both of 'em, I guess," Annie giggled. "Don't be shy about it, Brynn. You wouldn't be half-normal if you didn't think so." Brynn raised her eyebrows and nodded in agreement. "Do you like it out here? Michael says you're from some fancy city out east. Do you think it's dull and dreary in this little western town?"

"I have to admit to you, I did…at first. But Mrs. Johnson and your mother and aunts and you and…well, you give me hope," Brynn responded. "Here's my house. You must come in and meet my mother."

Annie dropped her eyes shyly, "I…I don't know. I heard she was a purty big to-do singer way back. I'd feel funny."

"She's just my mother. Now come on. She'll be offended if you don't."

Brynn opened the front door, allowing Annie to enter first.

Annie stepped into the Clarkston house and looked about nervously. "Mother? I've brought someone to meet you," Brynn called.

Ophelia appeared from the kitchen, drying her hands on her apron. "You've brought company, Brynn? How marvelous!" Ophelia stopped abruptly upon seeing the girl, and Annie fidgeted uncomfortably. "Oh, my! You are the very vision of your mother! You must be Annie!"

"Yes, ma'am," Annie answered, dropping a slight curtsy.

Ophelia rushed forward and took the girl's hands in her own. "Isn't she just the vision of Malaina McCall, Brynn?" Brynn smiled and nodded in agreement. "Now you come right on in here and sit down to dinner with us, Annie."

"Oh, no, ma'am…I couldn't possibly…impose…I…my brother will be…" Annie stammered.

"Nonsense. You must stay and meet Brynn's father!"

"Oh, but really, Mrs. Clarkston…I…"

"Come along then and talk to us while Brynn and I finish up dinner. Which, by the way, is getting cold. Did you hurry your father along, dear?" Ophelia inquired of her own daughter as she tugged at Annie, leading her into the kitchen.

"He'll be right along, I would think, Mother," Brynn answered, amused at the silence Ophelia had inspired in Annie McCall.

"Now, sit right here, and tell us all about yourself, dear," Ophelia instructed the girl, offering her a chair.

"There's not much to tell, ma'am," Annie sputtered.

"Nonsense! Tell us about life on a farm. Whatever in the world is a 'barn raising' anyway?"

Annie smiled and came to life. Her sweet babbled words spilled from her lips like an infinite waterfall. "Oh! Just the funnest thing on earth, ma'am. You see, each barn has to have a frame put up first. It really is the hardest part of buildin' a barn. So folks get together and put up the frame, and then there's food and dancin' and just plain fun for the rest of the day and night! It's wonderful! You all are going to Uncle Matthew's for his raisin', I hope."

"Oh my, yes! We wouldn't want to miss something so wonderful!" Ophelia chimed.

"Mama! Scottie is wipin' his nose on his sleeve again!" Sierra whined, bursting through the back door. "It's making me sick. Tell him to stop. He's doing it on purpose!"

"Well, all she ever wants to do play is house and get rescued by some dumb prince! I hate it, and my nose is running. What am I supposed to do, Mama?" Scottie defended himself, bursting in after his sister.

"You carry a handkerchief like a gentleman should, Scottie. Go change your shirt before dinner. I swear, you drive me to lunacy! And Sierra, try playing something Scottie might enjoy too once in a while, dear," Ophelia instructed. Then sighing, she turned to Annie and added, "You've now met Sierra and Scottie, Brynn's younger sister and brother. Please don't judge us too harshly by their behavior."

Annie giggled as Scottie stopped to stare at her for a moment before dashing off toward the back of the house.

"Good evening, cherished family," Richard announced, entering then through the back door as well. "I see we have a lovely guest. And judging from the uncanny resemblance, I would guess you would be a McCall?"

Annie nodded and said, "Yes, sir. I'm Annie McCall."

"How very pleasant to meet you, Miss McCall. I'm Richard Clarkston. I assume that you are above the age that would require you to attend school?"

"Yes, sir. I finished last year," Annie assured him.

"Ah. Then I won't have to inform the truancy officer, will I?"

Annie looked stunned, and her face paled. "No, sir."

"Only jesting, my dear. Merely jesting," Richard chuckled, kissing Ophelia affectionately on the cheek.

"The potatoes are far from hot now, dear," Ophelia scolded.

"Ah, cold, hot, or warm, it matters not to me. Potatoes are simply the staff of life. Don't you agree, Miss McCall?" Richard chuckled.

A knock on the door sent Annie leaping to her feet. "That's

Michael, and he's gonna be madder than an ol' wet hen at me for sneakin' off!"

"Nonsense, dear," Ophelia assured the girl. Going toward the door, she added, "We simply can't send the two of you home without a decent meal! Whatever would your mother think of me then?"

As Brynn watched her mother open the door, she drew in an anxious breath. Could it really be Michael McCall come to her very own house to collect his sister? As her mother exclaimed "Oh my!" upon opening the door, Brynn knew that it must, indeed, be Michael. "Oh my!" Ophelia exclaimed again as she turned and looked at Brynn curiously. "I'd guess you're Mr. Michael McCall."

"Yes, ma'am," came the answer in the deep voice all too familiar to Brynn. As he stepped into the parlor, Ophelia looked to Brynn again, raising her eyebrows, obviously impressed by what had just entered her home. "I'm…lookin' for my sister Annie. I thought maybe she mighta come on home with Miss Brynn," he explained, removing his hat immediately.

"Why, yes, she did. And I've told her that the two of you simply must stay for dinner," Ophelia told him.

"Hello, young man. I'm Richard Clarkston," Brynn's father said, stepping into the parlor and extending his hand to Michael. "We're very glad to meet you. You seem to have an exceptional family, my man."

"Thank you, sir," Michael said, taking Richard's hand and shaking it firmly. "We'll be gettin' outta your hair now, Mrs. Clarkston."

"Nonsense, Michael. You and Annie cannot possibly leave before having a bite to eat with us," Ophelia insisted, shutting the front door behind him. "Now come along, and sit down to dinner. We would love to hear more about you and your family. Brynn is simply too quiet and never lets us know a thing." Ophelia looked to her daughter knowingly as she motioned for Michael to follow her.

"You're very kind, ma'am. But Annie and I do need to be gettin' on home. We wouldn't want to impose anyhow," Michael argued.

"Now listen here, young man," Richard interceded. "You aren't wanting my dear wife to have her feelings hurt, are you?"

"Well, no, sir, but—"

"Then it's settled. You'll have dinner with us," Ophelia stated.

As Michael entered the kitchen behind Ophelia, Annie broke into nervous chatter. "I just walked home with Brynn, Michael. Honest! And Mrs. Clarkston was so insistent that I—"

"I ain't really dressed for dinner, ma'am," Michael said to Ophelia, though he glared at Annie.

Brynn smiled. The shoe was on the other foot, so to speak. It seemed that fate had placed Michael in the uncomfortable position this time. She dropped her eyes as he looked at her and smiled.

"You're dressed wonderfully, Mr. McCall," Ophelia assured him. "Now you sit right down. Richard, darling, would you call Sierra and Scottie? Why don't you sit between Annie and Michael, Brynn dear? They know you best."

Brynn's smile left her face immediately as Michael said, "That's dandy with me. How about you, Annie?" As Michael winked at her, Brynn looked quickly to her mother to see if she had detected the flirtatious gesture. She sighed with relief when she saw that her mother was busy taking the roast from the oven.

Brynn looked blankly at Michael as he pulled a chair away from the table and motioned for her to sit in it.

"For goodness sake, Brynn. Don't gawk at a gentleman when he knows his manners," Ophelia scolded.

Brynn allowed Michael to seat her at the table. Michael repeated the same service for Annie and then sat on Brynn's right.

"You must be Michael!" Scottie exclaimed, entering the room and staring blatantly at the male guest.

"Yes, sir. That's me," Michael chuckled, offering a hand to the young boy.

Scottie shook Michael's hand. It was obvious to Brynn that her little brother was intent upon impressing Michael.

"I heard you and your daddy get all manner of injuries breaking horses. I heard between the two of you, you've lost enough blood to fill a lake!" Scottie exclaimed in a whisper.

"I'm Sierra," Brynn's younger sister said, approaching their guest with her beautiful blue eyes as wide as lakes themselves. "You're very handsome, Mr. McCall."

Brynn wanted to sink into the floor and disappear at the brazen remark uttered by her sister, until she noticed the slight pink that colored Michael's cheeks.

"Shucks, Miss Sierra. What are you butterin' up an ol' goat like me for?" he said, tweaking her nose.

"You got any big, nasty cuts on you, Mr. McCall?" Scottie asked.

"Oh, one or two. But it wouldn't be polite to show 'em to you just now, boy," Michael chuckled. "Maybe later," he added in a whisper.

"Oh, boy!" Scottie exclaimed, excitedly taking a seat next to his father.

As the meal began and continued, Brynn listened intently to the questions her father posed to Michael and the answers he offered in return.

"Exactly what kind of farm do your father and uncles run, Michael?" Richard asked.

"Well, sir…Uncle Baker raises beef cattle. Uncle Matthew takes care of the wheat and alfalfa. My daddy runs the horse end of things with a little alfalfa thrown in," Michael answered. "It's a good life. My daddy and both his brothers were West Point graduates, but they're glad they went back to farmin' and ranchin' 'stead of goin' into the military permanent."

"I think your mother and your aunts are simply jewels!" Ophelia commented.

"Yes, ma'am. And ain't little Annie here the spittin' image of my mama?" Michael asked.

"My, yes!" Ophelia agreed. "Do you like farm life, Annie?"

"Yes, ma'am!" Annie assured her. "I can't imagine not havin' fresh air and carin' for animals. You'll have to come out and spend some time with me at our place, Brynn."

"That's a right good idea, Annie," Michael agreed, and Brynn gasped slightly as she felt his leg brush against hers for a moment. She looked at him suspiciously, but he only smiled and took a bite of potatoes. "These are right good mashed potatoes, Mrs. Clarkston."

"Aren't they, though?" Richard agreed, serving himself a second helping of the white vegetable.

Brynn found it impossible to eat. She could feel Michael, smell him, sense him with every ounce of her body and spirit. His arm brushed hers once, and she jumped nervously.

He chuckled and dropped his voice so that the others, who were all involved in a conversation about the recent stage and bank robberies in the state, couldn't hear. "Don't be so jittery, darlin'. You'll give us away." Then she felt him step lightly on her foot with his boot, and he winked at her.

She couldn't resist smiling at him, for he was so handsome and adorable. And polite! She couldn't believe his polished manners. She felt guilty for expecting any less from him.

Some time later, as they all were finishing their meal, Annie muttered to Brynn, "Mama's gonna wring my neck. Michael probably will too once we're gone."

"No. Your mama will understand that you couldn't possibly refuse dinner here! My mother would have been hurt," Brynn assured her.

"I hope you're right, Brynn," Annie sighed.

"Mrs. Clarkston, this was a dandy of a meal. I tell you, you could give my mama some right serious competition," Michael chuckled as he folded his napkin and placed it neatly beside his plate.

"Oh, must you rush off?" Ophelia pleaded.

"Yes, ma'am. I'm afraid so. Mama's gonna be a worryin' as it is. Not so much about me…but she worries about Annie bein' out."

"Well, thank you so much for joining us. You two drop in anytime you're in town, do you hear me?"

"Yes, ma'am," Annie answered sweetly. "If you really mean it, that is."

Ophelia laughed, "Of course I mean it, Annie! You're welcome anytime."

Richard started to stand as Michael rose from his chair. "No need for that, Mr. Clarkston. You let that fine meal settle awhile. Annie and me can see ourselves out," Michael said, reaching across the table and offering Richard his hand.

Richard shook Michael's hand and said, "It was wonderful meeting the two of you. We look forward to further associations with you and your families. Extend our greetings to your parents, won't you?"

Michael smiled, "Yes, sir. And thank you again."

"Walk me out, Brynn. Please," Annie begged, linking her arm through Brynn's. Annie fairly dragged Brynn along, chattering constantly. "Oh, your daddy's just a dream! Makes me wish I was still in school. And your mama! She's *so* pretty! And they're all so nice. Do you really think she'll mind if I come visit you again?"

"Of course not," Brynn assured her.

"Quit that gossipin' now, girls. It ain't polite," Michael said, stepping in front of the two young ladies and opening the front door for them.

Brynn avoided looking directly at Michael, for the warm sensation on her leg still burned from his earlier touch at the dinner table. Still, she could feel his eyes on her as she passed through the threshold with Annie.

"You all need a porch swing, Brynn," Annie commented as she noticed the lack of one on the Clarkston's front porch. "Michael could build one for you, couldn't you, Michael?"

"Why, sure. Porch swings are right necessary for certain… situations, you know, Miss Brynn," he chuckled.

Brynn looked up, her eyes widening as she saw him wink flirtatiously at her.

"That's right," Annie agreed. "Mama and Daddy sit out on ours every summer night sparkin' for hours!" Annie sighed heavily and continued on a different thought, "I guess we have to go. You have no idea, Brynn, how glad I am you've moved here. I can tell we're gonna be the best of friends. Can't you?"

"I agree," Brynn giggled. She was a bit startled when Annie embraced her quickly before skipping off.

"Hurry up, Michael! You want Mama to tan your hind end?" she called.

Michael chuckled, and Brynn looked away as the penetrating

blue of his eyes flickered mischievously at her. "Too bad the rain stopped earlier today, ain't it?"

Again she looked at him with widened eyes, her sweet mouth gaping open in astonishment at yet another insinuative remark.

"Careful, there, Miss Brynn. You might catch somethin' unexpected with that there baited trap of yours." Then he tipped his hat, smiled, and turned, following his sister into the sunset.

"My goodness, Brynn!" Ophelia exclaimed as her daughter entered the kitchen and began helping to clear the table. "That boy must have every unmarried female heart in the West palpitating!"

"Yes. He's very handsome, isn't he?" Brynn remarked casually.

"That would be putting it mildly, I think," Ophelia said, smiling knowingly at her daughter.

"I would be more prone to say that he is far from being a boy," Richard interceded.

"You're a boy too, Richard darling. 'Man' is just a general term, you know," Ophelia teased. "And he's so polite and well mannered. And that Annie! She's the very image of her mother. What a little chatterbox. I think she's adorable," she finished.

"I wonder if she really meant it when she said I should come out and visit their farm," Brynn said quietly.

"I'm certain she did, dear," Richard encouraged.

Late that night, as Brynn lay in her bed attempting to go to sleep, her mind was awhirl with thoughts of the day. Especially the morning in Mrs. Johnson's back room. She knew she would never forget the divine feel of Michael's skin against her palms nor the heavenly scent of leather and bacon that was his. Each time she thought of those moments when he'd asked her if she would slap him if he kissed her, her heart would swell to near bursting, and she would wish to herself that she hadn't answered so properly. For if merely being near to him sent her body and mind into fits of ecstatic delight, no doubt receiving a kiss from him would render her dead where she stood from ecstasy.

When she finally drifted off to deep slumber, she dreamed of the moments in Mrs. Johnson's back room again and again and again.

CHAPTER THREE

"So they have this box lunch sale, you see. All the young women in town make a picnic lunch. Then the sheriff auctions them off to the highest bidder. The man who wins the biddin' gets to have a nice little picnic with the girl of his choice. All the money collected goes to the school for deaf children over in Dove Creek. We all do it every year, honey. I hope you don't mind that I signed you up to make a lunch."

Brynn's mouth dropped open in astonishment at Mrs. Johnson's mentioning signing Brynn up for the town charity fundraiser. "Mrs. Johnson! It sounds so…heathenistic! Men bidding on women!"

"They bid on the box lunch, sweetheart. It's all in fun, and it's for a good cause. Shoot, if Mr. Johnson hadn't a bought my lunch so many years back in California…we might never have met and fallen in love," Mrs. Johnson chuckled.

"My mother won't approve, I'm afraid," Brynn told her.

"Oh, I already asked her about it when she was in this mornin'. She thought it was a sweet idea."

Brynn shook her head in disbelief. Her mother and father had both relaxed so much since their move west. Sometimes it astonished her how much more they enjoyed life.

"Hey there, Mrs. Johnson…you little vixen, you," came Michael McCall's voice from the doorway.

Brynn turned to see him standing, handsomely grinning at both her and Mrs. Johnson.

"Michael! How good to see you, boy. What are you in fer today? I see your shirt ain't fallin' off ya," Mrs. Johnson greeted him.

He walked to the counter and, folding his arms, leaned casually on the counter next to Brynn. "I just come in to see if you had anythin'…interestin'," he said, winking at Brynn. "Hey there, Miss Brynn. I ain't seen you in a week."

Brynn looked away, blushing. As warmth flooded her body, especially her rosy cheeks, she answered, "Yes. How have you been?"

"Oh, me? Just fine." Turning his attention to Mrs. Johnson then, he said, "I come in for some supplies, sweetheart. I'm buildin' a porch swing for Brynn's mama and daddy."

Brynn's eyes widened as she looked at him in astonishment. "What?" she asked.

"I just come from your house, Miss Brynn. I told your daddy I'd be more'n happy to put up a swing out there on your front porch. I told him that if he wanted me to feel more comfortable when I was out on the front porch asparkin' with his daughter that he needed to get a swing up."

Mrs. Johnson snickered as Brynn screeched, "What? You didn't really, did you?"

Michael chuckled sympathetically as he reached out and took her chin in his hand. "No, darlin'. Of course I didn't say that to your daddy. Now get that purty color back in your face."

Brynn sighed heavily with relief, but her breath was immediately taken away as Michael reached out and pulled her against him in a warm embrace. "I think I scared her, Mrs. Johnson," he muttered.

"You're a mean ol' tease, Michael McCall. Poor thing's as white as a sheet," Mrs. Johnson scolded.

Brynn's face had been smashed flat against Michael's massive and incredibly firm chest before he tipped her chin with one hand and looked down into her astonished and beautiful face. "I'm sorry, Miss Brynn. I was just teasin'. But I really am buildin' a swing for your mama. I asked her if'n she'd like one, and she said yes," he explained.

"That's very kind of you," Brynn stuttered as she gazed into his enchanting face.

"Well, Michael McCall! Whatever are you doing with that child?" Michael released Brynn abruptly at the sound of Annabelle Barrington's voice.

"If she ain't got the timin' of the devil," Mrs. Johnson muttered under her breath loud enough that Brynn still heard the comment.

"I scared her near clean out of her britches, Annabelle. Had to calm her down," Michael explained.

"Well, you have to be considerate of children. They take things completely to heart, Michael. Are you busy right now? Papa has a new pony! He's just brought it in from Denver, and he wants you to take a look at it," Annabelle cooed, linking her arm through one of Michael's.

"Is it really a pony, Annabelle? Or is it a horse? I don't deal much in ponies," Michael told her.

"It's a horse, silly. I meant to say that! I've just had a terrible time sleeping since I've returned from the east. It's too quiet here. Anyway, Daddy wants to know if you'll come and look the animal over."

"I'm pickin' up some things to build somethin' for Mrs. Clarkston. When I'm done here, I'll run by for a minute 'fore I head home," Michael agreed.

"Can't you come right now, Michael?" Annabelle pleaded, batting her eyelashes.

"I'll be along shortly, Annabelle. Run on home and tell your daddy that for me," Michael repeated.

"Well, all right. But can't I just wait with you here instead? I have a few things to pick up myself."

"If'n you're wantin' to wait, go right ahead," Michael said, detaching her hand from his arm. "Here's a list of what I'm needin', Mrs. Johnson. You point it out, and I'll get it. I don't want you luggin' this stuff over here for me."

"Whatever did he do to upset you so, Brynn?" Annabelle questioned when Michael and Mrs. Johnson had left the counter to go collect the things on Michael's list.

"He…he…was just teasing me. Nothing really," Brynn answered.

"Oh. Well, my Michael is a tease! He used to tease me something terrible when we were children. He even picked me up and dropped me in the creek at a town social when I was nine! I was so angry. But of course, who can stay mad at him for long? I forgave him promptly. Were you in the store to buy something or just to visit Mrs. Johnson? I suppose you are painfully aware that Michael always comes in here to see her when he's in town. No doubt that's why you come to visit so often."

Brynn drew in a deep breath to calm herself and then said, "Actually, I've become quite attached to Mrs. Johnson. I just happened to be in here when Michael arrived. It's not as if I sit across the street and watch for him every day and then just happen to show up anytime he's here."

Annabelle's triumphant smile faded, and her eyes narrowed. "You're a little young to be trying to catch his attention, Brynn."

"I don't have to try, Annabelle," Brynn retaliated. Then turning toward Mrs. Johnson and Michael, she called, "I'll be off now, Mrs. Johnson. I feel the need for some fresh air and a brisk walk. Thank you for the visit. I guess I'll be seeing you at our house soon enough then, Mr. McCall?"

Michael's eyes twinkled knowingly, and he said, "First minute I can get there, Miss Brynn."

"Good bye, honey! You come on by tomorrow, you hear?" Mrs. Johnson called, waving to the girl as she left the store.

"Have a nice day, Annabelle," Brynn chirped as she left the young woman standing in the store scowling angrily. She smiled to herself at her verbal victory over Annabelle—then scolded herself in the next thought for dropping to the girl's own petty level.

Later that afternoon, there was a knock on the front door.

"Brynn, dear…would you get that please? I'm up to my elbows in trying to find a way to bake a decent cake in this oven!" Ophelia sighed irritatedly.

Brynn did indeed answer the knocking, and the familiar thrill that filled her each time she found herself facing the man erupted once more as Michael McCall greeted, "Hey there, Miss Brynn. I come to take some measurements for our…the swing I'm buildin' for your family."

His smile was dazzling, and the toothpick between his teeth fluttered briefly.

"Is it that dashing young McCall boy I hear, Brynn?" Ophelia asked as she entered the parlor, drying her hands on her apron. "Hello there, Michael. Have you come to start on the porch swing?"

"Yes, ma'am," he answered, tipping his hat. "I don't suppose you could spare your lovely daughter for a minute here. I need to measure some things out front."

Brynn shook her head nervously, but her mother answered, "Well, of course, Michael. Whatever you need. You don't mind assisting him for a minute, do you, dear?"

Michael grinned slyly at Brynn and winked quickly. "Of course not, Mother," Brynn said and was startled when Michael took her hand and yanked her through the doorway with him the instant she agreed.

"I've got a cake or two to tend to," Ophelia called as she turned and walked back toward the kitchen. "You just let me know if I can help, Michael."

"Yes, ma'am," he called in reply.

"Your family's comin' to the barn raisin', right?" Michael asked as he handed Brynn one end of a tattered tape measure.

"Yes. We're planning on it. That's why Mother's in there trying to perfect her cakes," Brynn said, smiling.

"Hold that down there on the floor, like that," he said, pointing to the porch floor. "Well, it'll be fun. Lotta work for us menfolk… but it's well worth it when the frame's up and we get to eatin' those goodies all the women bake. You want it to be at least two feet off the floor, you know," he said as he stretched his arm up, holding the other end of the tape measure, placing it against the porch roof.

"Was Annabelle's father's horse a good one?" Brynn asked casually. She began seething at the thought of Michael spending time at Annabelle's home.

"It is purty good. I wasn't sure it would be. I thought maybe

Annabelle was just blowin' smoke. She's always out for attention. But it's a nice animal. He paid a purty price too. I know the feller he bought it from 'cause he buys from me." Michael smiled and dropped his voice. "I'll let you in on a little secret, darlin'. I raised that stallion from a colt. I own his sire!"

Brynn smiled delightedly. "Why didn't he just buy it from you?"

"'Cause I sold him to the feller up in Denver. I guess that the feller up there just saw what good stock he was and decided to make himself a profit by sellin' him to Annabelle's daddy. Believe me, he did make a profit!"

"I think that's funny," Brynn giggled.

"Yeah. Me too," Michael chuckled and dropped the tape measure. "What color are you wantin' this swing to be, Miss Brynn?" he asked.

"I don't know," she answered. "What would you suggest?"

"Won't matter none to me what color it is. I plan on sittin' on it in the dark anyhow," he answered, winking at her.

Brynn smiled and shook her head, all too pleased at his flirt. "You are far too playful, Mr. McCall."

"What makes you think I'm always just teasin'?" he asked in a whisper, his eyebrows raised questioningly.

"Because you…you…" she stammered.

"You just be sure you don't stand me up at that barn raisin' next week." Removing the toothpick from his mouth, he pricked her lip with it, placing it between her parted lips as he had once before. "I got plans for you, little Miss Brynn Clarkston." Then he tipped his hat and said, "Tell your lovely mama that I'll have that swing up for her 'fore she knows it." He winked at her and left.

Brynn watched him walk away down the street, fascinated by his way of walking in general. Little did she realize that Michael had meant his last remark literally. For the next morning when her brother and sister bolted out the front door on their way to school, they called to Brynn and their mother to come outside. There, hanging glistening white in the morning sun, was a finished and perfect porch swing.

CHAPTER FOUR

It felt like a dream. As Brynn rode in the back of the wagon with Sierra and Scottie, she pinched herself to make sure she was awake and not just dreaming. They were finally and actually on their way to Matthew and Mary McCall's farm for the ever-anticipated barn raising. It had been a seemingly endless wait for the day to arrive. Of course, her father said they could attend just after her mother had asked him about it. But to actually be going was simply unbelievable.

Brynn smoothed the skirt of her new dress and pinched at the sleeve heads to puff them. It had turned out nicely, and Brynn's mother had assured her endlessly that it was very becoming on her.

"That must be it there," Richard Clarkston said, pointing ahead of them. "Look at all the wagons! Must be every family and person in town is here."

"My, yes!" Ophelia agreed. "What fun this will be!"

Immediately, Brynn's stomach began to tie itself into square knots. The anticipation of seeing Michael McCall again was completely unnerving!

Brynn hadn't seen Michael since the day he had come to measure the porch for the swing a week before. She wondered if he would even remember the casual flirts he had bestowed upon her that day. Maybe he wouldn't even be in attendance at the barn raising. After all, it was his uncle's barn that was to have its frame raised this day, not his father's.

Brynn, unfortunately, had also had the opportunity to become better acquainted with Annabelle Barrington. This was not a positive experience, considering that Annabelle saw herself as far too elite and beautiful to comfortably associate with the other girls in town, especially Brynn.

Whenever Annabelle spoke to Brynn, she wore a painful sneer on her face, as if she'd just tasted something unpleasant. Several times Brynn had discovered Annabelle studying her from across the street. Always she wore a disgusted expression, but Brynn had reconciled herself to the reality that Annabelle was simply a cliché snob. Therefore, she tried to not take her expressions and condescending remarks too seriously.

"Oh, I suppose it is necessary to attend these…these…little gatherings," Brynn heard Annabelle's shrill voice chirping as Scottie and Sierra bounded off the wagon when it halted near the others. "Still, it's ever so dusty and dry out today. A girl's complexion might suffer dreadfully if she weren't skilled in protecting it."

Brynn caught sight of her then, standing nearby and talking to a tall, handsome young man that rather resembled Michael in some ways. As Richard assisted Ophelia in her exit of the wagon, Annabelle and the young man turned, Annabelle catching sight of Brynn instantly.

"Brynn! How delightful to see you! Haven't you a parasol, child?" the snobbish filly greeted with all the sweetness of maple syrup.

"No, I never bring one, Annabelle. I prefer to have a little natural color to my cheeks," Brynn answered, smiling sweetly.

"Touché, my dear," Ophelia mumbled, winking at her daughter.

Brynn felt triumphant and was again glad that she had taken her mother into her confidence and told her about Annabelle Barrington. She felt she had an ally, someone to support her should the other girl's subtle remarks start to penetrate her self-confidence.

"The Clarkstons?" the young man asked as he approached, his hand outstretched and offered in greeting to Richard.

"Yes. And you are?" Richard inquired, taking the young man's hand and shaking it firmly.

"Matthew Jr. I'm Matthew and Mary's oldest boy, sir. And it's glad I am to meet you."

Brynn felt the warmth gathering in her cheeks as the young man's gaze fell to her. A smile spread across his face, and he said, "You must be Miss Brynn Clarkston."

"Yes, sir," she sputtered.

"I heard tell of you. My—" The young man looked up quickly to Brynn's parents and then continued. "My…uh…my mama told me that there was a right lovely young lady in the Clarkston family."

Brynn blushed at the compliment and then was horrified as Sierra popped up almost magically at her side and said, "I'm a Clarkston too, you know."

Matthew squatted, tipped his hat back, and smiled at Sierra. "I can see that, sugar. And I'll tell ya a secret," he whispered. "My fancy runs to lovely young ladies with dark hair, big blue eyes, and angel kisses sprinkled across their noses."

Sierra smiled and said, "They're freckles."

"Some folks calls 'em freckles, sugar. I know they're little spots where the angels kiss people who are 'specially purty," the man said, tweaking the girl's nose before standing again.

"I'm Annabelle Barrington, Mr. and Mrs. Clarkston," Annabelle interrupted, stepping between Matthew and Sierra. "I don't believe we've met yet."

"Oh, but we've heard so much about you, dear," Ophelia chimed, smiling delightedly at the girl.

"I'm certain you have. I am just returned from finishing school. And as you know, that's a rarity in these small western towns," Annabelle informed them.

"My mama will be near to squealin' her head off when she finds out you've actually come, Mrs. Clarkston," Matthew said, taking Ophelia's arm and linking it with his own. "Do let me take you along to see her."

"Are all you McCall boys such gentlemen?" Ophelia asked.

"Every last one, ma'am. We get that from our daddies," he assured her.

"Come along, children. Let's go greet Mrs. McCall. Scottie… Scottie? Brad, darling, Scottie has run off already!" Ophelia sighed, shaking her head.

"Boys will be boys, ma'am," Matthew commented. "He'll be fine. Can't get into much trouble around here."

"You don't know my Scottie," Ophelia reminded him.

"No. But I remember myself as a youngster, ma'am," he chuckled.

Brynn smiled exaggeratedly at Annabelle as the family left her standing alone.

"Ophelia! Brynn!" Mary called as the Clarkston family approached the long table laden with every kind of baked good and food imaginable. "I'm so glad you've come! Did you have trouble finding us?"

"None at all, Mrs. McCall," Richard answered, placing Ophelia's perfectly baked and decorated cakes on the table.

"And I see you've met my Matthew." Mary smiled as she caressed her son's cheek lovingly. "Isn't he handsome, Ophelia?" she asked.

"Oh my, yes. And so polite and chivalrous," Ophelia agreed. "I have to admit the McCalls seem to have a very recognizable genetic heritage."

"Here's Matthew now," Mary said as a tall, attractive, older version of Matthew Jr. approached.

"I'm Matthew McCall. Mary's told me all about you," Matthew said, extending a hand to Richard.

"Richard Clarkston," Richard offered, shaking the man's hand.

"Here comes ol' Baker. Ain't he an ugly ol' cuss?" Matthew chuckled as another man approached.

Even though he was older, Brynn recognized this man from the picture in Mrs. Johnson's back room. "Baker McCall," the man said, shaking Richard's hand firmly. "And I'm the best-lookin' boy in the family. Matthew's just jealous," the man chuckled, slapping his brother soundly on the back.

"Brynn! Brynn! Finally! I've been waitin' all mornin' for you to get here!" Annie squealed as she rushed forward. "Come on! There's all kinds of folks you need to meet." Annie dropped her voice to a whisper and added, "Ol' Beevis Bellmont even slicked back his hair for this occasion," she giggled.

Brynn smiled and looked to her mother, who nodded, thus telling her daughter that it was all right for her to go off with Annie.

Once out of sight of the adults, Annie babbled endlessly. "Porter Jorgenson is here, Brynn! I can hardly contain myself! He's an absolute living dream! Wait 'til you see him…all tall-like and blond with the deepest brown eyes you ever saw! He's a bit older than me though. I don't think he knows I'm alive. But you wait—someday I'll get his attention. He's right over here! See him? That tall one. He's as tall as Michael, at least. Look. See him?"

Brynn looked in the direction that Annie pointed and did indeed catch sight of a handsome young man fitting Annie's description.

"Ain't he just a dream? I think I'm plum gone on him, Brynn. Dang it all anyway," Annie sighed.

"Believe me, Annie—I understand all too well," Brynn muttered, sighing heavily herself as she thought of Michael.

"But you're so pretty, Brynn! You catch everyone's attention! I'm so plain Jane and short. No one notices me." Annie sighed again, and Brynn looked at her, her own mouth gaping open in disbelief at the girl's perception of herself.

"Baitin' flies again, Miss Brynn?" came Michael's whisper in Brynn's ear. Goose bumps broke over every inch of her body as his breath warmed her neck. Whirling around to meet him, she smiled automatically at the sight of him in his clean white shirt and newer-looking Levi's. She liked the way Levi's looked on Michael, and she secretly uttered a silent thank you to the man who had made them so appropriate for hard-working men to wear.

"Mmmmmm mmmmm!" he exclaimed then, studying Brynn from head to toe. "Girl, you look good enough to eat."

Brynn's eyes widened at such a bold remark, but she managed a polite, "Thank you, Mr. McCall."

"What are you two little cats gawkin' at, Annie?" he asked, looking past them to the group of young men that stood some ways off.

"That dreamy Porter Jorgenson. And you just keep your big trap shut, Michael McCall," Annie whispered.

"Who's lookin' at him? You or Miss Brynn here?" Michael asked, winking at Brynn.

"Me! Now quit teasin'," Annie scolded.

"Well, Mama sent me over to get you two. They're gettin' ready to start the barn. You gonna come on over and watch my muscles bulge whilst I'm workin', Miss Brynn?" Michael chuckled.

Brynn blushed to her heels and said calmly, "I'm interested to see how a barn raising comes off, yes."

He winked at her as he offered her his arm. Rather cautiously, Brynn laid her hand in the crook of it as he offered his other arm to his sister. "Well, come along then, girls. I'll tell you what, Annie," he said, dropping his voice. "I'll see if I can talk ol' Porter into workin' without his shirt on. We wouldn't want him to get it dirty now, would we?"

Annie slugged her brother playfully in the shoulder. "Keep your mouth quiet, Michael. I got my own dirt on you as ammunition. Remember that." Michael chuckled.

The barn raising was indeed interesting and hard work. Brynn and her mother had both gasped aloud in astonishment when, simultaneously, every man present with the last name McCall who was working on the barn stripped his shirt off before beginning the task. Instead of gasping, Sierra had simply muttered, "Wow!"

Brynn giggled with Annie as they watched Porter Jorgenson strip his shirt off as well after talking briefly with Michael. Michael turned around then and winked at his little sister. Brynn smiled warmly, for it was so obvious that the siblings shared a sweet relationship.

Brynn's eyes never once left Michael's muscular and capable form as he worked with the other men to raise the barn's massive frame. She thought of what an excellent vision of her own ideal of the perfect man he was. She reflected on the brief moments in Mrs. Johnson's store when she had been embraced apologetically in his strong arms and against his firm, muscular torso.

A sigh escaped her lungs at the remembrance, and Annie said, "Porter is so handsome, isn't he?"

When the frame had been successfully erected, the men attacked the table laden with food as if not one of them had eaten in a month. Annie pulled Brynn to one side and whispered, "You wanna see somethin' so romantic it'll send butterflies soarin' in your tummy?" she asked.

Brynn nodded and followed her friend as she led her to the house. As they approached, Brynn could hear voices speaking in quiet intonations. Annie turned to Brynn and put an index finger to her lips to indicate that she be carefully silent. As the two girls peered around the corner of the house, Brynn's eyes widened at the sight that was before her.

The beautiful and sophisticated Malaina McCall was standing with her back against the side of the house and an intense blush brazen across her cheeks. Jackson McCall stood before her, a hand pressed firmly against the house on either side of Malaina's head. He was shirtless and leaning forward so that his forehead was pressed against his wife's.

"Come on, darlin'…you still like me best this way, don't you now? No shirt and trappin' you up against a wall?" Jackson said in a low voice.

"You have absolutely no manners whatsoever, Jackson McCall," Malaina giggled.

"Maybe not, but it's all true, ain't it? Everything I promised you I would be when we got married. I still get your heart racin' when I catch you like this, now don't I?" he chuckled.

Malaina took his face between her lovely hands and nodded. "Yes, you do, you monster. That's why I worry so about those boys of yours."

"Aw, they're just like their daddy, darlin'. No need to waste your time worryin' there."

Brynn watched, mesmerized as Annie's daddy then leaned forward, capturing his wife's mouth in a deeply passionate kiss. Annie tugged at her sleeve then, and Brynn followed her back to the others.

"Oh, my goodness! They are too wonderful!" Brynn exclaimed when they had returned to the gathering.

Annie sighed heavily. "Yep. I ain't gonna get married 'til somebody makes me feel the way Daddy does Mama. Even to Porter Jorgenson."

Brynn was startled then as a plate of blueberry pie was suddenly smashed against her.

"Oh, my! How carelessly clumsy of me," Annabelle gasped dramatically, having appeared from seemingly nowhere. "And blueberry, of all things. Your dress is no doubt simply ruined!"

"You did that on purpose, Annabelle Barrington! You ol' biddy!" Annie accused.

Brynn inhaled deeply as she wiped at the blueberries that clung to her bosom. "Fortunately it was an older dress, Annabelle. Don't concern yourself too much," Brynn said, forcing a forgiving smile. "I'll simply sponge it off a bit, and it will have to do for the rest of the evening." Then, leaving Annabelle looking quite vexed at not having provoked her, Brynn turned and left the others. As she walked away, Brynn could hear Annie still scolding Annabelle.

Once out of sight of the group of townspeople, however, the tears of anger, humiliation, and disappointment began to escape her lovely blue eyes and trickle freely down her cheeks. How she detested that Annabelle Barrington! Every beautiful inch of her. She could only be thankful that Michael had not been present to witness her humiliation at Annabelle's hands.

Going to a watering trough that stood near to the old barn, she sighed heavily and wiped the tears from her cheeks.

"You're a better man than I would've been, Miss Brynn."

At the words uttered by the familiar voice, Brynn spun around and found herself looking into the perfectly awe-inspiring face of Michael McCall.

"I'd a popped her square in the snout," he said, taking several steps toward her. His brow was puckered in a most unfamiliar frown as he looked at her, studying the large stain on her dress front.

"She would've triumphed then," Brynn responded, wiping at her tear-stained cheeks once more. "It's what she wanted me to do."

"I know. And I would've jumped at the bait myself," Michael grumbled. "But, I suppose—bein' the lady that you are—yer above such things, ain't ya?"

"Not really," Brynn said, looking away and trying to avoid his unsettling gaze. "I would've loved to have smashed the rest of that pie in her syrupy little face."

"Well," he chuckled, moving closer to her, "next time, you do just that, Miss Brynn."

Brynn cleared her throat nervously and turned, walking to a nearby tree. "Maybe I will. At least I would've felt better about the ruination of this dress."

Taking a toothpick from his back pocket and placing it in his mouth, Michael followed her to the tree. "It's a right purty one too. Ain't that the cloth you were pickin' out that first day I seen you in Mrs. Johnson's store?"

Brynn looked up at him then, entirely flattered that he would remember such a minor detail of their meeting. "Yes, it is," she answered. He smiled at her, and she noticed the sound of the breeze through the leaves of the willow beneath which they stood. She watched, entertained, as the toothpick in his mouth began to flutter up and down.

Michael reached up and took hold of a tree limb with both hands, leaning toward her a bit as he let the branch support some of his weight. "You know, Miss Brynn," he began, "blueberry is my favorite color."

Brynn smiled and said, "You're just trying to make me feel better."

"Oh, believe me, darlin'…I could make you feel better. And without saying one word."

Brynn blushed and shook her head in disbelief. "You're the worst tease I have ever met, Mr. McCall," she giggled.

"I ain't teasin', Miss Brynn. It's the truth." His grin was mischievous as well as tantalizing.

"You know, I should slap you for even speaking of such things to me," she reminded him. She thought of how utterly horrified her mother would be were she to overhear the conversation her daughter was involved in.

He chuckled, and as the musicians back at the gathering began to play a song, he let go of the tree limb and offered one hand to her. "May I have the pleasure, Miss Brynn?" he asked, bowing slightly as he looked at her.

The brightened smile left Brynn's face, and her hand went nervously to her collar and began anxiously toying with the cameo broach there.

"I ain't the best dancer, but I can handle waltzin' all right," he added, motioning to her to take his hand.

Tentatively she reached out and placed her small hand in his large one. The instant his fingers tightened around hers, she knew that she had made a grievous error in accepting his invitation, for every thread that held her being together was aware of his simple touch. And as he pulled her closer to him, placing his other hand at her waist, she had to battle with every muscle in her body, which threatened to bolt from him.

"Yer other hand goes on my shoulder, darlin'," he reminded her, chuckling knowingly. "You think I'm a mangy ol' flirt, don't ya?" he asked as he began to lead her in the waltz.

"What?" she asked, befuddled. The smell of leather and bacon filled her lungs as it had that day in Mrs. Johnson's back room. She could feel his breath in her hair and sense the warmth from his body. Uncertainly, she reached up and laid her hand lightly on his shoulder.

"You think I'm just teasin' you all the dern time. You probably think I tease every female in town the same way, now don't ya?"

"Yes."

He chuckled. "Now, ain't this romantic? Us waltzin' under a willer...all secluded like? Nobody eyein' us but the breeze in the leaves and the stars?"

Brynn looked up at him, startled by the sudden change in subject of conversation.

"Just the right weather for sparkin', I say," he muttered, winking at her playfully.

"Oh, no, no, no," she whispered as he stopped their waltzing, dropped her hand, and removed the toothpick from his mouth. "Oh, please no," she repeated as he pulled her body flush with his own.

Brynn was certain that he would be able to feel the feral hammering of her heart as it pounded within her chest. She could hear it in her own ears as it beat recklessly. She watched in silent awe as his head descended, and then she melted in his arms when his mouth touched her lips gently. She pulled away and averted her eyes shyly, but he took her chin and directed her gaze at him once more.

"I'm just gettin' yer feet wet, darlin'," he whispered. "Ain't nothin' to be afraid of where I'm concerned." He smiled at her, moistening his lips before bending to kiss her again.

His kiss was more intense the second time. Brynn feared that if he attempted to coax her any further, she might submit to actually returning the kiss. As it was, every strand of her being fought valiantly to keep from succumbing to him.

"Brynn! Brynn?"

Brynn gasped and looked at Michael, horrified. "My mother!" she whispered.

He smiled. "I guess she'll be findin' ya here in a minute, huh?" he whispered in return.

"Let me go!" Brynn pleaded, struggling.

"Kiss me back, and I'll let you go, Miss Brynn," he chuckled.

"What? Are you insane? She's coming this way!"

"Brynn? Oh dear, Malaina. I hope she's not too upset," came Ophelia's voice on the breeze.

"Ain't that nice," Michael whispered, smiling. "My mama's comin' on over too."

Struggling, Brynn pleaded, "Oh, please, please. Let me loose!"

"Kiss me first," he chuckled.

"Very well," she relented and quickly kissed his rugged cheek before commencing with her struggles.

"No, no, no, darlin'. They're gettin' closer. You better fold." And his mouth was fierce and demanding on hers. This kiss was different from the previously playful ones he had introduced before, and Brynn was instantly enticed into participating in it. This kiss was conceived by an all-powerful, provocative man obviously capable of rendering any female of the species willingly defenseless with one trifling touch. Though devastatingly brief, Michael's kiss exhausted the breath from Brynn's lungs, and she could only stare at him dazedly as he gazed down at her afterward.

"Now, you run along and put some dry stockin's on 'fore you catch cold, Miss Brynn," he whispered. Then, pricking her lip lightly with his toothpick, he placed it between her parted lips before quickly leaving her alone under the willow tree.

Only moments had passed when Brynn, still dazed from her recent experience, saw her own mother and Michael's standing beneath the tree with her.

"There you are, sweetheart. Oh, I'm so sorry that this had to happen," Ophelia comforted, truly understanding.

"Yes, Brynn. That Annabelle Barrington needs a good paddling if you ask me. But Mary's had her youngest girl run in and choose one of her dresses for you. You can change in the house and join us in a moment, okay?" Malaina asked.

"There, now that looks lovely!" Ophelia exclaimed as she studied her daughter.

"Yes! It fits perfectly. Now come on out and join us for the rest of the fun," Malaina chirped.

As Brynn and the two older women left the McCall house, Ophelia whispered aside to her daughter, "Sweetheart, I think you should spit that toothpick out somewhere before we return to the social, don't you think?"

Brynn hadn't realized until that very moment that she had, indeed, kept Michael's toothpick in her mouth the entire time she had been changing her dress.

"Yes, Mother," she agreed. Only she didn't dispose of it but rather tucked it into the pocket of her dress.

"Oh dear, Ophelia," Malaina began. "I hope she hasn't picked that nasty ol' habit up from my boys! Why, my Michael is forever and always chewin' on a…" Her words died away, and one of her lovely eyebrows rose as she looked at Brynn lingeringly then.

Brynn felt herself blush but was puzzled when Malaina only smiled happily.

☙

"See, they're just starting another waltz," Ophelia said as they approached the large bonfire that now glowed near the food tables. "Just be a lady and ignore that haughty tapioca-faced girl, Brynn."

"I'm fine, Mother. Really. You've no idea," Brynn said as she returned Annie's friendly wave.

Annie dashed over to Brynn, smiling radiantly. Brynn envied the girl, for it was painfully apparent that Annie would one day be Malaina's double.

"It fits perfect, don't it?" Annie squealed.

"*Doesn't* it," Malaina corrected.

"I'm so glad! Now you can come and dance and have fun!" Annie added, pulling Brynn toward a group of McCall relations.

"I'd a smacked her right in the kisser," Grant McCall stated as Brynn and Annie joined the group.

"Yeah, me too. She's such a stinker! I mean, it might be one thing if she were purty…but she ain't," another cousin added.

"Brynn's a lady. That's why she just walked away," Annie reminded.

"Next time I might be more inclined to conform to the general opinion," Brynn giggled.

"You get them feet all dried off, Miss Brynn?"

"Michael! Don't sneak up on Brynn like that! She nearly jumped out of her skin!" Annie scolded her brother as both she and Brynn turned to face him. Brynn blushed immediately upon seeing the knowing grin spread across his face. "And for your information, it weren't her feet that got wet. It was her dress," Annie added.

"Don't you let Mama hear you talkin' so bad! She'll tan yer hide," Michael chuckled, still looking at Brynn. "I come to ask Miss Brynn for a dance. Miss Brynn?" he said, offering her his hand.

Instantly Brynn's own hand went to the cameo at her throat and began to fidget.

"Oh, it's a waltz, Brynn! You have to!" Annie encouraged. "Where have you been anyway, Michael? Mama was lookin' all over for you."

"I…I had to change my shirt," he answered, still looking at Brynn knowingly. "You see, it's a long story…but there was this stain on—"

"I'd be honored, Mr. McCall," Brynn interrupted, taking his hand abruptly.

"You do ride by the seat of your britches, don't you?" he asked, chuckling as they began the waltz.

"I thought you were going to say—" Brynn began.

"I was. Turns out, I got yer blueberry stain all over the front of my shirt. Now how do you think that happened? Not that I wanted to explain it to my mama, you understand."

Brynn cast uncertain eyes to the ground. "Why did you…under the tree before? You shouldn't tease people like that, you know."

"Yer just miffed 'cause I was right," he muttered.

"What do you mean?" she asked, looking up at him again.

"I was right. 'Bout bein' able to make you feel better."

Brynn rolled her eyes exasperatedly. "You know what I mean. You shouldn't tease people like that."

"I don't tease people, Miss Brynn. Just you," he answered. He added then, "And I wasn't teasin' neither."

"You were," she whispered.

"I wasn't," he whispered. Then bending so that her ear could barely discern his breath from his words, he added, "That there last kiss that you let yourself have dern near knocked me on the seat of my pants too."

"Quit teasing me!" Brynn cried in a whisper, smiling innocently as another couple dancing nearby glanced over at her suspiciously.

"You think I'm playin' with you 'cause yer so young, don't you?" he asked. His amused smile was gone, and he wore a frown instead.

Brynn dropped her eyes guiltily.

"Well, I got some information for you, Miss Brynn Clarkston," he began. "You ain't a baby girl no more. Better face up to that fact, and prepare yerself for a grown-up man. Namely, me."

Brynn could only stare blankly at him, not believing what she had heard him say. As her mind fought to comprehend the meaning of his words, the music ended, and he bowed to her quickly.

"Thank you, Miss Brynn. Now, if'n you'll excuse me…I gotta little matter to discuss with Miss Annabelle." And before she could stall him, Michael McCall was across the way, offering his hand to Annabelle Barrington.

"Oh, my goodness," Annie exclaimed as she came to stand next to Brynn. "I hope he don't make a scene! I bet he's steamin' mad about her ruinin' your dress, Brynn."

"Oh! You don't think he'll mention it to her, do you?" Brynn asked. She didn't want the situation to be any worse than it was.

"Oh, he won't mention it to her, as such. He'll make some smart-aleck remark lettin' her know what a pain in the hind end she is. Then he'll walk away all smiles and muscles like nothin' happened. You watch. I know Michael like the back of my hand."

Brynn did watch as Michael led Annabelle in a waltz. She was irritated at having to watch them dance. Only she did fancy that he didn't hold Annabelle as closely as he had held her. Her stomach churned as she watched Annabelle smile sweetly up at Michael. Then suddenly, her smile faded, and she looked completely indignant.

"See. Here he goes," Annie giggled.

Brynn watched as Annabelle stiffened in Michael's embrace. Her eyes narrowed as she looked up at him, even though Michael grinned happily as he talked to her. When the music ended, Michael bowed slightly to Annabelle, who inhaled angrily, turned quickly, and stomped away.

"She won't never smash pie on you again, I can promise you that, Brynn," Annie giggled.

"Miss Annie, would you pleasure me with a dance?" came an unknown voice from behind Brynn.

Brynn and Annie turned, and Brynn was delighted when she saw Porter Jorgenson standing there offering his hand to Annie.

"Me?" Annie asked, unsure that he had actually spoken to her.

"Yes, ma'am," Porter assured her.

Annie nervously tucked a loose strand of hair behind her ear as she placed her trembling hand in the young man's. "Thank you, Mr. Jorgenson. I would be honored, of course," Annie said, smiling delightedly up at him.

Brynn smiled, overjoyed for her friend as she watched them enter the group of waltzing couples. She immediately stiffened, however, when Beevis Bellmont approached, grinning kindly at her.

"Miss Clarkston, would you do an ol' feller a favor and give me a dance?" he asked.

Brynn forced a friendly smile and placed her soft hand in his roughened, wrinkled one. "My pleasure, Mr. Bellmont," she answered.

Sadly, it was a dance to be bravely endured. And when it at last was ended, Brynn felt good that she had endured it, for the man seemed truly grateful.

"You're a kind soul, Miss Clarkston. Ain't many a young girl would go through a dance with me smilin' like you did. I thank you," the man said, tipping his hat.

"You're a very kind gentleman, sir," Brynn assured him, smiling sympathetically as Beevis left her with a bow.

"And you're a very kind lady."

The usual tingling sensation traveled through Brynn as she turned to face Michael. "Miss Brynn, I—" he began, stepping closer to her.

But he was interrupted when a young man rode up on a horse and shouted, "They done robbed the bank in Dove Creek!"

"Robert! What you talkin' about, boy?" Michael asked as the young man who greatly resembled Michael dismounted his horse.

"I'm tellin' you, big brother, this robbery stuff is gettin' mighty close to home. I was comin' through Dove Creek this mornin' when I heard it. Them bandits done robbed the bank at Dove Creek! Shot the sheriff to boot! Dang! That's not more'n thirty-five, forty miles from here!" Robert reminded.

"This here's my little brother, Miss Brynn. He's the adventurer of the family. Ain't home long enough to take a bath usually," Michael explained.

"Well, howdy do, Miss Brynn," the young man said, smiling.

"I'm Robert McCall. Not quite as handsome as ol' Michael here. But I do fine, don't you think?"

Brynn giggled. "Yes, I can definitely see the similar characteristics."

"What you doin' ridin' in like a tornado, Robert?" Jackson McCall asked, approaching his sons and Brynn.

"They done robbed the bank in Dove Creek, Daddy! Shot the sheriff too," Robert answered.

"Well, I don't like the sound of that. That's too awful close to home," Jackson mumbled.

Baker and Matthew McCall soon joined the group and the discussion about the recent robbery. Brynn, feeling uncomfortable, slipped away and found her parents preparing to leave.

"We'll be in town next week for the box lunch sale, Brynn," Annie assured her friend. "Then I'm gonna ask Mama when you can come out and spend some time with us on the farm! We'll have *so* much fun! You'll let her come, won't you, Mrs. Clarkston?" Annie pleaded.

"If I have your mother's approval, then I suppose it would be all right," Ophelia agreed.

"What are you so deep in thought about, Brynn?" Richard asked his daughter as they drove home beneath the stars that warm summer's night.

"What, Daddy?" Brynn said, when she realized she had been addressed. Her thoughts were back under the willow tree when the ruggedly masculine, fantastically attractive Michael McCall had favored her with the most tantalizingly, tastily passionate kiss she could ever have imagined.

CHAPTER FIVE

"Don't worry, Brynn dear," Annabelle Barrington whispered. "It can't possibly take the old goat more than an hour to eat his box lunch."

"What makes you so sure that Mr. Bellmont won't bid on you?" Annie snapped to Brynn's defense.

Annabelle rolled her eyes and sighed irritatedly. "Because there is a specific and very dashing young man who would never let my box lunch go to anyone but himself. And besides, I heard Beevis Bellmont tell Doctor Timmons that he intended to bid on Brynn's."

"Are ya'll ready?" Sheriff Barnes shouted suddenly. The crowd gathered in front of the general store cheered. "Well, let's get on with the biddin' then!"

Annie McCall and her box lunch were bid on first, and Brynn was horrified when she realized that the bidding was taking place with motions, nods, and indications from the crowd that made it impossible to tell who was bidding on what.

Brynn watched as Annie bit her lip nervously. As far as Brynn could see, Porter Jorgenson did little more than run his fingers through his hair and fold his arms across his chest.

Several moments later, however, Sheriff Barnes chuckled, "Sold for two dollars, folks! Now, remember…ya'll wait 'til the bidding is completely finished 'fore ya run up to get yer lunch!"

Annie smiled proudly and poked Brynn in the ribs with her elbow. "Two whole dollars, Brynn! That beats anybody I can ever remember. And I think it was Porter who bid on my lunch!"

"Don't get your hopes up too high, Annie. He hardly moved," Brynn reminded her.

"I know! I was watchin'!" Annie squealed.

Brynn swallowed with great difficulty as her eyes fell to the kind yet homely face of Mr. Beevis Bellmont, who sat grinning at her adoringly. Watch as she did, and like a hawk, Brynn could not tell who had bid on and won any of the other girls' lunches either. Then it was Annabelle's turn, and Brynn felt sick as she saw Michael appear seemingly from the air and prop himself against a hitching post across the street.

"Now we've got here Miss Annabelle Barrington and her box lunch. We all know what good cookin' Miss Annabelle turns out, don't we?" Sheriff Barnes shouted. "Who bids a quarter?"

Brynn watched intently, but Michael only took a toothpick from his pocket and placed it on his tongue.

"All right then…we've got twenty-five cents. Do I hear fifty?" Sheriff Barnes barked. "Fifty! A dollar. Do I hear a dollar?"

The bidding continued, and Brynn looked at Annabelle when the price reached three dollars. The prim princess of plumage smiled mockingly at her.

"Sold! Three dollars! Boy doggy! What a price!" Sheriff Barnes chuckled as the crowd cheered. "Now, the final and purtiest box lunch goes with Miss Brynn Clarkston. Do I hear a dollar?"

Brynn watched in horror as Beevis Bellmont tipped his hat to the sheriff. She looked to her mother, who nodded encouragingly in a show of strength and support.

"Good then. Do I hear a dollar fifty?" the sheriff barked out. Brynn could discern no movement from anyone in the crowd, yet the sheriff continued. "Hold on, hold on, folks. I've just had a bid… yes, I read that as five dollars! Is that right, sir? Are you biddin' five dollars on Miss Clarkston's box?"

Brynn looked desperately at Mr. Bellmont, who grinned triumphantly and nodded. She looked to Michael, who stood still, the fluttering toothpick in his mouth the only thing that moved.

"Sold!" the sheriff shouted. And the crowd applauded wildly.

"Five dollars! That's a town record, Miss Clarkston!" he congratulated. Brynn smiled, fighting to hold back the tears of humiliation and disappointment that pleaded for release.

"Now, if you boys'll come on up here and pay yer money, you can be on yer way for a nice picnic lunch with a lovely companion. I remind you…behave yerselves, boys," the sheriff chuckled.

Brynn watched in horrified wonder as several men began to walk toward the general store's porch. Among them were Beevis Bellmont and Michael.

"It's only an hour, Brynn," Annabelle cooed as she rose in anticipation of her patron.

"Don't listen to her, Brynn," Annie whispered. "She's just mad 'cause you brought more'n she did. Michael wouldn't let Beevis Bellmont buy me or you."

Brynn smiled and tried to appear relieved. She watched as Michael stepped onto the porch and took a money bag from his pocket. Beevis Bellmont had already given Sheriff Barnes his money and was walking toward her. She forced a friendly smile as he approached but nearly burst into hysterical tears when Annabelle tapped the man on the shoulder, halting his advance, and said, "She was hoping for someone else, Mr. Bellmont. But I'm sure you'll show her what a gentleman you can be."

Mr. Bellmont nodded, and Brynn rose courageously to greet him. "You're ready to go then, Miss Barrington?" he asked Annabelle casually.

"I'm sorry, what?" Annabelle asked.

"I done bought yer lunch box, Miss Annabelle!" Beevis announced, taking Annabelle's hand and placing it in the crook of his arm. "Let's go have us a picnic!"

Annabelle looked back at Brynn, who stood stunned, mouth gaping open. In that same moment, Michael pushed past Beevis, saying, "Excuse me, Beeve. Gotta get over here to my lunch. I got me a terrible appetite this afternoon."

Then he was standing before her, and Brynn looked up into his breathtaking face. "Close yer mouth, darlin'. You baitin' flies or what?" Michael chuckled as he took the box lunch from her, holding it securely under one arm and taking her hand in his. "Annie," he whispered aside to his sister, "ol' Porter oughta be comin' up any minute to claim you. You can relax."

Annie squealed with delight and began looking for Porter frantically. She giggled as she watched him pay the sheriff and approach her, tipping his hat.

"You? You bought me…my lunch?" Brynn asked Michael in a stunned whisper.

"Who did you think bought it, Miss Brynn?"

"But I was watching you. You never moved!"

"I told ya before, darlin'…a toothpick is a mighty handy habit. Sheriff Barnes knows me well enough too." He fluttered the toothpick in his mouth and laughed as he led her toward his wagon. "Yer face dern near drained of life when ol' Beevis started headin' on over."

Brynn smiled. She could smile because she was so greatly relieved and elated at the same moment. "I suppose he's a very nice man. I really shouldn't have reacted that way."

"Are you joshin'?" Michael asked. "He smells like mothballs and mice nests! Yer lucky you got me instead."

"Yes. I know," Brynn admitted.

"'Sides…I'm better lookin', ain't I?"

"More conceited, I'd say."

"No. It's just…well, I got an old hound at home that's better lookin' than ol' Beeve," Michael whispered.

Brynn smiled to herself. What a beautiful day it had turned out to be. She felt mildly self-conscious as people stared at them as they walked to the wagon. Michael would tip his hat and smile, muttering a pleasant, "How ya doin'?" to each of the onlookers that they passed. At last they reached his wagon, and Brynn felt her body being lifted effortlessly off her feet.

"Comfy?" Michael asked as he grinned up at her after lifting her onto the wagon. Then he climbed up, sitting next to her on the buckboard, and took the reins in hand, snapping them gently. "I know this perfect picnic spot, Miss Brynn. Don't you worry. You're in real capable hands," he assured her. "This spot's got a crick, a nice patch of bluegrass, and a big ol' weepin' willer tree to boot."

Brynn looked quickly to him as his words reminded her of her past experience with Michael McCall and a willow tree.

Michael winked slyly and added, "Gives off a lot of coolin' shade, you see." Brynn glanced away, blushing excessively. "What ya got in the box there for lunch?"

Brynn cleared her throat and looked to him once again. "Fried chicken," she stated.

"My favorite," Michael chuckled. "Anything else? I got me a mighty big appetite today. You're gonna have to satisfy it somehow."

Brynn began to wonder how much longer she could endure his implicative remarks and still remain unruffled. "Potato salad, fresh rolls, and chocolate cake," she answered.

"Mmmm. Sounds tasty. So," he said, changing the direction of their conversation as they traveled, "you're gettin' to be purty good friends with my sister, ain't ya?"

"Annie? Yes, I think she's fabulous! She's so very beautiful. She looks just like your mother," Brynn remarked.

"Yeah, she's a cutie. My mama is purty near to gorgeous, ain't she? You should see her and Daddy's weddin' picture! I tell you, they was quite the attractive couple."

"I'm certain of that!"

"Well, you just be sure you don't go listenin' to any of that hound slobber Annie goes around tellin' about me. I ain't half as bad as she makes out," Michael chuckled.

"She's only got good things to say about you," Brynn assured him. "You seem to get along so well together. I'm still too easily irritated by my siblings."

"We're older, Annie and me, that's all. You'll see…that little imp of a brother of yours will grow up to be one of your best friends. And that darlin' little sister—her name's Sierra, right? She's a sweetheart. I think she's plum gone on my cousin Matthew."

"This week," Brynn giggled.

"Oh, she's a fickle pickle, is she?" Michael chuckled. "I hope you ain't inherited that characteristic too!"

"No, no, no. Not me!" Brynn sighed, thinking of her sister's endless interest in romance. "I just have that one vision of—" She stopped herself from confessing her deepest thoughts to him. She had almost told him that ever since she was a small girl like Sierra, she had sheltered an ideal image of the man she wanted to spend her life with. She had almost confessed this secret to the very mortal envisionment of that ideal.

"Of what?" he prodded.

"Of…of…" she stammered.

"Of…" he prodded again.

"Of…of what a man should be," she finished awkwardly.

"Oh," he chuckled. "You mean you just have that one vision of me tucked away, huh?"

Horrified at his hitting the proverbial nail on the head, Brynn's mouth dropped open, and she stared at him in silence.

"I'm just joshin' with ya, Miss Brynn," he laughed. "No need to go baitin' bugs again."

Brynn immediately clamped her mouth shut and drew in an unsettled breath.

"Here ya go," he announced then, reining the team to a halt. "Purty, ain't it?"

Brynn nodded as she surveyed the lovely area he had driven them to. It was even lovelier than she had envisioned from his description. He jumped down from the wagon and motioned for her to follow. "Come on, darlin'. I'm starvin'," he said as she placed her hand tentatively in his own. "Watch this," he instructed, winking at her. Then he knelt down on one knee, making a step for her with his other thigh. "Purty impressive, huh? Learned this one from my daddy."

"Oh, I can't possibly…" Brynn began. But he tugged on the hand he held, and she involuntarily stepped down with one foot, which landed squarely on his thigh as he had intended. He took her other hand as she stepped down again and helped her steady herself as her feet finally met the ground. Then standing, he reached up and removed the box lunch from its place on the buckboard.

"Hold on here a minute," he said as he reached into the wagon and produced a plaid blanket. "See, I thought ahead."

Brynn raised her eyebrows and smiled as he took her arm, pushing her forward.

They enjoyed the lunch Brynn had prepared, all the while Michael making flattering comments about her culinary skills. When they had finished eating, Michael leaned back against the enormous willow tree, his legs stretched out long and straight in front of him, and taking a toothpick from his pocket began chewing on it.

"Now that was worth five dollars," he sighed, winking approvingly at her.

Brynn tucked her legs under her skirt and said, "No meal is worth five dollars, Mr. McCall. But I'm sure the deaf children in the home will appreciate your generosity."

"Weren't nothin' generous about it, Miss Brynn. I just wanted to get you out here alone under a willer tree again." He winked at her teasingly just before he pulled his hat down over his eyes.

"I wonder if Annie is enjoying her picnic," Brynn muttered, looking around her at the beautiful landscape.

"Oh, yes. I'm sure she is. I lent ol' Porter Jorgenson the two dollars to buy her with. I knew she'd a died if he hadn't been able to take her," Michael mumbled.

Brynn looked at him in pleasant surprise. "That is so sweet, Mr. McCall. She had her heart set on going with him."

"I know. I'm a sucker for my sister."

Brynn shook her head and marveled at his sentiment. He was too good to be real. No man possessed all the positive qualities that this one seemed to. She began to wonder what secret flaws were hidden within him. She must have sighed out loud at the thought because he lifted his hat from his eyes quickly.

"Gettin' tired of me already, huh?" he asked.

"Oh, no! Of course not!" she exclaimed.

"Well, let's go for a stroll. Ya wanna?" He stood up and replaced his hat in its proper position on his head.

"Very well," Brynn agreed, rising to her feet.

"There's an interesting little rock formation in the crick down here a ways. Come on, you'll like it," he said, taking her hand and pulling her along.

"This is such a lovely area," Brynn sighed as they followed the creek's downward babbling.

"Yep. Now, look here," he instructed, crouching down and peering into the water. "See that?"

Brynn knelt, bending over the edge of the creek's bank and peering into the clear water. She was startled to gasping when she immediately saw her own reflection looking back at her. Not the faint reflection from the water's surface, but an obvious mirrored reflection made by something that lay beneath.

"See. It's a real thick sheet of mica. Works just like a mirror. Ain't that kinda interestin'?" he asked.

"Oh, yes! I've never seen such a large piece before," she agreed.

Michael sat down on his seat and looked around. "This here's one of my favorite places. Just upstream a ways is where Daddy did ol' Black Wolf in."

Brynn looked at him quickly. "This close to town?" she asked.

"Yep. Me and Robert used to play in that ol' cave all the time. We ain't had no Indian trouble since I was a baby. Government packed 'em all off to the reservations." He stood up and drew in a deep breath. "I suppose I better be gettin' you on back to town. Don't want yer daddy comin' after me with a rifle, now do we?"

"I suppose," Brynn mumbled as every ounce of joy exited her body. It had been a dream come true, picnicking with Michael McCall in seclusion. It was over now, and he would go home to his way of life. She looked up as she felt him take her hand, and her breathing quickened as she beheld the serious expression on his face.

"I made sure I drug you off far enough that yer mama won't be callin' for you this time," he whispered as a mischievous grin spread across his face.

"You're right. We better be getting back," Brynn said, wrenching her hand free and walking briskly toward the tree.

Having returned to the empty box lunch and picnic blanket that still lay in the grass beneath the willow, she turned to face him as he said, "I'm sorry, Miss Brynn. I guess I shouldn't press you like that."

Brynn leaned back against the tree's trunk and sighed heavily. "It's just that I know you're only teasing me. You shouldn't play with people's feelings like that, Michael." Realizing that his first name rather than *Mr. McCall* had slipped from her lips, she looked up to find him staring intently at her. He moved closer to her, removing the toothpick from his mouth and flicking it away, and she realized that she was trapped between the tree trunk and the gorgeous specimen of masculinity.

"Now, I like that. You just mighta got away this time…" he mumbled as he bent toward her. "If you hadn't a called me Michael, Brynn." He bent toward her until his mouth was a breath away from her own. "I suppose you'd slap me if'n I tried to steal a kiss, right?"

"No," she breathed.

"Wouldn't matter either way, Brynn," he whispered.

His kiss was like warm cider on a winter's day. As his lips pressed firmly against her own, Brynn felt the blissful warmth of the kiss fill her body. She sensed his hand on her face and realized that he cupped her chin in it, pulling her toward him as if it were possible for her face to be closer. His voice saying her name echoed through her mind as her senses thrilled to his touch.

"You gonna slap me, Brynn?" he whispered, interrupting their shared interaction.

"No," she managed to mouth, though no sound escaped her lips.

Her chin still held gently in his hand, he tipped her head to one side, and she jumped as his mouth placed a moist caress on her neck just below her ear. Reflexively her hands gripped his forearm attached to the hand that held her face as goose bumps broke over her body like a tumultuous tidal wave. He released her chin and, taking her hands in his own, laced his fingers with hers. Then he pulled her body to his, holding their hands at her back as his mouth fiercely commanded hers to return the unrestrained ardor it incited.

His kiss was powerful, yet still bridled, and when he released her hands and let his arms fully embrace her, she instinctively allowed her hands to wander caressively over his broad shoulders. Brynn had never imagined that being held and kissed in such a manner would be such blissful delight. She knew that she was experiencing true and unequaled ecstasy at the hand of Michael McCall. His breathing was quickened and strained as his mouth guided hers in the impassioned exchange. He ended their bandying with softer, less threatening kisses, finally sighing heavily as he released her and straightened, clearing his throat.

"I better get you headed home," he said, mumbling something under his breath about having to talk with her daddy if they didn't leave then.

As they traveled back toward town, Michael asked, "You plannin' on bein' some big singer like your mama when you grow up?"

Brynn looked at him quickly, irritated by his inference that she was still a child. It vexed her so that he would even intimate it that she snapped back a little more defensively than she meant to. "No. My ambitions go more toward gaining a firm education. Women aren't as accepted as they should be in the universities, and I plan to be the exception."

"You mean, you plan on having a profession of your own?"

"Yes. Someday."

He became oddly quiet then, and Brynn wondered if she had angered him by her snapping remark.

"And you?" she asked finally, attempting to rekindle the conversation.

"Me?" he mumbled. "I'm just a poor farm boy, remember?" he spat sharply. "I ain't got no ambition 'cept livin' a long life full of hard work and fun, Miss Clarkston."

"I didn't mean to imply that—" she began.

"Ah, I know, I know. I fly off the handle too all quick. You just go on and be whatever you want, Brynn. An opera singer, university professor, or rich man's wife. It's your life to live, now ain't it?" he muttered.

"I don't want any of those things," Brynn exclaimed. A sense of panic was beginning to rise within her, and she didn't know why.

"You deserve those things. A girl like you…well, you ain't meant for these parts and the harshness that sometimes goes along with it. I don't know what your daddy was thinkin' movin' you all out here."

"He was thinking quite clearly, and I've only just now come to realize it," Brynn muttered. A thousand thoughts were flying about in her mind then. She remembered the noise and chaos of the city. The smell of burning tobacco, coal, garbage, stale liquor. She remembered the worry and fatigue that was always evident on her father's face when he returned very late each evening from the university. She noted the bronze and healthy pink that colored Sierra's and Scottie's faces now that they were able to play outside in the fresh air. She thought of her mother's lovely voice echoing through the house as it hummed or sang a tune almost constantly. Her mother's singing had been absent in their city home on a daily basis. She thought of the immaculately dressed young men that would come to call. Always clean and tidy they were, hair slicked flat on their heads, collars so high their ears could perch on the rim of them. She looked over to the indescribably handsome man that held a set of reins and sat next to her. His hair blew back slightly in the breeze, and his Levi's were clean yet worn, especially, she had noticed, in the seat. She blushed and scolded herself inwardly for noticing such things as the seat of Michael McCall's Levi's.

"Thank you for purchasing my box lunch, Michael," she said so softly it was nearly a whisper. "I don't know why you choose to be so kind and to…flirt with me so, but I do want to thank you."

"Thank you, Brynn. It was a mighty fine meal," he said bluntly.

"I've done something, haven't I?" she asked. She sensed the change in him, and it frightened her. The teasing, friendly manner she had come to know was gone. In its place was aggravation and distance.

"You ain't done nothin'," he sighed heavily. "Nothin' at all. And I apologize for my behavior back at the crick. It won't happen again."

Brynn felt tears sizzling at the brink of her eyes, and she stated angrily, "Please stop this wagon."

So commandingly did she order it that Michael immediately reined the team to an abrupt halt.

"I knew it," she cried as she fought to withhold the hot moisture gathering profusely in her lovely blue eyes. "I knew you were just a…just a…philanderer! I suppose you do this to every new girl that moves into town! Don't you? Just take her heart firmly in hand and squeeze it to death!"

"Philanderer?" he repeated.

"Yes! Philanderer!" she squealed as she quickly hopped down from the wagon and began marching toward town.

"That's a nasty name, Brynn," he called after her as he too jumped down from the wagon. "I don't take to name-callin'! Especially when it's me bein' called it!"

"And to think!" she shouted, stopping and turning to face him. "To think I let you…surrendered my…let you…actually force yourself on me back there! What a chuckle you must have had at my expense."

"Wait a minute!" Michael growled, taking hold of her arm. "You know that ain't it at all, Brynn. I ain't like that. You know that. It's just that now I realize you got other things in mind than I do."

"I don't. I only said those things because you spoke down to me so!" The tears ran down her cheeks at last as she was no longer able to contain them.

"Oh geez, don't cry, Brynn. I ain't got no backbone when it comes to women crying," he whined, frowning defeatedly.

"I'm not crying. And I am grown up. Whether old men like you think so or not," she said, yanking her arm free and marching forward once again. She gasped as she was suddenly caught in his arms as he pulled her back against his body. "Let me go!" she ordered, struggling in his embrace.

"I know you're grown up, Brynn. And…I believe it's time I started treatin' you that way, ain't it?" he whispered, and her body nearly melted as his mouth placed a moist, persistent kiss on her neck just below her ear. "You see," he whispered, brushing her hair aside and placing another kiss at the back of her neck. "I wasn't sure… you are young, whether or not you want to admit it, darlin'. Young enough that these sorts of situations might make you bolt and run. I have to watch my step. You understand that, don't you?"

"I understand that you're using me for your own amusement! You must think I'm terribly naive!" she sniffled.

Michael turned Brynn to face him. "I know I say a lot of teasin' things, Brynn. It's my way. But I ain't funnin' when I kiss you. That's just the man in me bein' a bit impatient, I guess." He brushed a strand of hair from her face and wiped a tear from her cheek with his thumb. "There's somethin' about you, Brynn Clarkston. Somethin' that gets ol' Michael McCall completely wrapped around your little finger." He kissed her forehead tenderly. "Don't you see? You could get me to do anything you wanted just by lookin' at me with them beautiful eyes of yours. First chance I get, I'm comin' over to talk to your daddy about you. We gotta get that new porch swing broke in, don't we?"

"You're teasing me," Brynn said.

Michael chuckled and pulled Brynn against him tightly. "I'm not! Dang, you're a humble little thing, you know that?"

"Do you mean it, Michael? You're not just mocking me because you know I…" Brynn stammered.

"Because I know what?" he prodded.

"Because you know," she repeated.

"Because I know that when I'm not around you think about me all the time? Because I know that sometimes when you're alone you wish I was holdin' you like I am now? Because I know that when I kiss you, you wish it never had to end?" he whispered as he tipped her tear-streaked face up to meet his own handsome one. Brynn's mouth dropped open slightly in awe at his words fitting her feelings for him so perfectly. Michael chuckled at the perplexed expression on her face. "You're wonderin' how I could know all that, ain't you?" His thumb traced her parted lips tenderly. "I know 'cause they're the same things I think about you, Miss Brynn Clarkston." Then, as his thumb continued to caress her lips, he whispered, "Now let's put that flytrap to use. You done caught somethin' this time, darlin'." And his mouth met hers in a moist and deeply sincere kiss. She was satisfied then with a sure knowledge that he was, indeed, honest in his feelings for her. His kiss was strong and commanding yet filled with integrity. Brynn knew then that by some blessed divine stroke of fate, she had managed to capture the attention of the impeccably developed, both physically and inwardly, Michael McCall.

CHAPTER SIX

The next morning, Brynn awoke with the euphoric knowledge that Michael found her interesting. Yes, attractive even. Any other young woman, say Annabelle Barrington for instance, would no doubt become slightly puffed up in her own vanity faced with such a wonderful revelation. Yet Brynn, blessed with boundless humility, still found herself doubtful that she had even experienced the previous afternoon's events in the company of Michael.

Sitting erect in her bed suddenly, she muttered to herself, "Maybe I simply dreamed it all!"

"Brynn! Quickly! Get up!" came Sierra's excited voice from the hallway. "The bank has been robbed, Brynn! Our very own bank! Right here in town!"

Brynn dressed quickly, and when she heard a knocking on the door, she rushed out to see who would be visiting.

"Oh, Ophelia!" Malaina McCall cried as she entered the Clarkston house. "Michael's missing! We can't find him! We haven't seen him since last evening at dinner, and that monster Sheriff Barnes has the audacity to imply that he may have been involved in the bank robbery late last night!"

"What?" Brynn gasped.

"Has he been here, Brynn darling?" Malaina asked frantically. "I thought he might be here!"

"No," Brynn answered, horribly anxious about Michael's well-being.

"He was here somewhat late last night, Malaina," Ophelia informed her friend. "He spoke to Richard about—"

"Yes, yes. I know. He spoke with us about it beforehand. Do you know where he went after that?" Malaina asked, dabbing at a tear on her cheek.

"No, I don't," Ophelia admitted as she began wringing her apron nervously.

"Whatever shall we do?" Malaina cried. "He's my baby! I'm so worried. He wouldn't do this unless something was terribly wrong! Perhaps he's been hurt somehow."

As the day wore on, the sheriff and his deputy, Clyde Tate, searched the countryside for the men who had robbed the bank. They looked for Michael McCall as well.

"Why was he here last night, Daddy?" Brynn asked her father as they sat together at the kitchen table that afternoon.

"I think you know why, young lady. At least I would assume that you did. Otherwise, I would judge you to be very naive indeed," Richard said, smiling at his daughter.

"What did he say?" Brynn asked, trying to appear casually curious.

"I think I'll let you hear it from him, sweetheart. He'll be back soon enough." And he was. In a mere few minutes.

"Michael!" Brynn exclaimed upon opening the door and finding him standing before her. "Michael! Your family is worried sick! Where have you—"

"I need to see your daddy right away, Brynn. Quickly," he interrupted, pushing his way into the house and closing the door behind him.

Brynn noticed immediately the profuse perspiration that trickled down his temples. Furthermore, his clothes were dirty, and his frown was frighteningly serious. "All right," she said.

She returned several moments later with her father, who immediately questioned the young man upon seeing him.

"Where have you been, Michael? Sheriff Barnes suspects you of taking the bank," Richard Clarkston stated.

"I'm sure he's lookin' for someone to pin it on, sir. He done it himself," Michael growled.

"What?" Brynn asked in disbelief.

"He done it, Mr. Clarkston. I seen him. I seen Sheriff Barnes and Clyde Tate comin' out of the bank late last night. That's why he's lookin' for me. He shot me, so he's probably wonderin' if I'm still breathin'," Michael explained bluntly.

"Where are you hit, Michael?" Richard asked, concern in his voice.

"Oh, it ain't hardly nothin', sir," Michael mumbled. But Brynn gasped again as her father took Michael by the shoulders and turned him around, revealing the back of his shirt, which was soaked with blood originating at his left shoulder.

"I need you to run out to my daddy's place and tell him to ride over to Telluride and get some law that ain't gone bad," Michael explained. "I'm sure Barnes is watchin' my family like a hawk, and I can't go there. Also, I'm in need of some bandages...maybe some soap? Then I'll be on my way."

"You're not going anywhere, Michael!" Richard ordered. "Brynn and Mrs. Clarkston need to clean that wound out! Of course I'll let your family know you're well...but I'll go for help. It would be less suspicious."

"I can't let you do that, Mr. Clarkston. This ain't your trouble," Michael stated.

"If the law officers in this town are crooked, it's everyone's trouble, young man."

"Daddy, Mother won't be home for some time. She's gone down with Sierra and Scottie to check on Mrs. Johnson," Brynn stammered. Michael was incredibly pale and appeared to be dangerously fatigued. "But I can do this. You need to leave now. There's no time to stand around."

"True. I'll be off then." Taking the young man's hand in his own,

Richard Clarkston shook it firmly. "I knew something like this was about. You're too good a man to be involved in thievery."

"I hope I'm not bringin' any danger down on your family, Mr. Clarkston," Michael muttered.

"I'd have hung you myself if you hadn't come to me," Richard assured him. "Clean him up well, Brynn. That bullet's been in there far too long. It didn't come out the other side, did it, Michael?"

Michael shook his head, frowning. "It's in there all right. I can feel it just under the skin of the front side here."

"Dig it out, Brynn," her father instructed as he took his hat from the hook behind the door. "You must remove it, do you understand?"

Brynn nodded obediently as she stared with terrified anxiety at the battered man before her.

"Be quick, Brynn. Then hide him well. They might suspect he'd come here for help." Brynn watched as her father closed the door behind him without another word. She wanted to cry out to him, to stop him from leaving her with such a terrifying burden as tending to the wound. But instead she took Michael's hand in her own and turned toward the kitchen.

"I can feel it, there…just under the skin, Brynn," he said. "I can't figure why it didn't just shoot on out. Hurts like the dickens, though."

"Sit down here," Brynn ordered as she pulled a chair away from the kitchen table for him. In silence, she went to the cupboard where her mother stored the medical supplies. Taking the things that she guessed she would need, she laid them on the table and lit the fire in the oven to warm the water in the kettle.

"Remove your shirt please, Michael," she commanded.

"Yeah, you like me best half-neked, don't ya?" he teased. The grimace on his face made it obvious that he was in great pain as he struggled to remove the shirt.

Picking up a pair of scissors that she had laid out, Brynn took hold of his collar and began cutting the shirt straight down the back. "It's ruined anyway, right? What's the point of causing you unnecessary discomfort?" she muttered to herself as she removed the bloody fabric from his body. She gasped when she saw the wound. It was ghastly and completely caked with dried blood. "Oh, Michael," she whispered as she felt tears brimming in her eyes.

"Go at it from the front, Brynn. Like your daddy said. Just cut me where I show you, and you'll find it easy," he mumbled.

It was only at that moment that she realized what both her father and Michael were instructing. She must cut into his flesh, scar his beautiful body, if she were going to even attempt to extract the bullet. Sitting down in a chair across from him, she said, "I-I can't. I can't possibly—"

"You have to, darlin'," he growled, taking hold of her arm firmly. "I can't do it myself. I'm too tired and weak. Listen to me. If I pass out..."

"What?" she exclaimed in alarm. "You can't! I need you to—"

"If I pass out," he began again, squeezing her arm firmly, "just dig that little cuss outta there. Wash the wound good with hot soap and water, back and front. Soap up your finger real good and clean it inside…as deep as you can go, darlin'. Now, don't lose yer head on me, Brynn. You want me to live long enough to corner you under that ol' willer outside of town again, don't ya?"

Brynn began shaking her head slowly as the tears leaped from her eyes and ran down her cheeks. "I-I…"

Reaching down, Michael pulled a large knife from his boot, offering it to her. "Here. Is that water hot yet? Dunk this in there, then I'll show you where to cut me."

Brushing the tears from her cheeks, Brynn did as Michael instructed. Sitting in a chair across from him once more, she said, "Very well."

"I'm gonna lay myself on the floor, darlin'. Might flinch too hard otherwise. You sit on my belly and—" he began.

"I can't possibly!" she shrieked.

Again he took hold of her arm firmly. "Brynn, ain't nobody else in this house, right?"

"No. They're all gone."

"Then somebody has to help hold me down just in case I turn out to be a pansy while you're cuttin'," he explained.

"You've never in your life been a pansy," she said.

"Ain't never had a bullet cut outta me in my life neither," he answered as he stretched out on Mrs. Clarkston's immaculate kitchen floor.

With great reservation, Brynn sat across his stomach and stared anxiously at the area of his chest he indicated.

"See there, it's bruisin'. Just cut like this," he instructed, motioning horizontally across the area. "You ready? Can't feel much worse than gettin' shot in the first place, right?" he said, attempting to chuckle lightly.

"I can't! I can't cause you such pain!" Brynn cried.

"Darlin'…ain't nothin' could hurt more'n it already does."

"Well, shouldn't I get you something to bite on?" Brynn asked. "A stick? Maybe a wooden spoon would do."

"Darlin', if'n I can keep my wits about me when you're this close, then I can certainly hold still while you're diggin' a bullet outta my body. 'Cause if there's one thing I've mastered since you moved into town, it's self-control." He attempted to chuckle at his own teasing. Then, taking the hem of her skirt and wrapping his right hand in it tightly, he said, "Okay now. Let's get it over with." Then he closed his fantastic blue eyes and waited.

Taking the knife firmly in her unsteady hand, Brynn cut the area quickly. Michael flinched slightly and without opening his eyes said, "You're gonna have to do more'n scratch it, Brynn."

She felt his grip tighten on her skirt, and her own tears spilled freely onto his chest as she tried once more, pushing the tip of the knife deeper into the fresh wound she had made. His body tensed fiercely beneath her own weight as she did so, and he grunted slightly. Brynn was nearly undone as she watched the bright red blood begin to trickle down onto the kitchen floor.

"It may be hard to get a hold on. You may have to make that cut bigger," he muttered in a voice that revealed an endurance of great pain.

"I'll get it," she whispered and pressed the wound with her thumb, trying to feel the threatening bullet there. "I feel it!" she exclaimed.

"Then dig it out, girl! It hurts like…" he mumbled.

With intense trepidation Brynn inserted her index finger into the wound. Immediately she felt the hardness of metal.

"Come on, Brynn! It's gonna take more'n one finger!" he shouted as his body stiffened.

Quickly she stuck her thumb into the wound as well. Oh! What a terrible feeling it was to be probing around in his wounded flesh with the knowledge that she was causing him such intense pain. Then, she felt the metal between her thumb and finger and yanked it hard, successfully extracting it from his wound. It slipped from her fingers, which were wet with his blood, and made a clicking sound as it skipped across the floor, leaving a trail of blood-red dots.

Michael sighed heavily, and his grip on the fabric of her skirt loosened. "Now clean it out quick. It hurts like…" he mumbled again.

Quickly Brynn did as he had previously instructed. Once she had washed and rinsed both wounds, she bandaged him and helped him to sit against the wall. His breathing was labored as if he'd just run a great distance, and the perspiration still hung in heavy beads on his face and forehead.

"I think I just need a glass of water, and I'll be fine, darlin'," he mumbled. His eyes closed again as Brynn rushed to the pump at the sink. Returning hastily, she held the glass to his lips as he drank. At some point she tipped the glass too much, and the water spilled over his chest.

"I'm sorry," she apologized, wiping at the water with her hand.

"Feels good. Ain't had me a tub since day 'fore yesterday," he whispered.

Brynn knew he was tired. Retrieving a pillow from the sofa in the parlor, she helped him to lay down on the kitchen floor, too afraid to move him any more than that motion alone required.

As his breathing steadied and slowed, Brynn knew he was resting, if somewhat fitfully. Going to the pump, she wet a cloth, wringing it out before using it to bathe his face, arms, and chest. When she'd finished, she glanced about her, noting the mess her mother's kitchen was in. The thought went through her mind that her mother would be nothing less than livid when she saw the chaos and blood, but propping herself up against the wall next to Michael, she closed her eyes for a moment. Removing the bullet and cleaning the wounds had taken every bit of strength from her.

"Wow! What a mess! Look at all that blood!"

Brynn's eyes fluttered open to behold her mother and Sierra standing over her, their mouths gaping open in astonishment. Scottie was running around the room, investigating Michael's blood-stained shirt, blood-stained knife, and the horrendous pool of blood that had begun to dry on the floor where Brynn had first laid Michael to work on him.

"Brynn!" Ophelia Clarkston whispered in awe at the sight that lay before her. "Is he…is he…"

"Is he dead?" Scottie finished for her, squatting down next to Michael and studying his face curiously.

"No," Brynn answered. Then, jumping to her feet, she spilled out the story Michael had told her father, explaining where her father had gone.

Ophelia inhaled determinedly and said, "You've got to take him out of here. Sheriff Barnes was asking me only ten minutes ago if you had seen Michael today. He said he'd like to come by and talk with you. Quickly, Brynn! Wake him! You must get him away from here," her mother ordered. Ophelia, being the courageous, cool-headed woman that she was, saw the danger and knew the solution. "Sierra, quickly…clean up this mess! Scottie, take that shirt out and drop it down the hole in the outhouse! Hurry! Brynn, get him out of here!"

"I'm sorry, Mrs. Clarkston," Michael said, pulling himself up to a sitting position. "I shouldn't have come here."

"Don't be ridiculous, Michael! Of course you should've come here. We know just what to do, don't we, Brynn?" Brynn nodded. "Don't come home until you're certain he's all right."

"I don't want her helpin' me any longer, Mrs. Clarkston. It's too dangerous. I'll be fine on my own," Michael grumbled, retrieving his bloodied knife from the floor and returning it to its place in his boot. But as he stood and tried to walk forward, he stumbled, barely catching himself on the table before falling.

"Quickly, Brynn. Get him away from here," Ophelia ordered. "They'll surely find him."

Brynn took Michael's right arm and placed it around her shoulders. "Come along, Michael. Hurry."

"Hurry, she says," he muttered as he stumbled toward the back door. "Just get me to where I'll be all right. Then I want you to get right home."

Evening was descending by the time Brynn was able to help Michael to the cave. She was thankful that the weather was warm, for she knew she would never find her way home in the dark even if she had harbored any intention of leaving Michael while he was injured or in danger, which she didn't.

"It's near the crick, darlin'. I'll be needin' water. Now you get home," Michael mumbled. His speech was slurred and unsteady. Brynn helped him to sit down inside the cave against one wall.

"I'm not leaving, Michael. And you are in no condition to fight me about that fact," Brynn whispered as she placed her hand on his forehead, which was uncomfortably warm.

"You got me there, darlin'," he admitted. "'Sides, I always wanted to spend some time alone with you in a dark cave." In the next moment, his breathing slowed, and Brynn knew he was at long last resting.

He would sleep deeply for some time, she was sure. And so, taking advantage of her time alone with him, she ran one hand caressively over his pale face. "I love you, Michael McCall," she whispered. He was so hurt and so handsome and so wonderful that tears filled her eyes once more at the thought of his having such considerate feelings toward her.

The rattle woke her instantly, for even though her own ears had never actually heard the sound before, she knew instinctively what originated it.

"Michael?" she whispered. But there came no reply, and Brynn sensed that he was not in the cave. Sitting up slowly, she turned and saw the snake coiled just behind her. Its hideous tongue flickered as its tail stood erect rattling. She knew it would strike, and she turned her back to it immediately, screaming when she felt the snake's fangs sink into the back of her left shoulder.

"Brynn?" came Michael's voice from just outside the cave's mouth. "Brynn!" he said again as he realized what had happened. Brynn watched, still stunned as Michael stepped firmly on the snake's head, pulled the knife from his boot, and sliced the reptile's head off swiftly. Then, spitting on the knife and wiping it on his pants, he shoved Brynn forward onto her stomach and sat himself soundly on her legs.

"Hold still," he ordered in a growl as he ripped the fabric of her dress, exposing the wound. Brynn bit her lip as she felt him cut her shoulder where the serpent's deadly fangs had pierced her body. Michael sucked on the wound brutally, spitting the blood from his mouth and then repeating the process repeatedly until Brynn could feel a numbing sensation replacing the pain of the bite. Then, quickly turning her over onto her back, he told Brynn emphatically, "It was a small snake, darlin'. You'll be fine. You might get sick, but you ain't done in, do you understand me?"

Brynn nodded and brushed the tears from her cheeks. Sitting up, she looked at the body of the snake, which lay near its decapitated head, still twitching now and again. Michael sat down against the cave wall, his eyes closing for a moment as his head fell forward.

"I shouldn't have left you here alone. I'm sorry," he apologized.

The shoulder where she had been bitten was painful and throbbing, yet Brynn could only think of the pallid lack of color on Michael's face.

"Are you all right, Michael?" she asked, moving toward him.

"No!" he shouted, looking up angrily. "I shoulda never come to your house! This here's all my fault! I shoulda tried to get home! I thought I was gonna drop dead of a heart attack when I come back in here and saw that danged snake had bit you! It took ten years offa my life, girl! I still ain't breathin' regular." He wiped the perspiration from his forehead with one hand.

"I meant, how's your shoulder? Are you feeling better than you did last evening?" Brynn asked, deeply touched at the effect her injury had on him.

"Oh, that. It's fine. It's sore, and I feel weak…but I'm fine. You feelin' sick yet?" he asked.

"No," Brynn answered honestly.

"Well, I musta sucked a pint a blood outta you. Maybe you won't get sick. At least, I hope you're well enough that I don't have to carry you home. I'm not sure I'm up to that just yet."

"I'm not going anywhere until it's safe for you to go home as well," Brynn informed him as she studied the torn fabric that hung open, exposing her shoulder.

"You're goin' home right here in a minute, Brynn. This ain't your problem, and I was wrong to drag your family into this. I didn't know what else to do, 'cause we can't let Barnes and Tate get away with this. I'm sure they're the ones that's been doin' all the robbin' in this area. I hope your daddy can get back soon. But I'm gettin' you home right now," he added, standing up again. He swayed slightly, and Brynn rose, taking hold of his arm to help support him.

"You're staying right here, and I am too, Michael McCall," she ordered. "You've lost a lot of blood, not to mention enduring the constant pain. Sit down here and rest."

"I promised your mama, Brynn," he mumbled as his hands went to his head. He swayed again, and Brynn was able to push him into a sitting position.

"My mother knows what kind of shape you're in. And it's no shape to be moving around," Brynn told him.

"You better check them wounds and make sure there ain't no infection startin'," he mumbled, closing his eyes as his head fell back against the cave wall.

Carefully Brynn removed the bandages that she had placed on his shoulder the night before. Fresh ones were needed, but the wounds, hideous as they were, looked clean and were beginning to heal.

"I meant the ones on your own shoulder, darlin'," Michael chuckled.

"Oh," Brynn realized.

Michael stood up slowly and pulled Brynn to her feet. "You still got that bar of soap that you used on me in your apron pocket?" he asked, extending his hand toward her.

"Um…yes," she said, withdrawing the soap from its place in her apron and placing it in his hand. "But I have to finish your bandages."

"First things first, Brynn. I didn't clean that knife too good 'fore I used it on you." Taking her hand, he led her from the cave and toward the stream. "It's gonna sting, you realize," he told her as he wet the bar of soap in the water and rubbed it between his hands, making a thick lather. Brynn nodded, and he began washing the wound. "Your daddy would shoot me in the kneecaps if he seen me rubbin' your bare skin like this," he muttered to himself as his hands and fingers worked to clean the wound. "But then again, I'm sure he wouldn't want no infection startin' in it."

Brynn winced at the pain and stinging that the necessary process caused, but at his touch, even in this specific circumstance, she asked her questioning thoughts out loud. "What were you doing at my home the night you were shot?"

"I was talkin' to your daddy," he answered plainly.

"About what?"

"About you."

"What about me?" she asked as her hopes began to soar.

"I done told you I was gonna have me a talk with him, Brynn. Didn't you take me serious?" Michael chuckled.

"What did you talk to him about? I mean…regarding me?" she asked, wincing as he scrubbed at her wound with the palm of his hand.

"I done told him the truth! What else? I told him that you were a brazen woman who tried to corrupt me under that ol' willer outside a town."

Brynn gasped, turning to face him, her mouth dropping open in horrified astonishment at his remark. Michael laughed, entertained by her expression.

"Oh, darlin'," he chuckled, taking her in his arms and pulling her against his warm body. "I'm only teasin' you. Of course I didn't tell your daddy that. Even though it's the truth."

"It is not," Brynn defended herself, letting herself be held tightly in his embrace.

"I'm sorry, Brynn. I'm sorry I've put you in danger. I never would've dragged you into this if I'd been in my right mind," he said as he stroked her hair gently.

"There's nowhere on earth I'd rather be, Michael," Brynn confessed in an inaudible whisper.

"What's that?" he asked.

"I said…I'm the one who dragged you out here," she answered.

"I owe you my life," he whispered.

"I owe you mine," she whispered, looking up into his handsome face, which wore an expression of tender appreciation.

Sighing heavily, Michael kissed her forehead gently. "Let's get this rinsed off," he said, releasing her and squatting down next to the creek. Filling his hands with water, he refreshed himself by drinking the cool liquid. Then he pulled Brynn down next to him and rinsed her wound, patting it dry with the torn fabric of her dress. Brynn's flesh tingled as Michael placed a light kiss on the bareness of her shoulder.

"I can't spend another night in that cave with you, Brynn," he whispered as his mouth caressed her neck teasingly. "Believe me…I have to get you home."

"Do you think badly of me because I'm not trying to…"

"'Cause you're not trying to get away from me?" he asked, turning her face toward his. Brynn nodded. "I'm glad you're not trying to get away, darlin'. I ain't got as much strength as usual to hang on to you." And this time Brynn didn't struggle when his mouth found hers. Instead she returned his kiss thoroughly, rejoicing in the power and passion that he radiated. His skin was smooth and warm and soft beneath her hands. He sat down promptly on the ground, pulling her onto his lap and cradling her in his arms as his mouth worked an enchanting spell of ecstatic passion with its skillful kisses.

Suddenly, however, Brynn felt the first horrid wrenching feeling in her stomach. Pulling away from Michael quickly, she doubled over as a sickening nausea engulfed her.

"Come on, darlin'," Michael said, helping her to her feet. "Let's get back to shelter and have you lay down."

"I'm fine, really," Brynn assured him as large beads of perspiration appeared across her forehead.

"Sorry little cuss," Michael muttered, glaring at the decapitated snake as he helped Brynn to sit down against the cave's inner wall. "I think we oughta eat it for breakfast."

Brynn clamped her hand over her mouth to help stop the heaving in her stomach at the thought of eating a snake. Michael put a hand to Brynn's forehead then said, "Come dark, I'm goin' back to town to fetch your mama and see if your daddy's back yet. I don't want to be draggin' you all over though. Here, lie down," he instructed her.

"What are you doing?" Brynn cried, startled when she felt Michael tugging at the hem of her petticoats.

As Brynn's petticoats slipped down from her waist and over her feet, Michael said, "Well, darlin', you need somethin' soft for your head. And unless you're wantin' to have a purty quick lesson in anatomy…I best not be takin' anything else of mine off." Wadding up the garment, he tucked it gently under her head. "I'm thinkin' maybe you're just hungry and that's addin' to your feelin' so poorly. I'll go out and dig you somethin' up to munch on."

"Oh, no! Stay here!" Brynn pleaded as fear gripped her.

"I'll be right back. There's some wild strawberries growin' not far off. Rest your little head, darlin'." And he left.

CHAPTER SEVEN

"So," Brynn said as she ate the last strawberry Michael had gathered earlier in the day, "what did you talk to my daddy about?"

Michael was fatigued, and his injuries were dealing great pain to him. Brynn could see that he was in need of sleep. Yet he would not rest. He had been correct about her need for nourishment, and after having eaten the delicious sun-warmed berries, she had felt quite recovered. He worried her. He was perspiring greatly again, and the color had left his face once more.

"Oh, horses, bridles, nails. Things the like," he mumbled as his eyes closed for a moment. "Did I ever tell you that my mama and daddy spent a night together in this cave 'fore they was married?" he asked, eyes still closed, changing the subject.

"No. Tell me," Brynn prodded, scooting up next to him. As she watched the sun already starting to set, she wondered why Michael was so evasive about revealing the particulars of his conversation with her father. She sighed, delighted by the brilliant pinks and purples that colored the sky like a freshly rendered oil painting.

Michael cleared his throat, eyes still closed. "You remember the ol' Indian that Daddy did in, right?"

"Mmmm hmmm," Brynn answered.

"There was a big blizzard goin' on, and Daddy couldn't get Mama home. She was in danger of freezin' to death, so he brung her in here to warm her up." He chuckled then, and his eyes opened as he turned toward Brynn. "Can you imagine how irate my mama musta been when my daddy forced her to put on a pair of men's red flannels?"

Brynn smiled and put a hand to his brow to wipe the beads of perspiration away. "What happened?"

"Daddy won a nickel," he said, his voice dropping and his words muddled. "I can't keep my eyes open, Brynn," he mumbled as his beautiful blue eyes closed once again.

"Don't try. You need rest," Brynn whispered to him as his breathing slowed and he fell asleep at long last. Folding her petticoats neatly, she pushed him gently, and he unconsciously leaned over as she helped his massive form to lie flat on the ground, his head placed on the petticoat pillow.

They couldn't build a fire, for no doubt the light would be seen by anyone riding near. Until Brynn's father was able to return with honest lawmen, it wasn't safe to reveal their location. Fortunately it was a warm summer night, and a fire wasn't needed. But as the sun set completely, the moonlight did not penetrate very far into the cave, and the wilderness noises and darkness began to unsettle Brynn. She had been far too fatigued the night before to be bothered. But tonight, as the wound in her shoulder throbbed and she sat next to the seriously injured and weakened man she adored, her strange surroundings frightened her.

She jumped, startled by the sound of an owl hooting somewhere just outside the mouth of the cave. She startled again as something warm touched her hand.

"It's just the night sounds, darlin'," Michael mumbled as his hand traveled up her arm caressively. "If you listen, you'll find a kind of strange security in them." She sensed he was pulling himself to a sitting position as he added, "Hear the crick? Don't that sound soothin'?" He tugged at her arm, and she scooted closer to him. "Hear that? That's a little ol' barn owl."

As Michael pulled Brynn against his warm body, she melted to him, completely comforted and knowing she was safe in his arms. "Please be well," she whispered to him.

"I'm fine, Brynn. Just needed a few extra winks," he assured her.

"Listen. You can hear Uncle Baker's new calf bawlin'. We ain't far from his farm, you know."

Brynn could hear something that was strange to her ears. It bothered her at first with its sad sound until she heard a low call that was similar.

"See? His mama found him fast," Michael whispered. "How's that shoulder?" he asked as his hand traveled gently over the sore area on Brynn's back.

"It's in much better shape than yours is," Brynn reminded him.

"I'm goin' then," he said. "You'll be fine here, Brynn." He made an effort to stand.

"Oh! No!" she pleaded, clinging tightly to his arm. "Don't leave me! I'll go with you!"

"I don't want you with me if I run into trouble, Brynn," he told her firmly as he stood completely and walked toward the cave's entrance.

"Please, Michael!" she cried, going after him. As he stepped out of the cave, the moonlight shone brightly on his tall, attractive form.

He smiled down at her and said, "I'm feelin' purty perky now, darlin'. And, well, I think it's best if we both get home as soon as we can."

"Well, of course, but—" she began.

"I told you before, Brynn," he said firmly, brushing her cheek with the back of his hand. "I can't spend another night here with you. It's too…too…I need to get you home or else your daddy's gonna change his mind."

"About what?" she asked, suddenly horribly curious.

"If they catch me, they won't get you. So if I ain't back by sunup… you start on home by yourself. Just follow the crick down. It goes right past town." He started to walk away.

"Michael?" she called, reaching out and taking hold of his arm. "Hurry. Please. I'm not very brave."

He reached out and took her quickly in his embrace. "Now that there's a lie if I ever heard one." He took her throat in one powerful hand, caressing her jaw with his thumb. Then without delay his delicious, masterful kiss was hers once more. His arms tightened around her like a vise, and his impassioned, demanding mouth seemed unable to quench his desire for her response. Interrupting their affections, he took her chin in hand and said, "Do you understand why we have to get back, Brynn?"

"Yes. To find out if my father's back so that you can be free from danger," she answered.

"No," he stated firmly. He bent, kissing her again with such intensity that his unshaven face scratched her own soft one. His mouth moved to her neck, kissing it briefly before finding the bareness of her exposed shoulder. "I'm a strong man, Brynn. But even the strongest men have their weaknesses. You're mine. Do you understand?"

"Yes," she answered, at last admitting to herself that his implication did indeed point in her direction.

He turned and left abruptly. When she could no longer see him in the dark of the night, Brynn returned to the cave and waited.

"Well, looky, looky. I believe we got the bait, Sheriff."

Brynn opened her eyes and gasped instantly as she looked up to see Clyde Tate staring down at her, a mocking smile branded across his face.

"We figured you woulda helped the boy out, Miss Clarkston," Sheriff Barnes chuckled. "But where's he run off to?"

"He's gone," Brynn stated. "He went to—"

"He left you here all by your lonesome, Miss Clarkston?" Sheriff Barnes asked as he reached out, pulled her roughly to her feet, and tugged at her torn dress. Brynn slapped his hand, then his face. He only continued to chuckle. "He'll be back, I've no doubt. Ol' Michael McCall wouldn't leave you here alone too long. He's too much of a danged gentleman for that. Besides, I bet he's wantin' to get his money's worth where you're concerned anyway."

"Oh, that's right. That ol' boy paid…what was it? Ten dollars for you, girl?" Clyde Tate asked, smiling impishly.

"I think it were fifteen total," Sheriff Barnes answered.

"What are you talking about?" Brynn snapped irritatedly.

"At the box lunch the other day. Michael gave ol' Beevis ten dollars to buy Miss Annabelle. Then he paid five for you. That's fifteen, I reckon."

"He's not coming back," Brynn said. "He's gone to some town up north to find some honest law officers."

Brynn winced and put her hand to the cheek that Sheriff Barnes had slapped brutally at that moment. "He'll be back. He's got his hat tipped for you, girl. What? You think the whole town is blind?"

"More'n likely. None of us saw through your yeller hide," Michael said from behind the two men.

Both men spun around to see Michael McCall facing them from the cave's opening.

"Michael!" Brynn cried. She was terrified now that he had been found by Sheriff Barnes and Tate. And he was alone!

"Leave her be, Barnes. You ain't got no fight with her," Michael said, frowning disgustedly at the two men.

"No. But we do with you. And I know if it weren't for the fact that this little filly is in our company, you'd put up a fight. You McCalls think you can lick anybody," Sheriff Barnes said.

"That's 'cause we can," Michael growled.

"Maybe. That's why we're glad we found your little petunie here first. You ain't gonna give us no trouble if she's in the middle, now are you?" Sheriff Barnes caressed Brynn's exposed shoulder lewdly.

"You touch her again, Barnes, and you're dead where you stand," Michael threatened.

Barnes and Tate both began laughing. "Look at you, McCall. You look like something the cat dragged in! You ain't in no shape to be a threatenin' us," Tate chuckled.

Brynn's mind was whirling. She knew they were right. Michael was battered and weakened. He couldn't possibly take them both on and triumph. She would be their tool to destroy him. But she was wrong. Michael lunged forward suddenly, kicking Barnes squarely in the stomach and laying Tate out on the cave floor with one swift blow of his powerful fist. Instantly Brynn dashed through the mouth of the cave, having seen the opportunity to escape provided by Michael.

"Come on! Annie's gone for help!" Michael cried as he took her hand and began running around to the other side of the rock formation that had housed them. Brynn heard the gunshot and saw Michael flinch, but he still pulled her with him. "Here! Get down!" he told her as he shoved her behind a large stone. With his back against the rock, he said, "I've gotta get you out of here!"

Brynn was petrified with horror when she saw the blood coming from a fresh wound at Michael's side. "Michael! You've been—" she began.

"It's only a graze. Let's go." Then, taking her hand again, he pulled her into an opening in between the rocks. A tree grew near the opening, and Brynn could discern at once that it would hide the crevice perfectly. Pulling her tightly against him, Michael said, "Sshh."

In the next moment, Barnes and Tate appeared and looked around carefully. "Where'd they go to?" Barnes growled. "There ain't nowhere to go!"

"It's that danged McCall blood. They's slipperier than snakes," Tate mumbled.

Brynn clung tightly to Michael. They would kill him if they found him. She knew that. They were ruthless criminals. Reaching down toward his boot, Michael drew the knife from its sheath that was hidden there. He looked at Brynn intently and mouthed, "Stay here." She shook her head adamantly and clung tighter to him. "Stay here!" his lips repeated. And he broke free of her, jumping out from behind the tree and driving the knife into Barnes's rib cage.

"You'll die like a dog!" Tate shouted as he fired. Michael fell backward, another fresh flesh wound vivid across his right forearm, and Tate chuckled triumphantly as he leveled his gun at the fallen hero. "You cocky pile of—"

His words were silenced as Michael threw his knife with perfect accuracy, sending it flying swiftly through the air and striking Tate squarely in the chest. The man stumbled forward and then fell to the ground motionless. Michael collapsed where he lay, and Brynn rushed over to him, falling to her knees at his side.

"Brynn!" Richard Clarkston called.

"Daddy! Quickly! He's been hurt again. Hurry!" Brynn cried as she cradled Michael's head in her lap.

Richard Clarkston, Jackson McCall, and two strangers wearing badges dismounted their horses. "Let's get him into town to the doctor," Jackson said as Richard helped him lift his son onto a horse. Jackson's expression showed plainly his worry and concern for his son. His face had paled immediately upon seeing Michael's condition, and Brynn wiped her tears on her soiled sleeve as Jackson's strong hands stroked Michael's hair. "Hang on there, son," he said. "Your daddy's come for ya now."

Barnes, still alive, raised his head, pointed his gun at Michael's limp form, and said, "That boy's under arrest."

Brynn watched as the brutally handsome father of the brutally handsome son walked to where the sheriff lay. "You dirty, yeller dog," Jackson mumbled just before his powerful fist met the man's jaw, rendering him unconscious once more.

CHAPTER EIGHT

"Wow! Look at all the bloody cuts and stuff!" Scottie exclaimed as Michael began rebuttoning his shirt after showing the boy his wounds. The wounds were still very gruesome to look upon, even two days after the doctor had finally been able to tend to them.

"You're so brave, Mr. McCall," Sierra sighed, gazing at him in wonderment.

"I was so glad when Michael found me and we knew the two of you were all right!" Annie exclaimed to Brynn. "I was just on my way to town to talk to your mother, Brynn, when I saw him. And I was so scared when he sent me for help. I thought sure that Sheriff Barnes would know I was up to somethin' when he stopped me on my way into town!" Annie put her hand to her chest as she reminisced the frightening moments.

"It wasn't thinkin' smart when I had Brynn take me to that cave in the first place," Michael said, standing and stretching his stiff limbs. "I shoulda known Barnes woulda thought of that cave sooner or later. Given its history concernin' our family and all."

Brynn nodded. "It's because he came to talk to Daddy that night. If he had stayed home…if…this would've never happened," Brynn mumbled.

"That ain't true at all, Brynn," Annie argued.

"Brynn?" Michael said. "Can I see you outside for a minute?"

"What's that I heard you sayin' to Annie?" he asked once they were outside the Clarkston house.

"It's true. If you had stayed home that night…" she began.

"If I'd a stayed home that night…I never woulda got to spend them nights alone with you," he chuckled flirtatiously, pulling her down so that she sat next to him on the porch swing.

"It's not funny, Michael! What was so important that you had to come out that late to see my daddy?" she cried as tears strolled slowly down her cheeks.

"You're serious, ain't you?" he asked, brushing the tears from her cheeks with his hand. "You're shakin' my confidence here a bit, darlin'."

"How am I shaking your confidence?" Brynn lacked vanity. Likewise, she was still afraid to believe that the fabulously handsome and older man sitting next to her could feel anything beyond friendship toward her. She was completely sincere in her question.

"What do you think I came to see your daddy about that night, Brynn?" he asked.

Brynn dropped her eyes to the ground but spoke the truth even though she faced certain humiliation. "I…I…I was in hopes that you came to ask…to ask if you could…court me," she managed to sputter.

Michael broke into amused laughter. And, humiliated, Brynn stood and began to walk away from him.

Catching her arm and stalling her, however, he said, "Darlin', you've got to be the humblest woman on this earth!"

"What do you mean by that?" she asked sharply.

Michael drew Brynn into his arms, and she struggled, angry with him for laughing at her. But when he quickly flicked the ever-present toothpick from his lips, and his delicious mouth coaxed hers into a tantalizing kiss, she ceased in her effort to flee.

"Don't you know, darlin'?" he whispered as he held her hand to his lips and kissed it tenderly. "I…I couldn't tell you before, during that time we was held up in the cave. I wasn't sure…well, I wasn't sure I'd be around to…" He chuckled and kissed her hand once more. "I asked your daddy if I could marry you."

"What?" Brynn asked, her mouth gaping open in disbelief.

"I knew that first time I saw you in Mrs. Johnson's store that I wanted you. Just you. You're perfect for me. I love you, Brynn Clarkston." Brynn looked away shyly. "You're not thinkin' of breakin' my heart, now are you?" he asked.

"Me? Break your heart?" Brynn asked.

"I gotta have you, Brynn. Your heart, your mind, your body. It all has to be mine. I can see my baby girls and boys in those blue eyes of yours. And if'n you don't say you'll marry me…well, I know a certain cave that is perfect for convincin' you," Michael whispered, smiling as he pushed on the porch floor, causing the swing to begin swaying back and forth slightly.

"I do love you," Brynn whispered, allowing her hands to caress his unshaven face. "I've always loved you. Did my daddy agree?" she asked, suddenly fearful that her father would've refused.

"He said I had to ask you," Michael whispered as his lips brushed her cheek.

"Then ask me," Brynn whispered as his kiss tickled her neck. It was true! She knew, at last, that it was true! Marvelously and blessedly true!

"Will you marry me, Brynn?" His voice was deep, quiet, and impassioned.

Brynn felt her heart swell with the exhilaration of a dream come to life. "Yes," she whispered. "You know I will."

"You're in for it now, darlin'. You realize, of course, I been holding back my best kisses," he said, kissing the corner of her mouth teasingly.

"That's impossible," she giggled. But then, Michael McCall proved to Brynn that, indeed, he had.

AN OLD-FASHIONED ROMANCE

To Barbara, Dixie, Karen, and Sheri,
See yourselves in my heart, my dears…
My laughter, my beacons of hope and joy,
My cherished friends.
My eternal love to each of you.

CHAPTER ONE

Breck McCall ran her fingers through her long, chestnut hair, sighing heavily as she waited for the traffic light to turn green. If she kept hitting every light on red, she would never make it to work on time. Still, she smiled as she watched the crossing guard motion for the group of distracted children to cross the street. The crossing guard—an elderly man with sparse silvery hair—waved to the children frantically with one hand, holding tightly to the stop sign in his other. Breck giggled, sympathetic as she watched one little red-haired girl tugging on her purple rolling backpack. It tipped over a moment later, of course, and the frantic crossing guard rushed over to help the child right it. The little girl and her purple rolling backpack were off again soon enough, and Breck smiled and waved at the tired traffic guard as the light turned green. She was on her way to work again.

Working at Wilson Investigation seemed the perfect career path for a young woman like Breck—just a week away from being twenty-one. Her coworkers were friendly enough, the work was far more than merely interesting, and it seemed that all should be well with Breck. But somehow, all wasn't well.

Descended from a long line of horse breeders, Breck's father had chosen the life of a big-city attorney instead of following his older brother into the horse business. Her mother and father were happy enough, but Breck had always struggled with city life. She remembered visiting her uncle's ranch as a child—the way she had always felt free, as if she could breathe better out there in southeastern

Colorado. Her father had always maintained she reminded him of his grandfather Michael McCall, who had loved the wide-open space of ranching life. Thus, Breck figured she was that child in every family who should have been born in a different era. But reality was that farming and ranching were vanishing lifestyles. And one didn't easily go from being a big-city girl, employed by one of the top detective agencies in the West, to plopping into the well-worn blue jeans of a farm girl. And so, Breck had finished her degree at Colorado State and had found a job at Wilson.

As she stepped off the elevator on the fourteenth floor, Breck heard the sounds of morning at the office. She could hear the copy machines and printers whirring away and low voices steeped in phone conversation—inhaled the familiar scent of stale doughnuts and old coffee.

"Good morning, Breck," Patty greeted from her seat behind the reception desk. "Having a good one?"

Patty was a sweet, pleasant-natured brunette woman of about forty-five, the main receptionist at Wilson.

"Yeah. And you?" Breck said.

"Fair enough. Mr. Henshaw has an appointment today."

Mr. Henshaw was a young, recently divorced man, a client of Mr. Wilson's. Patty thought he was the hottest thing since jalapeño bean dip.

Breck giggled and said, "Well, then your day should be a good one!"

Patty's smile widened, and she nodded, seeming to remember something a moment later. "Mr. Thatcher is already in this morning," she said. "He doesn't look like he's had a minute of sleep. Probably staking out a case on his own again."

"Probably," Breck agreed. Mr. Reese Thatcher was not only Breck's boss but also the handsomest man a woman had ever seen—and a bachelor. It was, quite often, difficult to work with him and not stare in awe at his good looks. He was the one reason Breck looked forward to going to work each weekday morning at Wilson Investigation—not that she wasn't well paid, for she was. However, her soul yearned for freedom somehow. But whenever she set eyes on Reese Thatcher, another emotion washed over her—euphoria!

"Have a good one, Patty," Breck called over her shoulder as she passed the reception area and headed for her desk.

"You too," came Patty's cheerful reply.

Setting her purse in the lower drawer of her desk, Breck tapped her computer keypad to signal her monitor display. The cool breezes of October had left her cheeks rosy and her disposition refreshed. She was ready for another day at the old grind. She noted that Mr. Thatcher had already set a pile of scribbled-on papers atop her desk. No doubt he'd been making notes all night again while he sat in his car staking out someone who was up to some dirty deed.

Breck sighed, feeling sorry for the handsome, brooding man who had to spend so much of his time with dishonest people who could not be trusted.

"Morning, Breck," Reese Thatcher mumbled as he stepped out of his office at that very moment.

"Good morning, Mr. Thatcher," Breck greeted as the scowling man approached her desk. Even scowling he was gorgeous—like some mix between a young Elvis Presley and a young John Stamos.

He ran his fingers through his black hair and forced a considerate smile as he said, "I tossed some notes on your desk when I came in this morning. Can you get them entered for me as soon as possible? I've already forgotten what's on them."

"I sure can," she answered.

He handed her a large black envelope next. "These pictures go in the Allen file. Michael Allen should be calling sometime this morning. Just let him know they're here whenever he wants his attorney to pick them up, okay?" he mumbled, running his fingers through his thick, ebony hair again.

"Sure," Breck answered. She felt a hard lump form in her throat, her stomach churning a bit. She'd done enough work on Mrs. Allen's case to know what must be in the black envelope—photos of Mr. Allen consorting with another woman. These kinds of cases always made Breck sick to her stomach, and unfortunately, there were far too many of them.

"Detective Taylor should be dropping some stuff by later too," Mr. Thatcher continued. "Bring it right in, would ya?"

"I will," Breck agreed.

She felt a slight blush rise to her cheeks as Reese Thatcher smiled at her a moment and said, "You look nice today, Breck."

"Thank you, Mr. Thatcher." Breck took his compliments not too much to heart, however. He always told old Mr. Wilson's assistant that she looked nice too. Mr. Wilson's secretary had been with him for forty years and was almost seventy—a fairly grouchy lady with a straight line for a smile and a perpetual frown.

"Another pumpkin sweater, I see," he noted.

"Yep," Breck admitted. Still, she was flattered that he would notice her passion for sweaters with pumpkins or orange patterns woven into them. "It is October, after all, Mr. Thatcher."

The smile he directed at her broadened. "Is it?" he teased. "And me without a pumpkin sweater to my name."

Reese Thatcher couldn't ignore the warm feeling sweeping over him at the sight of his attractive assistant dressed in yet another sweater paying homage to the ultimate orange squash. Over the past couple of weeks, he'd begun to wonder how much of her paychecks she spent on pumpkin-themed sweaters and where in the world she was able to find so many. It was one of the most adorable things about her lately, he noted to himself. But he buried that thought, not only quickly but deep.

Breck's smile broadened too at his teasing. He turned, and she couldn't help noticing how nicely his jeans fit, how the fitted, ribbed knit shirt he wore complemented his muscular build and broad shoulders.

With that black hair and those blue eyes, you'd look ridiculous in a pumpkin sweater, she thought. But she'd be willing to bet he'd look great in a red Christmassy one.

When he finally walked into his office, closing the door behind him, Breck exhaled a sigh of relief. Oh, how he rattled her! The epitome of the tall, dark, and handsome cliché, Reese Thatcher was one of those guys that a girl sees only one or two of in her entire life! He was tall, broad-shouldered, and in excellent shape physically. His eyes were a kind of light, light blue—almost sky blue—and his hair the deepest black Breck had ever seen in real life. His perfectly straight, perfectly white teeth added a movie-star quality to his smile, and he was simply the most handsome man Breck had ever seen! Not to mention that he was kind, well-mannered, and as masculine as they came.

Breck, in contrast, felt very plain. Green eyes, brown hair, medium height—not much to brag about. She did have a good figure, but still, she saw nothing unusually striking about herself. Thus, a man like Reese Thatcher intimidated the life out of her! She knew that every girl in the office daydreamed about him, and—the truth be told—she was no different.

Imagine kissing him, she thought to herself. *I'd drop dead on the spot, for sure.*

Sighing and trying to dispel any daydreams of being Reese Thatcher's girlfriend, Breck filed Mr. Allen's envelope in her desk file drawer and proceeded to put her phone headset on just as the phone rang.

With a, "Good morning. Wilson Investigation, Reese Thatcher's office. May I help you?" Breck's day at work officially began.

☙

The morning was uneventful at best. Breck worked most of the day preparing the information Reese had gathered for Mrs. Allen's file, and it put her in a rather foul mood. She kept thinking that someone ought to string Mr. Allen up by his toenails and torture him for cheating on his sweet wife. And the fact the couple had a brand-new baby only served to further infuriate her. By the time her lunch hour rolled around, Breck was more than ready for a break. And it promised to be a fun one—for she was meeting her four best friends downtown at Marcelli's.

Marcelli's was Breck's very favorite restaurant! It boasted the best

Italian food in three states and with affordable prices. Plus, Sherryl, Trixie, Kay, and Barb were meeting her there. In fact, she'd scheduled herself an hour and a half for lunch—to allow more time to visit with her friends.

Lunch with these girls was always an adventure! Nothing ever went smoothly, mostly because they were all laughing so hard they couldn't eat. The tips they all left were more than generous—because each of them felt a bit guilty for being overly flirty with the waiter of the day. Yep! Breck looked forward to time with her four dearest friends more than anything. She knew the girls would help lift her out of her *I wish someone would flog Mr. Allen* mood into a *I'll just enjoy looking at my handsome boss* frame of mind once again.

༄

Before the waiter had even shown Breck the table where her friends waited, she could hear them. Barb's laugh was literally contagious, and Breck heard herself giggle as she heard its magical melody drifting from one corner of the room.

No doubt Trixie (her real name being Marie) was already busy sculpting puppies with some bread and olive oil. Trixie couldn't leave her food alone to save her life! She was forever sculpting puppies, penguins, and even North America out of bread, leftover desserts, and pancakes. She was good at it too! Breck had often wondered why Trixie didn't take to sculpting with some substance more lasting and durable than leftover restaurant food.

Kay would have a list of books as long as her arm ready to share. Kay loved to read, and her sole purpose in life had become trying to find a book for Breck that would outdo Breck's beloved and favorite book, *The Highwayman of Tanglewood*. Kay knew it was a daunting task—one most likely never to be achieved. Still, Kay had given Breck some fantastic reading material over the years—even though nothing would ever beat out *The Highwayman of Tanglewood* in Breck's heart.

And then there was Sherryl. Sherryl was the "up-to-no-gooder" of the group. A well-known photographer by trade, Sherryl would inevitably have the girls up to their necks in mischief by the end of lunch. Whether it was flirting shamelessly with some poor waiter,

6

trying to solve the love-life concerns of some unsuspecting waitress, or simply cracking jokes all through lunch until everyone had indigestion, Sherryl was the clown of the clan.

Yes, as Breck approached the table and saw her friends, smiling faces ablaze with mirth, she knew this would, once again, be a lunch to remember.

"Did you pinch your boss's butt yet, Breck?" Sherryl inquired as Breck took her seat at the table. As usual, the waiters had the foresight to sit this group of women out of the way of normal, everyday folks.

"I could get sued for that, Sherr," Breck reminded with a giggle.

"So what?" Trixie said. "Your dad's a lawyer."

Everyone laughed, and Kay hugged Breck as she sat down. As always, Breck sighed as she scanned the faces of her beloved chums. These girls were real. There was nothing false or arrogant about them, and Breck loved them with all her heart—depended on them to help her through the ugly parts of life.

"I don't know how you keep your hands off that man," Barb said, shaking her head.

"I admit it…it's hard," Breck sighed. "Especially since it's painfully obvious that he wants me," she sighed dramatically.

Everyone laughed, and lunch began with Trixie's proud display of her latest restaurant appetizer sculpture—Italian bread smooshed and flattened into the shape of Texas.

The hour passed too quickly, and Breck's sides were aching from laughing so hard. Barb had laughed so hard at one point that the gulp of water she'd just taken left her body by way of her nose. And so it was that, with an overly full stomach and a heart full of mirth, Breck glanced over to where their waiter was seating a new set of patrons.

Her very audible gasp caused her friends to follow her gaze.

"Oh my heck!" Kay exclaimed in a whisper. "It's him!"

"Oh my heck, it is!" Trixie confirmed.

Indeed, sitting at a table just across the room was none other than Reese Thatcher! Breck felt hot beads of perspiration accumulate on her forehead as she looked and noted the rather beautiful blonde that was with him.

"And he's with a woman!" Sherryl exclaimed in a hushed tone.

"That ain't no woman," Barb corrected. "If she's with Breck's man…she's a hoochie."

"Ssshh! You guys! He'll hear us," Breck warned.

"Oh my heck! He *is* gorgeous," Kay whispered, ignoring Breck's warning. "Breck…you have to marry him!"

"For Pete's sake, Kay," Breck scolded, slouching down in her seat. "He'll hear you!"

"You definitely have to pinch his butt," Trixie added, winking at Breck. Breck couldn't fault them at all for teasing her. For were the shoe on the other foot—and it had been in the past—she would have been just as bad.

"Oh my heck! Oh my heck!" Sherryl warned. "He's looking over here!"

"I wonder why," Breck growled, unable to help but smile at her silly friends.

"Well, sit up straight, Breck," Barb ordered. "You don't want him to think you're a sloucher, for crying out loud."

Breck thought she might nearly drop dead when she heard Kay say, "Oh my heck! Oh my heck! He's coming over, Breck! Oh my heck!"

Breck plastered on a fake smile and looked up just in time to see none other than Reese Thatcher standing over her.

"Well, hello, Breck," he greeted.

"Hello, Mr. Thatcher," she managed to sputter.

"Girls' day out, huh?" he asked, waiting for an introduction.

"Yep," Breck confirmed. Still, she was completely tongue-tied and couldn't respond any further.

Fortunately, or rather unfortunately, Sherryl's tongue was all too loose.

"Well, hello, Mr. Thatcher," Sherryl greeted. "We're Breck's idiot friends."

"Nice to meet you all," Reese Thatcher said, smiling, obviously amused. "So…uh…is this an official meeting of the Pumpkin

Sweater Club?"

Breck closed her eyes for a moment, horrified as she, only then, realized she and every one of her friends wore sweaters with some sort of pumpkin design on them. Reese Thatcher smiled and looked to Breck.

"Um…no, sir. We just all like…pumpkin sweaters," she explained.

"Is that your girlfriend, Mr. Thatcher?" Barb asked. Barb was known as the blunt one of the group. She didn't believe in wasting time. *Cut to the chase and just find out what you want to know* was her motto. Breck was mortified—wanted to scream with embarrassment. However, Reese grinned, amused by the woman's brazenness.

"No…just a friend," he answered.

Breck was silently scolding herself for being so relieved that the woman wasn't his girlfriend. Further she was irritated with herself for caring so much.

Reese smiled at her, and Breck was certain that he pitied her for her discomfort. He said, "Well, I'll leave you ladies to your dessert. It was nice to meet you all." Then, winking at Breck, he added, "See you back at the office, Miss Pumpkin Sweater Club President."

"Okay," Breck managed.

Everyone at the table was silent—all five sets of eyes intent on Reese Thatcher as he sauntered away. And then Breck knew it would start. And it did.

"I cannot believe you haven't pinched that rear end," Trixie teased.

"I cannot believe you haven't thrown him down on your desk and smooched him!" Kay added.

"I cannot believe that he noticed we were all wearing pumpkin sweaters," was Sherryl's contribution.

"I cannot believe that you didn't run over there and claw that hoochie's eyes out…just a friend or not!" Barb concluded.

I cannot believe was a sort of verbal game that Breck and her friends played quite often during their conversations and adventures. And it was Breck's turn.

"I cannot believe that you guys are so crazy!" Breck exclaimed in a whisper. Then they all started to giggle, and Breck relaxed once more.

Reese couldn't help but glance over to the table where Breck and her friends were finishing up their lunch. He'd never heard such giggling and goings-on, and it made him smile. He suspected that Breck was completely caught off guard by his presence at Marcelli's, and he had enjoyed the look on her face when one of her friends had askÓed if the woman with him were his girlfriend.

Of course, he knew that the woman with him, Meagan Jetta, wanted to be his girlfriend. She'd made it quite obvious many, many times. But Meagan wasn't for him. She was nice, pretty, and fun—enjoyable to go to lunch with—as a friend. But he wanted nothing more serious where she was concerned.

In fact, he felt bad that he kept glancing to Breck's table, his mind wandering from the conversation he was having with Meagan.

"Your secretary is a little obnoxious, Reese," Meagan said. "And what's with all the pumpkin sweaters anyway?"

Reese smiled. He wasn't angry with Meagan. He had neglected their conversation since seeing Breck at the restaurant.

Picking up his glass, he took a drink of water and said, "Apparently it's a Pumpkin Sweater Club meeting."

Meagan rolled her eyes and breathed, "Whatever." Then looking at her watch, she gasped and said, "Oh! I've got to run, Reese! I've got an appointment at Jenkins and Jenkins in ten minutes. Thanks for lunch."

"Sure," Reese said as Meagan hopped up and left the table.

He felt guilty for being so relieved that she was gone. Now he could spy on Breck and her friends in private. However, when he looked over to their table, it was to see Breck waving and walking away. He watched as her friends lingered, whispering among themselves and glancing over at him. One of them hopped up and went to the window that overlooked the parking lot. And then, much to his dismay and delight, the four women rose from their table and began walking toward him.

When they reached his table, it was the skinny blonde who found the nerve to speak first.

"Um…excuse us. Mr. Thatcher?" the skinny blonde said.

"Yeah," Reese said, his curiosity more than piqued.

"Hi, I'm Sherryl Foster," the skinny blonde began, "Breck McCall's friend."

"Yes, we've met. Did you forget already?" Reese teased.

"Oh, no. Of course not," the woman assured him.

"What can I do for you ladies?"

The four young women giggled like high school cheerleaders talking to the captain of the football team—their eyes lit up with mischievous excitement.

"Well," Sherryl Foster began, "Breck's birthday is next Friday."

"Her twenty-first birthday," the dark brunette added. "I'm Trixie," she whispered aside to him.

"Yes," Sherryl confirmed, then continued, "and we've just come up with the greatest idea for her birthday dinner. And…and…"

"And we were hoping you'd be willing to help us out," the lighter brunette finished.

"Oh, really?" Reese asked.

"Barb," the lighter brunette told him. This was getting interesting. He was very intrigued. A surprise for Breck's birthday with these four chatterboxes involved would certainly be something to behold.

"Kay," the other blonde said. She nodded and then continued, "Now, don't worry. It doesn't involve a giant cake or you in nothing but a bow tie and your underwear."

Reese chuckled. "Well, that's good to know."

"Although," the darker brunette said to the lighter one, "that *would* be a nice finale for Breck's birthday dinner."

Reese chuckled as he watched their faces. It seemed they actually considered the idea for a moment—then realized exactly what had been suggested and began shaking their heads in unison.

"Yeah, yeah, yeah," the skinny blonde said. "A bit over the edge for a public display."

"For Breck anyway," the lighter brunette noted.

These friends of Breck's were funny, and it made him wish he could've been a fly on the wall when Breck had been with them at lunch.

"What *is* your plan, ladies?" Reese asked. He grinned, amused at the way they all looked one to the other in such a mischievous, conspiratorial manner.

"Well, Mr. Reese Thatcher," the dark brunette began, "Kay here is a fabulous seamstress."

❧

Thirty minutes later, Reese Thatcher sat in his pickup in Marcelli's parking lot. He couldn't believe he'd agreed to be involved in such a mess! For a moment he felt sorry for Breck. The attention would, no doubt, mortify her. Still, a girl who wore pumpkin-themed sweaters every day in October and owned friends who would concoct such a scheme—there was definitely more to Breck McCall than met the eye. Of course, he'd suspected that from the moment he'd hired her.

Still, he wondered what on earth had gotten into him. Shaking his head, he turned the key in the ignition. It was about time he did something fun—something to take his mind off the ghosts in his past, the muck he was knee-deep in at work. Pumpkin sweaters— that gave him another idea. Picking up his cell, he dialed and waited for an answer at the other end.

"Hi, Mom," he greeted. "I need a favor."

❧

Her lunch with the girls had completely revitalized Breck. Back at work and sitting at her desk once more, she felt refreshed and not so resentful about the condition of the world. She wished she could meet the girls more often, but at least she had dinner next Friday with them to look forward to. She smiled, knowing they'd make her twenty-first birthday dinner at Marcelli's a memorable one indeed. She suspected they had something wild up their sleeves, and it would be hard to wait over a week to find out what it was.

"Seems like you've got a good group of friends there, Breck,"

Reese Thatcher said as he approached her desk.

Breck felt herself blush. It had been so startling to see him at Marcelli's—so irritating to see him with that woman—so frightening to sit and wonder what her friends might say when they met him. Her emotions were in turmoil. Not to mention he looked particularly handsome at that moment. Lunch at Marcelli's seemed to agree with just about anybody.

"Yeah. They're a bunch of fun," she said.

"They certainly seem to be," he said, smiling. Breck blushed, flustered—wondering what else he'd witnessed of her luncheon at Marcelli's.

He turned to walk into his office but paused and looked back at her.

Pointing an index finger at her, he said, "Did I tell you, 'Nice pumpkin sweater,' yet today?"

Breck smiled at his teasing manner. "Yes, sir. You did."

He winked at her and closed his office door behind him.

He seemed oddly relaxed, Breck mused. But the smile left her face when she began to wonder if it were simply lunch at Marcelli's that had given him a lift. Or was it the woman—rather, the hoochie—he'd been lunching with?

CHAPTER TWO

Breck's twenty-first birthday dawned on a perfectly crisp and cool autumn morning. October's end brought with it a feel of frost in the air. Tired trees were shedding the last of their leaves of reds and gold, and piles of pumpkins dotted the front porches of Colorado suburbia. Breck felt more lighthearted than usual as she waited for the elevator doors to open onto the fourteenth floor and the Wilson Investigation offices.

In fact, she felt so excited—anxiously anticipating dinner at Marcelli's with Trixie, Sherryl, Barb, and Kay—that when the elevator doors did open at last, she rushed forward, plowing into Marty Sprague from accounting. The files Marty had been holding under his arms went flying everywhere, scattering quite efficiently over the floor in front of the elevator.

"Oh, Marty!" Breck exclaimed. "I'm so sorry. I wasn't paying attention."

Marty smiled down at Breck. "That's okay, Breck. No problem."

Breck returned Marty's friendly smile, on her guard however—for it was unspoken but public knowledge throughout the office that Marty more than admired Breck. He was a handsome one too—tall, very well built, and with brown hair and green eyes that flashed like emeralds when he was looking at something he liked. And his eyes were certainly flashing as he watched Breck drop to her knees and begin gathering his papers.

He hunkered down to help her retrieve the innards of his files, and Breck felt the heat of his stare on the top of her head.

"Rumor has it that today's your birthday," he said as they scooped up papers.

"Well, for once the ol' rumor mill is correct," Breck admitted. Even though Marty's attention unnerved her a bit, he'd never made any inappropriate advances toward her. He'd asked her out several times, and Breck had enjoyed his company well enough, but that was all—casual friendship. No butterflies took flight in her stomach when he entered the room; no goose bumps broke over her flesh at his touch. And that was what Breck wanted—butterflies and goose bumps.

"Not to spoil the surprise," Marty began, "but they've got a cake and are all waiting in the break room for you. The standard birthday snacks here at Wilson."

Breck smiled, pleased to work for a firm that recognized employees in such a kind manner.

"How neat," she said, smiling.

"I thought you'd think so," Marty chuckled.

All the papers having been gathered, Marty pushed the elevator down button on the wall and waited for his transportation to arrive.

"So…happy birthday, Breck," he told her, smiling.

"Thank you," she said, returning his smile.

The elevator doors opened, and Marty stepped in, turning to face her again. "Oh," he added, "and that's a nice pumpkin sweater you're wearing today."

Breck giggled and tossed him a friendly wave as the elevator doors closed. Sighing heavily, she turned to greet Patty. Patty wore her familiar, captivating smile that seemed to please and comfort anyone who saw it. A person couldn't help but smile back at Patty—her smile was that agreeable.

"He's sweet on you, you know," Patty told her.

"Sweet on me, Patty?" Breck giggled. "Patty, you sound like my grandma."

"Well, he is," Patty assured her.

Breck's smile faded a bit at the thought of what a handsome and kind young man Marty was. Why couldn't she like him? He was perfect. Wasn't he? No—sadly he wasn't. Not when you stood him next to Reese Thatcher. And that, after all, was the whole problem. It seemed no matter how nice a man was—how handsome or polite— Breck kept comparing him to her boss—her gorgeous, kind, out-of-reach boss. Reese Thatcher possessed a sort of vintage masculinity. It would be hard for any man to compete with that rare quality. Still, Breck knew how unobtainable Reese was to her, so it bothered her that his presence in her life would keep her from gravitating to a good man like Marty. But fact was fact—and Marty just wasn't the zinger.

"And a happy birthday to you, Breck!" Patty added.

"Thanks, Patty," Breck said. It was nice to have such kind and sincere birthday wishes—two already and she'd only just stepped off the elevator.

"I've got a little something for you," Patty told her, rising from her seat behind the reception desk and handing Breck a small package.

"Patty!" Breck exclaimed. "You didn't need to do that."

Patty smiled and nodded. "I know. But I wanted to. You're just such a sweet girl, Breck. You deserve to have some special attention on your birthday."

Breck giggled. "Can I open it now?"

Patty smiled. "Of course."

Breck admired the pretty wrapping of the package for a moment—pink paper with lavender and yellow ribbon tied around it. Then she quickly slid the ribbon off and tore away the paper to reveal a white box. Opening the box, she withdrew its contents and gasped with surprise and delight.

"Oh, Patty!" she exclaimed as she held the lovely snow globe in her hand. The globe housed a dainty fairy with wings of gold and green, sitting on a large pumpkin. Furthermore, instead of the traditional white snow that usually furled around when one shook or turned such a globe upside down, swirling Patty's gifted globe revealed tiny red, orange, and yellow leaves raining down on the pretty autumn fairy and her pumpkin throne. It was so beautiful and such an obviously personal gift that it brought tears to Breck's eyes for a moment.

"Patty," Breck said in a whisper, "it's the most beautiful thing I've ever seen. Truly!"

Patty smiled, delighted with Breck's reaction.

"Well," she began, "when Mr. Thatcher pointed out to me the other day that you'd been wearing pumpkin sweaters all month…well, I saw this in that little gift shop on Burlington, and…well…you just had to have it!"

Breck felt her heart rather leap in her bosom at the knowledge that not only had Reese Thatcher noticed her pumpkin sweaters, he'd talked about them to Patty. Impulsively she threw her arms around Patty's neck, hugging her.

"Thank you so much, Patty," Breck told her. "You'll never know how much I love this and how much your thoughtfulness means."

Patty returned her embrace and then said, "You deserve it, Breck. You're the nicest girl here." Breck smiled as Patty smiled at her. "There's something different about you, you know," Patty told her. "You're…well, it's as if you…I don't know. It's like you're from somewhere else…somewhere other than a big city. I think your heart is sweeter…more kind than most."

Breck smiled—touched beyond description at the woman's tender words.

"Now, you get on into your office. Mr. Thatcher was pacing the floors early this morning. I'm sure something is up with that Allen case. I heard him talking to Mrs. Allen on his cell as he stepped off the elevator," Patty told her.

Breck smiled. "Thank you again, Patty. It's so beautiful."

"You're very welcome, Breck," Patty said.

When Breck arrived at her desk, Reese was nowhere to be seen. So she set her lovely new snow globe—or rather, leaf globe—on her desk and tried to get to work. But she found it hard to concentrate. All she could think about was dinner at Marcelli's that night with the girls and, of course, Reese Thatcher. Seeing him at Marcelli's with an unknown woman the week before had greatly disturbed Breck. For some reason, the jealousy she felt every time she thought of it churned in her like an intestinal virus. She hadn't been able to get past it all week, and it bothered her. Furthermore, the physical reactions her body had been having in Reese's presence had also increased over the past few days. She felt rather shaken whenever he was around— nervous, giggly, uncertain of herself. It was driving her nuts!

And where was he anyway? Patty had made it sound as if he'd be waiting right there for her, ready to rant and rave about the Allen case.

Breck's phone rang then, and she answered it to find Barb on the other end.

"Happy birthday, Breck!" her friend greeted. "Mr. Wonderful around there close?"

"Haven't seen him yet," Breck answered, lowering her voice.

"Don't forget…we're picking you up at six-thirty sharp tonight," Barb needlessly reminded her.

"How could I forget," Breck giggled. "I can't wait!"

At that very moment, Reese rounded the corner. A severe frown wrinkled his brow, and he was heading straight for Breck's desk, his eyes deadlocked on her.

"Gotta go, Barb," Breck whispered.

"Okay," Barb said. "But it's your birthday today, Breck, and he owes you something. Be sure to pinch his—"

Breck hung up the phone before Barb had finished, for Reese now stood directly before her, glaring down at her—fury all too evident in his expression.

"Breck, will you get Michael Allen on the phone for me?" he growled. "I have something to say to him and can't find his number."

Breck sighed and adjusted the headset mike at her mouth. Reese was mad! She'd seen him like this several times before—usually when husbands or wives had done each other wrong. And fortunately she knew how to handle him—thus keeping him out of trouble.

"I will, Mr. Thatcher," she said calmly, "if you really want me to."

"I really want you to," Reese grumbled. Still, she could see him calming down a bit.

"Okay. But remember…you don't want to do anything that might jeopardize Mrs. Allen or her case in any way," she reminded him.

Reese drew in and exhaled a deep breath, closed his eyes for a moment, and then tilted his head to one side as he looked at Breck and grinned.

"Trying to keep me out of jail again?" he asked.

"Yes, sir. Trying," Breck answered, smiling at him.

She startled when Reese placed his fists on her desk and leaned toward her for a moment. Then, shaking his head and straightening to his full height once again, he said, "That man's an…idiot."

Breck couldn't stop the grin that spread across her face. She'd heard Reese call Michael Allen a lot of things while he was talking to various people in his office. *Idiot* was the tamest term he'd used.

"Yes, sir. He is," she agreed.

Another deep sigh to further calm his temper and he turned toward his office.

"Oh, wait," he said, however. Pointing an index finger at Breck, he said. "Wait right there."

Breck smiled. He was her boss—where did he think she was going? He disappeared into his office, only to return a moment later with a badly wrapped gift in his hands.

Breck felt her cheeks go crimson with a hot blush as he held the gift out to her and said, "Happy birthday."

"Thank you," she breathed as she accepted the gift from him.

"I wrapped it myself," he boasted, and Breck giggled. She loved a man who wrapped a gift so that it looked worse than a kindergartener's first attempt. First of all, it was purely masculine to be all thumbs with wrapping paper, tape, and scissors. Second, she'd always felt that a man attempting to wrap a gift on his own showed sincere care. Oh, it was fine in her book for a man to have his wife, his daughters, or a department store wrapping service fancy up his gifts. But attempting to wrap a present on his own—there was an adorable man!

"It's beautiful!" Breck lied as she noted the pink bow so obviously over-taped on the orange wrapping paper.

"I think it looks pretty good too," he said with the sweetest boyish pride. "But open it up. I want to see if it fits."

Breck giggled. Another cute man thing—unconsciously revealing the contents of a gift. For appearance's sake—after all, he had expended quite a lot of effort on his wrapping—Breck opened the gift carefully. She was unable to stifle another nervous giggle when she was fairly certain that whatever Reese had sheltered inside hadn't really come from "Uncle Ben's Fish and Tackle," as the stickers on the box indicated.

"You are gonna love this," Reese said, chuckling. Breck looked up at him, amazed by the mischievous twinkle in his eyes. He nodded and winked at her, biting his lower lip in anticipation. For Pete's sake—she was sure he was more excited than she was!

Breck's heart began to hammer rather intensely as she opened the box. Immediately upon seeing the color of its contents, she gasped, guessing at once what the item was.

"Oh, Mr. Thatcher!" She was so delighted, she nearly squealed the exclamation. An orange mound of knitted yarn was badly folded and cached in the fish-and-tackle store box.

With a chuckle, Reese told her, "It's a pumpkin sweater!" He chuckled, obviously very proud of his clever gift. "And I know for a fact that you don't have this one."

Breck's hands began to tremble as she took the sweater from the box and unfolded it across the top of her desk. It was truly beautiful! Knitted out of the softest orange yarn, it had several small pumpkins woven into the pattern here and there—each embellished with three leaves at its stem and accented by twisty green vine remnants. It was truly the most beautifully crafted—most beautiful in every way— pumpkin sweater that Breck had ever seen.

"Oh, Mr. Thatcher," she breathed in awe. "It's so perfect!"

She felt goose bumps break over her body as he knelt down beside her at her desk—his arm brushing her shoulder for a moment. She could smell him instantly too—the soft, masculine scent of Speed Stick and aftershave filling her senses.

"It's nice, isn't it?" he asked. Then looking to her, their faces only inches apart, he added, "Don't you want to know how I found a pumpkin sweater you didn't already have?" Breck held her breath. He was so close—so gorgeous! She could feel the warmth of his arm as he rested it on the back of her chair. Five inches forward and she could've kissed him smack on the mouth!

"Um…yes," she stammered.

"Well," he began, his eyes holding her mesmerized gaze, "at first I wondered if maybe you were sick of pumpkin sweaters. You know what I mean?" Breck nodded, intrigued and delighted by his boasting over his finding the perfect gift for her. "Like…you know…a guy… he finds a sports logo he likes, and he can stick with it for, like, forty years, you know?" Breck nodded again, amused by his analogy. "But a girl…no offense, Breck…but girls can be pretty fickle." Breck could only nod again. "However, when I saw you and your friends at the restaurant the other day…every one of you wearing some sort of pumpkin fanatic sweater."

Breck giggled at the memory.

"I figured…you're a collector. And collectors never have enough of whatever they collect. Right?"

"Right," Breck breathed again.

"So," Reese continued, "I called my mom."

Breck's heart began to slip into the pit of her stomach. He'd sent his mom shopping for her birthday present? All she could visualize then was the woman wearing herself ragged by running around trying to find an obligatory birthday gift for her son's secretary.

"Oh," Breck managed, forcing a smile. "It was so kind of her to look—" she began.

"No, no, no," Reese interrupted. "She knitted it just for you. It's a one of a kind."

"What?" Breck asked, her emotions bouncing back and forth so quickly it was giving her a headache.

"Yeah. My mom's a great knitter," he told her. "Look," he said taking the collar of the sweater and turning it down. "See there." He pointed to a small hand-sewn tag on the inside back of the sweater. "Made with love by Marjie Thatcher," he read.

Breck felt tears welling in her eyes. What a special thing he'd done! Sure, it had imposed on his mother, but not the way Breck had at first imagined. This was different! Asking his mother to make such a unique and individual gift? It was unbelievable.

Reese looked at Breck, studying her face for a moment. As Breck willed her tears to stay in her eyes and not escape down her cheeks, Reese said, "You like it, huh?"

"I love it," Breck admitted, her voice cracking a bit and betraying the depth of the emotion she felt.

Reese allowed a triumphant smile to spread across his face, a deep sigh of satisfaction escaping his lungs as he stood.

"I can't…I can't ever thank you enough," Breck told him. "Or your mother! What incredible sacrifice she must've made."

Reese chuckled. "Naw. She loves it," he assured her. "I can just see her now…sitting in her lounge chair, orange yarn and knitting needles flying at the speed of light." Breck smiled at the vision Reese's mind must be conjuring for him.

"Thank you, Mr. Thatcher," Breck said.

Reese smiled and winked at her. "You're welcome, Breck." Then—and Breck thought she might drop dead on the spot from the rapture of the sensation his touch sent through her—Reese Thatcher brushed her left cheek with the back of his hand and added, "Happy birthday."

"Thank you," was all she could manage. With a final grin in her direction, Reese Thatcher disappeared into his office.

The moment his office door was closed, Breck blinked, causing a flood of withheld tears to stream down her cheeks. Quickly, she wiped at them with the backs of her hands. Neatly folding the sweater, she placed it back inside the Uncle Ben's Fish and Tackle box before she rushed to the ladies room to splash some cool water on her face.

After five or ten minutes of regaining her composure in the bathroom, Breck was back at her desk, trying to get some work done. But the feel of Reese Thatcher so close to her as he'd been when he'd hunkered down by her chair—the knowledge that he'd been so thoughtful about a gift for her birthday—all of it kept her stomach in knots for the rest of the morning.

Breck had begun to fall in love with her boss the first moment she met him six months before when she interviewed for the position as his assistant. But during the past few weeks her feelings for him had erupted into a state that was beginning to worry her. And as she sat at her desk a few minutes before lunch—reading the handwritten sweater-washing instructions that Reese's mother had placed in one sleeve of the sweater—she began to feel frightened. He'd break her heart and not even know it.

Her anxious thoughts were interrupted when Patty came rather bouncing up to her desk and said, "Ready for lunch, Breck? The support staff is all downstairs waiting already."

It was a common practice at Wilson Investigation for all support staff members to take one another out to lunch on any given member's birthday. Breck had been excited that morning at the prospect of lunch with her friends at work. But since Reese had gifted her the sweater earlier in the day, her emotions were such a jumble that she wondered if she'd be able to settle down and enjoy lunch at all.

❧

Fortunately, she did. The little Mexican restaurant Patty had reserved for Breck's lunch provided quite the perfect party atmosphere. Many of her friends even brought gifts. And, of course, she was forced to wear the sequin-sloshed sombrero as the restaurant employees sang "Feliz Cumpleaños" to her.

Still, returning to the office left Breck feeling quite unsettled. She wondered if perhaps it was simply her excitement about her impending dinner with friends that night. But that theory was quickly squelched when Reese returned from lunch.

"Did you have a nice birthday lunch?" he asked her as he walked—rather sauntered—toward his own office.

"Yes, thank you," Breck answered a bit too politely.

"Did they make you wear the hat?" he chuckled.

"Of course," she admitted.

"Did they take a Polaroid picture of you in it and stick it up on the restaurant wall of humiliation?"

Breck nodded.

"Good," he chuckled. "Every one of us has been humiliated that way. It's about time you joined the ranks."

"I want a word with you, Reese Thatcher!" an angry voice shouted.

Reese frowned and turned toward the angry man storming his way toward them from the hallway linking the office spaces with the reception desk. Breck drew in her breath, unhappy at seeing Michael Allen suddenly standing in front of her desk, glaring at Reese.

"Go home, Allen," Reese growled. "Oh, wait," he added, his voice thick with sarcasm, "you don't have a home, do you? You kicked it right out the window."

Breck pushed her chair back from her desk and stood up, pressing the security button on her phone.

"Security," came Dave Pullman's voice on the other end.

"Dave," Breck whispered, "would you come down to Mr. Thatcher's office immediately?" There was no pause, simply a dial tone indicating that Dave was on his way.

"And what are you doing with my wife, Thatcher?" Mr. Allen shouted. "Providing the rebound vessel?"

"I am gonna kick your sorry—" Reese growled a moment before Breck climbed over the top of her desk and planted herself squarely between the two men. She put her hand over Reese's mouth to keep him from delivering a verbal assault that could get him in trouble.

"Go ahead!" Mr. Allen challenged. "I'll sue yours for assault!"

"Mr. Allen," Breck said to the man, turning to face him, "you need to leave. You shouldn't even be here." She could feel Reese's body against her back and knew that she was the only thing keeping him from going at Michael Allen with both fists flying.

"I can be wherever the hell I want to be!" the man shouted at her. Then, taking her chin in his hand, he growled, "You got something going on with him too?" Breck slapped the man's hand away but not in time to keep Reese in line.

"Oh, that's it, man! You're dead!" Reese threatened, taking Breck by the shoulders and moving her aside.

"Come on, coward," Mr. Allen said, trying to provoke Reese further. "You gonna hide behind your secretary all day?"

Breck caught Reese's arm mid-air, only just stopping the brutal punch he'd thrown at Michael Allen.

"Reese!" she shouted. "Reese! Don't let him provoke you. It's what he wants."

Reese pulled his arm from Breck's grasp and looked at her. His eyes were red with fury, his broad chest rising and falling with the heavy breathing of anger. Forcibly, Breck pushed at Reese's chest with all her strength, trying to get him to take a step back. When he finally did, she knew it was not because of the strength of her pushes but rather because he was obeying her.

"You're nothing but a low-life nobody, Thatcher," Allen growled. "Spying on people, taking pictures, and messing with other men's wives."

This time Breck had to turn to face Reese to keep him from going off at the man. Pushing him back against the wall, she took his face in her hands and made him look at her.

"Ignore him, Reese. It's what he wants," she told him as his jaw tightened with anger. "Give Dave a minute, and the guy will be out of here."

As if in answer to her prayers, Dave walked up behind Michael Allen at that very moment.

"Come with me, sir," Dave demanded. Dave Pullman was a huge man! At six foot seven, his size alone would intimidate just about anyone. Add to that the Marine tattoos on his forearms, his flattop haircut, and bulging biceps, and Wilson had just about the most intimidating security guard in the state.

"Yeah, I'm going," Michael Allen growled. But as Dave backed him out of the room, he pointed at Reese and added, "You stay away from my wife. We'll get things worked out without anybody's help."

Reese lurched forward, but Breck put a hand to his chest to stall him. Dave escorted the man from the room, and Breck relaxed the pressure she'd used to hold Reese against the wall.

"You all right, Reese? Breck?" Mr. Wilson asked as he hurried into the room.

"Yeah, yeah. We're fine, Roger," Reese grumbled.

"That right, Breck?" Mr. Wilson asked, obviously not convinced by Reese's appearance.

"Yes, sir," Breck assured him.

"Then you take the rest of the day off, Reese," the older man said. "You need to simmer it down a bit, you hear me?" Reese nodded and sighed. "Okay then. Everybody back to work." Old Mr. Wilson hobbled off, having made his demands.

Breck was startled as she felt Reese take her chin in his hand then and turn her to face him. His eyes were still narrowed with residual anger.

"Don't you ever let that guy, or anybody else like him, touch you that way again. Do you hear me?" he growled.

"Okay," Breck squeaked. He seemed more than protective— almost possessive. But Breck chased the hope from her mind as she gazed up at him. He was just teaching her how to further take care of volatile situations in the future.

"Okay," he mumbled, releasing her. Then, shaking his head, he added, "I'm sick of this—" He paused and looked away before finishing, "—crap." Then with a heavy sigh, he said, "I'm going home, Breck. You can go too, if you'd like."

"Okay," she said. She'd seen him like this before and imagined he was feeling the same way she was—that people were jerks, that the world was going to the dogs. And it only seemed to be getting worse. What happened to fidelity in marriage? To honesty in business? To family dinner around the table, children using their imaginations and playing outside instead of sitting in dark rooms watching television or having seizures caused by video game graphics?

Reese went into his office and retrieved some files from his desk. "Good night, Breck," he mumbled on his way out.

27

"Good night, sir," she called after him.

Collapsing in her chair, Breck let out a long breath of discouragement. What a day it had been! She couldn't remember the last time she'd experienced such a range of emotion in such a short period of time. From excitement about her birthday—delight over Reese's attention to it—to the bottom of the bog with anger, bitterness, and discouragement.

Closing her eyes for a moment, she remembered how good Reese had smelled that morning when he'd given her the sweater—how adorable his pride in his wrapping job was—how warm and strong his body felt under her palms as she had pushed him against the wall to keep him from beating the life out of Michael Allen. Gosh, he was fabulous! Secretly she liked that he could've and would've beat Michael Allen to a pulp. It seemed few people stood up for things (especially the honor and protection of women) anymore. Maybe they were too selfish—or too out of shape physically. Maybe they were scared of getting thrown in jail. Breck shook her head at how many cases she'd seen go through the office of good men who were facing lawsuits and jail because they'd manhandled some gang member that had bullied or beaten up their ten-year-old child. But what frightened her most was the thought that men like Reese were rare because the men of her day and age just didn't care.

Pulling out of her current thought process—for it was nothing but despairing—Breck gathered her things. She would leave work early because she wanted to enjoy her evening with her friends. And if she were going to, she needed a few hours peace and quiet to recapture her good mood. Home would do it. She'd run home, turn on some Harry Connick Jr., and have a piece of the pumpkin pie waiting in her fridge and maybe a short nap. That would help. Still, she wished Michael Allen had never shown up at the office. The idiot had cheated her out of three valuable hours spent in Reese's presence. Jerk.

CHAPTER THREE

Marcelli's seemed more exciting than usual that night. At least it seemed that way to Breck. The incident at the office with Mr. Allen had definitely dampened her spirits for a time. But after a nice long shower, some soothing music, and a little baking, Breck had felt quite revived. In fact, when she'd pulled on the beautiful pumpkin sweater Reese had given to her, she actually felt quite enchanted. Furthermore, the knowledge that Reese had inconvenienced his mother on her behalf—that he had wadded the sweater up, stuffed it in a fish-and-tackle store box, and wrapped it himself—it was too delightful! Wearing the sweater caused Breck to imagine being wrapped in Reese's arms—warm, secure. It was an incredible sensation and added to the bounce she had in her step as she entered Marcelli's with her friends to celebrate her birthday.

As Dean Martin sang "That's Amore" softly in the background, Breck and her friends ordered entrees, giggled, talked about life, and just generally had a wonderful evening. The atmosphere in the restaurant was especially perfect. Breck noted the lights were dimmer than usual. The delicious aromas of olive oil, garlic, and pasta blended perfectly with the low hum made by patrons in conversation, and Sherryl had arranged for their favorite waiter to attend their table that evening, allowing for more silly frivolity.

Later, as they waited for their desserts to be brought out, Breck relaxed against the back of her chair and sighed—content. Smiling, she quickly surveyed the scene before her.

There was Barb, laughing with merriment—Barb, who was married to the sweetest man—Barb, who had two sweet little toddler daughters only a year apart—Barb, who had spent two years before college leading troubled teens through the wilderness on survival treks. Breck shook her head, finding it hard to believe that this was the same woman who used to hunt and kill rattlesnakes for food. Now she was the vision of the perfect wife and mother and completely content about it.

Breck smiled again as she looked to Trixie, busily sculpting a rabbit out of the remains of her meat ravioli. Trixie was engaged now—to the man of her dreams, Bobby Jepson. She was quite the successful floral designer, and Breck was surprised she didn't sculpt more flora and fauna when they were out to eat. Trixie was the most patient person Breck had ever known, and she loved her for it.

Kay was a sweetheart! She'd been a forensic chemist in the days before she married. In fact, whenever Kay hosted a get-together at her house, she used large test tubes for punch glasses. And her home was completely covered in fabulous, handmade quilts! Kay could sew like the wind and anything she set her mind to. She was the crafty one of the bunch, and Breck admired her for it.

Now, Sherryl—Sherryl was the group clown. As Breck studied her for a moment—trying not to burst out into belly laughs as Kay snapped a picture of Sherryl with two straws hanging out of her nose—she wondered at how the woman kept up with herself! Sherryl seemed to have endless amounts of energy. And it was a good thing, for she was one of the best-known and most requested photographers in the city! Owning her own photography studio downtown, Sherryl kept a crazy schedule of portrait and product shoots. Still, with all the things that pulled her in every direction, she was careful to make time for her friends. Sherryl was dating a nice man—a landscaper—and Breck secretly hoped that wedded bliss would soon be the outcome.

As she sat studying and appreciating her good friends, Breck was too preoccupied to perceive the hush that fell over the patrons at Marcelli's in that moment. In fact, it wasn't until she noticed her friends all looking at her—smiles stretching from ear to ear—that she realized something was afoot.

"What?" she asked, glancing down at her beautiful pumpkin sweater. Had she spilled sauce on it?

She gasped as a black-gloved hand suddenly covered her mouth from behind. Next a man's voice—his breath hot on her neck—whispered in her ear, "Be still. The Highwayman of Tanglewood owns you now."

Breck recognized the phrase as one of her favorites from the book she so adored, *The Highwayman of Tanglewood*. However, she did not recognize the voice. The man's hand still covered her mouth tightly, but Breck could see the delight blazing across her friends' faces.

So this was what they were up to all week, she thought. They had hired someone to be her Highwayman of Tanglewood.

Breck tried to push the man's hand from her mouth so she could turn and see him. But he tightened his grip, coaxing her to rise from her seat as he whispered, "Do not struggle. I'll not harm you. I simply intend to have you." Whoever was playing the Highwayman was delivering his lines straight from the book and with perfection! As she stood, Breck began to giggle, for the expressions on her friends' faces were worth a lifetime of other expressions from other people. They were nothing short of entirely delighted with themselves!

Once she was standing, Breck felt the Highwayman's free arm encircle her waist from behind, pulling her back against his body. He bent, resting his chin on her shoulder for a moment before playfully nuzzling he neck.

"Come away with me, sweet Breck," the Highwayman whispered. By this time, every patron in Marcelli's large group dining area was staring at the scene. "What say you?" he added, removing his hand from her mouth and letting it rest at her throat.

Breck tried not to giggle, but it was all entirely too wonderful! A little more public than she would've perhaps preferred, but wonderful all the same.

"I say, who are you Highwayman?" she asked, quoting the book.

"Ah! But that you should know, sweet Breck," the man whispered.

At that point, the thought flittered through Breck's mind, *How perfect if you were Reese Thatcher!* Knowing that to be impossible, however, Breck began to wrack her brain for other possibilities.

Slowly, Breck began to turn in the man's arms in order to better view the secreted Highwayman of Tanglewood. But suddenly, the lighting in the room burned even more dimly—someone having turned them down. Still, enraptured by the entire event, Breck smiled as she saw she was standing in the arms of a man dressed head to toe in black. A large, draping cowl hung down over his already masked eyes and nose; a flowing cape drooped from his shoulders reaching nearly to the floor. Breck looked down to see that he was indeed wearing black breeches and black boots that cuffed just below his knee. Reaching out, she took the silky fabric of his shirt in her hand, unable to believe the perfect detail of his costume. She could hear the repeat of Sherryl's digital camera shutter clicking away at a mad pace as she tried to imagine who would be willing to involve himself in such an outlandish scheme. The light was too dim and Breck was held too closely in the Highwayman's arms to get a good look at him. Still, his mouth was easily seen. She tried to recognize the grin he wore, but his mustache and goatee hid even the shape of his lips well.

Sherryl was on her feet now, her camera shutter wearing itself out with her maniacal snapping. Breck reached out, running her hands caressively the breadth of the Highwayman's shoulders. Two could play at this game, and her friends deserved a good show for all their trouble.

"I know you not, sir," Breck said in a whisper. "Surely I would remember such a shape of a man." The Highwayman's grin broadened at her quoted banter.

"Indeed, would you?" he asked. Breck was certain he was doing more to disguise his voice than the simple method of speaking in a whisper, for she didn't recognize it at all.

"I would, sir," she answered.

"And the taste of his kiss, my sweet?" the Highwayman whispered. "Would you surely remember such a taste of a kiss?"

Breck giggled. She couldn't take it any longer. "Who are you?" she begged.

The Highwayman paused in answering—probably to allow her friends to stop laughing for a moment.

"It matters to you?" he asked, using another line direct from the book.

"You're good, whoever you are," Breck said, smiling. She wondered if the girls had pooled their money and hired a professional stage actor to portray her dreamy Highwayman.

"I will reveal myself to you," he whispered, pulling her body tightly against his own, "on one condition." He'd strayed from the book's text now, and Breck giggled with delight.

"What's that?" she asked.

"The promise of a kiss," he whispered even more quietly. Breck's eyebrows rose in astonishment, and she looked back to her friends as they joined the other restaurant patrons in an encouraging applause.

"I don't kiss strangers," Breck countered. She was enjoying the playful event, but kissing someone she didn't know would be a bit over the edge.

"I am no stranger. It is well you know me," he whispered, again quoting the book.

She looked over to Sherryl, who paused in her mad photo taking long enough to say, "You do know him."

"We promised him you'd kiss him too, Breck," Barb called from her seat at the table.

"What?" Breck exclaimed, spinning around to face her traitorous friends.

"You know him, Breck. I promise," Kay assured her. Kay wouldn't deceive her about something like this—Breck knew that.

Turning back to face the Highwayman, Breck studied him again. Was he as tall as Reese Thatcher? She measured every man's height against Reese Thatcher's. She fancied that he was perhaps even taller—and then it hit her!

"Marty Sprague!" she exclaimed. "You little devil!" Then turning to her friends, "How did you ever talk him into this?"

"You're sure you know who it is?" Trixie asked, giggling.

"Who else could it be?" Breck said. "Look how tall he is. It's Marty."

"Then…I'll get my kiss if I undress…uh…reveal my identity?" the Highwayman asked, still using his disguised voice.

Breck sighed, trying not to appear too disappointed. Marty was a sweet man, and how kind of him to be willing to go to such lengths to embarrass and delight her on her birthday. Would one kiss really be so bad? The only thing that worried her was the question of whether Marty would understand that a kiss between them would be a one-time "thank you" sort of kiss—not something to raise his hopes of anything more being possible. Still, how sweet he was to do this for her. Therefore, Breck relented.

"Okay," she said, causing her friends and the other restaurant patrons, waiters, and waitresses to cheer. Putting her arms around his neck to finally return his embrace, she said, "Reveal your identity, Highwayman of Tanglewood…and I agree to a kiss between us."

The Highwayman's smile broadened, and Breck felt her brows pucker in a frown. For as his grin grew into a smile revealing a nice set of pearly whites, Breck did not recognize it as Marty's. In fact, as he then began to tug on the well-made—however, false—mustache and goatee, Breck drew in her breath.

"It can't be!" she heard herself whisper.

But when the man then reached up, pulling back the cowl that draped his head and the mask that hid his eyes, Breck's knees gave way beneath her.

"Mr. Thatcher?" she breathed, and his arms banded around her tightly to keep her from slipping to the floor on rubbery knees.

"Now, Breck…surely you can be more familiar than that," Reese Thatcher chuckled. "Especially considering that we're about to become far more familiar than we've ever been before."

Breck felt dizzy for a moment—afraid she might pass out. Reese Thatcher? It couldn't be! Quickly she glanced to Sherryl—still wildly recording the event with her camera.

"We told you that you knew him," Sherryl giggled.

"B-but…" Breck stammered as she looked back to Reese. His smile was that of triumph. He knew she was rattled.

"Hey," he began, "I kept my end of the bargain and revealed myself. Now you need to keep yours."

Breck felt her eyes widen. Her side of the bargain? A kiss? She couldn't possibly!

Shaking her head—still in awed disbelief that it was Reese Thatcher who stood before her, Reese Thatcher holding her tightly in his arms, Reese Thatcher who had quoted lines to her from her favorite book—she whispered, "You're kidding, right?"

Reese chuckled. "No," came his monosyllabic answer.

"But…but…." Breck stammered.

"Kiss him, for Pete's sake, Breck," Barb demanded. "The man deserves at least that."

Standing there wrapped in Reese Thatcher's powerful arms—the restaurant patrons softly chanting, "Kiss him! Kiss him!" in unison—Breck felt her hands press against Reese's solid chest as his face moved closer to hers.

"I can't possibly," she told him.

He chuckled. "You have to," he told her. "They promised me."

"We did," Sherryl confirmed between shutter releases.

"Here," Reese said, turning Breck around so that her back pressed against the nearby wall. Then taking her face in his hands for a moment, he added, "Relax, Breck. It's just me."

Breck release a short, nervous giggle. Was he kidding? But in the next moment, she knew he wasn't.

His hands moved to encircle her neck—then one of his gloved thumbs moved slowly across her lips.

"Hold up," he mumbled, releasing her, stripping off his gloves, and letting them fall to the floor. Then his hands encircled her neck once more. His palms were warm—hot on her skin. And when his thumb caressed her lips again, slowly traveling from one side of her mouth to the other—as if preparing a canvas for the first stroke of a painter's masterpiece—Breck again thought she might literally pass out. His touch was incredible! It sent goose bumps erupting over her body—butterflies bursting forth from cocoons in her stomach! Just from his touch! If his simple touch had such an effect on her, Breck wondered if she could manage to live through a kiss from him. Could a woman drop dead of euphoria?

Instinctively, her hands gripped his strong forearms as his head descended toward hers.

"Mr. Thatcher, wait. I-I…" she whispered in an attempt to stall him. She truly wasn't certain she could remain conscious if he kissed her.

"It's Reese, Breck," he whispered a moment before his lips began to toy with her own.

Reese kissed her lightly at first—kissing first her upper lip and then her lower lip twice in succession.

"Oh my heck," Breck heard herself whisper. She heard Reese's low chuckle.

"Can I have my kiss now?" he asked.

"Well, yeah. But wasn't that—" Breck began. But before Breck could finish her sentence, Reese's lips took her own in a warm, powerful, driven kiss. And it wasn't a short peck of a kiss either! It endured on and on—deepened—warm, moist, and euphoric. Breck was instantly lost in it, returning the kiss as bravely as her shy twenty-one-year-old self could involve herself in a public kiss—with her boss!

Showers of wild, bright color exploded in her mind. Her heart seemed to skip several beats—her hands and feet going numb. And all from one kiss! She wasn't even aware of the cheering by restaurant patrons—for the roaring in her ears drowned out any noise. She didn't notice the super-fast snapping of Sherryl's camera shutter or the waitress that dropped a tray nearby—stunned at what was happening in her place of employment.

Reese paused for a moment in administering the driven kiss—again kissing Breck's upper lip once and then her lower lip twice. He smiled down at her for a moment—an expression of understanding evident in his bluest of blue eyes. Then he kissed her again, and she nearly melted in a puddle at his feet as the heated moisture of his mouth mingled with her own.

Their kiss ended far too soon, and Reese helped Breck to stand as the restaurant patrons cheered and whistled with delight.

"And now," he said, bending to retrieve his gloves from the floor. "I must go…before your father catches me and has me sent to the gallows for threatening his daughter's virtue." Gently he took her chin in his hand once more. "Happy birthday, Breck." He left then among the applause of the restaurant patrons and staff.

Breck's knees wouldn't support her any longer, and she slid down the wall into a sitting position on the restaurant floor.

"Oh my heck, you guys!" she breathed as her dearest friends gathered around her—delighted eyes aflame with mischief!

"Are we the greatest or what?" Kay giggled.

Barb and Trixie each offered a hand to Breck, and she accepted their help—grateful for the needed support to stand.

"I don't know whether to hug you guys or kill you!" Breck giggled as she began to regain her composure.

"Oh my heck! You've even got five-o'clock-shadow rash on your cheek!" Trixie squealed, having noticed the slight pink rash left on Breck's cheek as a result of Reese Thatcher's attention.

Breck buried her face in her hands, uncertain whether to take flight in the blissful memory of Reese's kiss or drop in a dead faint at the thought of having to face him at work come Monday morning.

"I say we blow this joint and head for my darkroom!" Sherryl said, waving her camera over her head.

"Yeah, yeah, yeah!" Barb agreed. "Don't you want to relive the moment through the magic of photography, Breck?"

Everyone hugged and giggled, and Breck could not ignore the delicious thrill running through her veins. Reese Thatcher had kissed her! It was her wildest dream come true! And it had been nothing but pure ambrosia. How could she ever be the same? She wouldn't—and she knew it. She knew that at some point, her heart would come tumbling down from the emotional flight it was on in those moments—but she would worry about that later. For now, all she wanted to do was live Reese's kisses over and over and over again in her mind. She hoped Sherryl's camera had captured a moment or two of their kissing on the memory card. How perfect to be able to look at their kiss—to verify to her mind that it actually had happened— that it hadn't been just a perfect dream.

Reese Thatcher chuckled as he wadded the cape, cowl, and mask into a ball, tossing them on the seat beside him. The look on Breck's face when he'd unmasked had been priceless! Utterly priceless! For a moment she'd looked like she would faint dead in her tracks. He'd never forget the way her eyes widened, how the blush rose to her cheeks when she realized it was her boss dressed up like an idiot. Her friends may have been silly, absolutely crazy, but she was lucky to have them. You had to love someone a lot to go to such lengths on their behalf. He envied Breck for having such good people in her life.

Reese had good people in his life too. But at that moment he realized how distant they had become—how distant he had caused them to become—and he felt deep regret. Still, he wouldn't think about it. Instead, he chuckled again at the memory of the look on Breck's face when she'd realized who he was. And he thought about her sweet kiss—how good she tasted—how soft her skin was—the vanilla fragrance of it. He thought how beautiful she looked in his mother's pumpkin sweater and was flattered that she'd been wearing it.

He hadn't been surprised he'd enjoyed kissing her so much—for he'd known he would beforehand. It was the fact that he'd almost not been able to find the self-control to stop kissing her when he did. He could've kissed her all night. Maybe it had been far too passionate a kiss for their first one, but he hadn't been able to help himself. She was just as delicious as he'd thought she'd be. More so! He shook his head, realizing that facing her at work—keeping his hands off her at work—would be all the more difficult now.

Still, he was glad he'd poked his head out of his shell long enough to be involved in Breck's friends' crazy scheming. Because that little trinket he called his assistant was getting under his skin, and he had to try to quench the thirst for her that had been building in him from the moment he hired her.

Pushing the clutch in, he started his pickup, shifted into first, and left Marcelli's parking lot with a smile and a desire in his heart to be a better man. Picking up his cell, he dialed.

"Hello?" came the sweet, beloved voice on the other end.

"Hi, Mom. You'll never guess what I've been up to tonight," he began.

↭

"One-hour photo be hanged!" Sherryl announced as she exited the darkroom. Sherryl was obsessive enough about her hobby-slash-profession that she always kept high-end photo editing computers and printers at home too. And tonight, Sherryl's talents were really going to pay off for Breck.

"Look at this puppy!" she exclaimed. "Straight off the cover of *Romantic Times*." Sherryl held up an eleven-by-fourteen enlargement, and a hot blush rose to Breck's cheeks as she looked at the picture.

"Whoa, baby! Look at that kiss!" Kay giggled.

And sure enough, there—nearly as large as life—was the perfect and tangible evidence of the fact that Reese Thatcher had indeed kissed Breck that evening at Marcelli's. A delightful shiver broke over Breck's entire body as she stared at the photo. As always, Sherryl had managed to catch the perfect moment. Her artist's eye and camera shutter had captured a moment of light in the universe—the moment when Reese's slightly parted lips had just touched Breck's—the split second before he'd pressed his mouth firmly to her own. It made for quite the intimate and thrilling photograph.

"This has to be the best kissing picture I've ever shot, Breck," the skinny blonde said. She added, "I'll have to do a sixteen-by-twenty… for your bedroom too. Mounted with a red matte, it will be perfect."

"Do we all get copies?" Trixie asked.

"I want mine with a red matte too…only eight-by-ten will be fine," Barb added.

"Done deal," Sherryl said.

Breck put her hands to her blazing-hot cheeks. "You guys are crazy. How am I ever going to face him at work on Monday?"

The women erupted into laughter as they looked to their friend.

"Who cares!" Kay exclaimed. "He was good!"

Breck blushed more deeply and smiled, shaking her head. "You guys are awful."

"No, seriously, Breck," Barb said. "It looked good. Was it as good a kiss as it looked…as good as it looks in the photo?"

Breck sighed, still light-headed from the experience. "Better," she said.

"He is so hot, Breck!" Trixie reminded them all, as if they needed reminding. "You have to have him."

"What?" Breck gasped, giggling. "You do realize he's Reese Thatcher, right?"

"Oh, honey," Kay said. "Believe me…we realize." Then she smiled and pointed to the picture, to Reese's parted lips. "Look at that kiss! Look at that man! How did you not drop dead on the spot?"

Breck shook her head as her arms and legs covered themselves in goose bumps at the sight of the photograph before her.

"I do *not* know," Breck answered honestly.

❧

Late that night, as Breck sat on the sofa in her apartment—comfortable in her flannel pumpkin-patterned pajamas and a mug of hot chocolate to relax her—she gazed at the picture Sherryl had given her of their kiss—hers and Reese's. She couldn't believe he'd done it—dressed up like some idiot, run into a very popular, very populated restaurant, and played her Highwayman! It was unbelievable. As unbelievable as the kiss he'd taken—given—shared with her. Again those imaginary butterflies that lie dormant in every woman's stomach waiting for the right man burst into flight, causing her to shiver. She tried to enjoy the memory of that wonderful kiss—the taste of it—the feel of his mouth to hers, his hands on her skin. But the knowledge of having to face him at work on Monday was drilling its way into her mind. Still, any man chivalrous enough to play the Highwayman of Tanglewood in public—surely he'd be chivalrous enough to realize how hard it would be for her to face him on Monday.

Taking a sip of the warm, sweet liquid from the mug in her hands, Breck closed her eyes and remembered how handsome—how absolutely gorgeous—Reese had been dressed in the period clothing of an aristocratic highwayman. If she concentrated very hard, she could still feel his thumb caress her lips—smell the aftershave on his cheek. What a perfect, fabulous night it had been. She would try to keep it in her dreams all weekend and worry about Monday morning on Monday morning.

CHAPTER FOUR

Breck spent Saturday and Sunday vacillating between euphoria and an anticipatory anxiety. Each time she looked at the pictures Sherryl had taken at Marcelli's—especially the one of the moment Reese's lips first touched her own—goose bumps, butterflies, and delightful shivers of every kind traveled through her body. It was truly a dream moment! And yet, whenever she thought of having to face Reese at work on Monday, she felt nervous, anxious, nauseated. Still, she knew he had made great sacrifices on her behalf. And there was the matter of the sweater he'd had his mother knit, as well. A major thank you was in order. And unable to think of anything else more appropriate, Breck arrived at work on Monday morning with one of her famous, and very delectable, homemade pumpkin pies in hand.

If there was one thing she'd noticed about Reese over the past six months as his assistant, it was that he had a huge weakness where baked goods were concerned. Anytime anyone brought homemade cookies, cakes, or pies to the office for any reason, Reese was always first in line to taste them. Therefore, Breck had put her faith in her pumpkin pie as being an apropos thank you for her pumpkin sweater. She'd worked for years—ever since she started baking as a young girl—to perfect her pumpkin pie filling recipe. And although she might not be very confident in other aspects of her life, she knew her pumpkin pie was a winner. She'd won first place at the Colorado State Fair seven years running with it.

As far as thanking Reese for the scene at Marcelli's—well, the pie would have to serve for that as well. The pie accompanied by verbal thanks, that was.

So with pumpkin pie in hand, Breck stepped off the elevator that crisp autumn Monday morning and smiled as Patty greeted her with a friendly wave.

"Hey there, Breck," Patty said, smiling. "What are you toting in this morning?"

"Something for Mr. Thatcher," Breck answered, adding, "and a thank you note for you." Balancing the pie carefully in one hand, Breck reached into her coat pocket and retrieved the thank you note she'd written for Patty regarding the lovely autumn snow globe she had gifted her.

"Oh, how sweet, Breck," Patty chimed. "You're so thoughtful."

"You're the thoughtful one, Patty," Breck told her. Then looking around quickly, she asked, "Is Mr. Thatcher in yet this morning, do you know?"

Patty shook her head and shrugged her shoulders. "Haven't seen him."

"Thanks," Breck said with relief. She wanted to get to her desk before he arrived—try to gather her composure.

But her plans to prepare herself to face him were thrown to the wind. For as she rounded the corner to her desk, she saw him standing in his office door, fiddling with his cell phone.

There was absolutely no way to avoid him. And so, drawing in a deep breath and trying to find an ounce of courage and composure, she walked directly to her desk.

"Good morning, Breck," Reese greeted with a knowing grin as she set the pie on her desk and began to remove her coat.

"Good morning, Mr. Thatcher," she said, unable to look at him and trying to sound nonchalant.

She heard him chuckle. "Oh, surely we're beyond 'Mr. Thatcher,' by now, Breck," he said. "Especially after the other night at—"

"You're right," she interrupted, a crimson blush already blazing on her cheeks. "And speaking of the other day," she began, "I owe you a truckload of thank-yous." Finally, she found the nerve to look at him and then wished she wouldn't have. He was too gorgeous—too knowing when it came to her discomfort! And what he was wearing was not only a bit different from what he normally wore to work but absolutely perfect on him! He often wore jeans to work, his profession and need to remain inconspicuous allowing for a more casual manner of dress. However, this day his jeans were adorably worn out! In fact, as he turned to remove a yellow sticky note someone had left on his office door, Breck noticed the dime-sized holes that were evident at the corner of each of the pockets on the seat of his pants.

For Pete's sake! she thought. She could see his underwear peeking through the holes—his white underwear! A raggedy, old blue-black baseball cap was partially shoved in one pocket too.

Complementing the rather intriguing holes in the rear end of his jeans were a pair of beat up, weathered, nearly ragged, black Roper boots Reese wore. And his shirt? Good grief! His shirt was nothing but a tight-fitting, red, rather faded, sort of misshapen T-shirt. He was absolutely drop-dead gorgeous!

"You do?" Reese asked, causing Breck to close her gaping mouth and frantically try to remember what she'd said before his adorable appearance had so completely distracted her.

"I do what?" she asked, unable to organize her thoughts.

He chuckled. "You said you owe me a truckload of thank-yous."

"Oh, yeah!" she said, nervous and giggling. "I do!"

With his familiar mischievous grin spreading across his face, Reese walked closer to Breck until he stood exactly in front of her.

Breck looked up into his face as he said, "Well?"

She was undone! How could she possibly ever remain calm in his presence again? Her eyes lingered on his delicious mouth, and she was reminded that she knew just how delicious it was.

"Well what?" she breathed.

Again Reese chuckled. "Is that pie plate on your desk my thank-you?"

The pie! Of course!

"Oh. Yes! It is," Breck exclaimed, turning from him and retrieving the pie from her desk. Holding the pie out to him, she said, "I hope you like pumpkin. I thought it appropriate, considering the beautiful sweater your mother made and all."

"Mmmm!" he hummed, removing the aluminum foil from the pie and inhaling of its mouth-watering fragrance. "Pumpkin pie is my absolute favorite," he told her.

"Oh! I'm glad," Breck said, swallowing hard. "Well then…I hope you enjoy it and—"

"So this is what I get for the pumpkin sweater?" he said, smiling at her.

"Yes. I hope it's okay. The sweater is beautiful. I know a pie doesn't really compare and—"

"What do I get for the thing at Marcelli's then?" he interrupted.

Breck felt goose bumps prickle at the back of her neck and on her legs. "I-I was thinking that…maybe the pie would do," she stammered.

He laughed wholeheartedly for a moment. Then winking at her and cupping her face in one strong hand for a moment, he said, "I'm just teasing you, Breck." Breck sighed with relief, but it was short-lived. "I was hoping for some copies of those pictures your friend took though." He smiled. "What do you think?"

"Oh. The pictures," Breck stammered. "Of course. I'll have her make some copies for you. I mean, your costume was incredible and—"

"It was fun, huh?" he said, lowering his voice. Breck looked up to find his eyes twinkling—bright with amusement at the memory.

"Fun?" she breathed. "Oh, yes. Yes it was…fun."

"We'll have to do it again sometime," he whispered in a low, very provocative tone.

"We will?" Breck choked. Reese chuckled and turned to leave her, intent on his office.

"Thanks for the pie, Breck," he called to her a moment before he shut his door.

Once Reese's office door was shut, Breck collapsed into her desk chair, trying to take in a deep breath. He was unbelievable! She'd almost grabbed the front of his T-shirt and pulled his head down toward hers to kiss him!

Fanning herself with one hand—trying to ease the temperature increase Reese had caused in her—Breck adjusted her headset just in time to answer the phone.

"Wilson Investigation, Reese Thatcher's office. May I help you?" she answered. The voice on the other line dispelled her euphoria.

"Miss McCall? This is Danielle Allen. Is Mr. Thatcher available to take my call?" the sobbing woman asked.

"Oh, Mrs. Allen," Breck stammered. "Let me see if he's in." Placing Mrs. Allen on hold, Breck beeped Reese's phone.

"Breck?" he answered.

"Mrs. Allen is on line one, Mr. Thatcher. She sounds very upset," she explained.

"I'll take the call. Thanks," he said. The teasing tone that had been in his voice only moments before was completely dissipated.

Breck resisted the urge to break company policy and eavesdrop on the conversation. Still, the thought of poor Mrs. Allen pinched her heart. Michael Allen was a jerk! And that was putting it mildly. Every time Reese was handed a case where one or the other member of a married couple was being unfaithful, she felt physically sick. What was wrong with people? Especially someone like Michael Allen. Danielle Allen was beautiful! Not only to look at, but she was a wonderful person. And their baby was adorable. What was wrong with that man? Secretly she wished she'd let Reese beat some sense into him the other day. But she knew that would've only landed Reese in trouble with some sort of wiener-spun lawsuit pending. Still, it made her angry. It hurt her heart.

A few minutes later, Reese opened his office door and stuck his head out, looking to Breck.

"Hey, Breck," he said. It was obvious he was infuriated. "Get me Lowel down at Stevens and Rodham, will you?"

"Sure," Breck agreed.

"Patch it in as a conference call on line one, please," he further instructed.

"Of course," she said.

❧

Breck spent the next two hours pulling stuff out of the Allen file and getting it ready to take over to Mrs. Allen's attorney. The more she worked on it, the more angry she became—the more discouraged. By the time her break rolled around, she felt like she'd been through an entire week of work. Her disposition wasn't very friendly at that moment, so she decided to just sit back in her chair and read the comics in the newspaper Reese always deposited on her desk when he was finished with it every morning. Something lighthearted—that's what she needed.

She'd almost finished the comic page of the newspaper and was just swallowing the last bite of her honey-roasted peanuts package when the door to Reese's office opened and he stepped out.

"There's something you should know, Breck," he said, striding to where she sat.

"There is?" she asked, wondering what in the world he was going to tell her. Was there more drama with the Allen case?

She was suddenly quite self-conscious and uncomfortable when he hunkered down next to her and took one of her hands between his own.

"Breck," Reese began. Breck could hardly breathe! Had Mrs. Allen taken matters into her own hands? Had she lost it and…and…

"That is…by far…the best pumpkin pie I have ever eaten," he said. There was no hint of teasing or amusement in his expression. But still, Breck thought, *He can't be serious.*

"Pardon?" Breck breathed.

Reese shook his head and inhaled deeply. "I never thought I'd say this to any woman," he began, "and part of me feels like a traitor even thinking this. But…but, Breck…" Breck waited for him to finish, unable to breathe or believe what he was saying. "That pie was better than my *mother's!*"

Breck let out a relieved sigh. What a kidder he was!

"Oh, oh sure," she giggled. He had her going for a moment. "I hope you enjoyed it all the same, Mr. Thatcher."

She was astonished, however, when he suddenly took her chin firmly in his hand, nearly glared at her, and said, "No. I'm serious."

There was not a hint of sarcasm in his voice or expression. Breck realized he was actually sincere in the compliment.

"Really?" was all she could say—a delighted smile spreading across her face. "Well, I'm glad you like it." She giggled a little, for he seemed unsettled.

"Do you realize what this means?" he asked, shaking his head.

"No. What?" Breck coaxed.

He stared at her for a moment, seeming to study her face with too much intensity to leave her comfortable. Then he stood up and simply said, "I've got to run over to Stevens and Rodham. Will you just forward my calls to my voicemail?" And he was gone.

Breck sat in her chair, completely perplexed. His behavior had been so odd—as if finding a pie that was better than his mother's was somehow life-altering. Still, she giggled, for his strange behavior had, once again, lightened her heavy heart.

Tucking the newspaper away in the recycle bin, she managed to get her headset on just as the phone rang.

"Wilson Investigation, Reese Thatcher's office. May I help you?"

Reese climbed into his pickup and laid his head on the steering wheel for a moment. He was in trouble! All weekend long he'd done nothing but obsess about what had transpired between him and Breck at Marcelli's on Friday night. Well, he'd worked on stripping his deck, gone to the game with Bill, and watched some Bruce Willis movie on TV. But mostly he'd had trouble getting the taste of that kiss with Breck out of his mind. And now this! No one—absolutely no one—made a better pumpkin pie than his mother! He was a bit unnerved that something so seemingly miniscule could throw him for such a big loop. The pie Breck had baked for him as thanks for "the sweater," as she put it, was absolutely the best he'd ever had. And there was no reason on earth that a man's office girl should bake a better pumpkin pie than his mother!

Maybe he'd just been deprived of pumpkin pie for too long. Maybe he'd just been really, really hungry, having skipped breakfast that morning. But he shook his head as he clutched and turned the key in his pickup ignition. This girl was getting under his skin—and long before the whole fiasco he'd involved himself in at Marcelli's—long before she'd made a better pumpkin pie than his own mother. Breck McCall was dangerous to the order of the life Reese Thatcher had chosen. She made him think of hazardous things like home, his cute little nieces, his ol' cow Honey—the last he'd raised at home before he'd left for the city and a big-city career.

He closed his eyes, trying to block out the image of Breck in that dang pumpkin sweater his mother had knitted. Tried not to remember how she'd melted in his arms when he'd kissed her—how delicious that kiss tasted.

Shifting into first, he peeled out of the parking lot. He'd drive around a bit. That would clear his head. Maybe he'd call his mother and ask if she thought ol' Honey would make it through the winter. He wouldn't tell her that he'd met a girl that made a better pumpkin pie than she did.

CHAPTER FIVE

Lunch with Patty had been unexpectedly soothing. Breck was amazed at Patty's ability to calm her down, help her remember the good in the world.

"Not everybody marries a jerk, Breck," Patty told her. They'd been discussing the Allens' situation. "Look at me and my Joe, for example. Twenty-five years of wedded bliss…and I mean it!" Yes, Breck enjoyed Patty's company, her positive attitude toward life, her hope in humanity.

However, when she returned from lunch and rounded the corner of the office to find Jamie Reynolds standing by her desk talking with another office girl, Breck felt her optimistic mood begin to evaporate again. One thing would sour a day faster than Michael Allen—and that was Jamie Reynolds.

Jamie worked in filing. She was a sharp-tongued, trouble-making "hoochie"—as Barb would call her—with the reddest of red hair and the most hateful green eyes Breck had ever seen. She was quite curvaceous and liked to remind everyone of it by wearing clothes that were far too tight and revealing. In actuality, Breck was surprised that old Mr. Wilson kept her on. She often wondered what blackmail material Jamie had cached away on Mr. Wilson, for she made everyone's life miserable. Furthermore, she was forever going on about which man at the office was pursuing her on any given day of the week. For some reason, however, she'd stayed clear of trying to link herself up with Reese through the gossip line. Breck thought this was because even a woman as ignorant as Jamie Reynolds knew no one would believe Reese Thatcher would consort with a woman like her.

As Breck approached her desk, she thought about how completely she hated having to feign friendliness to Jamie. But Jamie was the kind of girl that would chew you up and spit you out if you rubbed her the wrong way. Still, Breck loathed dealing with her—and it was obvious she would have to.

"Well, I've had it!" Jamie said in a lowered voice to the girl she had cornered. As Breck approached, she heard her add, "Someone needs to take him down a size or two, and I'm ready to do it."

Breck felt the hair on the back of her neck prickle, sensing something very bad was about to happen.

"What do you mean?" Breck sighed. First of all, she couldn't believe that Jamie was talking trash about someone while standing in her office. The girl knew Breck didn't like to hear all her dirty laundry.

"Your boss! That's what I mean!" Jamie exclaimed, raising her voice a bit. The girl who Jamie had been talking to before Breck arrived rolled her eyes at Breck as she made some sad excuse to leave Breck to the wolf.

"Mr. Thatcher?" Breck asked, a strange, nauseated sensation flooding her stomach. This was not good. Breck knew it.

"Surely you've noticed how arrogant and superior he acts," Jamie whispered. "Walking around with his nose in the air, never giving anyone the time of day. It's time he learned people deserve more respect. I'm gonna slap him hard with sexual harassment. We'll see how high and mighty he is then."

"What?" Breck exclaimed. What kind of an idiot would tell her—Reese's assistant—about plans to accuse him? Still, she thought it might be wise to feign the ally for a moment longer. At least until she knew more about what Jamie intended to do. "Reese Thatcher is the only gentleman around here," Breck growled.

"Exactly," Jamie sneered. "Or so he claims. Today I caught him looking dead at my chest…and don't tell me he wasn't checking me out."

Breck frowned and shook her head as she glanced down at the plunging neckline of Jamie's blouse—not to mention the two strategically placed, hot pink daisies glaring at her from each breast.

"Anybody is gonna look at that shirt, Jamie." Realizing this was exactly Jamie's intention, she added, "But I guess that was the plan."

Jamie glared at Breck. "You *would* defend him. I should've expected that you were too wowed by his good looks to see through him for what he really is."

Breck clenched her teeth tightly for a moment, trying to find the self-control to simply walk away. However, she couldn't. She was sick of women like Jamie—and the world seemed to have too many of them. It was time someone took one down.

"Jamie…it is so way obvious that you're just ticked off because Reese doesn't give you the time of day. And believe me, you try to accuse him of anything…and I'll make this conversation public knowledge."

Before Breck could even fathom what was to come, she felt the hot sting of a hard slap against her right cheek. Putting her hand quickly to her throbbing face, Breck looked back to Jamie in time to see (but not avoid) the painful slap across her other cheek. Jamie had paused just long enough between slaps to turn her chunky silver ring so that the gems were on the inside of her hand. In doing so she had assured that the second slap left a painful and now bleeding cut on Breck's left cheekbone.

Breck stood stunned—unable to believe the viciousness of the woman's attack. "You're crazy!" she exclaimed.

"Well, you're naive," Jamie told her. "No…you're plain stupid." She turned to leave but paused, turning back to Breck. Waving an index finger at her, she whispered, "You're an idiot if you think he's going to ever give you the time of day. And you're even dumber if you think Wilson won't pay me off when I charge him."

Breck pressed her wound with her fingers and then looked at the blood it left on them—still awed by what had happened. She was going to say something, even though she didn't know what, but when Dave Pullman rounded the corner, she decided to keep quiet. There was nothing she could say anyway.

As Jamie turned to leave again, she paused as she saw Dave and heard Reese's office door open.

"What's going on here?" Reese asked, perplexed. Patty appeared almost instantly, and Breck breathed a sigh of relief as she realized that Patty must've heard or seen something and called security.

"Tell him what's going on, Jamie," Patty urged. She glared at Jamie, folding her arms across her chest in a gesture of waiting for the woman's response.

"What do you mean?" Jamie asked, feigning ignorance. "We were just talking."

Reese looked to Breck, his frown deepening as he strode to where she stood. Taking her chin none too gently in his hand, he tipped her head and looked at the bleeding cut on her cheek.

"What're you doing, Jamie?" he growled.

"She's assaulting Breck, that's what she's doing," Patty said, "and planning to slap you with a sexual harassment charge too," she added.

Again Breck was thankful that Patty was always running to someone's assistance. She must've been in the hallway just outside Reese's office—heard the conversation prior to Jamie's violence and called security and Reese.

Reese nodded as he glared at Jamie, "Oh, I see," he mumbled. "Dave," he said, releasing Breck's face for a moment, reaching down, taking a tissue from the box on her desk, and holding it to her cheek.

"Yes, sir?" Dave nodded.

"You wanna take Miss Hellfire here to her desk, let her get *only* her personal items, and then escort her out of the building, please?" Reese ordered.

"My pleasure, sir," Dave answered.

"You can't fire me!" Jamie argued. "She hit me first!" she lied.

"She hit you first?" Reese shouted, enraged by the obvious lie. Reese took Breck's hand and placed the tissue in it as he turned toward Jamie. But Breck read the look on his face and knew if she let him continue toward the woman in his state of mind that he'd be facing an assault charge in the least.

"Dave," Breck said, calmly stepping between Reese and Jamie.

"Follow me, Miss Reynolds," Dave said, taking her arm carefully and directing her away from the scene.

"You haven't seen the last of me, Reese Thatcher!" Jamie shouted as everyone in the office began poking their heads out of office and cubicle spaces to see what all the commotion was about.

"You got that right!" Reese hollered after her. "You seem to have forgotten there's a security camera watching this space. We'll see who gets charged with what."

Patty took hold of Reese's arm. "Settle down, Reese. Settle down," she soothed. "She'll get hers."

Reese sighed heavily, trying to gain control of his temper. Then he turned his attention to Breck once more.

"Let me see," he said, pulling her hand away from the cut. He took her chin in his hand again and inspected the injury more closely. Then he turned her face to look at the other cheek. "Look at the welt she left here!" he growled. "Patty, have Dave get that security tape copied, please," he said to Patty, although still looking at Breck's face. "Breck," he said then, releasing his hold on her face, "can I see you in my office?" It was a command under the guise of a polite question, and Breck's heart began to hammer with anxiety. Would he be angry with her as well? Would Dave be escorting her from the building in the next few minutes?

Reese opened the door to his office and stood aside, motioning for Breck to enter first. Closing the door behind them, he said, "I am so sorry, Breck."

His apology was not only unnecessary but unexpected as well.

"Pardon me?" Breck said, uncertain whether she had heard him correctly.

"You shouldn't have to come to work and worry about whether or not you're going to end up in the hospital by the end of the day," he explained, taking her chin in his hand again. He studied the wound on her cheek, and Breck knew he must've tugged at it a bit because a sharp pain stung her there for a moment. "Yep," he muttered, releasing her chin. "You need a stitch or two."

"Really?" Breck gasped, going to the nearby wall mirror. As she studied the small but deep cut on her cheek, she felt tears welling up in her eyes. Suddenly, what had just happened with Jamie—the thoughts of poor Mrs. Allen—all the ugliness of the day—washed over her like a hot, horrible rain.

"Why are people so awful?" she cried, burying her face in her hands for a moment, unable to stop her tears. Her heart actually hurt because of the cruelty in her day, and she felt like she wanted to curl up and hide away from the world. She was angry too and looked up at Reese as everything she was feeling began spilling from her lips.

"Mrs. Allen is a good, kind, beautiful woman! How can her husband be such a creep? And that cute little baby. How can he not appreciate what he has…or rather had?" she corrected.

"I don't know," Reese mumbled, shrugging his shoulders.

But Breck's mind and mouth were bent on venting. "And Jamie," she continued. "She's just ticked off because you won't give her the time of day. So she decides to slap you with a sexual harassment suit?" Breck frowned and shook her head, still unable to believe what had just happened outside Reese's office. "I mean…you're the least harassing man I've ever met in my life! Did she really think she could make that stick? Well, in today's world…she probably could've! And to sink so low as to wear something so tacky as that stupid blouse with two big pink daisies smack on her…on her…bosoms!" By this time Breck was pacing back and forth in front of Reese as she rambled. He just watched her go back and forth, back and forth, like a spectator at a tennis match, as she raved on.

"I mean, who wouldn't look at her chest? I did! I mean, what happened to decency? Do you know what I mean?" she asked him. "Where are all the good guys? All the good girls, for that matter? And slapping me like that…at work!" She paused, waving an angry index finger at Reese and adding, "You know, I'd be justified in slapping her with an assault charge or two." Then she shook her head—felt her shoulders sagging defeatedly. "But then…would I be any better than her? And where would it get me? In debt to some attorney." Breck sighed heavily and rubbed at her temples for a moment. "What a rotten day," she muttered as she felt any remaining energy drain from her being.

"And it's only going to get worse, I'm afraid," Reese said, taking his keys from his worn-out jeans pocket, "'cause you do need a couple of stitches. Let's go."

Breck wiped the tears from her cheeks, but more still came as Reese nodded toward his office door.

"Come on," he said. "I'll take you to the Urgent Care down the road."

Breck shook her head. "You don't have to take me," she told him. After all, she didn't want to inconvenience him and add to his rotten day. "I can take myself."

"You'll be sitting there for at least two hours," he reminded her. "Urgent Care is just another term for Non-Urgent Care. But…it'll be faster than the emergency room." He grinned at her and opened his office door, gesturing for her to leave first. "You'll need something to do while you're waiting. You can talk to me."

Even with everything she'd gone through—the pain on her cheeks, the disappointment in humanity in her heart—she felt butterflies rise in her stomach, excited by the prospect of a couple of hours spent with Reese outside the office.

"Are you okay?" Patty asked as Breck reached under her desk to retrieve her purse.

"I'm fine," Breck lied.

"Patty…will you let Mr. Wilson know what's gone on, please? Will you tell him I'm running Breck down for stitches and that I'll get with him about this mess when I get back?" Reese asked.

"I sure will," Patty said, winking at Breck.

Breck was delighted when Reese then took hold of her arm and began walking with her out of the office. "Come on then, Miss McCall. Let's get you patched up."

Breck wiped a final tear from her cheek, knowing, however, that more would follow. It had been a terrible day, and even though she was in the company of her dreamy Reese Thatcher for now, she knew that anxiety would wash over her later.

❧

"Climb on in," Reese said as he opened the door to just about the most beaten-up old blue pickup Breck had ever seen. Breck smiled at him as she stepped up into the passenger's side of the truck. Given his attire that day and his mode of transportation, he looked as if he could've just stepped out of her uncle's barn on the old McCall ranch.

As Reese shut her in and walked around the pickup to get in himself, Breck took a quick look around inside. Now this was a real man's truck, she noted. Gum wrappers littered the faded dashboard; there was a long crack in the windshield running vertically down in front of her. The gearshift was so old and so well used that the gear numbers were completely worn off. There was a distinct aroma in it as well—a combination of Speed Stick, mint gum, and soil. Not the expected vehicle choice of a man who made far beyond six figures annually.

"Buckle up," he said, grinning as he hopped into the truck and turned the ignition.

Breck smiled as she buckled the vintage seat belt, lap belt only, across her tummy and cinched it tight. She thought she might burst into beams of joy as he pulled the old cap from his back pocket, slapped it onto his head facing backward, and pulled a stick of gum from the pack lodged in the ashtray.

How cute! Breck thought as she watched him toss the empty wrapper onto the dashboard. He kept the gum in the old ashtray and threw the wrappers around everywhere.

"Gum?" he asked when he caught her staring at him with a smile.

"Sure," she said, taking a piece from the tray.

As she began folding the wrapper, intending to put it in her purse, he said, "Just throw it up here." He tapped on the dashboard with one hand. "I'll get it later."

The local country music station playing on the radio and the way the old truck rode reminded Breck of her grandfather McCall's truck—heavy and tossing its passengers around like popcorn in a kettle.

Breck couldn't help smiling as she looked over at Reese, driving his old truck, chomping on his gum, and looking like a farm kid let loose in the city. He just kept getting better and better, and her heart felt heavy for a moment at knowing how slim her chances really were of winning him. Still, he had dressed up like her Highwayman. And he had kissed her pretty darn passionately. Breck studied him for a moment as he drummed on the steering wheel, matching the rhythm of the song currently playing on the radio.

"I know, I know," Reese said, smiling at her when he caught her staring at him. "Don't feel bad. Chicks always dig this pickup."

Breck giggled. "Chicks? Dig?" she teased.

"Yeah," he chuckled. "I think there's a song along those lines, isn't there?"

"Yeah," Breck agreed.

ॐ

Ten minutes later, Breck was sitting next to Reese, waiting her turn to be seen by an on-call doctor at the Urgent Care. Reese sat reading a pamphlet on hearing loss, and Breck looked around the waiting room trying to feign indifference to his presence.

"Yep," Reese said. "I'm a candidate."

"What?" Breck asked.

"A candidate. For hearing loss," he explained. "See? Use of loud machinery, listening to loud music, chronic ear infections as a child. It's a wonder I can still hear at all." Then he tossed the pamphlet to the chair next to him and began tapping his foot. "What do you want to do while we're waiting?" he asked.

"You don't really have to wait with me, Mr. Thatcher," Breck said, not wanting to inconvenience him any further. "I can call someone to—"

"How many times have you had stitches?" he interrupted.

Breck giggled. He was like a little boy trapped in a Sunday school meeting on an inviting summer's day.

"Never had any," she answered.

"What?" he exclaimed in sincere disbelief. "How can you never have had stitches before?"

"I don't know," she told him. "How many times have you had stitches?"

"Fifty-seven," he said.

"Fifty-seven?" Breck exclaimed. "How can you possibly have had to have stitches fifty-seven times?"

"The first time I slammed my finger in the door when I was two. Then there was the snowmobile accident I had when I was nineteen… drove my ride into a barbed-wire fence. Odds and ends and a couple of other big incidents. It's easy enough to need stitches," he told her. He talked so nonchalantly about it.

Breck shook her head, completely amused by his attitude.

"These won't hurt much though," he said, studying her cheek again. He took her chin in his hand and, frowning, looked at the wound more closely. "It ticks me off. I've been telling Mr. Wilson that Jamie was going to cause trouble. It makes me wonder what she has on him to make him keep her this long."

Breck nodded. "Me too," she admitted.

"Let her charge me with harassment," he growled. "I'll just insist she wears that shirt she wore today to court. Once the judge gets a load of that…I'll be fine."

Breck began to giggle—the sort of nervous giggle a person gets when a situation is too ridiculous, horrible, or both to believe. "That was the most outrageous blouse I've ever seen."

"Yes, ma'am," Reese chuckled. Breck glanced at him. There was something more real about Reese Thatcher that day. All the things that made him attractive were still there—surreal good looks, charming personality—but there was more. As Breck watched him sitting next to her, she sensed there was a part of him that had been hidden—or asleep—before. What was it?

"Do you have any brothers and sisters?" he asked, trying to make light conversation.

"One brother is all," Breck answered. "Jake. He's a Marine and stationed overseas."

"Really?" Reese seemed impressed. "Wow. Are you guys close?"

Breck shrugged. "As close as we can be now that he's so far away." She smiled at him. "You?"

"Two brothers, one older, one younger…and an older sister," he answered.

"That's great," Breck said, smiling. She liked imagining Reese as a child—playing and fighting with siblings.

"Mom and dad?" he asked.

"Yeah. They're in Europe for a few months."

Reese frowned. "So…you're alone here?"

"My uncles and cousins live a couple of hours away." Breck shrugged. She did miss her family. It broke Breck's heart the way families were separated by the necessity of earning a living or other intrusive elements of life. Modern times had wreaked havoc on the family unit. More often than not, Breck dreamed of living in the days when, in most cases, at least a few members of a person's family settled in close.

"Your mom and dad?" she asked, trying to change her lonely state of mind.

"One of each," Reese answered.

An awkward silence followed, and Breck understood why. Reese and she had shared only a working relationship, but the events that unfolded at Marcelli's a few nights before, coupled with today's goings-on, had given them a more intimate association—sort of.

"Why is it that you're not settled down…married and expecting a baby or two, Miss McCall?" His question was completely unanticipated and completely stunning.

"What?" was all Breck could muster.

Reese shook his head. "I don't know. You just seem…I mean, you're really good at what you do," he assured her. "It's just that…somehow I envision you in a little yellow house, surrounded by a white picket fence…a couple of babies crawling around while you bake chocolate-chip cookies or something."

Breck felt a crimson blush rise to her cheeks—accompanied by a delighted smile. It was as if he'd seen her soul! For in truth, that was exactly her secret, unspoken dream. Ever since she was a child she'd wanted to grow up, get married, and raise a family. But people, especially other women, seemed to frown on that way of life these days. And finding a man who wanted the same things seemed almost impossible. But here, sitting next to her in the Urgent Care…

"I'd love that!" she slipped. She hadn't meant to confess it to him so honestly. When he looked at her with curiosity, she continued, "It's just that…that's a vanishing way of life. Don't you think?"

He seemed thoughtful for a moment. "I guess so. But I think people allowed it to vanish. They get caught up in technology, entertainment. Or they run away from it for some reason." He looked at her again. "Had you pegged though. Didn't I?" He smiled.

Breck giggled. "That is what you do." After all, he wasn't a success in his field for no reason.

"That is what I do," he repeated. But as he looked at the pretty girl sitting next to him in the Urgent Care, he couldn't help pushing the issue.

"Why don't you settle down, raise a family? Bake some cookies?" he asked. Reese knew he liked this girl way too much. He wasn't even sure she needed stitches. He'd just wanted to find a way to whisk her away from that awful office. She didn't belong there. He'd known it all along. He'd become far too protective of Breck McCall and her refreshing wholesomeness.

He smiled as she squirmed, uncomfortable by either his gaze or his question. He couldn't tell which.

"I…well…the opportunity hasn't presented itself," came her canned answer. Reese was in far too teasing a mood to let her slip away that easily.

"Which opportunity?" he asked. "To bake cookies or have babies?" He could've sworn she blushed to the very tips of her toes.

"T-to settle down," she stammered. "I bake cookies all the time."

"Breck McCall?" the nurse called from the front desk. Reese was disappointed that they'd called her in so quickly. He'd been hoping for at least two hours in her company.

❧

"Here," Reese said, taking Breck's keys. "Let me get it." Reese unlocked the door and stepped aside to allow Breck to enter her apartment first. Breck smiled, delighted with his manners. It had been a very long time since any man under the age of fifty had opened a door for her. And Reese had held doors for her all day.

Breck stepped into the apartment and somehow felt nervous as Reese stepped in after her, closing the door behind him. She watched as he began to look around.

Yep. Even the decor in her apartment—the atmosphere inside, the perfect feel of it—added to Reese's knowledge that this girl was different from most. First of all, it smelled like apples and cinnamon, nutmeg and warm bread—aromas he hadn't enjoyed for a long time.

"Would you like some ice water? Root beer?" Breck asked. He smiled, delighted with her concern for him and further delighted by what she had offered him to drink. Most women he'd known lately would've started with, *Can I get you a drink before I slip into something more comfortable?*

"Water," he answered, smiling at her. It seemed odd, but she looked adorable with her two little cheek stitches. He was mad for a moment again then—mad that a woman like Jamie even existed to harm such a sweet girl as this.

As Breck left the room to retrieve his water, Reese wandered around slowly—taking in everything about it. There was a small entertainment unit on a nearby wall, a TV, stereo, and DVD player housed there. Along the top stood an ancient-looking clock, nine or ten old sepia-toned photographs of people from days gone by. Reese looked closely at all the photographs for a moment. One in particular caught his interest—a handsome-looking couple standing with a horse. The woman was dark-haired and quite beautiful—especially for the time period, which Reese guessed was the late 1800s. In the background was an arched entry typical of an old ranch that read, "El Costa Lotta—McCall Ranch." Reese felt his eyebrows rise as he recognized the name of the ranch. McCall horses had been a valuable commodity in Colorado for the past century, and he figured that his own little Breck McCall must be a relative.

He looked down then—having nearly stepped on a pile of CDs and DVDs that lay on the floor in front of the wall unit. He smiled as he recognized artists and titles of bygone eras—old movie musicals from the '50s, jazz artists and crooners from the '40s, counted among various Christmas music and romantic comedies.

Looking around the room, he noted several antique lamp tables topped with hurricane lamps, old books on several wall bookshelves, three thriving Boston ferns. Artificial pumpkins and turkeys were strategically placed here and there, reflecting the woman's adoration of autumn and the holidays.

Indeed, it was a cozy, warm, beautiful room that left Reese in a fog of nostalgia, comfort, and further confirmation of Breck's being unique from other young women of the day.

"Here you go," she said, returning and handing him a glass of water.

"Thank you," he said. Even the water from her faucet tasted better. Purer, colder, fresher.

She bit her lip nervously and finally said, "Do you want to sit down for a moment?"

"Sure," Reese answered. He couldn't help grinning at her because he knew he made her uncomfortable. It probably wasn't easy to have her boss there in her apartment so unexpectedly. Especially when he'd kissed her just days before—and wanted to kiss her again—although she didn't know that. Even so, he enjoyed watching her discomfort.

"So," he began, sighing as he took a seat on her sofa, "this is where you live and bake cookies."

"Yep," was all she managed to say.

"And pumpkin pies that are better than my mother's," he added. She smiled, obviously delighted by his compliment. "It's nice," he told her. "I like it. It's very…you."

"What do you mean?" she asked, seeming uncertain as to whether this remark were a compliment.

"You know…comfortable, cozy…smells good," he answered. He smiled as he saw her cheeks go crimson.

"Thank you," she said. Then she dropped her gaze for a moment, her hands fiddling in her lap as she nearly mumbled, "Thank you… for taking me to get stitches."

"You're welcome," he said. "But a girl shouldn't have to leave an office job to go get sewn up."

"Maybe not," she said. "But thank you anyway."

He smiled, feeling a little angry with the male members of the human race. Obviously, she wasn't used to any sort of chivalry or manners in men. And he resented his own gender for that.

Breck tried to breathe regularly—tried not to smile too much at the joy she was experiencing. He was there—right there with her in her own apartment—Reese Thatcher! That fact was definitely worth getting beaten and having to have stitches. She couldn't believe he was there!

"I'll pick you up for work tomorrow, and you can just leave your car at the office tonight," he told her.

"Oh!" she exclaimed. She had forgotten all about her car. "Are you sure that will be all right? I can take the bus in and—" she began.

"No way," he said. "I'll just pick you up in the morning."

"If you're sure," she agreed.

"Of course I'm sure," he said. "I noticed the pictures on your thing there," he said, pointing to the wall unit. "Are you related to the people that run the McCall ranch out east of Colorado Springs?"

Breck felt her heart swell. He knew about the McCall ranch? How could he know? Of course, Reese Thatcher did seem to know something about everything.

"Yeah," Breck admitted with obvious pride. "My uncle runs it now…but my great-grandfather, Jackson McCall, named it officially back in, like, 1889."

"El Costa Lotta," Reese chuckled. "That's funny. I didn't get it at first."

"Yeah," Breck giggled. "Jackson McCall and his brothers were known as quite the characters in their day."

"You ever spend much time out there as a kid?" he asked.

Breck smiled, delighted by his interest. "I did," she told him. "And I loved it out there. I always wished my dad had stayed in the ranching business. But…he didn't."

Breck retrieved a drink coaster from the end table and handed it to Reese. He smiled at her and placed his glass on the coffee table in front of him.

Dang, this girl was cute! Reese felt a slight anxiety rising within him as he lingered in Breck's company. She was dangerous to a man's stability. He could feel it. A rare and wonderful girl like this could distract a guy from his course in life. He knew he had better escape while he could. Too much time around Breck McCall could be risky.

So, with a heavy sigh, Reese stood to leave. "I better get going," he told her. Her forced smile told him that she didn't want him to leave. No doubt the events of the day were still weighing heavily on her mind. Still, to linger would not be a good idea. She was too cute and vulnerable with her little stitches and windblown hair.

"Thank you for everything, Mr. Thatcher," she told him. And then he knew he had lingered too long. For the devil in him was at the door.

"You mean for taking you to the Urgent Care?" he said, smiling at her as she stood to face him. "Or do you mean for dressing up like an idiot for your birthday?"

She smiled and blushed. "Both," she said.

He watched her glance away shyly when he took her hand in his and said, "I'm sorry about this mess today, Breck."

"It wasn't your fault," she assured him.

"It was. I know that," he said. "You stuck up for me and ended up with stitches." She shook her head and glanced down shyly again. "And the worst part of it is…she was right."

She looked up at him—frowning—puzzled. "What do you mean?"

Stop it right now, Reese, he told himself. But it was too late. The wolf in him was already prowling. He raised her hand to his lips and placed a lingering kiss on the back of it.

"Only…it wasn't her that I planned on harassing." He grinned, delighted at the way her eyes widened in astonishment at his inference. She was struck silent, of course, so the wolf continued to stalk its prey. "Still…does it count as harassment if it's after hours and not in the office?"

"What?" she gulped.

Somewhere Reese found his steady mark then, and instead of stealing a kiss as he'd planned, he simply asked, "Can I take you to dinner Friday?"

"What?" she repeated, obviously still rattled by his previous flirtations.

"To help soothe the sting of what happened today…let me take you to dinner, Breck." She paused, seeming uncertain, so he added, "I'd feel a little better if you let me make a sad attempt at repaying you for looking out for me today."

She smiled at him. "Sure," she agreed.

Reese smiled at her. He seemed genuinely pleased that she'd accepted his dinner invitation. Breck tried to remain calm—tried to still her excited trembling until she'd seen him all the way out the door and closed it.

"Seven okay?" he asked.

"Seven what?" she asked in return. Kisses? Sure! She'd take seven kisses from him any day!

He chuckled. "Seven o'clock at night on Friday. I'll pick you up at seven. Okay?"

"Oh, yeah," Breck breathed, blushing and horrified from being so brainless for a moment.

"Okay," he said. "Call me if you need anything tonight."

"Thank you," Breck managed.

Through her front window she watched him walk out to his

pickup. He smiled and waved to her a moment before he drove off into the sunset.

Breck sighed, content and delighted with the result of what had otherwise been a completely rotten day. Gently she touched the stitches that held the wound at her cheek. Yep! Well worth the pain to spend an afternoon with Reese Thatcher. How would she ever settle down, stay calm, and function normally until Friday night?

CHAPTER SIX

Tuesday, Wednesday, and Thursday seemed to drag by like months as Breck waited for Friday to arrive. Work seemed tedious at best, and working with Reese was all the more difficult now—for now she sensed she knew a part of him that had been dormant or hiding before. When she considered his willingness to play the Highwayman—thought of the way he had been dressed the day she'd been assaulted by Jamie Reynolds—even the type of vehicle he drove hinted at a hidden identity of some sort. For the most part, Reese perfectly fit the description of the up-and-coming, big-city businessman, but there was more to him than mere appearances. Breck was certain of it.

From the time Reese dropped her off at her apartment Monday afternoon until the moment the clock on her wall unit chimed seven on Friday night, Breck was preoccupied with anticipating the evening. How should she dress? He hadn't specified, nor had she thought to ask, what type of restaurant he was taking her to. So as she took a deep breath and readied to open the door to meet Reese, she smoothed the white angora sweater she'd chosen to wear with a jean skirt.

"Hi," Reese greeted her as she opened the door. He wore Levi's and a black long-sleeved shirt—perfect as usual and handsome as a dream!

"Hi," she replied.

"You ready?" he asked.

She nodded, taking her coat from the peg behind the door. Breck locked her apartment door and then began walking toward the street, where she could see Reese's pickup parked.

"You look great," he said, smiling at her and placing a hand at the small of her back. Breck felt herself blush and hoped he would think it was just the cool night air.

Opening the passenger door first, Breck was startled when Reese simply spun her around to face him, placed his powerful hands at her waist, and lifted her into the pickup seat.

"Don't want you to tear your skirt," he explained before closing the door.

"Thank you," Breck offered, blushing with the delight borne of his rather heroic gesture.

"I hope you like steak," Reese told her as his pickup's engine roared to life, "and company."

Breck felt her heart sink to the pit of her stomach. He'd invited someone else?

"Sure," she said, forcing a smile and trying to sound delighted.

"Good. 'Cause we're going to Bulls Eye's, and my mom is meeting us there," he explained. Breck glanced at him, her mouth gaping open in astonishment. Oh, it wasn't the fact that he was taking her to the most expensive steak house in the city that shocked her: it was the fact that his mother was meeting them there! His mother?

"Your mother?" she couldn't help asking.

"Yeah," he said, smiling. "She ran up to check on me today and decided to stay the night. I told her I had a date…but how could I leave her alone? You know?"

Breck shivered with excitement at his referring to their dinner as a date. Still, his mother?

"Of course you couldn't," she said. "I wouldn't expect you to."

"Oh, I would've just given her a book or the remote or something, and she would've been glad to stay home. But…" he continued, "she found out I was going with you. That's why she wanted to come."

Breck felt nauseated. "Why would it matter that it was me?" she ventured.

"Really?" he chuckled. "Are you kidding? You're the pumpkin sweater girl. I suspect she wants to see what kind of a girl would get me to go the extra mile for a birthday gift."

"Oh. I see." Breck swallowed hard. All at once her excitement about the evening had disappeared. His mother, for Pete's sake!

The rest of the way to the restaurant they talked about nothing in particular—the Broncos' last game, the Allen case, other things in the news. Breck thought her knees would fail her when, at last, they did arrive and Reese took her hand to help her down out of the pickup. He did not release her hand as he locked up the truck and started into the restaurant either. Her hand burned warm and tingly when he held it, and even when they entered Bulls Eye's to be greeted by Reese's mother, he did not let her hand go.

"Hey, Mom," Reese said, kissing his mother affectionately on one cheek. "This is Breck. The pumpkin sweater girl."

Reese's mother was a short, plump, merry-looking woman. Her eyes seemed to smile along with the rest of her face, which was framed by brown hair with just a hint of gray. She wore a bright red sweater under a denim jacket, a jean skirt, and a pair of red Ropers. She was absolutely the friendliest, most approachable-looking woman Breck had ever met.

"Oh, hello!" Reese's mother greeted, throwing her arms around Breck's shoulders in a familiar hug. "I'm so glad to meet you…Breck, is it?"

"Yes, ma'am," Breck said, smiling. "And it's so nice to meet you, Mrs. Thatcher."

"Oh, call me Marjie," she said, laughing.

"And I'd like to thank you for the beautiful sweater. I've never seen anything like it! It's so perfect," Breck said.

"You're welcome. Aren't you a sweetheart?" Marjie cooed, delighted by the praise.

As the waitress led them to their table, Marjie said, "I hope you don't mind my comin' along on your date tonight, Breck."

"Oh, of course not," Breck told her. And, surprisingly, she realized she meant it.

"I just swung up to town to check on Reese and do some shoppin' today…didn't think that he might have plans." Breck watched as the small woman squiggled into her chair at their table. It was like some sort of strange white light radiated from her. Breck would have sworn that she illuminated the room all on her own.

"Now, don't eat like a bird, Mom," Reese said as the waitress handed them all menus. "I mean for you to go home well-fed and rested."

"And I mean to go home that way," Marjie said, opening her menu and happily sighing.

Breck was feeling quite comfortable considering the circumstances. The more she thought about it, the more she realized how sweet it was that Reese was taking his mother to dinner with them.

"Reese tells me you're related to the McCalls out at El Costa Lotta," Marjie said as she flipped a page on her menu.

"Oh, yes. Jackson McCall was my great-grandfather," Breck explained.

"Good horses comin' out of there these past couple of years," Marjie said, nodding. "Ol' Goose was from the McCall place, Reese," she added.

"He was a good horse for kids," Reese said.

And then, it all became clear to Breck. How could she have been so naive? So blind?

"You're a farm boy!" she exclaimed, looking to Reese in astonishment. She could see it now—the polite manners, the sauntering way of walking, the pickup, the knowledge of the McCall ranch. Instantly, she felt like a cloud had been lifted from her mind.

Reese and his mother both chuckled. "It's been a long time since anyone called me a boy, Breck," he told her.

Breck giggled. "It just explains so much." Immediately she wished she wouldn't have said anything at all.

For Reese instantly asked, "Like what?" His tone seemed a little defensive, and when his mother reached over and patted his arm, Breck feared she might have offended him.

"Well…like your good manners, your old pickup…things like that," she stammered.

He sighed and smiled at her. "It shows, huh?"

"It better show!" Marjie said. "I worked hard raisin' you into a gentleman."

Breck couldn't quit smiling at Reese. It was like the last piece to the puzzle—the puzzle that was the man Reese Thatcher—had just been pressed into place. All this time Breck had tried to put her finger on just what was different about Reese other than heavenly good looks, success, strength—other than the obvious. Now she knew—and she loved him all the more for it! Yes, loved him, she admitted to herself.

☙

The meal was delicious, the conversation happy and light, and Breck began to dread its end. She concluded that Marjie Thatcher was an angel—a hard-working, old-fashioned girl who loved her family. Reese seemed to relax in his mother's presence to a state that Breck had certainly never witnessed, and it was wonderful—like sitting before a warm, cozy fire on a cold winter's night.

Breck was just finishing her last bite of chocolate cake when Marjie asked, "So, Breck…what are your plans for Thanksgivin'?"

Truly taken by surprise and not foreseeing what was about to come next, Breck stammered, "Oh, I…uh…" For in truth, she had no plans. With her parents in Europe and brother, Jake, overseas, she had simply reconciled herself to sitting at home with a turkey potpie.

"So you don't have plans?" Marjie prodded.

"Well, not really. My parents are in Europe this year, and my brother is in the military, so I thought I might just—"

"Reese!" Marjie interrupted, turning to her son. "You have to bring her out to the farm for Thanksgivin'!"

"Oh! No, no, no," Breck assured her. "I have a ton of people that I can—"

"No. I won't hear of it. You've got to come with Reese out to the farm and have Thanksgivin' with us," Marjie insisted. "Besides, if

73

Reese is given the responsibility of bringin' our guest…then he won't be able to find an excuse not to come."

"Mom," Reese scolded, "don't force her to come if she doesn't want to." He was shaking his head and smiling—amused at his mother's insistent manner.

"She wants to come. Don't you, Breck?" Marjie said.

This was uncharted territory for Breck. An invitation to Thanksgiving? From her boss's mother? What was she supposed to do?

"I couldn't possibly impose like that, Mrs. Thatcher. It just isn't done and—" Breck began to argue.

"Impose? Are you kiddin'? We would love to have you! You'll come out for the whole four days, won't you?" Marjie continued, "Reese, you are givin' her those days off, aren't you?"

"Four days?" Breck exclaimed.

"Yes, Mom…she has the whole time off," Reese chuckled. "But maybe she doesn't want to come."

"You do want to come, don't you?" Marjie pleaded.

"I-I can't possibly…" But the refusal stuck in Breck's throat like a horsefly, for the look on Mrs. Thatcher's face was so sincere—so pleading—and she knew refusal would hurt her. Reese's also wore an expression that said she should not deny his mother. A kind of *please don't hurt my mother's feelings* sort of expression.

"Of course you can!" Marjie announced, finally. "You can drive up on Wednesday night with Reese. Can't she, Reese?"

"Of course," Reese said, smiling at Breck. She knew he could sense her squirming under the pressure of the situation.

"Just pack up a few things and spend the weekend with us! I promise it will be worth your time," Marjie assured her.

"But, Mrs. Thatcher…I just couldn't. It would be…" Breck stumbled over her words like they were choking her. For one thing, she couldn't imagine anything more wonderful than spending four days in the company of Reese Thatcher. Add to it the fact that just being out of the city would be the stuff of dreams—but she couldn't possibly accept. Could she?

"I won't take no for an answer," Marjie said, smiling. "And, furthermore, I won't go home here in a few minutes so that Reese can take you out parking, if you don't agree."

Again Breck's mouth gaped open in astonishment—her face as red as Marjie Thatcher's sweater.

"Mom," Reese scolded, "quit trying to bully her into it." Then, smiling, he turned to Breck and said, "Come on, Breck. Just agree to it so we can go somewhere and park."

Breck could only sit, silent. Was he kidding? Was his mother kidding? But when they both looked at her—eyes smiling with mischief—she knew they had only been teasing her.

"Oh, please say yes, Breck," Marjie pleaded at last. "It will be a Thanksgivin' you'll never forget. I promise."

Breck looked into the woman's twinkling eyes. How could she refuse to go?

"Okay…I guess it would be all right," she managed.

Reese's mother clapped her hands together, delighted. "Wonderful!" she exclaimed. "Now, Reese…I'll just be on my way," she began, standing as if she were leaving. "I've got my key to the house, and I'll just put my little self sound to sleep in your guest room for the night. You and Breck finish up your evenin'."

"You're leaving?" Breck asked.

Marjie smiled, hugged Breck, kissed Reese on the cheek, and said, "Of course. I've spoiled your evenin' enough already."

As quick as that, she was gone. She was gone, and Breck sat stunned—unbelieving she'd been talked into going to her boss's parents' house for Thanksgiving.

"Don't worry, Breck," Reese said, motioning to the waiter to bring him the bill. "It'll be fun." Still she couldn't speak. Reese chuckled. "What's the matter?"

"I'm just wondering…" Breck began, "how I got here."

Reese put a hundred dollar bill on the table with the tab, stood, and pulled Breck's chair out for her. "That's my mother for you," he sighed. "When she likes somebody…she doesn't hide it. She'll be gushing on about you for days now."

"But I didn't do anything," Breck reminded him.

"That's the point," he said. "You were just you."

Breck noticed the way the women in the restaurant followed Reese's every movement as they walked between tables and past booths on their way out. She couldn't help the feeling of pride that swelled in her at being on the arm of such a man. On top of everything else, he treated his mother like a queen. Breck decided not to let discouragement or uncertainty overtake her. For the moment, she would just bask in his presence—bathe in everyone else's envy.

"How are your stitches healing?" Reese asked as the pickup hummed along the interstate.

"Fine," Breck said. "The redness is gone, and it doesn't hurt nearly as much now."

"It left a nice bruise though," he noted. And it was true. Breck had tried to forget about it. But, yes, her cheek was a lovely color of mingled purples, yellows, and greens. "It still ticks me off."

"At least she's not around the office anymore," Breck said. "It was worth getting a shiner just for that to happen."

Reese's silence implied that he wasn't sure he agreed with her. Therefore, she let the subject die.

"I'm planning on leaving the Wednesday morning before Thanksgiving," he suddenly told her. "I'll okay the day off for you too."

Looking to him, she said, "I just don't think I can—"

"Oh, there's no squirming out of it now, baby," he chuckled. Breck was a bit caught off guard by his rather endearing term. "Mom will have me skinned alive if I don't bring you now."

He'd called her baby, and she'd loved the way he said it—so naturally—as if he truly meant it!

"You better bring some warm clothes. There's already snow out at the place," he said. "And I'll tell Mom you'll bring some pumpkin pies."

"Oh, no!" Breck argued. If there was one thing she knew, it was that a woman needed to feel like she was the queen of her own castle. "Can't I bring something else?"

"No way!" Reese said, with the lack of understanding akin to a man. "Mom *has* to taste your pie."

Reese parked the pickup in front of Breck's apartment building, and she felt the cold rain of disappointment begin to envelop her. Her night with Reese was over.

He got out of the pickup, opened Breck's door, helped her out, and began walking with her toward her apartment. When they reached the apartment door, Breck pulled her keys from her purse and began to fiddle with them.

"Here," Reese said, taking the keys from her. He opened her door and let her step inside.

"Thank you for dinner," Breck said, feeling suddenly very shy— like a high school girl returning from her first prom.

Reese leaned in the door toward her. "You're not mad at me, are you?" he asked.

"Whatever for?" Breck asked, her attention falling to his mouth.

He grinned and said, "For bringing my mom to dinner with us."

Breck shook her head and smiled at him. "No. She's adorable. And it was so fun to watch the two of you together."

"Yeah, but now you're all committed to Thanksgiving. Heck, I'm all committed to Thanksgiving," he said.

Breck thought it odd that he should refer to himself as being committed to be with his family on the one holiday that most families tried to be together.

"Don't you usually go home for Thanksgiving?" she couldn't help asking.

Reese sighed. "That's a long story, Breck." She knew this was a sensitive subject, something he wasn't ready to reveal to her. Nor should she expect him to. Then looking at her, his eyes narrowing, a mischievous grin spreading across his face, he said, "That's a soft-looking sweater you're wearing."

"Thank you," she said, uncertain where he was going with this compliment.

But as he stepped through the door and reached out, taking her by the waist with one hand and brushing her sore cheek with the other, she began to hope—to hope and to tremble.

"And your poor little stitches," he mumbled as he seemed to look intently at her cheek for a moment. "You know," he continued, "it would make me feel a lot better about what happened on Monday if you kissed me good night."

"It would?" she whispered, awed by his suggestion.

"Oh yeah," he assured her, his grin broadening to a smile.

"But you're my boss," Breck reminded him.

"So?" he chuckled. "It isn't like we haven't done it before."

Breck felt his arms around her then, pulling her against his strong body. She looked up at him, her mouth moist with the desire for him to follow through with his implication—to kiss her.

"Hmm. This *is* a soft sweater," he whispered a moment before she felt him playfully kiss her upper lip. She gasped quietly, as he then kissed her lower lip twice in succession before finally pressing his mouth to hers in a tender, yet powerful exchange. Breck felt an overwhelming heat travel up the length of her spine, spreading throughout her limbs. The feel of Reese's roughly shaven face against the flesh of her face as he kissed her served to somehow further elevate her temperature, and she worried that she might melt dead away in his arms.

His kiss became driven—impassioned for a moment—then he simply pulled away from her, sighed heavily, and said, "And now…I better be going." Smiling at her, he added, "I guarantee you my mom did not go to bed when she got back to my place. She's waiting up to make sure I didn't let you squiggle out of coming for Thanksgiving."

Breck was speechless. All she could do was smile and nod at him. He turned and began walking down the sidewalk to his pickup.

As Breck watched him, he turned to look at her and said, "I'm beginning to like Friday nights, Miss McCall."

Breck smiled and waved as he drove away. What was happening? Could it be that she'd actually managed to capture Reese Thatcher's attention? Or had she simply captured his mother's attention somehow? All mothers wanted their sons to have nice girls in their lives. Still, Reese had kissed her again—and it was rapturous! She dared to hope then—dared to hope that Thanksgiving would be special. She just hoped she'd be able to find the courage to follow through with it. The girls would help her with that. Yes—the girls would help her find the strength.

That night Breck lay awake for hours unable to settle her mind or her senses, which had both been so completely stirred up by Reese Thatcher that evening. Thanksgiving was all she could think about. Four days with Reese, away from the city, away from work. Could another warm, delicious kiss with him be in her future? But what then? She wouldn't worry about what then. She'd simply worry about Thanksgiving.

Gazing at the picture of her and Reese kissing—the photograph of her and her Highwayman hanging on her bedroom wall—Breck tried to believe that there was still hope in the world—that people could stay faithful in marriage, that nasty troublemakers like Jamie Reynolds did not make up the majority of the population. Maybe dreams could come true. Maybe.

❧

Just as Reese suspected, his mother was sitting on the sofa, eyes beaming with curiosity when he arrived home after dropping Breck off at her apartment. He chuckled, for he could see that Marjorie Thatcher was near to exploding from the pressure of so many withheld questions.

"Well?" she asked.

"Well what?" He'd toy with her a bit. It always amused him how wound up his mother got about certain things—like Christmas, new puppies, and the possibility of romance in the lives of her children.

"Oh, don't play dumb with me, Reese Thatcher!" she scolded. "What's goin' on with you and that lovely girl?"

Reese shrugged. "What do you mean, Mom? She had a bad day at work on Monday. She's my assistant…thought I'd take her to dinner to—"

"She's your assistant who had a bad day, my hind end." Marjie wagged an index finger at her son. "You didn't flinch once when I

79

invited her for Thanksgiving. Day was you would've walked in here ranting and raving like a madman had I done that." Again Reese shrugged. His mother continued, "And I don't ever recall you havin' me knit anything for a girl before."

"Calm down, Mom," Reese told her, still smiling. "You're getting all worked up over nothing."

Marjie sighed, defeated. Waving an arm in the air as she turned toward the guest room, she said, "Oh, you just go on ahead and act like I can't read you like a book, boy. 'Cause I can. And that girl is on your mind."

"Good night, Mom," he called after her. It was true. She could read him like a book—always had. But he wasn't ready to tell her anything about Breck. He was still too unsettled himself. And the truth was Breck was getting deeper and deeper under his skin.

He shouldn't have kissed her just now. He was her boss! But he couldn't resist her—there in that soft, furry sweater, those two little pitiful stitches on her tender, bruised cheek. Besides, he'd waited a week to kiss her again. And considering the feelings that had been rolling around in him since that night at Marcelli's, he figured he'd done a pretty good job at keeping his hands off.

However, four days down at his parents' farm? Temptation would be thicker than the November fog. And Reese Thatcher knew one thing—he'd lost himself years ago, and until he was found, he'd have to avoid dragging anyone else down with him.

As he lay in bed late that night staring out the window at the stars, he knew there was something very different about Breck McCall. For one thing, she kept distracting him from all the down and dirty cases he was working on at the office. She was like a sweet beacon of sunshine beckoning at the mouth of a dark cave of worldly sludge.

With a heavy sigh, Reese rolled over, punched his pillow a couple of times, and mumbled, "Guess I'm going home for Thanksgiving this year." He caught himself smiling at the thought.

CHAPTER SEVEN

"This is it!" Sherryl squealed, leaping up from Breck's sofa like a recently released jack-in-the-box. "Home to meet the family? Oh, this is big!"

"You guys," Breck began. From the moment her friends had shown up for a night of silliness at Breck's apartment—from the moment two weeks ago when she'd told them all about her dinner with Reese and his mother, her invitation for Thanksgiving—not one of them had retained a calm thread of sanity. "She was just being nice," Breck continued.

"A woman doesn't invite just anybody to Thanksgiving dinner— hold on, Thanksgiving weekend—hold on, the entire four-day break. A woman just doesn't invite anybody…and certainly not just to be nice, Breck," Trixie interjected.

"That's right," Barb agreed. "My mother-in-law still doesn't invite me." Everyone giggled.

"And you'll have to bring something as a token of your thanks," Kay mused, frowning.

"I've got it!" Sherryl exclaimed. "I'll make an enlargement of that picture of you and Reese making out at Marcelli's!"

"Funny, Sherr," Breck giggled. "Very funny." Her friends were absolutely no help, and that's why she loved them. Oh, they had plenty of serious talks together—heartfelt sobbing over trial and tribulations. But moments like these—moments when all care was thrown to the wind, discouragement vanquished in favor of glee and fun—those were the moments that pulled Breck through. Those were the moments she most looked forward to.

"But, Breck," Kay began, clasping one of Breck's hands in her own. "Don't you feel it? Something big is about to happen."

Breck inhaled a deep breath, trying to calm her nerves. She did feel it. But was it a premonition of good—or an ominous throbbing of impending disappointment?

"You should definitely take your pumpkin flannels," Trixie suggested.

"Heck, no!" Barb argued. "You need something more alluring… like that flannel nightgown with the little pink sheep on it."

"Absolutely not!" Sherryl exclaimed. "She'll look like a pilgrim."

"Well, it will be Thanksgiving weekend," Kay pointed out.

"Guys…no one will be seeing my pajamas while I'm there," Breck said. Her friends exchanged skeptical glances.

"Ten to one…they're the kind of family where the mom makes everyone matching pajama bottoms for Christmas," Barb said. "They probably eat breakfast in them."

"They're farmers, Barb," Breck pointed out. "They probably do two hours of chores before breakfast."

"Still, you can never go on the assumption that you won't be seen in your nightwear," Kay instructed.

"What about those plaid ones she has?" Trixie asked. "They're kind of silky and pretty."

Breck giggled and covered her face with her hands for a moment. These friends of hers were unbelievable! Here she was, on the verge of the most nerve-wracking weekend of her life, and all they could discuss was what she should wear to sleep in. Oh, how she loved them for it!

❦

Oddly enough, the weeks since Reese's mother had invited Breck to visit for Thanksgiving had passed fairly quickly. Work had gone smoothly—save the fact that Jamie Reynolds had attempted a lawsuit against Wilson Investigation. That had been quickly vanquished, however—the moment Jamie's attorney had seen the security camera footage of her slapping Breck. Even the Allen case had simmered down for the moment. Still, there were plenty of ugly cases hitting Breck's desk. Reese had been gone for a few days, and Breck found it much easier to work with him out of the office. He was more distracting to her than ever. Fortunately, the girls—Trixie, Barb, Sherryl, and Kay—had helped Breck to remain calm, to look to a positive outcome concerning her trip to Reese's home.

And now, unbelievably, here she sat, in Reese's pickup—on her way to his family's farm for Thanksgiving.

"I can't believe I'm doing this," Breck mumbled as they hit the interstate and headed south. All at once her nerves twisted themselves into knots, and she worried she might be ill. "I think you better take me back. I'm not sure I can go through with this," she told him.

Reese smiled, "You're not going skydiving, Breck," he told her. "You're just going to the Thatcher's farm for Thanksgiving."

For a moment, Breck considered how much easier skydiving seemed. Rather a few minutes of terror than an entire weekend of it.

"But this is so out of my comfort zone," Breck explained.

Reese chuckled. "It's a little out of mine too…if it makes you feel any better," he said.

"What do you mean?" she asked. He was going home for Thanksgiving. She assumed he would be excited—view it as a holiday routine. Hadn't he always gone home for Thanksgiving?

"I haven't gone home for Thanksgiving for the past two years," he confessed.

"What?" Breck was stunned. "Why not?" Immediately she realized she probably shouldn't have asked the question. Most likely Reese's reasons for not going back were personal.

But he shrugged broad shoulders and said, "I always came up with a good excuse. At least, I thought they were good excuses."

"Why wouldn't you want to go?" Breck pressed. She was too deeply interested now to worry about being considerate.

"Honestly?" he asked. She nodded. "I think I didn't want to be reminded how great it was."

Breck was puzzled. "Why not?"

"Oh, it's a long story," he sighed. "And it's…it's…"

"Personal?" she finished. A girl! That was what it had to be. He'd had a girlfriend, and she'd broken his heart. Breck was immediately jealous of whoever the mystery girl was. She loathed her instantly.

"No, not really," he said. "Just stupid."

"Will you tell me?" she asked. She couldn't believe how bold she was being. But this had happened to her before. Every time she went out to El Costa Lotta to visit her cousins, in fact. Once she'd left the city, the pollution, the crowds—it was as if her soul could breathe again. She always felt free to be herself—more confident in who she was when she was away from the city.

Reese grinned and looked at her. "Are you serious?"

"Of course," she confirmed. "I can't imagine why a farm boy would rather stay in that smelly old city for Thanksgiving instead of escaping back home to family and good cooking."

Again he smiled. "You're certainly chatty this morning."

Breck shrugged. "Well, we do have…what? Two hours to kill. You might as well tell me your deepest, darkest secrets." She smiled at him, and he shook his head, amused.

"Well, if you insist on being bored to tears," he began, "I'll confess it all to you."

Breck smiled, snuggled down into her coat, and anxiously waited for him to begin.

"Okay, I'm ready," she said.

He chuckled, shook his head again, and turned the heater up a notch. "Okay, Miss McCall. But it's not a happy story."

A bit of Breck's enthusiasm was lost—but she was still far more than very interested.

"Well," he began, releasing a heavy sigh, "as you know, the grass is always greener."

"I know," she said, understanding the cliché. Things often looked better, more exciting, when you looked into the neighbor's yard.

"When you're young you think you know everything and associate all your troubles with the place you're at. You know?"

Breck nodded.

"Well, when I was about nineteen," he continued, "me and my friend Tom Holms were out on the snowmobiles. Just having a regular day of fun in the snow." Reese checked his rearview mirror, and Breck looked at him, waiting for him to go on with his story. "I'd had an accident earlier in the month…ran my ride right through a barbed-wire fence, and Mom had nearly grounded me from the snowmobiles for life," he continued.

"One of your fifty-seven sets of stitches?" Breck prodded.

Reese smiled, "Yeah. A big set." He continued then, "But Tom and I were daredevils. You know how boys that age are." Breck nodded. "Well, we were out by Simpson's Woods, a few miles east of our old farmhouse…and all of a sudden, I hear a rifle go off." Breck felt the hair on the back of her neck begin to prickle. She sensed this wasn't going to be one of the more lighthearted farm boy stories that Reese probably owned.

"It's not that unusual to hear gunfire out there…especially during elk season. But I stopped to check on Tom anyway, and when I turned around…his ride was stalled, and he was lying facedown in the snow." He paused, and his eyes narrowed with the unpleasant memory. "By the time I stopped and got to him, the snow around him was already red with his blood, and…he was dead."

Breck's mouth gaped open in surprise. She certainly hadn't expected such a revelation. She'd expected him to say he had become bored with farm life, had his heart broken by some girl, or something. Nothing like this.

"Reese!" Breck exclaimed in a whisper as she looked up at him.

"Nobody ever found out where the shot came from. It was elk season, after all, and people in town speculated that someone was out hunting, and Tom was hit by a stray shot. Or maybe some kids were messing around with guns somewhere. Either way, the sheriff's department never did figure it all out."

"I'm…I'm so sorry, Reese," Breck stammered. How did someone respond to such a story other than with an awkward apology?

Reese shrugged. "I left home that next year…earned a bachelor's in three years…then flushed it down the toilet and joined the Denver PD."

"A policeman?" Breck nearly gasped.

Reese smiled at her. "How do you think I got on at Wilson?" he asked. "Yep…went off to become a cop to make sure that every case in the entire world didn't remain unsolved like Tom's."

Breck felt her insides begin to tremble. The thought of Reese as a policeman unnerved her somehow. "But you quit," she offered.

"Yeah. Mom convinced me to. She said she could see how dealing with the scum of the earth was bringing me down. Plus, she worried a lot," he continued. "Farmers die of old age, heart attacks, or getting kicked in the head by a horse. The idea of me getting shot by a drug dealer was really causing her a lot of stress…depression. So when Mr. Wilson heard about me—that I was a good detective and how fast I had made it up the ladder—he offered me a job, and I took it." He paused. "Still trying to save the world…but with a little less danger to my person. Easier on my mother's nerves."

"Officer Thatcher?" Breck said, still stunned at Reese's revelation.

"Yeah," he chuckled. "Hard to imagine?"

"Well…sort of. Yes," Breck admitted.

"It wasn't for me. Mom knew that," he said. "It would've killed me one way or the other…physically or mentally."

Breck shivered at his statement—completely undone by the thought of Officer Thatcher being killed in the line of duty.

"And so…there you have it, Breck McCall," he sighed. "I got to where I just didn't go home very often because…I felt weak when I did."

"Weak?" Breck didn't understand. How could going home have made him feel weak? Strong families usually drew strength from one another.

"Yeah," he said. "Every time I go home, it gets harder and harder to leave. And I have to."

"Why?" she plainly asked. She knew she certainly wouldn't have left if she'd grown up at El Costa Lotta.

He smiled at her. "Boys are different than girls, Breck," he explained. "Initially I was angry…angry about Tom being killed and no one being able to tell me why. Then I took it upon myself to save the world from unsolved crime. Turned around and I was old enough I needed to make a living somehow, and I'd fallen into a great job that let me do both." He reached over and turned the heater down a notch. "But recently…recently I've been wondering if I really want to do what I'm doing."

Breck began to panic. Was he thinking of leaving Wilson? He couldn't! She would die without him there!

"So there you have it," he said, interrupting her thoughts. "My deep, dark secret."

"Wow," she breathed. "That's kind of hard for me to top."

He chuckled. "But you have to try. I told you one of mine. What's yours?"

But she couldn't possibly tell him. Her deepest, darkest secret was she was falling hopelessly in love with him! More and more every day. That she could not reveal.

"I don't think I have one that can measure up," she said.

"Hey. Fair is fair. You gotta spill something," he told her.

Breck searched the files of her memory for something, some secret she could share. But still the only one she could think of was she was in love with her boss.

"Come on now, Miss McCall," he chuckled. "Pay up."

But try as she might, she couldn't think of one thing, one delicious secret to share with him. "Can I have a few minutes?" she begged.

Reese playfully glared at her. "Okay. I'll let you off the hook. But just this once."

"My life just isn't as…as…involved as yours," she explained.

"Sure," he said.

Just then something clanked in the pickup bed as they hit a bump in the road.

"Did you pack those pies safe enough?" Reese asked, sincerely concerned. Breck smiled, amused by his infatuation with the four pumpkin pies he'd talked her in to bringing.

"Yes. They'll be fine," she assured him.

The knot of nerves began to form in her stomach again. What was she doing? She couldn't be going home with her boss for Thanksgiving. It was too…

"So let me tell you about the Thatcher family so that you'll be prepared. Okay?" Reese began. He was so talkative—and Breck liked it.

"Okay," she said.

"Mom you've met," he began, and Breck nodded. "And with Mom, or 'Marjie,' as she'll have you call her for now…what you see is what you get." He smiled. "Dad is hilarious. You'll like him. His name is Ben, and he's a typical farmer…hard-working, good sense of humor, and worn out by the end of the day." Breck smiled, knowing she would like Reese's dad for being a typical farmer. "My older sister, Katie, is married to Keith Donaldson, and they have a little girl who's, like, about four, I think…and another one who's, like, two." Reese paused, pensive for a moment. "Yeah. Four and two. Their names are Lizzy and Sarah. Then there's Bobby. He's just under Katie and not married yet…still living with Mom and Dad. I'm next, and my little brother, Nick, is the youngest. He's twenty by now. He lives with Mom and Dad too." He smiled at her. "And there you go," he said.

"Sounds quite intimidating," Breck sighed.

"There's nothing to worry about. You'll love my family," Reese assured her. And Breck had no doubt about it. "And they don't know anything about your weird friends or how they talked me into being a piece of beefcake for your birthday, or anything like that."

"What?" Breck exclaimed, blushing vermilion.

Reese laughed and then said, "Come on, Breck. You gotta admit, those girlfriends of yours go to some extreme measures." Breck could only nod in agreement. He was right, after all, and many were the times she'd been on the planning end of the measures. "All I have to say is you're one heck of a good sport."

"No," she corrected. "You're one heck of a good sport."

He nodded. "Yes, I am. But…I wasn't entirely the innocent participant you may think I was."

"What do you mean?" she asked.

"You seem to have forgotten that I placed a condition of my own on the event."

Breck thought back, but all she could remember now was how fabulous he'd looked in the costume of the Highwayman—how thirst-quenching his kiss had been.

"They paid you?" she thought out loud. She was horrified at considering it.

But before she could be totally crushed, he answered, "No. I told them I better get a kiss from you out of the deal. I made them swear to me you'd kiss me before I agreed to do it." Breck's mouth was gaping open again, and he laughed as he glanced at her. "I guess I'm just spilling secrets left and right."

He was right! She remembered now. *We promised him you'd kiss him too, Breck*, Barb had said that night. But amid all the excitement and passionate kissing, Breck had completely forgotten.

"You were a little freaked out, making it a little short-lived," he chuckled. "But it was nice. Wasn't it?" He was smiling at her, knowing full well how embarrassed she was.

She was mortified! She was elated! She was horrifyingly delighted! He'd wanted to kiss her. That's what it all boiled down to. He'd wanted to kiss her!

"You're redder than a beet in a basket," he laughed. "And with that, I'll let you off the hook for a minute or two." He chuckled some more and tuned the radio to a country station.

Breck had to fight the urge to pinch herself to make certain she wasn't dreaming. It couldn't possibly be real—riding along with Reese Thatcher in his pickup, on the way to spend Thanksgiving with his family—his confessing that he had wanted to kiss her that night at Marcelli's? Suddenly she wanted to throw her arms around him, kiss him square on the mouth, and thank him for being so wonderful! But she resisted and simply smiled at him as his hands drummed on the steering wheel in time to the music.

❧

Eventually Reese led Breck to more comfortable lines of conversation, and the remaining trip out to Reese's parents' house was more at ease.

Breck had watched the snow on the side of the roads getting deeper and deeper the more isolated the roads became. But just before eleven, Reese pulled up in front of a cozy-looking farmhouse—much newer than Breck had expected—and she felt a bit disappointed.

She'd been in the old ranch house out at El Costa Lotta. No one lived there now, but her Grandpa and Grandma McCall had lived their entire married lives. It was creaky, drafty, and needed a load of work. But it spoke of the past, of simpler times, of love, and of comfort, and Breck had adored it. She'd secretly hoped Reese's family home was a bit older—a bit more weathered. Still, the warm light that flooded the snowy ground outside the front window spoke of all the things farmhouses did—old or new.

No sooner had Reese helped Breck down from his pickup than Marjie Thatcher was racing out the front door, arms flung wide in greeting, jolly red apron strings flying at her back.

"Oh, there you are, you sweet girl!" Marjie greeted Breck, throwing her arms around her and hugging her tight. "And Reese, my baby," she cooed, releasing Breck and nuzzling into Reese's powerful embrace.

"You cooking already, Mom?" Reese asked.

"Of course!" Marjie said. Immediately she began to ramble, "Did you two have a nice trip up? What do you think of the drive, Breck? Reese said he was going to force you to bring some of your pumpkin pies. He says they're better than mine." All the time she rambled, Marjie smiled—looking like some sort of kitchen angel and smelling like flour, butter, and brown sugar.

"Oh…oh…I'm sure mine aren't nearly as—" Breck began.

"Nonsense," Marjie interrupted. "If Reese says they're better, then they are, and I can't wait to taste them."

Marjie put her arm around Breck's shoulders and began walking her toward the house. "Did Reese drive the speed limit? It scares me to death, these back roads. And in the winter…whew! Let me tell you, it's downright dangerous."

Reese smiled. Breck looked back at him over her shoulder as his mother pushed her along toward the house. She looked scared to death, and he chuckled—though feeling sympathy for her at the same time. She'd be fine once she was inside and everyone had gushed all over her. Breck would be fine with his family. But would he? He wondered if he had his head on straight enough to have come home for Thanksgiving and not make any rash decisions. He wondered if he had his head on straight enough to keep his hands off his adorable little assistant, Breck McCall. *Probably not*, he thought. And he chuckled, recalling the astonished look on her face when he'd told her he'd bargained with her friends to steal a kiss. He shook his head and swallowed the extra moisture that had flooded his mouth at the thought of kissing her. Four days out in the middle of nowhere? It could get interesting.

CHAPTER EIGHT

Mrs. Thatcher pushed Breck into a warm, cinnamon-scented home, filled with welcoming, smiling faces. Taking a quick inventory, she guessed everyone in Reese's family was there. Two little dark-haired girls sat in front of the fireplace playing with a pile of banged-up looking baby dolls. Two handsome young men with dark hair and striking resemblances to Reese stood with another young man with lighter hair. The three seemed to be steeped in conversation with an older, gray-haired man, lounging in a recliner nearby. And as Reese closed the door behind him, a very pretty young woman with Mrs. Thatcher's twinkling eyes squealed with excitement and threw her arms around Reese's neck.

"Oh, Reese!" the young woman laughed. "It's so good to see you." Then turning to look at Breck, she added, "And this must be Breck." She put a friendly arm around Breck's shoulders and hugged her briefly. "I'm Reese's sister, Katie. And Mom has told us all about you."

Breck felt like a new toy on Christmas morning. She drew back slightly as Reese's father, brothers, and the light-haired young man made their way toward her. Stepping back—intimidated by the four men approaching—she heard Reese chuckle as she bumped into him.

"Don't worry, Breck," he whispered in her ear. "They won't eat you."

But Breck wasn't so certain. What had she been thinking when she'd accepted Mrs. Thatcher's invitation to visit?

"Nick Thatcher," one of the dark-haired men said, offering her his hand.

Breck accepted it and managed a timid, "Breck McCall," in response.

"Bobby Thatcher," the other young man with darker hair said.

He too offered Breck his hand, and she took it saying, "Nice to meet you."

"Keith Donaldson. I'm Katie's husband," the blonde man said, taking her hand as well. Breck managed another smile.

"And I'm Ben Thatcher, pretty girl," Reese's father said, moving to stand next to her and putting a strong arm around her shoulders. Breck smiled when she caught the scent of wind and hay as he hugged her. "And I'm sure you're just about plum overwhelmed with all us, now aren't you?" Ben Thatcher chuckled, and Breck noticed how much his chuckle sounded like Reese's.

"Katie and I are just whippin' up some barbeque for lunch, kids," Mrs. Thatcher said. "Would you like to give us a hand in the kitchen, Breck?"

Breck sighed, relieved at being saved by the women, who no doubt understood her discomfort at being inspected from head to toe by the men in the room. "I'd love to," she said and smiled as Katie took her hand and led her away from the towering grove of Thatcher men.

"Reese, that there…that's worth livin' in the city for," she heard one of the men say in a lowered voice as she left. She heard the other sounds of men greeting each other, their low chuckles, and suddenly felt safer somehow—safer than she'd felt in years.

"We've just got some potato salad, baked beans, barbeque sandwiches, and chips," Marjie Thatcher said. "Thought we'd just pile each of them up a plate and slop 'em where they stand."

Even though she was quite overwhelmed with new people, an unfamiliar place, and being a stranger in her boss's family's home, Breck did begin to feel herself settling down. The Thatcher home was inviting—safe—the perfect haven for relaxation. As she entered the kitchen, she glanced around quickly, smiling at the quaint vintage decor and architecture. If it hadn't been for the microwave oven and other modern-day appliances, she could've sworn she'd stepped right into the 1940s. It was fabulous! The windows were dressed with yellow gingham valances and lace sheers, and a yellow tablecloth covered an old kitchen table. It was warm, fragrant, and beautiful.

"You wanna just plop a big ol' spoon of potato salad on each plate, Breck?" Katie asked, handing Breck the largest serving spoon she had ever seen.

"Sure," Breck said.

She began putting potato salad on each plate Mrs. Thatcher handed her, handing each plate in turn to Katie, who added a sandwich. When they'd finished and had deposited a plate heaping with good food into the hands of each man in the other room, Mrs. Thatcher, Katie, and Breck sat at the kitchen table to eat their lunch.

"Gotta slop the hogs before we can settle down to eat, don't we?" Katie giggled. Then, taking a sip from her cup of water, she asked Breck, "Did you have a nice drive down?"

"We did," Breck answered. "It seemed to go really fast too."

"Well, I don't know how," Marjie Thatcher sighed, "in that beat-up old thing Reese calls a pickup."

"Mom, you know he's got, like, 250,000 miles on that thing?" Katie said.

"I know it. He'll drive that thing 'til its guts fall out somewhere," Marjie remarked. "It probably jostled your kidneys clean to death," she added.

Breck giggled. "No. Not too badly."

"Makin' all that money and he still prefers to drive that old thing," Katie said. "Guess he's not as far from bein' home as he likes to think." There was a moment of quiet.

But not too long a moment before Marjie said, "So tell us about yourself, Breck."

Breck was feeling quite comfortable and asked, "What do you want to know?" It was a loaded question.

"Is my brother as good a kisser as he always bragged he was?" Katie asked.

Instantly Breck felt her face turn crimson. "I-I…"

Katie giggled and, aside to her mother, said, "Must be."

Marjie patted Breck on the hand, understanding her discomfort. "We tease a bit now and then, honey. You just let it roll off, and you'll be fine." Then, smiling warmly, she added, "Now, tell us…where did you grow up exactly?"

❧

Breck spent most of the afternoon in the yellow kitchen talking and laughing with Katie and her mother while Reese and the other men visited in the other room. Katie and Keith's little girls came in periodically for drinks of water, help with baby doll diapers, and cookies from grandma's cookie jar. But for the most part, the two toddlers stayed fairly well entertained by the men. Breck could remember being a small girl and sitting in front of the fire or in the old kitchen at El Costa Lotta—listening to the low, comforting hum of the adults as they visited. Those were some of the most secure, happy times of her life, and she relished the opportunity to be in a home permeated by a similar atmosphere.

Dinner came and went as well, and it wasn't until afterward that she even had the chance to talk to Reese again. Yet just knowing he was there in the other room gave her comfort.

However, once dinner was over and Reese's brothers were busily doing up the dishes, Reese walked into the kitchen smiling. Breck noticed how relaxed he looked. The frown that often puckered his brow at work was gone.

"You wanna go with me to bust up the ice in the watering tanks?" he asked.

Breck smiled. "Sure," she said.

"Well, grab a coat 'cause, baby, it's cold outside," he said, taking her hand and pulling her to her feet. Instantly, his mother and sister broke into a verse of the popular song from the 1950s, whose title Reese had just quoted.

As they sang, Reese unexpectedly pulled Breck against him, leading her in a two-step as he joined his mother and sister in a chorus. Breck giggled, delighted by Reese's unexpected knowledge of one of her favorite old songs. When they'd finished their chorus, and it was quite well done, he took her hand and led her toward the door.

"We're going to bust up the troughs," Reese told his father as he helped Breck on with her coat.

"Yep. Bustin' up the troughs," Nick chuckled. "That's what Katie and Keith used to call it too." Breck felt herself burn a terrible blush. She was somewhat relieved as Reese made an attempt to defend her.

"Now, Nick," he began, "Breck's not used to such teasing. You behave." Still, she saw him wink at his brother and continued to burn a blush.

Once outside, Reese shivered a low, "Brrrr!" and pulled his gloves on. "It's gonna get cold tonight. I hope you brought some warm pajamas."

"I did," Breck assured him.

"Come on then," he said, pulling her toward a four-wheel ATV parked nearby. Reese hopped on the four-wheeler, and it roared to life. "Hop on," he instructed, looking over his shoulder at her. "And hold on."

Breck smiled, delighted at the prospect of riding behind Reese on the four-wheeler and wrapping her arms tightly around him. Climbing on behind him, she put her arms around his waist and rested her chin on his shoulder. He smelled divine—like Speed Stick, chewing gun, and aftershave.

"Hang on," he told her again. In the next moment, they were riding through the night, the cold air stinging the tip of Breck's nose, but she didn't care. The air was fresh—still—alive with frost, and she was snuggling up against Reese Thatcher.

Not too far away from the house, they stopped. Reese climbed off the four-wheeler and told Breck to wait while he broke up the thin layer of ice that had formed over the top of the water in the tank. Even before he was finished, a group of cows began ambling their way toward the tank.

Climbing back on the four-wheeler, Reese let go another, "Brrr!" before adding, "They'd better tank up for the night. I'm not coming out before three in the morning. I want a good night's sleep."

"Three a.m. is a good night's sleep?" Breck asked.

Reese simply chuckled and started the four-wheeler toward the next watering tank.

❦

That night Breck lay in bed staring over at the warmth of the wood-burning stove, still aglow with the dying embers of a fire. She was staying in Katie's old room, and the bed was soft and covered with well-worn quilts. Marjie had explained that in the morning Katie would be over to help prepare Thanksgiving dinner. Breck could imagine the excitement in the kitchen, the heavenly aromas.

She sighed, smiling as she listened to the low mumbles and chuckles coming from the room next door—the room where Reese was bunking in with Nick and Bobby. She wondered what they were talking about—family, friends, and the farm—maybe even her. It had been a wonderful day. Especially the hours spent in the pickup with Reese on the way to the farm—and the hour spent riding around with him as he broke up the ice in the water tanks. That had been blissful! She thought of the way he'd tweaked her cold nose after they'd finished—the way his eyes twinkled as he looked at his mother. Reese Thatcher had come home. And he'd brought Breck with him.

CHAPTER NINE

Thanksgiving morning on the Thatcher farm dawned cold, crisp, and frosty. The sun was trying to peek through the clouds, but Ben Thatcher said he was doubtful that it would succeed. Breck had awakened to the homey sounds of clanking dishes and the heavenly smell of frying bacon. She could hear the delighted giggles of little girls and figured Katie and her family had already arrived. She was thankful for the bathroom adjoining Katie's old room. It gave her privacy and enabled her to get ready for the day very quickly.

Stepping into the kitchen, she was met with the warmth and smells of a kitchen on Thanksgiving Day.

"Good morning," Katie said, smiling and giving Breck a quick hug. "Did the girls wake you?" she asked.

"Oh, no," Breck said. "The smell of bacon did."

"Well, now you sound like Reese," Marjie said, smiling at Breck. "That boy eats far too much of it, and if I don't cook enough, no one else will get a lick." Breck smiled as Reese's mother motioned for her to come over to where she stood at the stove frying the bacon. "Did you sleep well, honey?" Marjie asked her, hugging her with one arm as she slid the bacon around in the skillet with the other.

"Yes, thank you," Breck assured her. "And I'm sorry I slept so long."

"It's only six, Breck," Katie explained. "But Keith dropped me and the girls off on his way into town. I forgot the cranberries and had to send him to the store for some."

Breck looked around, but there wasn't a Thatcher man in sight. "Is everyone else still asleep?" she asked.

"Yep," Marjie said. "They went back to bed after breakin' up the ice in the tanks this mornin'."

Good. Breck hadn't wanted Reese to be up before her.

"But don't worry," Marjie added. "The smell of this bacon will have them up before long."

"Daddy ate one of your pumpkin pies for breakfast before he went out this morning, Breck," Katie said. "The whole thing! In one sitting!"

"I hope you don't mind, honey," Marjie said. "He loves pumpkin pie for breakfast on Thanksgiving morning and wanted to try one of yours."

"Oh, that's fine. I brought them for you," Breck told her.

"Well," Marjie began, "I did have a bite before he gobbled it down completely, and I do have to admit…Reese is right. Your pumpkin pie puts mine to shame." Marjie winked as Breck began to shake her head. "Oh, now don't go tryin' to be humble, Breck. Shout it from the rooftops. I'm pleased as punch about it."

Breck smiled, uncomfortable with the fact she might make a better pumpkin pie than the lady of the house.

Breck looked around then when she heard Reese mumble a "Good morning, ladies" as he entered the kitchen.

Her eyes widened as she beheld him wearing nothing but a pair of flannel pajama bottoms. The pajama bottoms were littered with cartoon character, but that wasn't what made her jaw go slack in astonishment. It wasn't even how adorable he looked with his hair tousled or the fact he rubbed his eyes with the heel of his hand like a tired toddler. What stunned her into shocked silence was the sight of him bare from the waist up! Quickly she closed her gaping mouth and turned around, going to stand closer to the stove next to Marjie—feigning interest in the frying bacon. Reese's torso was supreme in its muscular structure. His body looked more like a professional body sculptor's than a guy who worked an office job at an investigation firm.

"Happy Thanksgiving, Kate," she heard him tell his sister. Still, she didn't dare turn around and look at him again. It wasn't until she felt his arm—his bare arm—go around her shoulders as he stepped between her and his mother that she looked at him again. Even this time she only glanced up at him quickly.

"Happy Thanksgiving, Mom," he said, pulling his mother tight under one arm as he kissed her cheek affectionately.

"Breck," he said then, and she held her breath as he kissed her cheek too.

"Happy Thanksgiving, sweetie," his mother said, raising herself on her toes and kissing his whiskery cheek.

"Yes," Breck said as he looked down at her, smiling. "Happy Thanksgiving."

Reese inhaled deeply—exhaled a happy sigh. "How many pounds did you do, Mom?" he asked.

"Four, Reese. And that will be plenty, do you hear?" Marjie chuckled.

"That leaves three for everybody else to share," Reese said aside to Breck. Breck wished he'd take his arm from around her shoulders. Well, not really. She liked having him touch her. But it was making her terribly nervous. She wished he'd at least put a shirt on! Well, not really. But his state of undress was making her even more nervous.

"The ice in the tanks was an inch thick this morning, Mom," Reese said, releasing the two women and going to sit down at the table.

"It got pretty cold last night," Marjie said.

"Uncle Weese?" It was one of Katie's little girls—the oldest, Lizzy. Breck turned to watch the sweet child climb up onto Reese's lap and lock her hands at the back of his neck.

"What, sugar?" he asked, chuckling and twisting a lock of her hair around one finger for a moment.

"Why don't you have any babies?" Everyone laughed at Lizzy's sweet, innocent question.

Reese continued to chuckle as he answered, "Well, Lizzy…I don't have a wife. And a man needs a wife to have babies." The child looked at him and seemed pensive for a moment.

Then, to Breck's utter horror, Lizzy pointed to *her* and said, "I bet she could do it for you, Uncle Weese." Breck thought she might drop dead from the heat of the blush that rose to her cheeks. Marjie, Katie, and Reese erupted into laughter and giggles, but Breck remained red-faced.

"I bet she could," Reese managed to respond.

"I think she'd have pretty babies for you," the child prattled on.

"Yes, she would," Reese managed again—though his eyes were watering with mirth.

Breck wanted to dash from the room—escape the embarrassing situation. What could she possibly say? She felt Marjie pat her understandingly on the back, but it didn't really help to soothe her predicament.

And then the situation got worse as Reese said, "Why don't you ask her if she's up to it, sweetie?"

"What?" Breck gasped.

"Okay," Lizzy said, happily hopping down from her uncle's lap.

"Now, Reese, you quit," Marjie halfheartedly scolded.

Breck forced a smile at the little girl as she approached and took Breck's hand.

"Hey, lady," Lizzy began. Breck hunkered down so the child could address her more easily. "You wanna have some babies for my Uncle Weese?"

Breck glanced up to Reese, who was bent over withholding his laughter. He winked at her—offering no salvation.

"I-I…" Breck stammered. What could she possibly say? "That's a big question, Lizzy, and I just got here yesterday," she said.

Reese burst into laughter, and Marjie and Katie were beside themselves.

Lizzy frowned for a moment. But then her face brightened. "Okay," she said, a disappointed sigh escaping her tiny lungs. "I'll tell him he has to wait a while longer." Breck breathed a sigh of relief herself and even managed a giggle when the child turned back to her and added, "Could you maybe have some kittens for me instead?"

∽

The morning passed quickly with so much to be done to get such a big meal ready. Keith arrived with the cranberries, and Reese had followed him into the den, allowing Breck to survive the embarrassment she'd suffered at the hands of him and Lizzy. She'd even managed to keep breathing when he'd hugged her after breakfast—still bare-chested— telling her what a good sport she'd been.

Katie and Marjie were absolutely wonderful! They treated Breck as if they'd known her their whole lives—involving her in every aspect of preparing the meal. Once in a while throughout the morning, the three women would take what Marjie called "a cider break"—sit down at the kitchen table and sip a glassful of freshly made apple cider. They asked Breck questions, and she answered and asked her own. It was a beautiful, dreamy morning.

Furthermore, Breck had never seen such a perfectly prepared Thanksgiving dinner! The turkey was roasted to perfection and stuffed with fresh rosemary, thyme, and sage. Marjie Thatcher served her cornbread stuffing on the side, and it was unlike anything Breck had tasted since her Grandmother McCall's! Mashed potatoes, homemade gravy, candied yams, cranberry sauce, deviled eggs, black olives, green beans, and the lightest, sweetest dinner rolls Breck had ever eaten.

Reese's father had said the blessing before the meal and even thanked the Lord for their "beautiful addition, Miss Breck." However, the best part of the meal wasn't the antique china, the perfect food, or the friendly, loving conversation. It was the fact that Breck was seated next to Reese, who would put his arm across the back of her chair and rest his hand on her shoulder each time he leaned back to give his food time to settle.

Once in a while, he'd bend over and whisper something in her ear too. Something like, "Do you want me to get you anything else?" Or, "They're hilarious, aren't they?"

Breck simply cherished every moment spent at the table that day. She laughed with everyone else as Lizzy and Sarah put a large black olive on each of their fingers, popping them into their mouths one by one, then starting over. She smiled when Reese's father unfastened the button at the waist of his jeans to "allow for more fixin's," as he put it.

And when the feast was finished, she was amazed when Marjie and Katie led her into the living room while the men cleaned up before disappearing into the nearby den to hoot and holler over football. It was a day made of dreams come true, and Breck savored it as best she could.

Sitting in the living room on the sofa in front of the fireplace, Breck could see Marjie and Katie were as sleepy as she was.

Finally, Marjie said, "Time for a nap, girls…or we'll never make it to dessert."

"I'll have Keith watch the girls," Katie yawned. "Can I bunk in with you, Breck?"

"Of course," Breck said. How incredibly fast they'd accepted her. How incredibly comfortable she felt with them. It was strange—and wonderful!

❧

"Breck? Breck?" his voice whispered again. Breck forced her eyes open to find Reese standing over her, smiling.

"Oh," she said. He put an index finger to his lips and pointed to Katie, still sleeping next to Breck on the bed. Sitting up carefully, she smiled at him.

"Do you want to go with me to bust up the ice again?" he asked. Breck's smile broadened, and she nodded. "Grab your shoes and a coat. I'll meet you outside." Breck nodded again and tried to hush the butterflies flapping around in her stomach.

It was already dark, and frost was again falling through a clear sky as they rode the four-wheeler from trough to trough to make sure the stock would be able to stay watered through the night.

Breck was surprised when Reese didn't head back to the house after checking on the horses but drove in an unfamiliar direction instead. Suddenly Breck could make out the shape of a house in the distance, silhouetted in the moonlight. There were no lights coming from it, however, and when Reese stopped the four-wheeler in front of it, she could tell that it was empty. Empty, but charming and beautiful!

"This is the house I grew up in," Reese told her as she stepped off the four-wheeler and followed him up the front porch stairs. It was hard to make out the exact architecture of the house in the dark, but Breck could tell it was old—an old Victorian-era house, complete with front bay window and two-story turret.

"We built the new house when I was about fourteen," Reese explained. "But…I still think of this one as home. I miss living in it." He pulled his keys from his pocket and sorted through them until he found the one he was looking for. Breck smiled—touched that he would still carry a key to his boyhood home.

"Want to see inside?" he asked, an expression of mischief blatant across his face.

"Certainly!" Breck assured him. She watched as he unlocked the door and pushed it open. It creaked to a stop, and Reese motioned for her to step inside.

Breck stepped cautiously into the old farmhouse, and Reese stepped in after her, flipping a switch on the wall. Instantly the room before them was illuminated, and even though it stood empty now, somehow the echoes of times gone by—of lives lived in it—somehow the house still seemed welcoming and happy.

The house was the perfect example of an old farmhouse. The hardwood floors were worn but beautiful. The walls were once white and needed new paint badly, but what walls in an old farmhouse didn't? It smelled closed up, but not unpleasant like some old houses did. She imagined how cozy and warm a fire blazing in the nearby fireplace would be.

Reese smiled and lowered his voice, as if revealing a great secret. "Fifth, sixth, and seventh stairs up squeak." He pointed to the staircase that led from the front or parlor area up to the second floor. "Mom and Dad always knew when one of us was trying to sneak out or in…'cause those three stairs would squeak, and if we tried to skip them and hop up to the eighth, the thud was too loud." Breck smiled at the image of three teenage farm boys trying to sneak to bed after having missed curfew.

"That bay window is beautiful!" Breck exclaimed. "A perfect Christmas tree spot," she mumbled, speaking her thoughts out loud.

"That's what my mom always said," Reese chuckled. "Every year she complains about not having a good spot for the tree in the new house."

"Well," Breck said, going over to stand in the bay window area, "it is the most important part of a house, you know." She smiled when Reese shook his head, obviously amused by the priorities of some women. She turned and looked out the window to the clean, unmarred winter scene beyond. Snow and trees—just snow and trees—no other buildings as far as she could see—frost sifting through the air, sparkling like glitter in the moonlight.

"Many are the Christmas Eves that I stood just there, peering out the window, hoping to see Santa and his sleigh fly by," Reese chuckled.

"It's the perfect spot to watch for him," Breck said. She sighed, enraptured by the entire moment.

"This house," Reese said, coming to stand beside her and following her gaze out the window into winter, "it's…it's…"

"Magical," Breck finished for him. A strange tingling sensation caused her to shiver.

"You cold?" he asked, having noticed her shivering.

"A little," she lied.

"We can go, if you want to," he said. "Mom will have hot chocolate waiting, and we can warm you up."

Breck nodded, even though she paused in wanting to leave the house. Somehow, she'd fallen in love with it, as well as the boy who grew up embraced in its loving walls.

ᕼ

"So," Reese's dad began, "tell me about this girl."

Reese feigned ignorance as he sat on the sofa next to his dad's lounge chair. He smiled as he watched the fire burn and heard his sister, mother, and Breck giggling over a game of rummy in the other room. He knew his father wouldn't be deterred, but it was worth a try.

"What do you mean?" he asked.

Ben Thatcher chuckled. "You know what I mean, boy." He leaned back in his armchair and waited for an answer.

Reese grinned, shaking his head. "She's my assistant at work."

"So you're seducin' your secretary, huh?" his father said.

"It's been done before, Pop," Reese said, smiling.

"That it has, son. That it has." Ben sighed—a sign that he was finally relaxing for the day. "What are your plans then?" he asked.

Reese shrugged. "You mean plans for life…or for Breck?"

"Both. I reckon they're about to become one and the same."

Reese chuckled. "Pop…she's just—"

"She ain't *just* nothin', son," his father interrupted. "Come on now…tell me. What does she put you in mind of?"

Reese was trapped, and he knew it. Once his father got something stuck in his brain, there was no deterring him until he was satisfied. He could spot a lie a mile away too. So there was nothing left to do but 'fess up.

"She puts me in mind of…of changing careers, for one thing," Reese admitted. "I'm tired of dealing with criminals, infidelity… basically all the crap involved with my job. Not that there are many jobs where a man doesn't have to deal with it. Just that…"

"You're finally rememberin' that although there're a few piles of manure out in the barn…they ain't as ugly as what you're dealin' with at Wilson."

Reese nodded. "Still…somebody has to shovel it, Pop. Somebody has to fight for the good people who need help."

"Somebody does, Reese. But that don't mean it has to be at Wilson." His dad leaned forward—a serious scowl on his face. "Ranchin', farmin', and the like…it's hangin' on by the skin of its teeth, Reese. Everybody knows it. But as long as someone's fightin' to keep it…this country won't go completely to the dogs." His dad sighed again, and Reese didn't balk the argument he'd heard so many times. For one thing, he agreed. "And…I'll tell you this," Ben added.

"You wouldn't be keepin' such a tight-fisted hold on that old house and the acreage you own here if you didn't know it."

Reese nodded. "I'll admit to you, Pop. Lately…I've been thinking about…about…"

"Just say it, son. You ain't gonna explode for sayin' it out loud," Ben urged.

Reese drew in a deep breath and admitted, "I've been thinking about…about coming back out here, fixing up the old house, running a few cattle…"

"It's the girl that got you thinkin'?" his father asked. Reese shrugged—but his father knew him too well. "Good! I like a girl who makes a man reevaluate his life. And she's a pretty little thing. Comes from good stock too."

Reese smiled. "You like her 'cause she's got horses in her blood," Reese chuckled.

His father smiled. "I like her 'cause she's gettin' under your skin."

"She ain't getting under my skin, Pop," Reese lied, standing to leave.

"Oh, she's under your skin all right. Never known you to bring a girl home for Thanksgiving, local or otherwise," Ben said, yawning.

"Mom invited her, remember," Reese said.

"And you invited your mom out to dinner that night, boy," his father countered. "And besides…I saw you takin' her out to the old place."

"I just wanted to show her where I grew up," Reese told him.

"Hm-hmm," his father chuckled. "That's why I took your mother out there the first time too."

❧

Breck couldn't sleep. Even by midnight she was still wide awake, all the wonders of the day replaying over and over and over in her mind—that morning in the kitchen, Reese's kissing her on the cheek, Lizzy's baby questions, the beautiful dinner, and the evening ride out with Reese to the old family home. It was marvelous, and all Breck could think about was the wonder of it all and how she would ever go back to everyday life. Even watching the family's favorite Christmas movie that evening before everybody went to bed. It was perfect! She covered her mouth to muffle her giggles as she remembered Reese's father wiping the tears of joy from his cheeks as the little boy in the movie was daydreaming about getting a BB gun for Christmas. All of it, the entire day—all of them—it had been perfect. And Reese! Reese had been perfect! Perfectly cute in his cartoon character pajamas—perfectly gorgeous with his shirt off—perfectly attentive and flirtatious. And there were still three days to go!

Getting to sleep soon was not an option, and Breck knew it. Perhaps a piece of pumpkin pie would do the trick. Yes— carbohydrates always helped relax her.

Quietly, she stepped into the hallway, peering right, then left to make sure no one else was about. On her way to the kitchen, however, she smiled as she saw the dying embers in the fireplace burning orange and inviting. Maybe a few minutes in front of the fire would find her eyes heavy.

Breck sat down on the sofa in front of the fire. She could still feel its warmth—even for its ending. She smiled, imagining what the next day would bring. Marjie had explained that it was "Christmas tree hunting day!" The family always went out for a bit of snow play and to get a Christmas tree the day after Thanksgiving.

"Who wants to go shopping and mess with the crowds?" Marjie had said. "The day after Thanksgiving…we do our tree."

Breck was excited about the prospect. For one thing, she was certain it was quite the event to behold.

"Sneaking out of bed, eh?" Reese whispered.

Breck startled and put her hand to her chest to still the wild thumping of her heart at the sound of Reese's voice.

"You scared me nearly to death!" she told him in a whisper. Quickly she made sure her pajama top was buttoned all the way up. The top buttonhole was stretched, and it sometimes came unfastened. Breck was suddenly very self-conscious about her all too casual attire. But her state of dress in which she appeared was soon driven from her mind when she noted that Reese again wore nothing but pajama bottoms.

Plopping down beside her on the sofa, Reese stretched his legs out in front of him, crossed his ankles, and began eating handfuls of bacon from the bag of bacon bits he'd obviously snitched from the kitchen.

Breck felt her eyebrows raise, accompanying her amused smile as she watched him eat his bacon bits.

Reese smiled and winked at her, holding the bag out toward her and asking, "Bacon?"

Breck paused for a moment and then nodded, holding out her hand. He poured a nice fistful into her hand.

"Don't worry. Eat as much as you want," he told her. "There's tons more out in the freezer. And they're real bacon. Not that imitation junk."

Breck smiled, amused at his addiction to breakfast meat.

"I'm glad Mom invited you and made me come home…and thanks for coming," he said.

"Me too," Breck admitted in a whisper. "Thanks for bringing me," she told him, glancing down at her lap.

"Thanks for bringing *me*," he told her. "It was time I came home."

Breck smiled at him. He belonged here. She felt it.

"So, tell me about this book," he said, dumping some bacon directly from the bag into his mouth.

"What do you mean?" she asked. His nearness was unsettling. Breck felt an uncomfortable warmth begin in her stomach and fan out through her body. "What book?"

"This book that has this highwayman guy in it that you like so much." He grinned at her. "I mean, you must really like it for your friends to go to all that trouble in finding a guy to dress up like this highwayman for your birthday and all."

Not this again. She'd never hear the end of it—from Reese or her friends. Breck blushed, and the warmth spreading through her body worried her. What if she actually began to perspire from it? She looked at him for a moment—tried not to notice the perfectly sculpted muscles of his chest and stomach—tried not to think about how even more handsome he was with his hair tousled, wearing flannel pajama bottoms covered in cartoon characters.

He tipped his head back, shaking the last few bacon bits out of the bag and into his mouth before smiling at her and saying, "Come on. Tell me about the book."

Breck knew she was cornered. There would be no changing the subject. But after Lizzy's questions about babies—could anything be worse?

"There's really nothing much to tell," she lied. "It's just a silly book that I've always liked."

"Well," he urged, "tell me about it. What's the title?"

She felt so overheated! However, she sighed heavily and figured there was no escape. After all, he deserved to know about it since he did go to all that trouble on her birthday. Besides, hadn't he told her one of his deepest secrets on the drive down?

"Well…it's pretty cliché really," she began. "It's called *The Highwayman of Tanglewood*." He nodded, set the empty bacon bits bag on the floor by the sofa, and looked at her expectantly, indicating that she should continue.

Taking hold of the hem of her pajama top and twisting it nervously, she continued, "It's about this guy who does the Robin Hood thing, sort of. You know, he dresses up like a highwayman and robs rich, criminal-type aristocrats and gives the money to the poor. And when he's dressed up like the Highwayman, he keeps running into this one girl…who of course is enamored of him."

"Enamored?" Reese interrupted, smiling.

Breck tensed as Reese scooted closer to her on the sofa. "You know…she was bewitched, captivated…enchanted by him," she explained, brushing a stray strand of hair from her cheek.

He smiled at her. "I know what it means. I just thought it was cute…the way you used the word."

Breck felt more heat rise to her cheeks as Reese rested his arm on the sofa behind her shoulders. He was flirting with her! Surely she was imagining it—the mischievous twinkle in his eye, the way he grinned almost seductively at her. The day had been too busy—filled with too many other people for her to have a chance to get nervous in his presence most of the time. But now—now that they were alone in the dead of night…

As her heart began to hammer hard within her chest with the thrill of his nearness, Breck prattled on, "Anyway…the girl always finds herself in his path. And of course he's quite the rogue…flirting with her, always saving her from peril…"

"He's a rogue?" he said, smiling. "Well…he would be, wouldn't he? Being a highwayman and all."

Breck's entire body broke into goose bumps as she felt Reese's hand leave the sofa back, slip beneath her hair at the back of her neck, and come to rest there. She looked at him quickly, denying the urge to throw herself against him and kiss him straight on the mouth.

"Anyway," she continued nervously, "it turns out she knows him when he's not dressed as the Highwayman too, of course. They're acquainted in real life as well, you see…"

"Kind of like the whole secret identity thing, right?" he asked, lowering his voice and weaving a strand of her hair through his fingers.

"Yeah," Breck choked out. She looked away from him and tried to focus on the light of the dying embers in the fireplace—tried to ignore the way his fingers kept caressing her neck as he toyed with her hair. "You see, she's a maid in the house that he…" But she stopped abruptly as she realized how desperately she did not want to reveal the heroine in the story actually worked as maid in the Highwayman's own house.

But it was too late. She heard Reese chuckle, and then he said, "Ohhh. I get it. He was her boss."

Breck couldn't help but smile and glanced down to where her hands were more violently twisting the bottom of her top. "Yeah," she admitted.

"I'm *your* boss," he needlessly reminded her.

"You are," was all she could force from her throat.

He chuckled again and said, "You've got some impish friends, Miss Breck."

"Believe me, I know it," she admitted, still afraid to look at him—still afraid that he could hear the mad hammering of her heart—sense her unbearable attraction to him.

"Does it all work out in the end?" he asked, lowering his voice as he moved even closer to her. She was tucked securely under his arm now and had to remind herself to breathe.

"Yes," she whispered.

"Does he seduce her into—" he whispered.

"No, no, no," Breck interrupted. "He's a gentleman. He…"

"But he does kiss her a lot, right?" he whispered.

"Yes," Breck managed.

He leaned toward her, his lips hovering just a breath away from the flesh of her neck just below her left ear, and whispered, "I've always wanted to kiss you, you know."

"Y-you have kissed me," she reminded him without turning toward him. She was going to fly apart! Explode into a million tiny particles! She could feel his breath on her neck—sense his lips just above her skin.

"That doesn't count," he whispered. "The first time you thought I was Marty Sprague," he reminded her. "The second time was after dinner with my mother. Neither one counts."

"What?" she asked. He just chuckled. "And anyway, I knew who you were that night at Marcelli's," she countered, trying to steady her emotions. "You'd already taken your mask off."

Her heart pounded so fiercely in her chest that she wondered if it might just burst through! She hoped he couldn't tell that she was having trouble regulating her breathing.

She heard him chuckle again. "Why are you so nervous?" he asked.

"I'm…I'm not nervous," she lied, twisting her pajama top even more violently.

He took her chin in one hand and turned her face to his. Instantly, her gaze fell to his delicious, grinning mouth. She felt warm moisture flood her own as she thought of his lips on hers.

"You're a liar," he told her. "You're ready to jump up and run."

"It's just that…" she stammered. "I've never…had anyone just tell me…just talk to me about it…"

"Well, if it's making you nervous to talk about it," he whispered as he lowered his head toward hers, "then I won't."

Breck gasped a moment before Reese kissed the corner of her mouth softly. Slowly, lingeringly, he kissed her upper lip, then her lower lip. Breck tried to draw in a quick breath, knowing she would black out if she couldn't find a way to start breathing again. But nature has a way of keeping a person alive, even during the most intense moments of their lives, and when Reese kissed her lower lip again, taking her face in his hands a moment before his mouth took hers fully, Breck found her body relaxed enough to breath—at least for a moment. His kisses didn't remain soft for long. In the next moment, she felt passion rise in him, his mouth working a spell of bewitching ecstasy with hers as hot, deep kisses erupted between them.

Reese Thatcher had had a lifetime of practice at impassioned kissing! It was the only explanation Breck's fevered mind could conjure for such a skill possessed by a man in kissing. The way his lips, his mouth worked to draw passion from hers while simultaneously taking her breath away over and over—it just wasn't normal!

Another moment and Breck knew she would be lost, unable to stop kissing him. So rather abruptly she pulled away from him, placing her hand over her mouth to keep herself from going back as she tried to catch her breath.

Breck had been kissed before, but none of the other kisses had undone her so completely. None had threatened to break her heart so thoroughly as Reese's did. And she knew why—because she loved him. And yet the world was the way it was, and most men and women didn't save the ultimate intimacy for marriage. But Breck *was* saving it, and it was impossible to imagine a man like Reese Thatcher— gorgeous, fun, strong, seductive—would not be expecting more than kisses from such a situation. All at once, she wondered if he'd agreed to bring her home simply because he thought he might benefit from the deal. But surely—surely he was a better man than most.

Breck had never feared such a situation with Reese because

she'd never entertained the thought that it could actually happen. But it was happening! And he was a gorgeous, no doubt passionate man. Her stomach churned at the thought of the other women he'd probably known in his life.

Breck felt tears welling in her eyes as Reese asked, "What's the matter?" He placed a hand to her cheek and caressed her lips with his thumb. "Am I that bad?"

Breck looked at him to find him grinning at her—an expression of understanding on his face. But understanding from a man in this day and age would be too much to expect. Especially a man like Reese, who could, no doubt, have his way with any woman he chose.

Still holding back tears and trying to stall the ache that had begun to throb in her heart, Breck shook her head, smiled, and whispered, "I think you know you're not bad."

"Then what's the matter, Miss Breck? Can you think of a better way to spend your Thanksgiving vacation than making out with your boss?" he whispered, kissing her cheek tenderly.

Breck breathed a giggle. He was so charming—so refreshingly blunt. "No. I mean…" she stammered, embarrassed.

"Then what?" he asked. "I know you don't have a boyfriend. I asked your skinny blonde friend."

Breck looked to him, rather astonished. "What?"

He smiled at her, brushed her cheek with the back of his hand, and said, "Just tell me what's wrong. You're holding back from me. I can tell." He ran his index finger the length of her nose and said, "I want to kiss you, Breck. And I'm pretty sure that you want to kiss me back. So what's stopping you?"

Breck swallowed hard—held onto her tears. In truth, she wondered for a moment if her conviction would stand where Reese was concerned. Was she too in love with him to resist if he decided to try and lead her down the hallway to his bedroom? And yet she knew she was strong enough—strong enough to break her own heart and push him away with the truth.

"It's just that…will you still want to kiss me after I tell you that I don't…" she stammered. Reese would turn away too. Just like every other man she'd dated. And Reese was different; her feelings for him were different. It would break her heart to lose a chance to win him for her own.

"After you tell me that you don't what?" he prodded, softly. He took her hand in his and raised it to his lips, kissing it firmly. When she still paused, he said, "Just tell me, Breck."

Breck looked down at her mangled pajama top hem and, taking a deep breath, said, "After I tell you that I don't…that I'm an old-fashioned girl. That I don't…" she stammered in a whisper.

She heard Reese sigh and looked up to see him smiling at her. Again he caressed her tender lips with one thumb as he held her face in his hand.

"Oh, I see," he said. She looked away shyly as he continued, "When you tell me that you're an old-fashioned girl…and kissing is as far as you go, right?"

Breck closed her eyes and nodded. Two tears escaped and traveled slowly down her cheeks. But she gasped when next Reese pulled her into his arms—kissing her neck several times in succession, sending goose bumps erupting over Breck's arms and legs. It was only natural that she return his embrace, and the warmth of his skin felt fabulous beneath her palms.

"Well, guess what, Miss Breck?" he whispered as he kissed the top of her head. Then he released her from his embrace, took her face between his powerful hands, and, as she looked up at him through tear-filled eyes, said, "There are still a few old-fashioned boys around."

"What?" she breathed. He couldn't be serious! Surely he was teasing her. Still, hope rose in her bosom like a phoenix from the ashes as she searched his eyes for any sign of deceit. She found none.

"Just kiss me, Breck," he whispered. "You can trust me." And she believed him. She could see the sincerity in his eyes.

"Okay," she whispered as his head descended toward hers. She felt fear and heartache evaporate from her soul—thrilled at the knowledge his kiss would be hers again. Softly he kissed her upper lip—teasingly kissed her lower lip twice in succession. He nearly took her mouth with his, pausing only a breath before their lips would've met.

"However," he began in a low, alluring, entirely seductive tone, "that doesn't mean that I wouldn't want to or be very tempted to…to help you have a litter of kittens for Lizzy if the opportunity presented itself," he said. "It just means…that I wouldn't."

She smiled and melted into his arms as his mouth captured hers in a kiss borne of dreaming.

CHAPTER TEN

Everyone at the Thatcher farm awoke, rose, and dressed early the next morning. Breck had enjoyed heavenly dreams—thanks to Reese's delicious affections the night before. She enjoyed helping Marjie whip up a quick breakfast of pancakes (and, of course, bacon) before Katie, Keith, and the girls arrived. As soon as they did, everyone in the family piled into various beat-up pickup trucks and were off on the "adventure of the year," as Marjie had called it.

Every year on the day after Thanksgiving, the Thatcher family (now accompanied by the Donaldson family) spent all morning playing in the snow: sledding, inner tubing, snowmobiling—the works. Then, by about noon, they'd take a break, warm up with some hot cocoa and muffins, and set out to find the Thatcher family Christmas tree. Since Katie had married Keith, there was twice the fun, for there were two trees to hunt down.

Mrs. Thatcher had packed extra snow boots, coats, hats, and mittens, and now Breck found herself sitting next to Reese in his pickup, his brother Nick beside her, on her way to her first snow play day in years.

"Wooo whooo!" Nick shouted, a huge smile lighting up his face. "I love the snow!"

Reese chuckled. "We're heading up to Doe Ridge, Breck," he explained. "Great hills for sleds and tubes!"

Breck nodded, rather nervous. It was so strange, all of it—sitting next to Reese in the pickup, his acting like nothing out of the ordinary had passed between them the night before. She still had goose bumps cropping up now and again just at the memory! But he seemed as relaxed as ever he had been since they'd arrived, and so she tried to act as normal as she could.

"Did Reese ever tell you about the time he ran his ride into a barbed-wire fence, Breck?" Nick asked.

"He told me that it happened but didn't offer any details," Breck answered.

"Well," Nick began, "ol' Reese nearly lost his movie-star looks that day, I'll tell you."

"Shut up," Reese whined at his brother.

But Breck was interested. "Really?" she prodded.

"Yep," Nick continued. "We were out in Simpson's Woods…out east of the old house, remember, Reese?"

Reese nodded and said, "Oh, I remember."

"We were riding fast…really pushing the limit on Pop's snowmobiles," Nick explained. "Rrrrrrr! Rrrrrrrr!" Breck smiled as the young man made snowmobile sound effects and held his hands out in front of him to simulate where his hands would've been on the handles of a snowmobile. "Yep! We were flyin'!"

"We were, weren't we?" Reese smiled at the daring memory.

"We were flyin' so fast and racing, of course," Nick said.

"Of course," Breck said. She could just imagine it—two farm kids out on their father's snowmobiles, mortality being something that only other people had to deal with. She remembered how her cousins out at El Costa Lotta behaved.

"And the sun was so bright on the snow that day. Remember, Reese?" Nick asked.

"Ohhh, yeah." Reese did remember.

"Anyway," Nick continued, "we're flyin' along, me and Tom and Reese…and, well, you know what a maniac Reese is, right, Breck?"

"Sure," Breck agreed, though she hoped he'd settled down a bit since he was nineteen.

"All of a sudden, I see Reese go flying out of the seat of his ride! It looked like he'd hit an ejection button or something! Then I saw the fence—the snowmobile got all caught up in it. Well, by the time we got over to him, it looked like he'd been starring in some sick slasher movie, you know?" Breck wrinkled her nose and shivered a bit at the thought of Reese so terribly hurt. "Fortunately for the ladies, the worst damage was across his chest…like, just below his collar bone. Have you seen the scars?" Nick asked.

"No," Breck answered, trying hard to remember if she'd noticed any scars on Reese when he'd been prancing around shirtless the morning and night before.

"That's right!" Nick explained. "'Cause we took him all the way to Denver! They had a good plastic surgeon come in and stitch him up. He's still got the one scar on his forehead that's pretty ugly though. Show her, Reese."

Reese didn't pause but reached up, pulling his hair off his forehead.

"See? Right there at his hairline," Nick pointed out. Breck did see a scar about four inches long at the point on Reese's head where Nick had indicated.

"I was wearing some good goggles that day too," Reese told her, "or else that wire would've clean poked my eyes out or cut right through them to my brain."

Breck wrinkled her nose and shivered, horrified again at the thought of Reese in such peril.

"Three-hundred and twenty-three stitches total. Right, Reese?" Nick asked.

"Yep," Reese confirmed.

"But we were flyin' that day, weren't we?" Nick chuckled.

"Dang right!" Reese laughed, meeting Nick's upheld hand with a slap from his own.

"No barbed wire where we're headed today, right?" Breck asked. She hadn't enjoyed the retelling of the story as much as the men had.

Both men laughed, and Nick put a comforting arm around her shoulder. "No. But there are a lot of good places to go for a roll in the snow…if you know what I mean."

Breck blushed as Reese said, "You got that right!" and handed his brother another high-five.

"Mmm mmm," Reese whispered, leaning over and seeming to inhale the scent of Breck's hair. "I can't wait to roll down a hill with you, baby!"

"What?" Breck exclaimed, simultaneously blushing from head to toe.

Nick and Reese both chuckled—amused at her reaction.

"Nothing like making out in the snow," Nick sighed.

"What?" Breck gasped, blushing deeper.

Reese chuckled. "Don't worry, Breck. I'll make sure everything else stays warm too…not just your mouth."

Again Nick and Reese high-fived over Breck's head. She couldn't believe how forward he was being. He always seemed so guarded at work. But then again, he did work with women like Jamie Reynolds.

Breck smiled as Nick and Reese began talking about other terrifying adventures they'd had as youth. It was wonderful to hear them talking, laughing, enjoying each other's company. But mostly she smiled at the prospect of Reese kissing her in the snow. It did sound delicious!

એ

And it was! The morning of playing in the snow with Reese and his family was incredible—from watching Lizzy and Sarah squeal with delight as their Uncle Bobby sent their sled racing down a five-foot incline to hearing Ben's and Marjie's laughter as their inner tubes collided on Doe Ridge. But most of all, it was the moments when Reese would suddenly tackle Breck (however gently) and roll her down a snowy hill, capturing her mouth in a molten kiss drenched with playful passion, that were Breck's favorites!

She'd watched Reese frolicking with his family—awed at his easy manner, his careless smile and laughter. She'd return his kisses, embraces, and smiles, enraptured by his untroubled ease and confidence. And his family—they didn't seem at all surprised by his behavior toward her! In fact, they acted as if—as if they'd expected it all along. It was wonderful! Breck felt as if she were carried away in a movie or a dream…some surreal fantasy that couldn't possibly be actually happening. And yet—it was! And it was wonderful!

After a quick snack and some hot hot chocolate, everyone formed two lines—one behind Marjie and one behind Katie. It seemed the matrons of the family were the leaders on the trek into the woods to find the perfect Christmas trees. It wasn't an easy walk either. Apparently Marjie and her daughter were not women to be pampered into settling for second best when it came to Christmas trees. It took nearly two hours before trees were found that received everyone's approval—including Marjie's and Katie's. It was delightful, and after Ben, Reese, Nick, Bobby, and Keith had chopped, sawed, dragged, and loaded the wonders of nature into the back of Ben's and Keith's pickups, everyone else hopped in the with the trees for the ride home. Everyone, that is, except Breck—she wanted to ride in the cab of Reese's truck with him.

With Nick in the back of Keith's pickup with his nieces, Breck was left alone with Reese in his. Initially, she'd jumped in on the passenger's side. But Reese had quickly taken hold of her arm, coaxing her to sit right next to him.

"You're a bit different out here," Breck told him as they drove back toward the farmhouse. She laughed as she watched Lizzy and Sarah bobbing around in the back of the pickup, holding on to their beloved Christmas tree—protecting it from harm as their daddy drove it home.

"I suspect I'm a lot more than a bit different out here, Breck," Reese admitted. "Do you like me more…or less?" he asked.

"The same," Breck told him. And it was true. She loved him when they were at work or out finding his mother's perfect Christmas tree.

"So," he began, the familiar grin of mischief spreading across his face, "all these months we've been working together…you would've let me kiss you all along?"

Breck blushed and took a chance, revealing, "Yes."

"You mean, I've wasted all this time…afraid you'd think I was a…a…"

"Philanderer?" she finished for him.

He laughed. "I can't even say that word…but yes!"

Breck shrugged. "You're Reese Thatcher," she told him, simply.

"So?" he said. He was sweet. He truly wasn't aware of the effect he had on women—people in general, for that matter. When she didn't respond, he added, "And to think of all the trouble I went to tricking you into it….the Highwayman of Tanglewood. Oh, brother."

But Breck smiled and snuggled against him as he put his arm around her shoulders. In that moment, it truly seemed that all her dreams were about to come true.

⁓

Breck leaned back against Reese's chest. She could feel his firm muscles against her back as he wrapped his arms around her, folding them across her waist. Sighing heavily, she glanced at the fire, burning low but still burning in the fireplace. The sofa was soft, Reese was strong, and the tree…the tree was beautiful!

It had taken the entire evening for the Thatcher family and Breck to decorate the Christmas tree. Breck smiled as she remembered the way Marjie had handed out orders to Ben as he awkwardly wrapped the lights around the noble fir.

"Don't tell me how to put the lights on, woman!" Ben had grumbled. "I've been doing it for thirty years, haven't I?"

Once the lights were on, Marjie opened two boxes of old, yet still shiny, glass ornament balls—red and gold. Everyone helped hang these, and Breck again smiled when she caught Marjie rearranging them all a bit.

"My boys just don't quite have the eye for it, you know," she had whispered aside to Breck. "But they try."

After all the colored balls were perfectly arranged, it was time for the specialty ornaments. Marjie had several boxes full of them. There were little wooden soldiers made out of old-fashioned clothespins—various reindeer, snowmen, nutcrackers, and Santas—tiny wooden mice with beds or nests made from small matchboxes or walnut halves. There were nativities and stars, even real candy canes. Each ornament seemed to mean something special to one or the other of Marjie's sons. She explained that she'd made or purchased a new ornament for each of her children every Christmas since they were born.

"Katie took hers when she got married and hangs them on her own tree now," she told Breck. "I wish one of my boys would get married. Then I'd have some room for some new things." She winked at Breck, and Breck blushed—flattered but uncomfortable with Marjie's implication.

The final tradition before the tree would be completed with the addition of silver strands of icicles was the moment when Marjie handed each of her sons their new ornament. Breck found she was suddenly overcome by emotion as she watched this tradition unfold.

Bobby took the small box his mother handed to him and chuckled when he withdrew a small snowman ornament. He thanked his mother, kissing her on the cheek and winking at his father, who sat in his lounge chair, obviously amused by the proceedings.

Nick's box contained a small reindeer made out of clothespins, and he too thanked his mother before finding a place for it on the tree.

Reese's ornament was a nutcracker, and it was then Breck realized one theme of the tree.

"I loved nutcrackers as a kid, so Mom always gets me a new one. Don't you?" Reese explained, lovingly kissing his mother's cheek, then finding a place for his newest nutcracker.

"And this is for you, honey," Marjie said, holding out a small box to Breck.

Breck was stunned. Already she'd had a hard time withholding her tears—the entire evening was so wonderful—but this was too much.

"I hope it's all right," Marjie said as Breck took the box in her trembling hands.

"You didn't have to—" Breck began.

"Oh, nonsense!" Marjie interrupted. "Now open it. See if you like it at all."

Reese was smiling understandingly at her, and Breck heard Ben chuckle from his seat in his lounge chair.

Breck gasped as she pulled the fragile ornament from the box.

"I thought of you the moment I saw it!" Marjie exclaimed.

Breck tried to keep the tears from spilling onto her cheeks, for there in her hand was the prettiest little porcelain doll Breck had ever seen. The little doll's head was covered in brown ringlets, a lace dress was her fashion, and in her lap she held, of all things, a tiny pumpkin!

"It's beautiful!" Breck whispered. "I can't believe you've gone to all this trouble."

Marjie giggled with excitement. "It was no trouble." Then hugging Breck, she said, "Now…find a place on the tree for your dolly."

"On *this* tree?" Breck asked. Surely Reese's mother wasn't inviting her to hang her ornament on Reese's family tree!

"Of course!" Marjie exclaimed. "After all, don't you want to see her there when you come back for Christmas?"

"Christmas?" Breck asked. She heard Reese chuckle.

"You're about as subtle as a train wreck, Mom," he said.

"Of course, Christmas! Reese says your family will still be away. That means you can come and spend it with us!" Marjie jingled.

"I-I couldn't possibly," Breck tried to argue.

"Nonsense," Marjie said. "Now put your dolly on, and we'll finish up with the icicles. Ben? Are you going to help?"

"I suppose you'll skin me if I don't," Ben mumbled, groaning as he exited his lounge chair.

There was nothing she could do. Carefully, Breck hung the beautiful little doll on a tender branch of the Thatcher family Christmas tree.

"Perfect!" Marjie exclaimed. "And now you *have* to come for Christmas!"

Breck looked to Reese, who winked at her and nodded. She knew she'd still have to argue the point for appearance's sake—but could it be? Could she really be coming home with Reese again? And for Christmas?

❧

"Mom helped us kids to make those the year I was twelve," Reese was saying. Breck pulled her attention back to the moment at hand. He chuckled, "Those danged old clothespin soldiers. I remember how mad she got when Nick, Bobby, and I started dipping toothpicks in the red paint and gluing them onto the soldiers' chests so it looked like they'd been stabbed." He laughed again. "Katie started crying and telling Mom that we were going to ruin Christmas, so Mom made us start all over."

Breck looked at the little clothespin soldiers with their black pom-pom hats. She could just imagine what a mess the Thatcher boys had made of their mother's craft project that year.

Oh, the tree was so beautiful, twinkling in the darkness of the room. The glass ornaments and silver icicles on the tree caught all the colors of the tree lights, casting color on the walls and ceiling, making pure magic of the moment. The only other light in the room was coming from the fire in the hearth, and it sent the comforting aroma of cedar wafting through the warm air, soothing the night even more. Reese's mother had left her Christmas music playing on the stereo, and the soft, restful sound of Nat King Cole's honey-coated voice singing a familiar Christmas song completed the atmosphere of contentment in the room.

"We'll have to leave the Tuesday before Christmas to come out," Reese said unexpectedly. "And early too, 'cause the snow is usually pretty bad out here by then. It'll take us longer to make the drive."

"I cannot possibly come here for Christmas, Reese. It's…it's rude," Breck told him, hoping he would argue.

He did. "It's not rude, and you are coming. And besides, I promised Mom," he told her.

"Do *you* want me to come home with you for Christmas?" she couldn't help asking. Everything seemed so perfect—so perfectly dreamy—too dreamy to be real, somehow. She worried that perhaps it was only Reese's mother who wanted her to come out to the farm for Christmas.

Reese chuckled and took hold of Breck's chin, turning her face toward his. "Who do you think planted the thought in her mind?"

Breck smiled up at him. He was wonderful! Could this all really be happening to her? And what would happen when they got back to the city? To work? To the real world?

In the next moment, Reese bent, kissing her upper lip. His kiss lingered on her lower lip and lingered there once more before he turned her in his arms and took her mouth with his own. Instantly Breck's heart seemed to swell—her breath was labored—she couldn't embrace him tightly enough. She let her hands caress his neck as they kissed—let her fingers run through his thick, soft hair. She wouldn't worry about work or the city or Monday. She'd have this gorgeous, masculine, fun, powerful man all to herself for as long as she could. She'd imagine she was worthy of him—that he found her as attractive as she found him. She'd be shoved back into reality soon enough. But for now she'd bathe in his embraces—soak in his kisses. And for now—she'd imagine that it would never end.

CHAPTER ELEVEN

Chatting with Patty as she stepped off the elevator had been nice. Even fighting the post-holiday, grouchy-driver traffic hadn't been too bad. But when Reese hadn't shown up for work by eleven that Monday morning, Breck had begun to feel quite insecure.

The drive back to the city from the Thatcher farm had been fine. Breck sensed Reese was having as much anxiety as she was about returning. Having to leave his mother standing on the farmhouse porch in tears hadn't helped matters. Still, when he'd dropped her off at her apartment Sunday night, he'd kissed her good bye—a long, passionate kiss, at that—and said he'd see her in the morning. Yet, here it was eleven a.m., and he was nowhere to be found.

In fact, it wasn't until after lunch that she received a message from him—on her voicemail. It seemed he'd be working out of town. Something he couldn't talk about requiring him to stay away for some time.

"I'll be gone until the fifteenth," his voice told her on the recorded phone message. "But don't worry, I'll call you."

Breck shook her head in disbelief. The fifteenth! That was two weeks! Certainly he'd had cases take him away for that long before, but things were different now. Weren't they? How would she endure? Already she'd been feeling very insecure about what had transpired between her and Reese at his parents' home over the holiday weekend.

Was it just a weekend fling? she wondered almost every moment throughout the day. Would he return and decide he'd made a mistake in getting involved with someone from work? She became so anxious she nearly threw up!

Even when the girls came over that night after work—Sherryl with chocolate-dipped strawberries—Kay with a new quilt square she'd been working on—Barb with her no-nonsense commands of "Buck up! He loves you"—even Trixie and her soothing manner— even with her best friends surrounding her, Breck felt hopeless, anxious.

Then, at about nine p.m. as Breck sat with her friends, trying to tell herself that all was well, the phone rang.

"Hello?" Breck answered, her voice quivering with hopeful anticipation.

"Breck?" It was Reese. Breck sighed and let a tear escape and travel down one cheek.

"Reese!" She couldn't stop the frantic sound in her voice. "H-how are you?" she stammered.

"Terrible," he grumbled. "I'm here, and you're there." She smiled, and a small wave of relief broke over her.

"Is everything okay?" she asked. "When you didn't come into work this morning…I was really worried." It was hard to concentrate with four other women nodding and mouthing questions to her.

"I know, I'm sorry. I was going to call you last night before I left, but it was so late," he explained. "Hey, I can't talk long…but everything is fine. Okay?"

She wanted to shout to him, *But everything is not fine! I need reassurance. I need you!* Instead she managed, "Okay."

He must've heard the anxiety in her voice. "Breck…I really do have to go now," he told her. "But I mean it. Everything is fine. I don't want you to worry…about anything."

"Okay," she managed again.

"Hey…I'll tell you what," he began, "put in for a day off on the sixteenth. Tell personnel that I okayed it. I'll be back on the fifteenth, and the sixteenth we'll…do something. Okay?"

Breck felt mildly relieved, but she wondered if he was only trying to pacify her. Something was wrong.

"All right," she said. "Um…Reese?"

"Yeah?"

"Are you really okay?" she asked. There was a long pause, and it worried her.

"I am," is all he said.

"Well, I-I guess I'll see you on the sixteenth then," she mumbled.

"I'll call you in a couple of days," he told her. Then he added, "Breck, I have…I have to do this right now…before we go home for Christmas. And I know you're a worrier, so I don't want you to worry about anything while I'm gone. Everything is fine."

"All right, Reese," she managed. She felt better, for it sounded like he was still planning to take her back to the farm for Christmas. "I'll try not to."

"There's nothing to worry about. I promise," he told her. "I'll call you soon."

"Okay," she said, wiping the tears from her cheeks.

"And we'll make out…oops," he chuckled. "We'll make *up* for lost time when I get back."

Breck smiled. Maybe everything was going to be fine. "We will?" she asked.

"Oohhh, yeah!" he told her. "Good night, baby."

"Good night, Reese," she said. And he hung up.

❧

"Well, I'm glad to see you've come around, Reese," Ben Thatcher told his son from his seat in his lounge chair by the fire. "It took a good many years…but it looks like you're finally over whatever sent you runnin' off."

Reese turned off his cell phone and sighed heavily. "Oh, I don't know if I'm over it, Pop. Just…just beyond it." He looked at the Christmas tree—his mother's beautiful Christmas tree—and thought how beautiful Breck had been when he'd dropped her off at her apartment before heading back to the farm.

"What did ol' Wilson say when you told him?" Ben Thatcher asked his son.

Reese chuckled. "He said, 'Good for you, Reese!' Though I know it puts him in a corner…trying to replace me."

"Oh, he'll find someone," Ben yawned. "A good investigator is easy to find. A good, hard-workin' man, however…ain't." Ben yawned again, this time adding a stretch for his back. "Still, I think you should've told your little treat there what you're up to."

Reese hung his head. He did feel guilty for not telling Breck that when he'd dropped her off the night before, realizing his mind and soul were whacked—that his life was messed up—he'd turned back around and headed for home. But he had a plan, and he needed time to implement a few things—get his head together before he faced her again.

"I know," Reese admitted. "But I think she'll understand someday."

"Oh, she will," Ben said. "She's a jewel. And you're a lucky man."

"I know," Reese said. "I just hope I can stay lucky."

❧

That night after the girls had gone—as she lay in bed attempting to find a way to get some sleep—Breck thought over the phone conversation she'd had with Reese.

"Stay calm," she told herself out loud. "Just stay calm."

If only he'd said, "I love you, Breck." If only he'd said, "I miss you," or something simple like, "I can't live without you." Then she'd be able to endure two weeks without him. But he hadn't said any of those things, and she was left to find a way to function for the next two weeks.

❧

Breck did function for the next two weeks. Perhaps not very efficiently, but she did function. She woke up, went to work, came home, and baked herself silly trying to stay busy. She tried to breathe and live—attempted to find ways of not worrying about Reese and what the future held or didn't hold for her where he was concerned. Still, it was more than merely difficult. For ever since returning from the Thatcher's farm—ever since Reese had kissed her and left her in her apartment that Sunday night over two weeks before—Breck had been unable to find a moment of happiness. Yes, he'd called her every few days, and each time he encouraged her—told her not to worry, that they'd spend time together when he returned. But it was hard. If only he'd give her more—a confession of sorts—of love. Of course, she hadn't told him she loved him—for what if he hadn't been ready to hear it? Then things might truly be ruined.

With each passing day, city life depressed Breck more and more. She was dissatisfied with it—angry with it—unsettled. Each time she'd think of Katie and Keith and their two adorable little girls—each time she'd think of Marjie and Ben and Nick and Bobby—each time she'd remember the sensations that ran through her body at being held in Reese's arms and kissed by him—every time she thought of the life she'd led for four days over the Thanksgiving holiday—she experienced despair.

Oh, she realized that everything about that weekend had been glamorized in a way. No one had worked from sunup to sundown trying to make a living off farming. No one had gotten hurt or hurt anyone. No one had worried about bills or making ends meet. She knew the weekend was rosy. Still, she also knew Reese belonged to that life. She'd seen it in him every moment they were there—the way he worked so physically hard helping his dad and brothers with chores, the contented smile on his face when he looked out to the pastures to see nothing but snow and cattle and sky. And she remembered the smile on his face when they'd stood inside the old farmhouse Thanksgiving night. Reese loved that house, and it loved him. Breck had felt it wash over her like a warm rain. She'd loved the house too, and the memory of it had helped her a bit over the past couple of weeks while Reese was out of town. If she felt tears of discouragement coming on, she'd take a moment or two and daydream—dreams of being married to Reese Thatcher and living in the old Thatcher farmhouse—dreams of rounding up cattle in the fall, calving in the spring, bringing in wheat and alfalfa in the summer—and dreams of walking through the woods near the old farmhouse, hunting for the perfect Christmas tree.

It was cruel, that's what it was, she often thought. Cruel to place such a man in her path if she couldn't have him. Cruel to show her such a wonderful life if she couldn't live it. Still, Reese had called her every few nights while he was gone, and tomorrow—tomorrow he would be back. Wouldn't he?

☙

December fifteenth had been an excruciatingly terrible day for Breck. So much had gone wrong at work. The Allen case was getting very ugly; the Morgan and Dalton cases were worse. After work, Breck plopped down on the sofa in her apartment with a spoon in her mouth, a jar of peanut butter in one hand, and a package of milk chocolate chips in the other. On days like this, Breck wondered if she could keep going. Especially now that the part of her job she'd always enjoyed was absent—that being Reese. She choked back the tears that welled up in her eyes at the thought of him. She was hanging on for tomorrow—maybe by the skin of her teeth, but she was hanging on. Tomorrow Reese would be back, and she would know: had he changed his mind about her or not?

There was a knock on the door, and with a heavy sigh, Breck set down the peanut butter and chocolate chips, but not before filling her mouth with one last delicious blob of the two combined. Therefore, when she opened the door to see Reese standing before her, for once her mouth didn't drop open in astonishment—it couldn't! It was glued shut with peanut butter.

"Hi," he said, smiling rather apologetically at her.

"Hi," Breck managed after finally choking down the stuff in her mouth. It was an awkward moment, and uncertainty hung heavy in the air.

"You wanna grab a coat and come out with me for a little while?" Reese asked. Breck felt anxiety and joy at the same time, and it was rather uncomfortable.

"Work go okay today?" he asked once they were in his pickup. Breck swallowed hard. He was making small talk. Not a good sign. Her insides began to quiver with apprehension. Was he taking her out to break off everything with her?

"It was ugly," came her honest answer.

He smiled. "I can imagine," he said.

"How was your trip?" Breck couldn't help but ask.

"Very productive and enlightening," he answered.

"Oh, that's nice," she said.

A few minutes later, Reese parked the pickup in an empty field just outside of the city limits. Breck was afraid to look at him. What would she see—guilt, regret—pity?

"Come on," Reese said, stepping out of the pickup. Breck opened her door and slowly stepped out too. "Come here," he said, and she watched, puzzled as he took an old quilt from behind the pickup seat and spread it over the hood of the pickup. She was startled when he suddenly took hold of her waist, lifting her up and setting her on the hood. He climbed on beside her, stretched out on his back, tucked his hands behind his head, and sighed, "Ahhhhhh."

Breck was completely confused.

"Look at those stars," Reese mumbled. Breck looked up to see the clear night sky sparkling with bright starlight. "You can't see them from the city. You have to get out here away from the lights to see them."

If he were getting ready to let her down easy—throw a fish back in the lake—this seemed a strange way to do it. Breck braced herself. It had been wonderful, her weekend romance with her boss. It had been fantastic actually, and she would remember it forever. That's what she kept telling herself—better to have loved and lost, as the old cliché went. Yet she could feel the hard lump developing in her throat—the nausea rising in her stomach.

"Wait until we get back out to the farm," he said. "Remember how amazing stars are out there? I'd forgotten how amazing they were until we were there for Thanksgiving."

"You mean…you still want me to go there for Christmas?" Breck asked. She couldn't help it! Her heart was hammering so fast she thought it might knock her off the pickup altogether.

Reese frowned and looked over at her. "Of course," he said. "You haven't changed your mind, have you?" The expression on his face was truly that of panic.

Breck smiled, relief beginning to find its way into her body. "No. No, of course not."

"Whew!" Reese sighed, shaking his head. "You scared me. I thought you'd gone off and found yourself a better man while I was gone."

Breck breathed a sigh of relief. *Men are so clueless*, she thought. Accidentally then, she spoke her thoughts out loud.

"Like I'd ever find a better man than you," she mumbled. She blushed when she heard Reese chuckle.

"You didn't worry too much while I was gone, did you, Breck?" he asked her, sitting up and taking her chin in one hand.

Breck gazed into his eyes. They were so beautiful; *he* was so beautiful.

"I want you to tell me the truth…because…I've been a little wrapped up in getting myself straightened out these past couple of weeks, and…and I want to make sure that you didn't worry too much…you know…doubt me…my feelings for you," he said.

The moment had come, and Breck knew it. Oh, everything had been perfect over Thanksgiving—the place, the man, the flirting, the romance, the kissing. But life wasn't perfect, and if she hoped to really have Reese in her life forever, she needed to confide in him—be honest with him—let him know her true feelings.

"I-I did worry," she confessed. "I thought you…I thought you had changed your mind and decided that Thanksgiving was nice but reality was back now."

He closed his eyes for a moment and exhaled a guilty sigh. "I'm sorry, Breck. I-I was kind of messed up after Thanksgiving. Not about you…about me. I had to get some things straight in my mind, and to be honest, I had to be where I couldn't get my hands on you in order to think straight. Do you understand?'"

"Of course not," she said, smiling at him. But she did understand—and she was flattered as well as encouraged.

"I'm sorry," he said again. "But I'm cool now. I know what I need to do, where I need to be, and…and who I need to be with," he said, reaching over and taking her chin in his hand.

Suddenly then, he pushed her down so she was lying on the hood of the truck, reached over her, and pulled the quilt up, wrapping them in it.

"I wasn't just messing around over Thanksgiving, Breck," he told her as he hovered over her—his mouth a mere breath from her own. "But you sure did a number on me."

"Really?" she couldn't help asking. For she still needed reassurance. The past two weeks had been a miserable mess of worry, doubt, and loneliness.

"Oh, yeah," he said, grinning at her. Breck sighed as she felt him kiss her upper lip gently. "Come on, Breck," he whispered, kissing her lower lip once. "Throw me for another loop." He kissed her lower lip again. "I promise, I'll land on my feet this time."

And with that Reese's lips blended with Breck's in a kiss of reassurance—at first. Reassurance quickly gave way to desire and passion—affirmation—and Breck knew then that whatever the future may bring to her where Reese Thatcher was concerned, his attention to her, his affections, had been and were sincere. No, he hadn't professed love to her. But she hadn't professed it to him either. Maybe he was as frightened to confess it as she was. Maybe he just liked her an awful lot. But *like* could eventually grow into love. Couldn't it? She knew it could. And so she reveled in the moment—in the feel of being wrapped in his arms under a sky full of stars. Reveled in his kiss and the knowledge that she "did a number" on him. And besides, Christmas was coming! Perhaps Christmas would be as magical as Thanksgiving had been. Perhaps come Christmas morning, she would find Reese Thatcher waiting for her under the tree. Oh, what a gift that would be!

CHAPTER TWELVE

"Breck, can I see you in my office for a minute?" Reese asked as he walked by her desk after lunch. Tomorrow—they were leaving for Christmas with his family tomorrow! Breck could hardly wait! The days since Reese's return from being out of town had been wonderful. He'd come over to her apartment every night, and they'd talked or watched movies—laughed and kissed. Breck was feeling much more confident of the sincerity of Reese's feelings for her. And now—now work was almost over for more than a week, and they would be back at the farm by tomorrow night!

"Yes," Breck answered. "I'll be right there." Reese had been working like a plow horse trying to get some loose ends tied up before leaving for Christmas. Breck couldn't believe how much time he was putting in at the office. In fact, she'd been amazed he'd even taken lunch that day.

Stepping into his office, she obeyed when he said, "Close the door, will you?" Once the door was closed, she gasped, dropping the yellow legal pad and pen she'd been holding in her hand as Reese took her shoulders, pushing her back against the door before smothering her in a hard, driven kiss. Breck wrapped her arms around his neck—instantly lost in the depth of their kiss. He was like a hungry lion—kissing her with a sort of ravenous appetite, a barely restrained desire! Oh, how she loved the feel of being kissed by him—the way his powerful hands traveled over her arms, resting at her waist a moment—his fingers pressing the small of her back, his thumbs briefly tracing the curve of her ribs. She sighed when he gathered her in his arms at last—gathered her in his arms and against the strength of his warm, strong body. Anyone would've thought he hadn't kissed her for a month rather than a mere sixteen hours.

After several minutes, his mouth left hers, and he smiled down at her, still holding her against the door. "Just needed a little dessert after lunch," he chuckled.

"Oh my heck!" Breck exclaimed with a smile. She was again amazed at his ability to keep her blushing.

"Now, you get back to work," he told her. "Quit trying to distract me. I have a lot to do before I can leave tomorrow." She shook her head and gasped when he swatted her on the rear end as she opened his office door.

"Reese!" she scolded in a whisper, looking up at the angle of the security camera above her desk and hoping it hadn't caught anything on tape. Still, she smiled at him—delighted—for, although her mother would've had a fit at his spanking her like that, she'd seen Reese's father do the same thing to his mother at least twice a day over Thanksgiving—and she liked the idea Reese would think of doing the same to her.

Still, it was hard to concentrate on anything after being ravaged in his office. Breck was even more distracted—fumbling papers, dropping pens. But the end of the day did come, and somehow, Breck felt as if work would never be the same again. It had been very different when she'd returned from her last visit out to the farm. But now—now she sensed it would be even more so on her return from this one. A small flicker of worry began to spark in the back of her mind because she knew Reese belonged away from the city, out in the open, working hard. But this trip back—what if he began to know it too? What if he decided to stay?

Breck shook her head, trying to dispel her worries. It was going to be wonderful—Christmas with Reese's family. And she was going to enjoy it.

❧

"Oh, you're here, you're here, you're here!" Marjie Thatcher greeted, wiping the flour from her hands onto her apron and throwing her arms around Breck's neck. The house felt and smelled like heaven—warm, friendly, the scents of pine and gingerbread heavy in the air. "We thought you'd never get here," Marjie explained. "Were the roads pretty bad, Reese?"

The roads had been bad. A big snowstorm had begun dumping snow about an hour from the farm, and it made for a stressful drive.

"There're roads out there?" Reese teased. He smiled and embraced his mother. "The last twenty miles were really bad. I stopped and chained up, though. And we're fine." Marjie stood on her toes and kissed her son's cheek.

"Well, you're here now, and, Breck, we've got gingerbread men going in the kitchen. Do you wanna help?" Marjie asked.

Breck couldn't help smiling. It felt like—like *she'd* come home—not just that Reese had.

"Of course!" Breck giggled.

"Not before I get my hug," Ben said, approaching then. Breck smiled as he wrapped her in his strong arms and kissed her cheeks. "Welcome back, sugar," he added.

"Thank you for having me," she told him. Reese helped Breck take off her coat, hanging it on the coatrack behind the door.

"Better get in the kitchen. Mom will have my hide if I mess up her gingerbread men," Reese chuckled, kissing Breck quickly on the cheek. Yes, they'd have to share one another now—with Reese's family. But somehow, Breck didn't mind too awfully much.

"Hey, Breck," Nick greeted as Breck followed Marjie into the kitchen.

"Hi," Breck responded with a smile.

"Man! Reese hasn't been home this much in years!" Bobby told her. Breck was curious when Nick jabbed Bobby in the ribs with one elbow.

"You've eaten the heads off again?" Marjie exclaimed. "You boys...get out! Out! Get in there and mess up your daddy's project!"

"Daddy never has projects, Mom," Bobby said. "Besides, yours taste better." Picking up another gingerbread man off the cooling rack, Bobby bit off its head and smiled when his mother spanked him as he left the room.

Nick followed his brother out, and Marjie said, "Look at that! They always do this. Every year when I'm making my gingerbread men, they sneak in here when my back is turned and bite the heads of at least a dozen!"

Breck couldn't help smiling at the sad remains of a dozen headless gingerbread men.

Her smile broadened as she watched Marjie begin popping the remains in her mouth, saying, "Still, it gives me an excuse to taste my own baking." Holding out a half-eaten gingerbread man to Breck, she added, "Try one. See what you think."

Eat a cookie after Nick or Bobby had already bitten it? Normally the idea would've churned Breck's stomach. But there was something about Reese's family—something clean and safe. So she took the cookie offered to her and ate it.

"Mmmm!" she mumbled. "Mrs. Thatcher! This is delicious!" Breck enjoyed the smile of pride that spread across Marjie's face.

"Thanks. I think they're pretty good myself," Marjie said.

Marjie helped Breck tie a red apron on, handed her a blob of gingerbread dough and a rolling pin, and asked, "So…how has work been?"

Breck looked quickly to her. Her question had sounded like she already knew the answer. "Okay. We have some nasty cases in right now…and they kind of wear on me."

"I can imagine," Marjie said. "Do you…do you think you'll work there for long?"

Breck shrugged. "I don't know. It does pay well. But…"

"Money isn't everything," Marjie stated.

"That's for sure," Breck agreed.

"Has Reese been behaving himself? Where you're concerned, I mean?"

Breck blushed slightly. How embarrassing to have your boyfriend's mother asking such a question. And after all, she did consider Reese to be her boyfriend.

"Of course," Breck assured her.

Marjie sighed with relief. "I'm sure it's hard for him…but he's a good boy." Marjie smiled and popped a pinch of dough into her mouth. "Katie and the girls will be by later," she said. "Can you believe tomorrow is Christmas Eve? Whew! It sure snuck up on me this year."

"I-I brought a few things for everyone, Mrs. Thatcher," Breck told her then. "Would it be okay if I put them under your tree? I noticed you've got quite a pile going already."

Breck adored the way Marjie's eyes lit up at the mention of gifts. "Of course, sweet pea! But…you really didn't need to bring anything."

"I wanted to. You all have been so kind to me…letting me impose on both of your major holidays and…" Breck began. She paused, however, when she felt Marjie place one hand over her own.

"You are not imposing, sugar," Marjie said, looking Breck squarely in the eyes. "You're…like one of the family." Breck felt a sweet, honeyed warmth drizzle over her. This woman was an angel, and Christmas was going to be wonderful.

❦

As usual, Breck found herself lying awake by four a.m. Christmas Eve morning. All her life she'd loved Christmas Eve even more than Christmas Day! Christmas Eve seemed to hold a certain wonder and magic for her that somehow vanished an hour or so after rising on Christmas morning. She knew Reese's mother left the lights on her tree burning all night, and she figured they'd be beautiful in the darkness of early morning.

Quietly, she dressed and tiptoed out into the hallway. Even in the hallway she could see the colorful shadows on the walls of the front room beyond, assuring her the tree was indeed aglow. Stepping into the front room, she sighed with delight at the sight of the tree. Someone had been up before her too, for there was a fire blazing in the fireplace.

Breck startled as she sat down on the sofa when she heard Ben say, "I like a woman who can get out of bed in the morning." Breck turned around to see Ben lounging in his favorite chair. No doubt he'd been out already. Probably the boys had been too—feeding the stock and making sure the ice in the watering tanks was busted up.

"I'm sorry," Breck told him. "Am I disturbing you?"

Ben chuckled. "Me? No," he assured her. "Reese, however…now that's a different story, isn't it?" Breck blushed. "I like the way you got him thinkin', Breck. He needed to do some hard of it."

"I'm sure I didn't have anything to do—" Breck began.

"Oh, I'm sure you did," Ben interrupted. "His mother and I have been poundin' our heads against the wall for years now." The man sighed and shook his head. "That deal with Tommy…it just cut him so deep. I don't think we realized how angry and hurt he was at the time. But it wasn't long before we realized he'd suffered some severe damage emotionally."

Breck didn't say a word. She wanted nothing more at that moment than to hear what Reese's father had to say.

"I think he felt guilty at first," he continued, "I think he felt bad that Tom died and he didn't. Then it turned into fear…a realization that a man can die. Boys…they have this misconception of being immortal, you see. When they're young they think they're so tough that nothin' can touch them. It's a hard thing to see your first friend die…and it sure hit Reese the wrong way.

"After the guilt left and the fear set in, anger was next. He was infuriated that the sheriff couldn't give him an answer….about what had happened to Tom. He ranted and raved and swore for weeks about it. Rage turned to blame…blaming farm life and small-town mentality for the accident and for not finding an answer. He decided then that he could single-handedly save the world." Ben smiled at Breck and added, "Personally, I think he read one too many superhero comic books as a kid."

Breck giggled.

"So for years we've been watchin' him struggle, tryin' to find himself, where he should be and the like," Ben said with a sigh. Then he smiled at Breck. "Then you come along, and he finally seems to be pullin' his head out of the bucket."

"I'm sure it's not me," Breck told him. And she was sure.

"Maybe…maybe just coming home at Thanksgiving—"

"He wasn't plannin' on comin' home for Thanksgiving…'til you came along," Ben explained. "Ahh…but I'm interruptin' your peace and quiet here," he said, pulling the handle at the side of his chair and sitting upright.

"Oh, no!" Breck argued. "I love talking with you! It's the first chance we've had to talk, really."

Ben chuckled, rather swaggering over to her and cupping her cheek in one strong, roughened hand. "We'll find our time, pretty girl. Don't you worry." And with that, he left Breck alone with the fire and the tree and the feelings of happiness and comfort.

☙

As day broke, everyone else in the Thatcher family trickled into the front room and kitchen. Breck could feel the excitement in the air. Everyone was excited about Christmas Eve, including the men. Katie and her family arrived just after breakfast, and Breck giggled as she watched Lizzy and Sarah shaking the gifts she'd set under the tree for them the night before. She hoped that the stuffed cat with her stuffed litter of kittens would soothe some of the child's disappointment at Breck being unable to produce a living litter for her. She smiled at the memory of Lizzy asking her if she'd have some babies for her Uncle Reese. It *had* been a funny moment.

Most of the late morning and early afternoon, Breck accompanied Marjie as she delivered various baskets filled with breads, cookies, nuts, meats, and cheeses to family friends of surrounding farms. It was wonderful. Reese had volunteered to drive his mother on her errands—being that the storm the night before had left driving a bit dangerous—and it was wonderful, sitting next to Reese in his pickup as his mother chattered away excitedly. It seemed she told Breck the entire family history of every family she visited, and Breck giggled at her merry mood.

Christmas Eve dinner at the Thatcher farm proved very traditional, with ham, potatoes, and all the fixings. Breck nearly burst into tears as she watched Ben coax his granddaughters up onto his lap as he sat in his lounge chair and began reading from the book of Luke—

the story of the birth of the Christ child. The tree twinkled, the fire burned, and Reese, his brothers, Katie and Keith, and Marjie sat in awed quiet as Ben read to the girls.

After the bible story, Marjie handed Ben a large, beautifully illustrated copy of *The Night Before Christmas*. Breck watched as Lizzy's and Sarah's eyes widened with excitement at the prospect of catching Santa leaving presents under their own tree.

All during Ben's reading the stories, Breck had been bathing in the warmth and power of Reese's embrace as he held her. But he rose suddenly, excusing himself to do a couple of chores outside.

"Do you want me to help?" Breck asked.

Reese smiled at her. "Not just now. You stay inside where it's warm."

Instantly, Nick plopped down next to Breck on the sofa. Bobby followed shortly, sitting on the other side of her.

"Don't worry, Reese," Nick chuckled. "We'll keep her warm for you."

"You boys behave," Marjie scolded, giggling at the same time.

"I'll be back in a minute," Reese assured Breck.

And so she settled back down and watched Lizzy and Sarah hop down off their grandpa's lap when the story was through and go back to investigating the presents under the tree.

Everyone was talking about Christmases past—laughing and telling stories.

"Remember that dog-ugly tree Pop brought home the year mom had her surgery?" Bobby asked.

"How could we forget?" Katie sighed as everyone else laughed.

"It looked like a big twig with a few pine needles on it," Nick told Breck.

"That there was a good tree," Ben defended himself. "It looked just fine when I first chopped it down."

"But then you rolled your pickup with the tree in the back…and by the time he got home…it was a twig with a few pine needles," Nick laughed.

"It was a lovely tree, Ben," Marjie assured her husband. She smiled at him, and he winked at her.

Reese returned then, brushing the snow off the sleeves of his coat.

"Hey, Breck," he said, "you wanna grab your coat? I've got something to show you."

"Sure," Breck said. She was excited about the prospect of spending some time alone with Reese. She didn't care if she froze to death riding on the back of the four-wheeler while they traveled around breaking up ice in water tanks. She just wanted some time alone with the man—with the man she loved.

Reese helped Breck put her coat on, and she frowned, puzzled as the entire family rose from their seats and followed them to the front door. And when Reese opened the front door to reveal an old sleigh—adorned with jingle bells and hitched to a strong-looking mare—she gasped, and everyone smiled at her.

"Wanna go for a ride?" Reese asked her.

Breck smiled at him, her eyes filling with tears of joy. "Of course!" she told him.

He helped her into the sleigh, tucked an old quilt tightly over her lap, and climbed in next to her. As he snapped the reins lightly on the horse's back, the sleigh lurched forward, and everyone stood on the front porch waving. It wasn't long before the horse was trotting along at a steady pace—the bells jingling, matching its rhythm.

"It's a 'one-horse open sleigh,'" Reese pointed out.

"I got that," Breck giggled, wrapping her arms tightly around one of his strong ones.

They rode in silence for quite a while, for it seemed that neither one of them wanted to talk and ruin the music of the bells and the sleigh sliding along in the snow. Frost fell through the air, sifting onto the surface of the snow-covered ground like a billion tiny diamonds. The stars were twinkling overhead—bright, happy, and beautiful. It was a moment borne of dreams.

"You're quite the romancer," Breck said quietly.

Reese smiled. "I try," he told her.

Some time later, Breck looked ahead of them and recognized

the silhouette of the old Thatcher farmhouse on the dark horizon. Only—this time—something was different. As they turned toward the front of the house, Breck gasped when she saw the beautiful twinkles of color dotting the snow on the ground in front of the house. A brightly lit Christmas tree stood in the bay window at the front of the house, shining out like a beacon of heaven.

"Reese!" she gasped and heard him chuckle.

"Do you like it?" he asked her, pulling the horse to a stop in front of the house.

Breck shook her head and let one tear escape each eye. "It's…it's too beautiful for words!" she whispered.

Reese smiled and climbed down from the sleigh. "Come on then. I have something to show you."

Breck stumbled once as he helped her out of the sleigh, for she couldn't take her eyes off the tree in the window. It seemed to illuminate the entire outside of the house as well. She could've sworn the paint looked fresher.

"Now…stand right here," Reese instructed, positioning her in a spot in the front yard directly in front of the house. "Don't move, okay?"

"Okay," she agreed. She continued to stare at the beautiful tree—at the happy-looking house. It was amazing what a Christmas tree did for a house: it made it a home.

Reese dashed up the front porch stairs and hunkered down for a moment. And then, suddenly, the outside of the house lit up as cascades of tiny white icicle lights glimmered from every eave and trim.

Breck gasped again—breathless for a moment as she took in the wonder of the lights. Reese jogged down the porch steps and came to stand next to her, inspecting the wonder himself.

"Pretty nice, if I do say so myself," he said.

Breck looked at him. "Y-you did all this?" she asked.

"Yeah," he said, pulling her into his arms. "I about broke my dang neck too."

Breck returned his embrace, smiling up into his handsome face. "I'm glad you didn't."

"Me too," he whispered before kissing her upper lip lightly. Breck felt the butterflies take flight in her stomach as his kiss lingered on her lower lip then. He'd kiss her lower lip twice before really kissing—she knew it. He often started their kisses in the same teasing manner. It was as if he were preparing her for greater things to come. And greater things always did.

They stood there in the snow in front of the old farmhouse—lost in their warm, moist kisses as the frost sifted down over them.

All at once, Reese pushed her away from him and, grinning at her, said, "Come on. There's more."

Breck giggled, delighted as he pulled her up the front porch steps and into the house. Once he'd closed the door behind them, Breck looked up and drew in a quick breath as she saw the fresh beauty of the room.

"Reese," she breathed. It was incredible. The lights from the tree cast color on the freshly painted, white walls. A fire burned warm in the fireplace, and the floor had been polished.

"It still smells like paint…but it looks good, huh," he told her, tugging on her hand, coaxing her further into the room.

"It looks perfect," Breck whispered. And it did!

Reese clapped his gloved hands together and nodded with pride. "I worked hard to get it this way."

Breck frowned and looked up to him. "*You* worked hard?"

"Yep," he told her. "I know you assumed I was working a case while I was gone, Breck," he confessed. "But I was here…working on the house…and working some things out in my mind. Are you mad?"

There was a part of her that was angry. He'd been here on the farm enjoying his family and the escape from the city, while she'd been worried and miserable in the city? And yet, it was *his* family— his family's farm. She had no right to be angry, and suddenly—she wasn't. Fear, however, began to creep into her mind and heart. Reese had obviously put a lot of time and effort into fixing up this old house. Why? Was he thinking of returning? Would he leave her in the city and…

"I quit," he said, his smile fading.

"What?" Breck asked. Her heart began to hammer hard in her chest—an anxious, frightened kind of hammer.

Reese nodded. "That night we got home from Thanksgiving…I dropped you off, turned around to drive through the city back to my own house, and…and never made it. I came back here and spent some time talking with my parents. Then I worked on this house… worked hard physically, you know? I've missed that."

"What do you mean?" Breck asked. He'd quit? If he'd quit his job at Wilson Investigation, then Breck could only guess what was coming next—or at least part of what was coming next.

"I own this house, Breck," he told her. "I bought it from Mom and Pop a few years back…the house and about two thousand acres."

"You're moving back?" she ventured. She felt light-headed—sick to her stomach. He was leaving the city—he was leaving her!

"You don't think I should?" He seemed concerned—seemed to doubt his decision—and Breck knew she must encourage him, for it was where he belonged, where he would be happy. And she wanted him to be happy.

"Oh, no," she stammered. "I…I think…I think it's wonderful."

Reese grinned then, his eyes narrowing as he searched her face. "Hold on a second," he told her. Then he walked to one corner of the room, lifted the lid on an old record player, and next—next Breck heard the melody of one of her favorite old Bing Crosby Christmas songs begin to play. Instantly, tears began to roll down her cheeks. It was a beautiful moment. The most beautiful, most heartbreaking moment she'd ever known. Reese was so excited about his decision to come home—wanted her to be excited for him. He'd gone to the trouble of finding her one of her favorite Bing Crosby songs, and all she could do was cry because she was devastated.

"Dance with me?" he asked, taking one of her hands in his. Breck wiped the tears from her cheeks and tried to smile.

As he led her in an old-fashioned waltz, he asked, "What's the matter, baby? Don't you like the house?"

"I love the house," she sniffled.

"Well, guess what, Miss Breck McCall?" he said, lowering his voice and stopping their waltz. Taking her face in his hands, he gazed down into her face and said, "I love *you*."

Breck closed her eyes for a moment, letting more tears escape down her cheeks. He'd said it! At last he'd said he loved her. But it was almost bittersweet. A long-distance relationship? Still, she loved him, and she didn't want to lose him.

"I love you too, Reese," she whispered, opening her eyes and looking up at him. "And I want you to be happy…here. You belong here."

"Do I?" he whispered, taking one of her hands in his, raising it to his lips, and kissing it tenderly.

"You do," she managed.

Breck gasped then, her tears turning to tiny rivulets as they streamed down her face—for Reese raised his other hand then—his fisted other hand. He opened it a moment later to reveal a beautiful diamond solitaire ring lying in his palm.

"You're all I want for Christmas," he said. "Every Christmas," he added, pushing the ring onto her appropriate finger. "Will you marry me, Breck? Will you quit your job in the city, give up everything you've worked so hard to achieve there…and be a farmer's wife?"

Breck buried her face in her hands and sobbed. This couldn't be happening! She shook her head, trying to dispel the dream—but it stayed. Reese stood there—wiping the tears from her cheeks, kissing her forehead, and chuckling. It was real!

"Will you, Breck?" he asked again.

With rivers of tears rolling down her cheeks, Breck nodded and said, "Of course, I will!"

Instantly, she was in his arms, his mouth taking her own in a driven, passionate exchange. He was hers! Reese Thatcher would belong to her!

He released her, raised her hand to inspect the ring on her finger, and asked, "Do you like your Christmas present, baby?"

Suddenly, Breck gasped, horrified as she remembered something. "I only got you an electric razor!"

Reese laughed and pulled her into his arms again. "I love you, Breck McCall. And you found me...helped me remember who I was and what I love." He cupped her face in his hands and gazed down into her eyes. "Thank you."

Breck smiled and brushed the tears from her cheeks. "*You* are my dreams come true," she confessed.

Reese smiled, caressing her lips with his thumb. "Then I guess here...in this moment...in *our* house...all is right with the world. Isn't it?"

Breck nodded, and there in the old Thatcher family farmhouse, fragrant with the scent of a cedar fire and warm with the beauty and color of Christmas tree lights, Reese kissed her again—a long, adoring kiss that spoke of promised happiness and everlasting love.

EPILOGUE

It had been fun having the girls and their families out the day before. Breck couldn't believe how big Barb's, Kay's, Sherryl's, and Trixie's children were getting. But then again, her own children were growing up faster than she liked too. Breck shook her head, unable to believe for a moment that her daughter Bobbie was already five years old—and Scottie would be three next month! How time had flown since that first Christmas she and Reese had spent together—that first Christmas when he'd driven her out to their house on a horse-drawn sleigh and asked her to marry him.

Breck dusted the rest of the residual powdered sugar off the counter and into her hand. It was Christmas Eve day, and it had been wonderful! Breck had delivered baskets with Reese's mother in the morning and later watched Katie's girls show Bobbie and Scottie how to sprinkle powdered sugar over the gingerbread houses to look like snow. She giggled, thinking the children got more powdered sugar on themselves and the floor than they did the gingerbread houses.

And Reese would be home soon! How she missed him every minute he was away from her. Anytime he was gone from the house doing chores or working with his father and brothers, she missed him. Their life together was wonderful! Oh, they worked hard and had their share of worries and challenges, but it was a life she'd once dreamed of—and her dreams had all come true. The new baby due in June would only add to Reese's joy and hers, and Breck knew that, come what may, the love she and Reese shared was deeper and stronger than most, and she was thankful for it.

She heard the kitchen door close and looked up to see her handsome husband brushing the snow from his coat sleeves. He stomped his work boots on the mat several times to free them of as much slush as possible before pulling them off and setting them aside. He took off his coat, hat, and gloves and laid them on the counter by the door.

"Hey, baby," he said, taking Breck in his arms and kissing her hard on the mouth. "Kids in bed?"

"Just now. They're waiting for you to tuck them in," Breck told him. "Brrr! Your cheeks are cold!"

"It's cold out there tonight," he explained. "But the sky is clear. Santa won't have any trouble finding our house," he chuckled.

"Well, I hope not," Breck giggled, "'cause Santa still has to assemble that dollhouse he's bringing for Bobbie."

"I'll run up and tuck them in." Reese smiled and kissed her cheek again. "Meet me in the front room in three minutes," he whispered. With a wink and a mischievous grin, he added, "I wanna make good use of that mistletoe you hung up in there."

He quickly kissed her cheek, and Breck giggled as she watched him saunter across the room in his stocking feet, bounding up the back stairs toward the kids' bedrooms.

Sighing with the pure contentment borne of love and Christmas Eve, she went into the front room, sat down on the sofa, and watched the lights of the Christmas tree twinkling in the bay window. Bing was crooning softly on the stereo. It was one of those rare moments a woman experiences when her mind, body, and soul find complete tranquility. She closed her eyes for a moment and breathed in the scent of their home—the warm aroma of fresh-baked cookies—of a cedar fire—of love.

"Merry Christmas, Mrs. Thatcher," Reese said. He took her hand, pulled her to her feet, and wrapped her in his arms.

"Merry Christmas, Mr. Thatcher," Breck whispered as he kissed her upper lip softly. He gently kissed her lower lip once—then a second time—and Breck's heart began hammering inside her chest as wildly as ever it did when Reese kissed her. His mouth captured hers for a moment, and she sighed—bathed in the warmth of love and desire.

Reese abruptly broke the seal of their kiss, distracted by the familiar squeak of the seventh step on the staircase.

"Kids? Get back to bed," Reese growled, in his most fatherly voice.

Breck smiled as she heard Bobbie's and Scottie's playful giggling as they scampered up the stairs and back to bed.

"They'll never get to sleep," Reese chuckled. "We'll be building that dollhouse 'til four in the morning."

Breck nodded and ran her fingers through her husband's hair. He needed a haircut. She let her fingers trace the outline of his mustache and goatee and then raised herself on the tips of her toes and kissed him softly on the mouth.

"Thank you for making all my dreams come true, Mr. Thatcher," she whispered.

"I love you, Mrs. Thatcher," he told her, tracing the curve of her face with the back of his hand.

"I love you too," she said, kissing him once more.

Again they were interrupted by one of the squeaky stairs, and Reese chuckled as they looked up to see their two little black-haired, freckle-faced babies, peering down at them through the wooden banister rails.

"We can't sleep, Daddy," Bobbie whined.

"Wead us a stowy, Daddy," Scottie begged. "Pwease?"

Breck smiled as her husband sighed. She knew he was tired. He'd worked hard all day getting everything finished so he would have minimal work the next. Still, she knew how the children tugged at his heartstrings.

"Okay," Reese agreed. "But you have to be in bed before I get up the stairs," he said, releasing Breck and sprinting for the staircase.

Bobbie and Scottie erupted into giggles, fleeing up the stairs and down the hall to their bedrooms. Breck could hear their delighted laughter as Reese tickled and teased them before finally settling them for his own rendition of *The Night Before Christmas*.

Breck glanced to the beautiful Christmas tree standing in her bay window. She watched its lights for a moment—admired its beauty. Her life was more wonderful than she'd ever dreamed it could be. There were still good people and good things in the world. There was still true love—the unsurpassed kind—the kind she shared with Reese.

"Mommy!" she heard Scottie call. "Come hear the stowy wiff us."

Smiling, Breck climbed the stairs of the old Thatcher farmhouse to where her husband and children sat waiting to cover her face with kisses, warm her with their hugs, and keep her heart forever safe—enfolded in their love.

AUTHOR'S NOTE

The Foundling
(Formerly released as *Desert Fire*)

You're probably wondering why in the world this trilogy edition has been published, considering that each individual book has been in print for years. Well, I tell you what my heart has been whispering for a long time: "The McCalls want to be together!"

I know it probably sounds corny to you, but it's true—I've wanted the three stories that incorporated different generations of McCalls to be all together in one book for a very long time. I've also taken advantage of the publication of the McCall Family Trilogy as an opportunity to address a little "burr under my saddle" that's been pricking at the back of my mind since the day the title of one of my favorite books, *The Foundling*, had to be changed to *Desert Fire*. Yep! In this here McCall Trilogy, *Desert Fire* finally has the chance to wear its original title, *The Foundling*.

Oh, I know that everyone loves the *Desert Fire* title; I do too! But it's the only book (so far) I was ever forced to change the title to, and it kind of always bother me—you know?—pricked and pricked at the back corner of my mind. And so, even though *Desert Fire* will always be *Desert Fire* to you, it has always been *The Foundling* to me and to those early friends and readers who loved the story when it was still in only xeroxed copy manuscript form. Thus I've settled on this compromise for my own haggard little brain—*Desert Fire* is *Desert Fire* on its own but is *The Foundling* in this trilogy. Thank you for allowing me that little OCD satisfaction.

Actually, now that I think about it, do you even know the story of how *The Foundling* became *Desert Fire*? I just realized that maybe that little tidbit isn't common knowledge. Well, sit back and relax, because I'm about to launch into the story behind how *The Foundling* became *Desert Fire*!

Picture this: way back in 2005, I agreed to let a small publisher publish *The Foundling*. *The Foundling* was actually the very first western romance I had ever written and very close to my heart. Thus, I was nervous about letting it go—about giving up my publishing rights and so forth.

For one thing, *The Foundling* held many, many fond memories for me. I had written it at a time when several of my dearest, dearest friends lived in my neighborhood. Oh, the fun we had one night when one of my friends offered to read *The Foundling* aloud to us all at a party held just for that purpose (well, for that purpose and the purpose of eating all things sugary and delicious). To this day, I can still remember some of the one-liners my friends came up with that night during the reading. I can still see us all lounging around in my front room, listening to our friend reading the romantic adventure of Malaina and Jackson. It was a wonderful evening, and hearing *The Foundling* read aloud made me enjoy the story in a way I never had before. It was fabulous!

The Foundling was also one of the books that my dear friend Dixie read as I was writing it. The comments she would leave in the margins cracked me up! Dixie was so hilarious with her margin comments, so supportive, and we were involved in our daily "walks" at the time—you know, the kind of walks where we would walk up and down hills, wear ourselves out trying to lose weight, and then promptly go to her house and eat half a loaf of homemade bread slathered in homemade strawberry jelly as our reward. Hysterical!

But I'm getting off track here. Blah, blah, blah—and then I agreed to let this little publisher publish *The Foundling* in 2005. I actually agreed to it because I had moved during that spring and hadn't finished *The Touch of Sage*, which was the book I had promised the publisher they could publish that year—and so the publisher ended up with *The Foundling*.

Well, one day, the VP of the company (whom I dearly love) called me up and asked me if he could change the title of *The Foundling*. I assumed he wanted to change it because it was such a common title.

(Seriously! Have you ever looked to see how many books there are with the title *The Foundling*? Even Georgette Heyer has one!)

But no! Overuse wasn't the reason the publisher wanted to change the title of *The Foundling*. The reason was this: the owner of the publishing company had come into the office one day, and as he was sashaying through one of the rooms, he saw a manuscript lying on the table.

Pausing and wrinkling his brow with puzzlement, he asked, "We're publishing a book titled *The FONDLING*?"

Yep! At first glance, the owner of the publishing company thought the book title said *fondling* instead of *foundling*. Thus, the VP of publishing decided that if the owner of the company had made the mistake, then perhaps others might too. And so he wanted to know if I would allow him to change the title.

As it happened I was in the town where the publisher was located soon thereafter and agreed to a meeting. Kindly the VP had agreed to allow me to help retitle *The Foundling* (even though I was loath to do so—remember by this time *The Foundling* had been *The Foundling* for nearly a decade to me!). And so there we sat—me, the publisher's VP, and a couple of other people that worked with him.

In truth, it was one of the most pleasant meetings I've ever attended. Everyone was fun and had a great sense of humor. We chit-chatted awhile, joked, laughed, and just casually visited.

Then it was time to address the title issue. Now, everyone who worked for this publisher at the time was very familiar with my "tag" of having the hero strip off his shirt cleverly implanted into every one of my books.

Therefore, the VP's first new title suggestion for *The Foundling*: "How about we call it *Hairy Chests Forever*?"

Naturally, we all cracked up, thankful that we hadn't been drinking root beer. (It hurts when you laugh root beer out your nose, you know.)

Next someone offered, "*Bare Chests in the Desert*!" And we all laughed some more.

Now, oddly enough, though everyone in the room began popping out ridiculous new titles for *The Foundling, Bare Chests in the Desert* struck a chord with me. (I suppose it would, right? Considering all the bare chest scenes in the book.) Therefore, at one point, when someone asked me what the book was about, and I began explaining that Jackson finds Malaina out in the desert, and they fall in love, it came to me—*Desert Fire*! You know, desert for the fact that Jackson found Malaina in the desert, and fire because they were so passionately in love. Passion…fire. It just made sense. I mean, if they were going to strip away *The Foundling* just because someone might misread it as a nasty title, then *Desert Fire* was good enough for me. At least that's what I tried to convince myself at the time—and for years and years afterward.

And so now you know why the title page of *The Foundling/Desert Fire* appears the way that it does—as *The Foundling* (Formerly Released as *Desert Fire*). Just a little something I wanted to share with you before I rattle off more trivial tidbits about the three novellas included in this book. Okee dokee? (P.S. I'm going to refer to *The Foundling/Desert Fire* as just *The Foundling* throughout the rest of this Author's Note, okay?)

The Foundling has always been one of my favorite stories that ever played out in my imagination. I'm not sure why exactly. But I love it! For one thing, I love the opening scene—you know, Jackson checking Malaina for critters and all. I love the McCall brothers too—all three of them. I love Old Root, the cantankerous bull—and that reminds me of something else…

Old Root's character (and after all, he *is* a character to me, even if he is a bull) is based on a real bull that lived years ago—Rockrose Jane's Conqueror. Yep! "Old Conq" was one of my dad's grand champion milking shorthorns back in the early 1960s.

The stories my family (Dad, Mom, and especially my mom's parents and siblings) tell about Old Conq are legendary! Literally legendary! It's one of those legendary stories of Old Conq's shenanigans that inspired Old Root in *The Foundling*.

While my parents were living in Oregon, my dad became seriously ill. He and my mother decided to head back to Canyon

City, Colorado, and stay with my mom's parents until Dad recovered. For my Dad and my Uncle Wayne (Uncle Wayne being sixteen at the time), loading a one-ton bull (Old Conq) and some other cows into a boxcar and bunking in with them for the trip from Oregon to Colorado was an adventure it itself, especially considering how ill my dad was. (But that's a story for another time.)

***Here are Rockrose Jane's Conqueror and my dad
in the early 1960s.***

However, once Old Conq and the other cattle, Uncle Wayne, and Dad arrived in Canyon City, Old Conq began weaving the stuff of legends with his antics. The one that inspired Old Root was this. My uncles, Wayne and Russell (ages sixteen and thirteen), went out one night to check on Old Conq. (Being that Conq was always wreaking havoc, apparently it was the wise thing to do to check on him every night.) My Uncle Russell always tells me that he was scared to death of Old Conq, and whenever he begins describing the way that he and Uncle Wayne crept out to the old corral in the pitch black of night, it makes me giggled to see the excitement leap in his smiling eyes, even after fifty years. Anyway, Uncle Wayne and Uncle Russell went out one night to check on Old Conq. They had one lantern with them, and Wayne was holding it. (Uncle Russell always tells this part so well—I wish he were here to tell it to you!) With great trepidation, the two teenage boys approached the corral, horrified when they saw that the gate was open! Uncle Russell always says that when he turned to look at Uncle Wayne, terror struck. Uncle Wayne was already gone—vanished—nowhere in sight.

Uncle Wayne then picks up the story by saying that he and Russell knew Old Conq was loose and that as they stood there in the dark, Uncle Wayne could hear Old Conq breathing but couldn't see him anywhere! All he could do was stand there in the dark, listening to that heavy breathing and knowing a one-ton bull was somewhere near.

Then the story really heats up! They knew they had to get Old Conq back in the corral, dark of night or not. So naturally my dad and Uncle Wayne and everyone else available (Grandma and Grandpa to boot) went out to try and round him up. Remember, it was pitch black outside—no light at all!

Eventually, Uncle Wayne and my Dad located Old Conq by listening for him, and when the bull took off running, Uncle Wayne and my dad paced him until (inserting my Dad's own words here) "we run up beside him in the dark and I got my hand on his shoulder and reached around and got hold of the ring in his nose."

There you have it! Old Root's legend was borne from Old Conq's. Old Conq has inspired other bull scenes in my books too. I find that a bovine can be the perfect muse sometimes.

I suppose I've rambled on long enough about titles and old bulls, right? But I just thought those were a couple of little side notes you might find interesting—or not.

There is one other thing. You know the cave scene where Malaina bets Jackson a nickel she can kiss him without touching him? Well, that is one little trick drawn from my real life. I knew a guy who liked to pull that trick on girls (including me), only he used a dime instead of a nickel. Pretty sneaky, huh?

Here's another photo of my dad and Old Conq. There's my grandpa sitting on the fence to the far left.

To Echo the Past

And now let's move on to *To Echo the Past*, shall we? One thing I will confess to you is this—*To Echo the Past* was originally written as a birthday gift to the teenage daughter of one of my friends. The girl's birthday was fast approaching, and she was such a supportive fan of my stories that I'd thought I'd write one just for her. And since *The Foundling* was her favorite of my books at the time, I decided to write a sequel to it, starring her!

In fact, the names of the heroine and her family were originally very different than they appear in the published version of the book. I changed them for many, many reasons. However, some characteristics of Brynn's family members remain the same as my friend's family. As for the name Brynn, it's the middle name of a friend who entered my life at a time when the names in *To Echo the Past* needed changing. And so, there you have a little trivial character names history.

As for other things—I *love* a man with a toothpick! Don't you love a man with a toothpick? My husband is an awesome toothpick twiddler, just like Michael McCall. And yes, that is from whence I drew my toothpick twiddling habit for Michael—from Kevin! From Kevin and the fact that my grandpa and uncles (the ones that helped my dad chase down Old Conq in the dark) always had a toothpick handy or clenched between their teeth. I don't know what it is about toothpicks that I like; I just like them. A man is more attractive if he's good with a toothpick, don't you think?

In other news, Michael McCall was my first less brooding hero; at least at the time I was writing *To Echo the Past* that was the case. He appeared in my mind already a fun-loving, blatantly flirtatious hottie. As Jackson McCall's son, his hottie-ness was a birthright, of course. But you'll notice that Michael doesn't quite have the scars, literal or otherwise, that his daddy does. You know, he wasn't a war veteran and all. Michael had a more stress-free upbringing and was nurtured in a home where his daddy and mama were passionately in love and lighthearted. And yet there was drama and tragedy in his family history—obviously. But Michael managed to own the knowledge but not dwell on it. Do you know what I mean?

And speaking of Michael, that leads me to thinking of porch swings! What a travesty it is that front porch swings are a vanishing thing in this world. It kills me! Have you ever seen the Disney movie *Summer Magic*? There's a scene in it where everyone is sitting around on the porch and Burl Ives sings a song entitled, "On the Front Porch with You." I love that song! I used to sing it to my kids all the time when they were little, to soothe them and settle them down. And I wish so badly that front porch swings were still something everyone owned. In truth, I wish that spending evenings lingering on the front porch was something everyone still did. And that's exactly why Michael built a porch swing for the Clarksons. Well, actually, we all know he built the porch swing so he could sit and spark with Brynn on it and make some brownie points with her mother at the same time. But either way, I love a good old-fashioned, handmade porch swing. (And if you haven't seen *Summer Magic*…you must! It's one of my favorites, and I love the way Hayley Mills gets the better-looking guy in the end! Love it!)

An Old-Fashioned Romance

Do you know what the funny thing is? When I first wrote *An Old-Fashioned Romance*, I thought everyone would hate it! I was so scared that my first contemporary story wouldn't be well-received that I included an Author's Note at the beginning of the book. It read thus:

An Old-Fashioned Romance *is different than most of my other stories. First of all, it takes place in the here and now, rather than the past. It is also a mirrored reflection of many things and people I cherish.*

In truth, I've been very unsettled about releasing this story…afraid it reveals too much about myself or that it doesn't have enough adventure to entertain the reader. However, those who have read it adore it—and it seems to strum a chord in their hearts…a tender chord often overlooked.

Therefore, I entrust it to you now, hoping you will enjoy reading it as much as I enjoyed pouring my heart into it.
To all of us…
And those 'Old-Fashioned' everythings we miss.

As the little "Author's Warning Label" read, I was afraid that sharing so much of my personal self might provide a target for hurt and harm—not only to my own heart and feelings but for loved ones making an appearance in the book as the fictional characters Barb, Kay, Sherryl, and Trixie. However, *An Old-Fashioned Romance* didn't crash and burn. In fact, it is often listed as a reader favorite—and I'm so glad!

Therefore, having been inundated with requests for details about the inspiration for the book, I'm delighted to have this opportunity to add a little something to it for you—to once again give the reader a little insight into the workings of my mind and the beloved things of my heart that helped inspire this book.

Let's begin with pumpkins. Ah! Wonderful pumpkins! Oh, how I *love* pumpkins! Few things make my heart soar the way the vision of a field of pumpkins does. Yes, I've seen fields of tulips—acres upon acres of tulips blooming in fields that stretch off into the horizon nearly as far as the eye can see. I've see the waves of the sea rolling in—lapping or crashing upon the sand or rocks of the shore. I've seen snowy mountains—majestic in their white cloaks of winter beauty. Yet none of these thrill me the way a field of pumpkins does. I love them! I love the fascinating squash, so resplendent in orange, so perfect for making pie and jack-o'-lanterns, or for simply lingering on a front porch in glorious autumn. It's a happy thing, the pumpkin, and I love it! I write poetry about pumpkins, collect ceramic pumpkins for my kitchen, wear pumpkin-themed sweaters as often as I can September through November. I even had a pumpkin-themed guest room in my house in Colorado, and currently my office is blissful in pumpkin color and decor. In short, pumpkins make me happy! Just the sight of one (or a ton) lifts my soul to the very zenith of joy. Thus, in *An Old-Fashioned Romance*, Breck loves pumpkins too.

Breck's adoration of the King of Squash is a not-so-secret reflection of my own pumpkin passion! (P.S. I *love* pumpkins!)

Pumpkin pie for breakfast on Thanksgiving morning? Of course! In the book, Reese's mom mentions that Reese's father likes to have pumpkin pie for breakfast on Thanksgiving morning. Well, who doesn't? My children can thank my kind, loving, understanding mother for that family tradition. Although we didn't have pumpkin pie for breakfast on Thanksgiving morning when I was growing up, we did have it for breakfast the following day. Once Kevin and I started our own family, pumpkin pie for breakfast became a tradition not only for Thanksgiving Day but also for two or three days following! I usually make ten or eleven pumpkin pies for Thanksgiving if we're having company for Thanksgiving dinner—a few less if we're not. That way there's always plenty of pumpkin pie for breakfast, lunch, and dinner! Breck's tried-and-true pumpkin pie recipe (included at the end of this Author's Note) is, in truth, my own recipe. Mmmm! I love pumpkin pie!

When I was six years old, my mom took me to a little craft evening with some ladies at church. There we were provided with old-fashioned wooden peg clothespins, red and blue paint, black yarn pom-poms, and some gold braid. Guess what we made? That's right—toy soldiers to hang on the Christmas tree! I remember making the toy soldiers—very vividly remember making them—and I remember hanging them on our Christmas tree every year after that. I love them! To me they were simply magical, and I cherished them because I remember Mom and me making them. When I left home, Mom gave me two of them, and my children hung them on our Christmas tree. Well, one year (being that I have three children and only had two toy soldiers) I sat down with my own children at our kitchen table, and we made some wooden peg toy soldiers of our own. Of course, my boys eventually began breaking up toothpicks, dipping them in red paint, and gluing them onto a few extra toy soldiers to make it look like they had been in battle. Needless to say, I felt the project needed to come to an end—and so did Reese's mom. I love those simple little clothespin soldiers my mom and I made when I was six. I wholeheartedly treasure them.

Some of my most tranquil moments have been spent in front of a Christmas tree, late at night, when all else is quiet and calm. In those moments I love to turn out all the lights (except for the ones on the tree, of course), put on a little *Christmas with Conniff* or *White Christmas* by Bing Crosby, and just sit in mesmerized wonder at the beauty of the Christmas tree and the season. Sometimes when I'm stressed—worried and feeling tired and perhaps discouraged—I can climb into bed, close my eyes, and envision those Christmas tree moments. Ahhh! I love the soothing, rather healing power of a Christmas tree.

Between 1992 and 1994, I met four women that would literally change my life—individuals that would become four pieces of my heart. Barbara, Dixie, Karen, and Sheri were and are absolute blessings from heaven—given to me to entertain, strengthen, support, and teach. The five of us met when we all lived in Rio Rancho, New Mexico, between 1992 and 1995—and such kindred spirits I could never have imagined. The laughter we've shared has nearly hospitalized us at times! The tears we've shed have kneaded our hearts near painfully. I really can't imagine my life without having been touched by these incredible friends.

The thing about the Groovy Chicks (as we came to be known) is that not only was our group relationship something to behold but my personal, individual relationships with each Groovy Chick is profound. Oddly, we came from about every different walk of life and had every different hobby or interest that you could imagine. Yet there's something—an invisible thread of commonality that glued us together. Barb, Kay, Trixie, and Sherryl are quite obviously based on my friends the Groovy Chicks.

As a collective group, you've never seen more waiters and waitresses have a better time serving customers or get bigger tips than those that served us anytime we were together. What fun we have with restaurant staffs! Furthermore, the one-liners that fly around the room anytime we're together could rival any favorite stand-up comic. To sum it up, when the Groovy Chicks convene, so does the entertainment.

Individually, each Groovy Chick has taught me, helped me, inspired me—been infused with my heart. I met Karen (Kay) first—a super sweet, book-reading quilter. Karen really does quilt and sew like the wind! Her house is always immaculate—very white and blue and homey—and she's a cookbook author. Karen's humor is borne of the fact that it is often unintentional—just something she says that comes out hilarious when she didn't necessarily mean it to be that way. She's the "sweet" chick, and we all adore her. Karen sprinkles serenity and smiley-faces in her wake. She's like a little pink petunia that makes you feel as if all is right with the world when you're with her. Karen—the book-reading, quilting, cookbook-authoring, seamstressing Groovy Chick.

Dixie is one of the three farm girls in the Groovy Chick contingency. I once heard her get onto one of her kids for chewing with his mouth open. "Close your mouth. We don't need to see you chewing your cud," she told him. If that doesn't reveal the farm girl in her, I don't know what would. Dixie makes the most delicious homemade bread and rolls—by hand! In fact, she had to have carpal tunnel surgery. The cause of her carpal tunnel—kneading so much bread dough! Dixie is also hilarious. Some of the things that shoot out of Dixie's mouth can leave the rest of us rolling on the floor with laughter at the moment and bursting into random giggles when remembering it years later. Furthermore, Dixie (like Trixie) really does sculpt her food! I have photos of pancake remains jigsaw-puzzled together to form North America, French fries stacked into a perfect little log cabin, and cake frosting literally sculpted into a bird. You never know what the remains of Dixie's meal are going to end up as—artistically speaking. Dixie—the patient, self-sacrificing, sultry-voiced, food artist Groovy Chick.

Now, Barbara—she's the adventurer of the group. A one-time "survival guide," Barbara could get you through anything! And she'd catch, cook, and feed you a rattlesnake while she did it. The camping, hiking, rattlesnake-cooker of the group, Barbara doesn't mince words. She's straightforward and matter-of-fact, and she has the most contagious laugh I've ever heard in my entire life! Just hearing Barbara burst into laughter can send you into your own peals of chortling— whether or not you even heard what made her laugh or thought it was funny yourself. She's also a classic one-liner artist. One of my favorites (which we all still quote): upon practicing a group song to be performed at an assisted living place and asked to sing alto, Barbara said, "You have to have a chest hair to sing that low!" I'm certain it's one of those *you had to be there to appreciate it things*, but I promise, it was hysterical! Barbara—the rattlesnake-cooking, one-liner dropping, "sheepishly jogging" (that's a long story), contagious-laugh laugher Groovy Chick.

And then there's Sheri. Oh my heck, Sheri! Sheri is not only the professional photographer of the group but the comedy relief! Sheri lightens my heavy heart and can add a glimmer of spark to my soul when things seem darkest. Sheri's my crazy-silly-fun friend! The adventures we've had where betta fish, tulip festivals, funny videos, and "The Twelve Days of Christmas" are concerned are literally indescribable. Sheri can grow anything; any plant loves her and thrives for her. She's an incredible photographer and *totally* would've captured the meeting of Breck and the Highwayman of Tanglewood with her camera. Most of all, she's hilarious! For example, she sent me a copy of the cover for my one of my books, *The Windswept Flame*, wherein she had computer-manipulated a photo of herself into the image to appear as if she were riding on the back of the horse with the silhouetted cowboy, changed the title to *The Windswept **Friend***, and inserted back cover text that titled another book as *Sheri and The Caballero*. Sheri—the photographing, green-thumbed, adventuring, comedic Groovy Chick.

My friendships with Barbara, Dixie, Karen, and Sheri have been absolutely life-changing! Each of these four friends has enriched my life in ways they probably will never know or understand. I'm thankful for them—know that I am blessed to have them—and I'm grateful for the inspiration they offered for this book.

An Old-Fashioned Romance Trivia Snippets

Snippet #1—Reese really did get his name because my favorite candy is miniature Reese's Peanut Butter Cups!

Snippet #2—In 1985 I babysat two little boys every day for a time—brothers, ages five and three. Just after the youngest was born, the older brother asked his mom if she would have some kittens for him next!

Snippet #3—One of the Groovy Chicks had a real-life experience that inspired the rotten, hoochie character Jamie in *An Old-Fashioned Romance*.

Snippet #4—As a child, one of the Groovy Chicks actually experienced "finding the perfect angel costume in the back of her mother's closet"—which, of course, inspired the entire "sexy angel" thread in my book *Love Me*.

Snippet #5—One of the Groovy Chicks is an incredible grammarian and owns an awe-inspiring vocabulary! I first heard the word *monosyllabic* (used in this book) drop from her lips, and long ago she challenged me to use the word *emasculate* in a book—which I did, in *Indebted Deliverance*.

Snippet #6—One of the Groovy Chicks loves rain—thus, the inspiration for the "kissing in the rain" scene in *Sudden Storms*.

Snippet #7—Each of the Groovy Chicks has at least one Marcia Lynn McClure book dedicated to her. In each of those books, there are hidden, personal tributes to that particular Groovy Chick.

Snippet #8—In *Shackles of Honor* the swans that are ever-floating over the surface of the lake whenever Cassidy is there are representations of the Groovy Chicks, as are the four elderly widows in *The Touch of Sage*.

As usual, I've babbled on too long. But before I go, please allow me to thank you for being there when Jackson found Malaina in the desert. Thank you for being as mesmerized by Michael McCall's skill with a toothpick as I am. And thank you for wandering through *An Old-Fashioned Romance* with me. I'll leave you now to run off and whip up a pumpkin pie and enjoy The McCall Trilogy all over again!

~Marcia Lynn McClure

Breck's Pumpkin Pie

2 nine-inch (uncooked) pie crusts (already placed in a pie plate, edges fluted, and set aside)

3 eggs
1 large can (29 oz.) of pumpkin
1 cup sugar
½ cup brown sugar
1 teaspoon salt
5 teaspoons pumpkin pie spice
2 ¼ cups evaporated milk
4 tablespoons flour

Combine all ingredients, and pour into crust in pie plate.
Place in oven, lightly covering with a sheet of aluminum foil. Bake at 425°F for 15 minutes, and then reduce oven heat to 350°F and cook for 60 to 75 minutes more—or until knife inserted into the center of pie comes out clean.
Cool before serving with fresh whipped cream!

My everlasting admiration, gratitude, and love…
To my husband, Kevin…
Proof that heroes really do exist!
I Love You!

ABOUT THE AUTHOR

Marcia Lynn McClure's intoxicating succession of novels, novellas, and e-books—including *The Visions of Ransom Lake*, *A Crimson Frost*, *The Pirate Ruse*, and most recently *The Chimney Sweep Charm*—has established her as one of the most favored and engaging authors of true romance. Her unprecedented forte in weaving captivating stories of western, medieval, regency, and contemporary amour void of brusque intimacy has earned her the title "The Queen of Kissing."

Marcia, who was born in Albuquerque, New Mexico, has spent her life intrigued with people, history, love, and romance. A wife, mother, grandmother, family historian, poet, and author, Marcia Lynn McClure spins her tales of splendor for the sake of offering respite through the beauty, mirth, and delight of a worthwhile and wonderful story.

BIBLIOGRAPHY

Beneath the Honeysuckle Vine
A Better Reason to Fall in Love
Born for Thorton's Sake
The Chimney Sweep Charm
A Crimson Frost
Daydreams
Desert Fire
Divine Deception
Dusty Britches
The Fragrance of her Name
The Haunting of Autumn Lake
The Heavenly Surrender
The Highwayman of Tanglewood
Kiss in the Dark
Kissing Cousins
The Light of the Lovers' Moon
Love Me
An Old-Fashioned Romance
The Pirate Ruse
The Prairie Prince
The Rogue Knight
Romantic Vignettes-The Anthology of Premiere Novellas
Saphyre Snow
Shackles of Honor
Sudden Storms
Sweet Cherry Ray
Take a Walk With Me
The Tide of the Mermaid Tears
The Time of Aspen Falls
To Echo the Past
The Touch of Sage
The Trove of the Passion Room
Untethered

The Visions of Ransom Lake
Weathered Too Young
The Whispered Kiss
The Windswept Flame

www.ingramcontent.com/pod-product-compliance
Lightning Source LLC
Chambersburg PA
CBHW070616260626
47161CB00007B/2452